THE INSURMOUNTABLE EDGE

Thomas H. Goodfellow

THE INSURMOUNTABLE EDGE

A Story in Three Books
BOOK TWO

CONTINUED FROM BOOK ONE

SPENSER PUBLISHING HOUSE

Spenser Publishing House, LLC
11661 San Vicente Boulevard, Suite 220
Los Angeles, CA 90049
www.spenserpublishinghouse.com

ISBN 978-1-7346130-1-8 (hardcover)
ISBN 978-1-7346130-4-9 (paperback)
ISBN 978-1-7346130-7-0 (e-book)

Library of Congress Control Number: 2020902685

Cover and interior design by Lisa Ham at spaceechoes.com
Image by peterschreiber.media

FOR J.A.G.

What is a fair lifespan for a human being? And if that life be taken by another before its natural end, what debt shall be owed?

Inscription on a stone tablet found on the island of Mykonos. Author unknown, circa 1200 B.C. Translated from the Greek.

PART IV

MALIBU

Continued from BOOK ONE...

CHAPTER 59

Haley stopped the film and I told her I'd get back to her. I switched off the computer monitor. I turned around to face Kate who had been leaning over the back of my chair staring at the monitor.

"I'm sorry, Kate," I said. "I didn't mean for you to see that."

Kate didn't respond. She just stood there, unmoving, staring at the now blank screen, her face frozen. I got up out of my chair to go to her side, but Kate shook her head. I sat back down.

Minutes passed.

Occasionally Kate's eyes narrowed ever so slightly, widened, then narrowed again. It was as if she was rolling something over in her mind, seeing it one way, then another, then returning to where she started.

More time passed.

Finally, Kate turned her head away from the monitor and looked at me. Her eyes were intense and seemed full of fury as they bored into me. I began to feel uncomfortable. I didn't know what to do, so I just sat there. Kate's body took on a posture that radiated a fierce, almost animal-like brutality. I had seen men look like that on a battlefield, but it wasn't the kind of thing I had expected to confront in the persona of a beautiful woman doctor-businessperson in her multimillion dollar home in Malibu.

Silly me.

"I want them dead, Jack," Kate said, her voice an angry hiss. "Every single goddamned one of them. I don't want them brought in to stand trial. I don't want them to be judged by a jury of their peers. I want them dead. Do you understand?"

"Yes," I said.

"And you'll do it?" Kate said.

"Kill them?" I said.

"Yes," Kate said.

"I will," I said.

"But before you kill them...," Kate said.

Her voice stopped and her face froze again. I was pretty sure I knew what she was going to say next.

"Before you kill them," Kate said, "I want you to make them suffer. I want them to suffer like NASAD's murdered engineers suffered. I want them to feel the same pain Sam, Lizzy, Sarah, and Paul's parents felt when their lives were being taken. I want them to know there's no way out, that they're going to die right then and there, just like my father and my husband must have known there was no way out, that death was coming for them, as they plummeted to earth trapped in that burning plane. And as night follows day, while I know with absolute surety that my father and husband went to their deaths with the bravery with which they lived their lives, I also know that if you do as I ask, whoever did this to them will go to their deaths in terror. Do you know why?"

"I can guess, but I'd rather hear it from you," I said.

"Because they're cowards, that's why," Kate said. "So, can you guarantee it? Can you guarantee those accursed people that murdered Sam, Lizzy, Sarah, Paul's parents, the NASAD engineers, my father, and my husband will die a horrible death? A death filled with pain, suffering, and terror?"

Boy, the women I was working with on this project were tough. Actually, merciless might be a better word. Van Zant, Haley, and now Kate.

"Yes," I said.

"You goddamn better," Kate said.

"You have my word," I said.

"Good," Kate said.

Kate took a deep breath. Some of the fire went out of her eyes and her body seemed to relax.

"Now," Kate said, "how long have you known?"

"Known what?" I said.

"Don't play games with me," Kate said. "How long have you known that the story about my father and Paul dying in an accident was bullshit? That my father and Paul were murdered?"

"I wasn't sure until I saw what you just saw," I said.

"I don't believe you," Kate said.

"Really," I said. "I didn't know until I saw the film."

"But you suspected it, otherwise you wouldn't have asked to see the film," Kate said.

"Yes," I said. "That's true."

"So?" Kate said.

"'So,' as in so how long have I suspected it?" I said.

Kate nodded. She also arched her eyebrows. I squirmed in my chair.

"Stop squirming," Kate said.

"Aren't you tired?" I said. "I'm really tired. Maybe we should both go back to sleep and we'll talk about it after we've both had a chance to rest."

"I'll get you a cup of coffee," Kate said.

Before I could say anything, Kate turned and headed off in a direction that I assumed led to the kitchen. A few minutes later, she came back with two cups of coffee, handed one of the cups to me, and grabbed my wrist.

"Come on," Kate said.

She pulled me out of my chair and led me between more of the room's chairs, sofas, and tables. We stopped at the room's western edge, which was also the part of the room closest to the sea. The moonlight and the FBI's tower-mounted halide lamps provided enough illumination so that I could see the waves breaking between a portion of the cliff line that darted inland. It was a very peaceful view for a moment. Then the FBI helicopter dove low out of the sky between me and the waves. Two of the German shepherd FBI guard dogs howled at the chopper as it flew back into the darkness.

Kate said, "Sit. And button your shirt."

I looked down. My shirt was open and my bare chest was exposed. In my haste to find a computer as Haley had requested, I'd left the bedroom without buttoning up.

"Sorry," I said. "I hope I haven't offended you."

Kate smiled.

"Offended?" Kate said. "No, not offended. Distracted, yes."

"Oh," I said. "Is that distracted in a good way?"

"Too good," Kate said.

"Okay," I said. "I'll button up. But maybe you should do the same."

Kate appeared taken aback for a moment, then looked down at her robe. It had slipped open a bit making it clear she had nothing on underneath and revealing a fair amount of the bare skin of her inner breasts.

"Oops," Kate said. She reached for the robe's belt and cinched it tighter.

"Of course you don't have to if you don't want to," I said.

Kate rolled her eyes. I buttoned my shirt and sat down on one of the chairs facing the sea. I surreptitiously looked down at my groin to see if I'd forgotten to zip my zipper like I'd forgotten my shirt buttons. Nope. No problem there.

Kate sat down in a chair next to me, demurely repositioning her robe over her naked thighs as she did. I stole a glance at her pretty feet. Up close, her toenails were an even more brilliant scarlet than I had seen through the sniper scope the previous morning.

We both took a sip of coffee.

"So, when did you first start suspecting and why?" Kate said.

I sighed.

"Yesterday morning," I said. "When you told me all the NASAD drone sub engineers had died in accidents. I started thinking maybe the chain was longer."

"That's not possible, Jack," Kate said. "Like I told you, since the three engineers were killed in Las Vegas last week, we've been closely guarding the engineers who are still alive. I'd know if anything had happened to them."

"I meant in the other direction," I said.

I cringed inside as I said that.

Kate's eyes narrowed. Kate must have thought I was being deliberately difficult. I didn't know what more I could say. Kate had just seen the satellite tape of her father's and husband's murders, she'd just told me to essentially torture the perpetrators to death, and yet she still must have been in some form of denial. I looked at her as calmly and supportively as I could.

"The other direction?" Kate said.

"Yes," I said.

Her eyes slowly un-narrowed. It was as if a light went off in her head.

"I'm an idiot," Kate said.

"Anything but," I said.

"It was right in front of me all this time and I never saw it," Kate said.

"It's a pretty painful leap," I said.

The FBI helicopter again dove out of the sky and into the beams of the halide lamps. The dogs barked at the chopper as it journeyed skyward a moment later. In the distance, I once more heard the sudden increased roar of the Coast Guard cutter's engines. Had a set of large waves rolled in? Was there a rock in the boat's path? Or was the cutter hunting a potential threat? I had no way of knowing.

"Maybe," she said. "Why didn't you tell me what you were thinking yesterday?"

"If I told you, and I was wrong, all I would have done is opened up an old wound for no reason," I said.

"It's always been open," Kate said. "Now it's just more open."

"Yes," I said.

"But that's not your fault," Kate said.

"I know," I said.

"From now on, though, I need to know everything you know," Kate said. "No holding back."

"Okay," I said. "Let's both get some sleep and go over everything later this morning."

I began to get out of my chair.

Kate reached over and pulled me back down onto its seat.

"Now means now," Kate said.

I had pretty much learned by then that fighting Kate was a losing battle. Which was another thing about Kate that reminded me of Grace - I could never win with Grace either. So, I didn't argue with Kate or try to get back up out of my chair. I just surrendered.

I told Kate about Bobby and Timmy and the man they had seen dancing as he had filmed the stoning of Sam and Lizzy - a man I presumed to be Asian since he had spoken English with a Chinese accent and had been wearing a Chinese dragon mask - the two Caucasian men in the party bus that Bobby and Timmy had said were American, the fact that the driver of the bus had a fancy gold racing watch, the Afghans and their pitcher's mound, the fence stakes to which Sam and Lizzy had been tied, the Kazakhs' tattoos and the pork rind wrapper, the ongoing hunt for Paul Lennon's sister Professor Margaret Lennon, the NASAD technology that had probably been used to fake the EPIRB signal and radar trace of her father and husband's flight from Homer, and Hart and CENTCOM's theory about how the Chinese believed they had an insurmountable edge in the war that could soon commence. I then relayed to her my suspicion that the insurmountable edge was the source of the grave risk Dr. Nemo had warned about - and therefore the edge could have originated from, and now reside within, a product made by NASAD - and advised her it would be best if she did not discuss the insurmountable edge with anyone other than me, as I didn't want to risk our enemy being tipped off that my mission at NASAD also included searching for the edge. Lastly, I apologized for the fact that earlier I hadn't been completely forthcoming about the method of death for Sam and Lizzy's mother Sarah and Paul Lennon's parents - Kate's children's grandparents - but that it had been decapitation for all three of them.

Kate didn't immediately speak when I finished, but seemed to take a moment to gather herself and perhaps further consider what I had told her. While she did that I kept my head pointed at her face, but what I was actually concentrating on was the bare, tanned skin of her neck and the part of her upper chest outlined by her robe. It was hard to believe such beauty could actually exist outside of dreams.

"Why didn't you tell me about Paul's sister Margaret when you told me about what happened to Paul's parents and Sarah?" Kate said.

"I'm sorry," I said. "I guess I was so concerned about how upset you were after I told you about Paul's parents and Sarah, it just slipped my mind."

"Okay, that makes sense," Kate said. "You're sure Margaret's not dead?"

"I'm not sure about anything," I said. "But since Paul's parents and Sarah were found where they'd been murdered in their own homes, Margaret was seen alive well after all of them had been murdered, and there's no signs of any violence at Margaret's house, I think there's a good chance Margaret is still alive."

"God, I hope so," Kate said. "Margaret is a good woman." She paused, seemed to mull something over in her head. "So, is that everything?"

"Everything that's important," I said.

"That's not what I asked for," Kate said. "I asked for everything. I sense there's something you're not telling me about."

Which was true. I hadn't told Kate my thoughts that our enemy's apparent interest in the drone submarine division was most likely a diversion. I hadn't told her because I didn't want to take the chance she might somehow reveal my diversion theory to someone else. If she told

General Hart he might try to force my investigation to focus solely on the drone subs, which again, was something I did not want to do. If Kate unwittingly allowed my theory to leak to someone other than Hart, and that someone in turn leaked my theory to my enemy, then my enemy - assuming, of course, my diversion theory was indeed correct - would know I was on to them.

I didn't want my enemy to know I was on to them. I wanted them to believe they had succeeded in misleading me. Because, if they believed I had been misled, there was a good chance the first time they noticed I was on to them would be when I was already upon them. It would be too late for them to defend themselves against whatever hell I would unleash.

"You're persistent," I said.

"Energy and persistence conquer all things," Kate said.

"Maybe if you're Ben Franklin," I said.

"I'm impressed you knew that," Kate said.

"Hang around General Bradshaw long enough and there isn't much you won't know," I said. "Like it or not."

"Understood," Kate said. "Now tell me."

I felt like I had to tell Kate something, otherwise she would keep pressing me. I didn't want to be pressed. The only things I could think to tell Kate about that I hadn't already told her about were the biker-drug dealer-football players and Foster Mom.

I hadn't told her about the bikers and Foster Mom since it really didn't relate directly to our current problems and I didn't want to appear to be tooting my own horn - not that I'm above tooting my own horn at times. However, it seemed my adventures with the bikers and Foster Mom might work to get me off the hook as those adventures had the advantage of being true. Kate wouldn't be able to sense I was lying because I wouldn't be. So I told her.

"I knew there was something," Kate said. "That was very kind of you getting all those children and the dog to safety."

"Thank you," I said. "So we're done?"

"Almost," Kate said. "I have some questions."

Again the FBI helicopter buzzed outside the window. Again the helicopter was followed by the barking of the patrol dogs.

"Can't the questions wait until after I have just a little sleep?" I said.

"I don't have that kind of mind," Kate said.

"You don't have the kind of mind that will let a guy get some sleep, or you don't have the kind of mind that can wait to get its questions answered?" I said.

"Both," Kate said.

I took a sip of coffee.

"Good to know," I said. "Shoot."

"Does the fact my father and my husband were murdered change how we're thinking about who might be behind the attacks on the NASAD drone sub engineers?" Kate said.

"I don't think so," I said. "While we still can't fully explain the motives of the people who murdered the engineers, I currently believe it's highly likely that those people are the same people who murdered your father and Paul, and that they murdered them for the same reasons they murdered the engineers. The only way my thinking would be changed is if we came to believe that Milt and Paul were murdered solely to gain control of NASAD. But since you and Freddy are the ones that took over at NASAD for your father and Paul, and you said Freddy is not the murderous type, then gaining control of the company seems an unlikely motive."

"Pennsylvania Avenue Partners bought ten percent of NASAD after my father's and Paul's deaths," Kate said. "If my father had been alive, he never would have allowed PAP to have anything to do with NASAD. Maybe PAP murdered my father and Paul?"

"PAP could have done that," I said. "But the murders of the NASAD drone sub engineers, your father, and Paul have caused tremendous harm to your company. As we discussed before, it's hard to imagine how PAP profits from harming NASAD."

"What if PAP murdered my father and Paul to gain their ownership share, but someone else killed the drone sub engineers?" Kate said.

"I think it's much more likely that the same entity killed the engineers, your father, and Paul," I said.

"I guess you're right," Kate said. "It seems very improbable that NASAD would have two entirely different murderers, with two entirely different sets of motives, active within the company at the same time."

Kate appeared to think for a moment. The sky above the hills to the east of Kate's estate was beginning to brighten. A line had formed between the blackness of the night sky and the small strip of softly glowing orange light beneath the blackness. The sun would soon arrive.

"I'm wondering about Dragon Man, the Asian man that those children Bobby and Timmy told you about?" Kate said.

"Yes?" I said.

"If the Afghans at the stoning site were working for Dragon Man, couldn't the Kazakhs who came after me at the Coso Junction rest stop also be working for him too?" Kate said.

"They could be," I said.

"Since Dragon Man is Asian and was wearing a Chinese dragon mask, couldn't he in turn be working for the Chinese?" Kate said.

"That's a definite possibility," I said.

"Hart and CENTCOM believe the Chinese may have an insurmountable edge that could have arisen out of something NASAD produces, correct?" Kate said.

"Correct," I said.

"What if Dragon Man is working for the Chinese in regard to that edge?" Kate said.

"That's also very possible," I said.

Kate paused. Her eyes narrowed for a moment as if something was upsetting her.

"By the way, I know the sensitive nature of what we're doing," Kate said. "I never would have told anyone about the edge, or anything else, for that matter. You didn't need to tell me to keep my mouth shut."

"I don't think I told you to keep your mouth shut," I said.

"You know what I mean," Kate said.

"I do," I said. "And I'm sorry I may have appeared to doubt you, even for a moment."

"Apology accepted," Kate said.

Kate appeared to think again.

"You know, I've listened to Dr. Nemo's tape over and over again," Kate said. "Nemo says that there is a grave risk and that NASAD will be blamed if something bad happens, but he never explicitly says that the source of the risk is NASAD."

"Agreed," I said.

"But, then again, if Nemo's a NASAD employee, it's likely what he is warning about has something to do with NASAD," Kate said.

"Also agreed," I said.

"Which would mean the odds are good that what you said about Dr. Nemo is correct," Kate said. "Nemo's warning is about the Chinese insurmountable edge."

"I think we have to proceed as if that's true," I said. "Even if it's only because we don't have anything better to go on."

"That doesn't sound very encouraging," Kate said.

"I'd love to have something better to go on," I said. "But when you're stumbling around in the dark like we are, you just have to go with your best guess until you get a better one."

"But we could be right about this one," Kate said.

"Could be," I said. "And hopefully are."

CHAPTER 60

Kate was quiet for a moment as she seemed to think over everything we had just talked about. I watched as the FBI helicopter swooped low across the cliff bordering the seaward side of the estate then banked sharply up into the sky. The Coast Guard cutter's engines kept up a low roar out at sea. Two FBI agents and their dogs were traversing the estate about twenty-five yards away from us and heading towards the cliff. The tower-mounted halide lamps shone down on the agents and dogs from all directions so that both men and dogs seemed to be moving in an eerie, shadowless world.

Kate appeared to come out of her reverie. She took another sip of coffee.

"The technology that misled the rescuers who were searching for my father and Paul's plane was produced by NASAD, correct?" Kate said.

"Unfortunately, yes," I said.

"So since it was a NASAD product that was involved, isn't it likely there is someone at NASAD who is behind all the murders and the attempt to harm NASAD?" Kate said.

I took a sip of coffee.

"I've thought a lot about that," I said. "While it is a definite possibility it is someone at NASAD, there are just too many other entities or individuals who also could have gained access to the NASAD technology."

Kate raised her eyebrows.

"It could be people in the military who made use of the technology or supervised its development, or anyone in another branch of government who was involved in the technology's procurement or development," I said. "It could be one of NASAD's subcontractors, or a government or military contractor. It also could be anyone who hacked any of those entities' computers or NASAD's computers."

"That's a long list," Kate said.

"Yes," I said.

"I think we're going to have to find Dr. Nemo or crack his code," Kate said. "It seems doing either of those is our best hope to figure out who's attacking NASAD."

"It keeps coming back to that, yes," I said. "Oh, shoot. I just remembered there's something else about Dr. Nemo I should have told you."

"What?" Kate said.

"The team at MOM believes he is a NASAD male programmer between the ages of eighteen and thirty-two," I said.

"We have a lot of men that would fit that bill," Kate said.

"MOM said it was around fifteen hundred," I said.

"That sounds about right," Kate said. "Is Dr. Nemo empathic?"

"I know I told you the profilers might be able to figure that out from the voicemail, but this time they couldn't," I said.

"Okay," Kate said.

"Can you think of any NASAD programmers that might have visited your house?" I said.

"You're asking me because of what we said about someone who knew their way around the house possibly being the person who left the phone with Dr. Nemo's message under my pillow yesterday evening?" Kate said.

"Yes," I said.

Kate appeared to think for a moment. She shook her head.

"I can't think of any NASAD programmers who have been in the house," Kate said.

"Well if anyone comes to mind, please be sure to tell me about it," I said. "Obviously, it could be important."

Kate nodded.

"You know, maybe it's selfish, but there's something else that bothers me," Kate said.

"What's that?" I said.

"NASAD is supposed to be on the side of good," Kate said. "What we produce is supposed to help protect this country and keep our soldiers out of harm's way. I don't want something NASAD worked on to be turned against the United States."

"Then we're just going to have to make sure that doesn't happen," I said.

Even with the coffee, I was still brutally tired. I thought that moment was a good time to once again try to escape to my bedroom. I put my coffee cup down on a table next to my chair and stood up.

"Time for some shut-eye," I said.

"Sit down," Kate said. "I'm not finished."

"You're not?" I said.

Kate shook her head.

"No," Kate said.

I sat back down.

"Did the FBI decide to check up on Paul's parents and his sister on their own?" Kate said.

"No," I said.

"You told them to look?" Kate said.

"Yes," I said.

"Good," Kate said.

"Good?" I said.

"I was testing you," Kate said.

"Did I pass?" I said.

"Yes," Kate said. "Ray Carpenter seems to be a smart guy, but I don't think he's as smart as you. I'm sure Ray would have thought of checking on them at some point, but with it having been done so quickly, I had a pretty good hunch you'd asked him to do it. Your answer told me you're still remaining truthful and that nothing, not even false modesty, is holding you back."

I'd heard what Kate had said, but didn't respond. I'd drifted off into a world of my own, having shifted my attention from her neck and chest to her eyes. I was very interested once again in what I took to be the infinite depths I saw in them. As if her soul was revealing itself to me. I felt myself floating to the moon on gossamer wings. Kate, Cole Porter, and me. It was just one of those things.

"Didn't we just talk about you not looking at me like that?" Kate said.

"Huh?" I said.

"You heard me," Kate said. "I need your professional attention."

The way she said 'professional' jolted me back to reality.

"I'm nothing if not a professional," I said.

"That remains to be seen," Kate said. "Did you think Paul's parents and sister were in danger after you learned that Dragon Man had murdered Sam and Lizzy?"

I nodded.

"Yes," I said. "His filming. His dancing. His party bus. It seemed personal."

"Personal?" Kate said.

"I'm sorry," I said. "I should have mentioned it to you when we spoke about the motives for the killings of your father and Paul. One of the things Jeff and I have been considering is that someone may be also be conducting a personal vendetta against Paul."

"That could explain why they killed Paul's parents and Sarah couldn't it?" Kate said.

"It could," I said. "Can you think of anyone who would hate Paul enough to brutally murder his relatives?"

Kate seemed to ponder this.

"I can't think of anyone like that," Kate said.

"If you do, be sure you tell me," I said.

Kate took a sip of coffee.

"Dragon Man's probably getting off on the film of Sam's and Lizzy's murders right now, isn't he?" Kate said. "Probably replaying it over and over."

"Wouldn't surprise me," I said.

The sun finally showed itself over the mountains to the east, and there was then enough light to see the details of the wispy leading edges of the fog bank rolling in over the ocean. I could also make out the wide, red, horizontal stripe on the Coast Guard cutter's bow, and an American flag flying over the boat's wheelhouse.

"What was the point of the murderers putting Sam and Lizzy in clothes with my kids' names in them?" Kate said.

"That's kind of a hard one," I said. "But I've been thinking a lot about it. The way I look at it, if we proceed on the assumption that the killing of Sam and Lizzy was part of some personal vendetta against Paul, then just the act of killing Sam and Lizzy would appear to be enough to satisfy the portion of the vendetta dealing with the two children. The names in the clothes wouldn't appear to be a necessary part of that vendetta, would they?"

"No," Kate said. "It doesn't seem so."

"And if the names in the clothes aren't part of the vendetta, then they must be something else," I said. "We have very little direct evidence to support what that something else is, but I think we have enough circumstantial evidence for me to hazard a guess."

"What's your guess?" Kate said.

"I think the bad guys responsible for the murders of Sam and Lizzy wanted to send a message to terrify you," I said. "To make you feel what it would be like if your children were dead, to make you believe that if they could murder Sam and Lizzy, they just as easily could have murdered your children."

"Why would they want to terrify me?" Kate said.

"So you'd cooperate with them," I said.

"Cooperate how?" Kate said.

"I think in regard to Dr. Nemo," I said. "I think the bad guys want to know what Nemo told you. But that's just a guess, a guess based on another guess - which is that the Afghan and Kazakh mercenaries were brought here on an emergent basis to deal with a crisis regarding the Chinese insurmountable edge. The crisis is Dr. Nemo. He represents a threat to the bad guys' plans regarding the edge."

Kate seemed to think this over. A deer ran out of the brush lining the northern wall of the estate. Two of the FBI patrol dogs spotted the deer. The dogs barked and strained at their leashes. The deer pirouetted in midair and disappeared back into the brush.

"So you're saying the bad guys just found out about Dr. Nemo?" Kate said.

"Yes," I said. "I think Nemo's contacting you probably tipped the bad guys off to his existence."

"But how could him contacting me possibly have done that?" Kate said. "I thought you said everything Nemo sent to me was encrypted?"

"I don't know how the bad guys learned of the contact," I said. "I just think that they did. It would explain both the timing of their attempted kidnapping of you, and the extraordinary lengths to which they appear to have gone in support of that attempt."

Kate seemed to think again.

"So the bad guys didn't think my looking into the deaths of the NASAD engineers was much of a threat, otherwise they would have come after me a long time ago," Kate said. "But the fact the bad guys are coming after me now, suggests not only that the bad guys are aware that

Nemo contacted me, but that they believe Nemo is a real threat to them?"

"I believe so, yes," I said.

"Since the bad guys are coming after me, wouldn't that also suggest that Nemo's fears and the warnings in his voicemail are real?" Kate said.

I took a sip of coffee.

"It would," I said.

"And the bad guys' overall plan was to kidnap me, then kill Sam and Lizzy to terrify me into believing there wasn't anything they wouldn't do to achieve their goals, so that once they kidnapped my own kids, I'd tell them whatever they wanted to know in regard to Dr. Nemo?" Kate said.

"Correct," I said. "But I also believe Dragon Man would have killed Sam and Lizzy anyway as part of his vendetta against Paul."

"Like Dragon Man probably also had Sarah and Paul's parents killed?" Kate said.

"Yes," I said. "And for that matter, Paul himself as well."

Kate's brow furrowed.

"Something doesn't add up," Kate said. "If I'd been kidnapped, I never would have known about my children's names in Sam and Lizzy's clothes. I mean, I found out about that in the morgue. How could I be terrified by something I didn't even know?"

Ray Carpenter suddenly came into view. He was walking along a path close to the edge of the cliff. Carpenter appeared to be heading for two FBI agents I had seen patrolling a section of the compound that bordered the cliff.

"The news had nonstop coverage about the stonings," I said. "The bad guys make you watch the news, then show you a picture of the bloody clothes with your kids' names in them. Your imagination would have filled in the rest."

"Okay...I can see that," Kate said. "It's lucky then that neither my children nor I were kidnapped. Lucky that you were with me at the rest stop, and lucky that Elizabeth spotted that van following her and my children after they left Disneyland and went right to the police."

"Lucky, maybe," I said. "But it's probably more than just luck. As you said, Elizabeth Wells is good at her job."

"So are you," Kate said. "I guess what I should have said, though, is that it was lucky I had both of you taking care of me and my children."

I didn't say anything.

Kate seemed to think about something again.

"It appears that what really needs to be done," Kate said, "is to find the intersection between someone who has a personal vendetta against Paul, and who also could somehow be involved with NASAD to such a degree that they would have access to something NASAD produces that would qualify as the Chinese insurmountable edge."

Outside, the German shepherd patrol dogs began to bark loudly. I looked in the direction of their barking, saw their FBI handlers flip on their flashlights. The handlers scanned the area in front of them, but seemed to find nothing. They turned off the flashlights and calmed the dogs.

"Well put," I said. "When I told Jeff what was going on, he said something similar. Jeff thinks Dragon Man will be at the intersection of the killings of Sam and Lizzy and the NASAD drone sub engineers."

"Do you think Dragon Man could work at NASAD?" Kate said.

"I don't know, but it's something we need to check out," I said. "In any event, I'm in agreement with both you and Jeff in regard to the importance of looking for an intersection between someone who might be seeking some kind of personal revenge against Paul and the killings of the engineers. That intersection is something I've already started searching for. When I find it, there's a good chance I'll have found the person or persons who are behind everything."

"You mean when *we* find it," Kate said.

"*We?*" I said.

"We're doing this together," Kate said.

"Way too risky for you to get involved in the next steps," I said.

"Why is it way too risky for me, but not for you?" Kate said.

"One, you've never been trained how to take those risks," I said. "Two, you've never experienced those risks, and so have no reservoir of responses to fall back upon. And three, you brought me here to do this job, and you should let me do it without having to worry about your safety any more than I already do."

"Except things have changed since you agreed yesterday to come with me," Kate said.

I knew what Kate was talking about.

"Paul and your father," I said.

"I think that entitles me to fully participate with you," Kate said. "Risks be damned."

"Are you sure you're a doctor?" I said. "Because you sound more like a lawyer."

Kate said nothing.

"How are your children going to feel when you get killed?" I said.

"You're just going to have to make sure that doesn't happen," Kate said.

I suppose I could have continued arguing with Kate, but if I'd been in her shoes, and just learned my father and my husband had been murdered, I'm sure I would have felt exactly as she did. Who, then, was I to deny her what she wanted, what she felt she needed? It was risky, but I thought I could protect her. And, as I said before, fighting Kate, just like fighting Grace, was pretty much a losing battle.

"You're going to have to stick close to me, or with security personnel I feel comfortable with," I said. "No going out on your own."

"I can live with that," Kate said.

"That's the goal," I said.

"Funny," Kate said.

The fog continued to roll in. The Coast Guard cutter intermittently disappeared within its mist, just as the helicopter nearly vanished whenever it flew out of the cones created by the halide lights. I remembered then that there was still one thing I had not yet discussed with Kate - the plan I had made with Adelaide and Jeff.

"You should know that while you're sticking close to me you also might wind up spending time with Adelaide and Jeff," I said.

"Why is that?" Kate said.

"I told them to come down here," I said.

"You miss them?" Kate said.

"I'm worried about them," I said.

Kate appeared to think this over.

"Seems like a good idea to me," Kate said. "I'm sure they'll be a big help."

"You are?" I said.

"From what I saw, that little hellcat is a great sniper," Kate said. "And I assume Jeff wasn't awarded all those medals in your den for nothing."

"No," I said. "Jeff definitely earned them."

Kate picked up her coffee cup, took a sip, and put it back down. Something seemed to cross her mind. Whatever that something was, it appeared to make her feel uncomfortable.

"What's wrong?" I said.

"Who says something's wrong?" Kate said.

"What's wrong?" I repeated.

"Jeff," Kate said. "I'm worried about his PTSD."

"Your worry is certainly justified," I said.

"Why aren't you worried?" Kate said.

"I am worried," I said. "But I think Jeff's progressing, and I think now's as good as any time to see where he's at."

"What does Jeff think?" Kate said.

"Jeff's eager to give it a go," I said. "He wants to test his immersion therapy theory."

"I suppose his theory is going to get a real test, then, isn't it?" Kate said.

"Yes," I said. "Hopefully whoever Jeff runs the test against will live to regret it."

"Or not live," Kate said.

"I like the way you think," I said.

"Thank you," Kate said. She paused. "What about Adelaide's ankle monitor? I thought she wasn't allowed to leave the ranch?"

"Technically she isn't," I said.

"Couldn't she get in trouble with her probation officer if she comes here then?" Kate said.

"She would if the officer actually knew she was here," I said.

"If Adelaide has the monitor on, how could he possibly not know?" Kate said.

"Adelaide has a computer program that can fool her monitor and make it appear like she's somewhere she isn't," I said. "She's running it right now and it's showing she's at the ranch. I discovered she had the program yesterday evening when I was watching her monitor's online tracking app and it showed she was in the ranch's kitchen, only she wasn't."

"Where was she?" Kate said.

"She'd gone to Carson City and was going to enlist in the Army," I said.

"Jesus," Kate said. "How'd you find out?"

"Jeff told me," I said. "It wasn't like he was ratting her out. He did the right thing. Anyway, it's all fine now. I stopped her."

"Well, that's good!" Kate said. "But what will you do if her app stops working?"

"Go to option two," I said.

"Option two?" Kate said.

"Pray the probation officer gives us a pass when I tell him Adelaide was by my side the whole time," I said.

"My guess is that he does," Kate said. "After all, you are a general." Kate appeared to think for a moment. "Was it Adelaide's app that gave you the idea of what might have happened to my father and husband's plane? That someone had used something similar to fool the searchers about the location of the crash?"

"The app gave me the idea, yes," I said.

"You know, if I wanted to be a real stickler I could say not telling me about the app falls under the category of holding something back from me," Kate said.

"That wasn't my intent," I said. "It completely slipped my mind earlier."

"I believe you," Kate said.

I picked up my coffee up and took a sip of coffee.

"So," I said, "I still don't know Adelaide and Jeff are going to stay when they get here. Do you have any suggestions?"

"You're kidding, right?" Kate said.

"I'm not," I said. "I don't know Malibu."

"They're staying in my house, Jack," Kate said. "I wouldn't have it any other way."

"You're serious?" I said.

"Of course I'm serious," Kate said. "You've seen this place. We could put a whole army in here."

"Thanks," I said.

"You've got someone to take care of the dog and the horse?" Kate said.

"Yeah," I said. "We have a neighbor."

"I didn't see any neighbors," Kate said.

"He lives twenty miles away," I said. "But he's still the closest neighbor we have."

"Of course he is," Kate said.

"Can I go to sleep now?" I said.

"Um-hmm," Kate said.

We both stood up. Kate stepped in close to me and hugged me. I felt her breasts flatten against my chest and the touch of her soft blond hair against my face. I took in the sweet scent at the back of her neck. She whispered in my ear, her warm breath sending tingles from my skull to my groin.

"I just realized something," Kate said.

"What's that?" I whispered back.

"If the enemy is so worried about me because of what Dr. Nemo told me," Kate said, "they must be even more worried about Nemo himself."

"I believe that's true," I said.

"We have to get to him before they do," Kate said. "We have to save his life."

"Save his life and find out what he knows," I said.

"We find out what Dr. Nemo knows, and find the intersection of both our enemy's attacks on NASAD and their personal vendetta against Paul, maybe we can stop a war," Kate said.

"That's the plan," I said.

"Let's get an early start," Kate said. "8:00 a.m. sharp."

"Great," I said. "That gives me a good two hours to sleep."

"Off to bed you go," Kate said.

"You know," I said, "I sleep better when I don't sleep alone."

"Maybe one day you won't have to," Kate said.

"Today's a day," I said.

"It certainly is," Kate said. "But..."

"But what?" I said.

"It's not *the* day," Kate said.

CHAPTER 61

Once in my room, I set my alarm for 7:45 a.m. and quickly fell asleep again. I soon began to dream. The coyote returned, this time with Foster Mom's mangy dalmatian in tow. The dalmatian had a blue canvas leash attached to its collar, and the coyote had the leash's other end in its mouth.

"We've got another song for you," the coyote said.

"Why am I not surprised?" I said.

A pitch pipe magically appeared in the coyote's mouth and the coyote blew into it. The two canines got in tune using the pipe - at least what seemed to pass for being in tune to them, although all I heard was a high-pitched screech that was indistinguishable from the sound of fingernails scratching a blackboard - and this is what they sang,

'At the end of a dream

If you know where I mean

When the mist just starts to clear

In a similar way

At the end of today

I could feel the sound of writing on the wall

It cries for you

It's the least that you can do'

The words sounded familiar even if the tune did not. Of course it wasn't a surprise the words sounded familiar to me, otherwise how could they have showed up in my dream? Still dreaming, I took out a dream iPhone and started up an app that can identify songs. The app told me the song was 'Long Live Rock 'n' Roll', by the group Rainbow.

"Am I supposed to understand what this means?" I said to the coyote.

"You certainly are," the coyote said. "But it's not quite as obvious as it seems."

"Not quite as obvious as it seems?" I said. "It's not obvious at all!"

"Maybe you should work on the sound," the coyote said.

"But you're the one singing!" I said.

"We're singing that way because you made us do it," the coyote said.

Just then my real iPhone's alarm went off. I woke up and the dream, along with the coyote and the dalmatian, vanished. I hadn't a clue what the dream was trying to tell me. I kept thinking about the dream as I got out of bed, dressed, and made my way downstairs. It was 7:55 a.m. by the time I crossed the atrium, exited the house's giant steel swinging front doors, and was standing on the marble landing waiting for Kate.

Kate's and my plan was to get me started at NASAD's headquarters in Westlake Village by talking to people in Human Resources and looking for clues to the identity of Dr. Nemo. I was wearing a light blue work shirt and blue jeans. The work shirt was about as dressy as I ever got.

The scent of the sea and the sound of its breaking waves both seemed to have grown stronger since the previous night. The fog bank had stayed at bay and the air was crystal clear and still cool. The morning light allowed me to more clearly see the Coast Guard cutter as it cruised just outside the wave break, the seawater foaming behind its stern. I could also make out a dozen or so crewmen on the cutter's deck and a 50 millimeter machine gun mounted on the cutter's bow. The crewmen were dressed in blue short-sleeved shirts, blue pants, and blue caps.

FBI dog teams continued to patrol the estate's grounds. Overhead, the helicopter circled in the sky. The tower-mounted halide lamps had been doused.

Manu and Mosi drove up in the Maybach. Manu parked the Maybach at the foot of the landing's stairs. Agent Ray Carpenter's black FBI Suburban, silent as a cat, pulled up behind it. No one got in or out of the Suburban, and there was not a peep from within.

The giant Samoan twins got out of the Maybach and walked up to me. They were identically dressed in light blue suits, white shirts, dark blue ties, white socks, and black wingtips. Their suits were snug and the sleeves and pants were too short, just like the black suits I had seen them wearing on the ranch had been. It made me wonder whether they had bought the clothes that way, or if the huge brothers had simply continued to grow since they had purchased them.

"Good morning, sir," Mosi said. "We heard Jeff and Adelaide are coming down this afternoon."

"News travels fast," I said.

Manu said, "We're thinking maybe we can get in some jump training."

"You have a jump tower hidden around somewhere?" I said.

Mosi gestured with his giant chin toward the seaside cliffs.

"We could use the cliff," Mosi said.

"I don't know about that," I said. "Sea breeze kicks up you two could get smacked pretty hard against the cliff wall."

Mosi scratched his head.

"I guess we didn't think of that," Mosi said.

"Of course if the breeze shifts in the other direction, it might take you out to sea," I said. "I've seen how you guys swim."

Manu said, "Mosi, perhaps we should give this a little more thought."

Kate came out the front door. Her hair was swept back off her face, and two diamond stud earrings sparkled in her ears. She wore a well-tailored grey business suit, white blouse, and heels. Her skirt, which ended just above her gorgeous knees, nicely accented her hips. Her suit jacket hugged the curves of her breasts and was tastefully drawn in around her thin waist. The hugging and the drawing in were light years away from the twins' bursting-at-the-seams style.

"A general, two bodyguards, and a Suburban full of heavily armed FBI SWAT agents," Kate said. "What does a girl do to deserve all this?"

Manu opened the Maybach's right rear door for Kate. I was watching Kate's skirt ride up the back of her thighs as she stepped into the car, when suddenly, a loud, somewhat high-pitched voice erupted from the direction of the other house on the estate.

"Kate!" said the voice. "Hold up."

Kate backed herself away from the car, and she, Manu, Mosi, and I turned to look. A short, overweight, prematurely balding man was running towards us. The man appeared to be in his early thirties and was then about seventy yards away from us. His dark brown suit was rumpled and three sizes too big. His pale yellow shirt was wrinkled and its shirttails were falling out of the front of his pants. The man's tie, which was yellow and dotted with some kind of oddly shaped white geometric forms, was crooked.

The short man appeared to be moving as fast as his little legs could carry him. His gait was a mixture between a waddle and a stumble, and his arms flew every which way, completely disconnected from the action of his lower body.

The short man quickly closed the gap between him and us. He

stopped a few feet short of us, bent over, and put his hands on his knees as he tried to catch his breath. He was perspiring profusely. When the short man appeared to be able to breathe a bit easier, he lifted his head and looked up at Kate.

"I'm glad I caught you," the short man said.

"Jack, this is my brother Freddy," Kate said. "Freddy, General Jack Wilder."

Freddy glanced over at me. I extended my hand. Freddy remained bent over by bracing himself using only his left hand on his knee and took my hand in his right. He shook my hand, though he appeared to do so reluctantly. Freddy's hand was cold and clammy and I felt like I was squeezing a jello mold. Freddy did not have an attractive face. His nose and ears were large and misshapen, there were bags under his eyes, and his lips protruded. He had what looked like a two-day growth of stubble on his cheeks and chin. I was then close enough to him to see that the repeating geometric forms on his tie were white Yale University Bulldogs leaning on blue 'Y's. His shoes were worn brown leather, and his socks, which had holes in them, were a match for his tie - yellow with white bulldogs and blue 'Y's. If Aristophanes were there, he probably would've had no problem shouting 'brek-ek-ek-ex ko-ax, ko-ax' with all the feeling he had originally intended. I dearly wanted to shout that as well, but I felt it best to at least try to make a good first impression.

"Nice to meet you, Freddy," I said.

"Same here," Freddy said, pulling his hand from mine. "I guess."

Kate's eyes widened.

"That was rude, Freddy," Kate said.

"So?" Freddy said.

"General Wilder is one of the most decorated soldiers in the history of the U.S. Armed Forces," Kate said. "He's here to help us."

"I don't think so," Freddy said.

"What the hell does that mean?" Kate said.

"Never mind," Freddy said. "You're not leaving are you?"

"What does it look like?" Kate said.

Freddy's breathing stabilized. He pushed his hands off his knees and stood up.

"Well you can't," Freddy said.

"Excuse me?" Kate said.

"We voted yesterday morning," Freddy said.

"Who's we?" Kate said.

"The board," Freddy said.

"I'm on the board," Kate said. "I didn't vote."

"Come on Kate," Freddy said. "We voted after the FBI found out your kids were dead. We're trying to protect you."

"My children are alive," Kate said.

"You know what I mean," Freddy said. "It's too dangerous for you to leave the compound."

"What's too dangerous is to sit here and do nothing but wait for another attack," Kate said.

"That's what the FBI is for," Freddy said. "Special Agent Burnette feels they're close to breaking the case."

"Really?" Kate said.

"Yep," Freddy said. "He told me so himself."

I looked up at the roof of Kate's house. The snipers there appeared to be keeping a close eye on all of us. The agents with the German shepherds had also stopped what they were doing and were watching us from about fifty yards away.

"Aren't you special," Kate said.

"Burnette trusts me," Freddy said.

"You're both such good judges of character," Kate said. "So I assume Burnette knows who the disgruntled employee is?"

"It's not a disgruntled employee," Freddy said. "It's terrorists."

"And who will it be tomorrow?" Kate said.

"What?" Freddy said.

"Forget it," Kate said. "I just cast my vote for me leaving."

Kate got into the car. Freddy grabbed her arm.

"You can't leave," Freddy said.

"What are you doing, Freddy?" Kate said. "Let go of my arm."

He did. I hadn't expected him to let go so easily. Maybe it was a brother-sister thing.

"Sorry," Freddy said.

"Freddy, I'll be fine," Kate said. "I have a great team escorting me."

"With all due respect to General Wilder," Freddy said, smiling at me with what appeared to be a very phony smile, "he is not allowed on the campus of NASAD. He can only provide security for you here at home."

"Another one of the decisions made by the board?" Kate said.

"Yes," Freddy said.

"You said the board met yesterday morning," Kate said. "No one even knew General Wilder was coming then."

"Burnette's people also got all the board members on the phone at around 2:00 a.m. last night," Freddy said. "Burnette warned us about General Wilder."

"'*Warned*' you?" Kate said.

"It's for the best," Freddy said. "I'm sure you can see that."

Freddy again smiled at me with his phony smile.

"How can you possibly object to Jack helping us?" Kate said.

"Oh it's *Jack,* is it?" Freddy said.

"What are you implying?" Kate said.

Freddy said nothing, just raised his eyebrows. He appeared to be trying to leer. The leer came out looking like he was suppressing a burp, though.

"Shut the hell up, Freddy," Kate said.

"I didn't say anything," Freddy said.

"I was talking about your face," Kate said.

Freddy just raised his eyebrows again.

"I don't believe this," Kate said. "What exactly is the board's objection to General Wilder helping us?"

"There are many," Freddy said. "First off, what if he is working for another defense company? We have trade secrets to protect."

The helicopter made a low circle above us. I felt the wind from its rotors wash over my head.

"The general is on leave, but he's still in the Army," Kate said. "He's not allowed to be employed by a private company."

"Are you really that naive, Kate?" Freddy said. "It's done all the time."

"Not by NASAD," Kate said.

There was a strange little flicker behind Freddy's eyes then, and he seemed to try to keep a smile from forming on his face.

"I don't like that look, Freddy," Kate said. "Tell me you haven't done something stupid."

"Of course not," Freddy said.

Freddy turned to me.

"General Wilder, are you aware that U.S. soldiers are prohibited from performing law enforcement duties on U.S. soil?" Freddy said.

"Posse Comitatus is the relevant statute, I believe," I said.

Freddy screwed up his eyes.

"Are you a lawyer or something?" Freddy said.

"No, but I like to talk like one sometimes," I said.

Freddy seemed unsure what to make of what I said. Kate stepped between us.

"He's not performing law enforcement duties, Freddy," Kate said.

"Oh yeah?" Freddy said. "What about that little shootout at the rest stop yesterday?"

"General Wilder saved my life," Kate said.

"Not according to Burnette," Freddy said. "Burnette says the general escalated a situation that could have been easily managed without violence into a bloodfest."

"Burnette wasn't even there," Kate said.

"You know what I think?" Freddy said.

Kate said nothing.

"I think you have an irrational dislike and distrust for the FBI," Freddy said. "Which is counterproductive, since they're the only ones who can get us out of this mess."

"You can think what you want," Kate said.

"Besides, too many cooks spoil the broth," Freddy said.

"Meaning?" Kate said.

"We don't want anyone getting in the way of the FBI and hindering their investigation," Freddy said.

"I've heard enough," Kate said. "Since I didn't get to vote yesterday, I now cast my vote for the general to take an active role in finding out what is going on with our company."

"Fine," Freddy said. "You're still outvoted, though."

"Ask me if I care," Kate said.

Kate gestured to Manu, Mosi, and me.

"Let's go," Kate said.

Freddy reached for Kate's arm again. Kate scowled at him. Freddy pulled his hand back.

"Alright, you want to be that way, be that way," Freddy said. "But you've left me no choice, Kate."

Freddy turned to face Manu and Mosi.

"Manu, please give me the keys to the Maybach," Freddy said. "Then I'd greatly appreciate it if both of you get back to my house."

Manu and Mosi looked at each other, unsure of what to do.

Kate said, "Leave Manu and Mosi out of this, Freddy. You said they could stay with me until the company's issues are resolved. I'm not letting you take them from me."

Freddy snickered.

"As I remember it, you didn't want any extra security," Freddy said. "You said you were fine without it."

"Things have changed," Kate said.

"Whatever," Freddy said. "The keys, men."

Manu and Mosi still appeared unsure of what to do. Kate sighed heavily and marched over to the Maybach driver's side door. She reached inside the cabin and grabbed the keys off the center console where Manu must have left them. She ducked back out of the car and waved the keys at Freddy.

"You want 'em, come and get 'em," Kate said.

It was Freddy's turn to appear unsure of what to do.

"Come on, Freddy," Kate said. "It'll give me an excuse to kick your ass."

Freddy glared at her.

"Screw you," Freddy said.

He stomped off.

"Wow," I said to Kate. "That's the last thing I ever expected to see."

"I'm his older sister, remember?" Kate said. "I've been kicking Freddy's ass his entire life. Now, let's blow this joint."

CHAPTER 62

The Maybach, with the FBI Suburban in tow, made its way over Kanan Dume Road in the opposite direction the Corolla and I had traveled the night before. I realized I had forgotten to eat anything after I woke up, so I made a breakfast out of some of the snacks in the Maybach's refrigerator. Thirty minutes after we'd left Kate's estate, and following a short jaunt up Highway 101, we were outside the gates that defended the entrance to NASAD's headquarters in Westlake Village. The gates, made of black-painted reinforced steel, were thirty feet wide, ten feet tall, and spanned an opening in a twelve-foot-high wall made of large blocks of golden limestone. The wall, much like the walls surrounding Kate and Freddy's estate, seemed to run on forever in both directions. Manning the gates were a team of NASAD's own security guards, along with a small squad of FBI agents. The FBI agents wore body armor and toted Heckler and Koch submachine guns.

Apparently, the stonings of Sam and Lizzy in the desert, the murders of the children's mother and grandparents, and the heavy fortifications at Freddy and Kate's Malibu compound continued to be a media sensation. A dozen news crews were lined up against the wall on both sides of the gate. Each crew consisted of a satellite broadcast van, a reporter, and a cameraman. The crews, who appeared to have been drinking coffee and socializing with each other prior to our arrival, all suddenly jumped into action. They rushed the gate and trained their cameras on the Maybach. Thanks to Carpenter's reminder the day before about the Maybach's windows being tinted, I resisted the urge to wave.

The NASAD security guards opened the gates and waved through the Maybach and our Suburban escort. The vehicles climbed a gently sloping brick road that was bordered by lush, freshly mown green grass. At the top of the slope, we came to three thirty-story office buildings whose exterior walls consisted of maroon-colored marble interspersed with large, green glass windows. The three buildings made a triangle that framed a parklike area. The parklike area had its own man-made, acre-sized lake that was filled with sparkling blue water.

We stopped in a circular drive that lay in front of the marble and glass building furthest from the top of the brick road. Kate got out of the Maybach, but I took a moment. My left knee had tightened up again and was painfully stiff. I rubbed it, carefully flexed and extended it a few times, then gingerly rotated it out of the car, and placed my foot on the ground. It felt like someone had hammered a railroad spike into my knee joint, but there wasn't much I could do about it other than push through the pain.

Once out of the car, I took in the smell of the newly mown grass as it wafted on a gentle breeze. Standing at my full height, I then also gained a broader perspective of NASAD's campus than I'd had within the Maybach. The campus appeared to encompass over a hundred acres of grassy rolling hills dotted with oak trees. The breeze I felt caused the oak leaves to quiver and the water in the lake to ripple.

One hundred yards away from me, and to the west, lay NASAD's private airstrip and heliport. No planes or helicopters were present, but drone aircraft with six-foot wingspans were taking off and landing on the heliport's surface. The drones appeared to be stealth drones - their wings had the distinctive flat shape of airplanes designed to be radar evading. I looked up at the building's windows, trying to perhaps catch a glimpse of the drones' pilots, but the sun glinting off the windows nearly blinded me, and forced me to turn away.

Kate and I were about to walk up the building's front steps, when Kate grabbed my arm and held me back.

"I'm sorry," Kate said. "I just realized that I was so pissed off at Freddy back at the house, that I forgot to apologize to you for his behavior."

"No need to apologize," I said. "He seemed to bother you a lot more than he did me. Is he always so annoying?"

"Always," Kate said. "He was born that way. It's almost like he's got a preternatural ability to annoy."

"Is it an ability that's improving with age?" I said.

"Definitely," Kate said. "I believe Freddy's following Moore's law."

"By that, do you mean Freddy's ability to annoy others doubles every two years like the computing power of integrated circuits?" I said.

"Yes," Kate said.

"That's scary," I said. Then gesturing at the surrounding buildings, I added, "You know, this place looks a hell of a lot different than the last time I was at NASAD."

"Last time was at the Chatsworth campus?" Kate said.

"Uh huh," I said. "A bunch of World War II era corrugated steel Quonset hut style warehouses next to the railroad tracks."

"Which campus do you like better?" Kate said.

"Well, honestly, Chatsworth was more my taste," I said.

"Me too," Kate said. "Taj Mafreddy would have remained only a gleam in Freddy's eye if my father hadn't died. Freddy started building this campus a few weeks after the plane crash, and construction was finished only a month ago. After we moved in, Freddy had the Chatsworth campus razed to the ground."

"Taj Mafreddy the official name?" I said.

"As long as it's officially said behind Freddy's back," Kate said.

"Must be a lot of that going on," I said. "So, our first stop is HR?"

"Yes, we're seeing the head of the department," Kate said. "Mary Beth Lankowski."

"I think I know her," I said. "Did she play middle linebacker for the Pittsburgh Steelers?"

"Hardly," Kate said.

We entered the building's lobby through fifteen-foot-tall glass doors whose green tint exactly matched the building's windows. The lobby was thirty feet high, its floors polished white marble, and its walls thick sheets of dark red mahogany. Kate took a badge out of her purse and clipped it to the lapel of her suit.

There were two guards at the lobby's security desk. The guards were young, well-groomed men dressed in dark blue blazers, pants, and caps, and light blue shirts. Above the left breast pocket of their shirts were the words 'NASAD Security'. Each man had a Glock in a black leather holster that was worn next to his hip. One of the guards gave me a badge similar to Kate's and I clipped it to my shirt pocket.

Kate and I walked toward an elevator bank at the far end of the lobby.

"There are microchips in the badges," Kate said.

"So NASAD security can track my every move?" I said.

"Yours and everybody else's," Kate said.

"What if I take the badge off and toss it down a stairwell or something?" I said.

"Security will know immediately," Kate said.

"They will?" I said.

"The badge's sensors can tell whether the badge is being worn or not," Kate said.

"What if I put the badge on a dog?" I said.

"I don't know," Kate said. "I never tried it."

"What about a monkey?" I said.

"Haven't tried that either," Kate said. "I'm sure it's not a good idea though."

"Bunch of big guys with machine pistols show up?" I said.

"Close," Kate said. "If the movement sensors report someone moving around without a badge, the elevator doors and exit doors on the floor surrounding that person instantaneously lock."

"I'd be trapped?" I said.

"Yes," Kate said.

"Sounds like a Stephen King novel," I said.

"Exactly," Kate said. "Once you're trapped, a car with a mind of its own runs you over and then a deranged nurse beats your shins with a sledgehammer. When the nurse is done, our chief of security comes in and lights you on fire with just his eyes."

"What do you charge for this?" I said.

"For you, it would be on the house," Kate said.

Kate and I arrived at the elevator bank. Kate pushed the up button.

"We're going to meet Mary Beth in my office," Kate said. "I thought it would shield us from any prying eyes in HR. I also gave my secretary the morning off."

The elevator arrived. Kate and I stepped in, and Kate pushed the button marked '30'. The doors closed. We were the only passengers.

We arrived at the thirtieth floor, exited the elevators, turned right, and walked down a long corridor. The corridor had the same polished marble floors and wood paneling as the building entrance lobby. At the end of the corridor was a window that looked out on the NASAD campus. A drone aircraft similar to the ones I had seen on the heliport hovered in front of the window, then disappeared.

Kate and I reached the last door on the right. The door had a plaque that read, 'Kate Lennon. Director'.

Kate and I entered the anteroom to her office. The anteroom had spectacular views out over the NASAD campus. The oak trees and rolling green hills seemed to go on forever. The sun was well above the mountain ridges to the east, and the sky was a shimmering blue. The drone aircraft were then so far below us that they looked like small blackbirds circling the heliport.

The anteroom was decorated with dark walnut paneling, oriental throw rugs, a black leather couch with matching armchairs, a glass coffee table, and a large secretary's desk made of walnut that matched the paneling. The secretary's desk had a plush mauve executive chair behind it, and on top of the desk was a computer monitor. The desk was immaculate, with nary a paperclip or pen out of place. Against the room's left wall was a cherry wood credenza. On the credenza was a silver serving tray with a silver pitcher, china coffee cups, small china plates, sugar, cream, and chocolate chip cookies.

The most remarkable thing about the anteroom was not the furniture or the view, however, but the woman sitting on the couch. She was one of the most gorgeous women I had ever seen - not as gorgeous as Kate or Grace, but gorgeous nonetheless. As soon as the woman saw Kate and me in the doorway, she stood up and approached us. She appeared to be in her mid-twenties, was about five foot nine, had straight blond hair that fell just above her shoulders, and wore a tailored blue wool suit that clung to her hourglass figure. The suit's skirt stopped just above a pair of incredible knees. The woman's brilliant blue eyes smiled as brightly as her full red lips and her perfect white teeth glistened between the lips.

"Hi, Mary Beth," Kate said.

"Good morning, Kate," the woman said.

"This is Mary Beth?" I said to Kate, my voice hoarse.

"Yes, this is Mary Beth Lankowski," Kate said. "Mary Beth, General Wilder was expecting a middle linebacker for the Pittsburgh Steelers."

Mary Beth frowned one of the most charming frowns I had ever seen.

"So sorry to disappoint you, General," Mary Beth said in a silky southern accent.

I said, "Disappointed? I don't think I'm disappointed. Am I disappointed, Kate?"

Kate rolled her eyes.

"He's not disappointed, Mary Beth," Kate said.

Mary Beth said, "It's an honor to meet you, General."

"The pleasure is all mine," I said.

Mary Beth extended her hand. I shook it. Her handshake was firm, but her skin was soft and warm.

Kate said, "Mary Beth, I didn't know the general could be so gracious. You should have seen the greeting I got yesterday at his ranch."

Mary Beth said, "If I know you Kate, you probably showed up all unexpected and uninvited. Am I right General?"

"Don't answer that, Jack," Kate said.

"Sorry, Mary Beth," I said. "But orders are orders."

Mary Beth said, "Spoken like a true fighting man, General."

Kate said, "Mary Beth has been with NASAD for over twenty-five years. She joined us right after college and finishing up her stint as Miss Georgia. She was always my father's favorite employee and knows everything there is to know about our personnel. All seventy-five thousand of them."

I could buy the part about Mary Beth being Kate's father's favorite employee, but not the part about Mary Beth working at NASAD for the last twenty-five years. That would mean she was in her late forties.

Mary Beth smiled when she caught my stare.

"I forgive you, General," Mary Beth said.

"On top of everything else, you're a mind reader too?" I said.

"I can see you making calculations in your head," Mary Beth said. "I also know that most people make the mistake of thinking I'm younger than I am. But there's no magic to it. Just good genes."

"I must be out of practice," I said.

"At what, General?" Mary Beth said.

"Being cool and inscrutable," I said.

Kate and Mary Beth laughed.

"I'll get you both some coffee and cookies before we get started," Mary Beth said.

Kate and I sat down on the couch. I watched Mary Beth's rear as she walked to the cherry wood credenza. I didn't care how old Mary Beth really was, any twenty-five year-old, hell, any nineteen-year-old, would have been happy to have that rear. Kate, apparently catching me staring at Mary Beth, gave me a sharp elbow to the ribs.

"Sugar and cream with your coffee, General?" Mary Beth said.

"Black, please," I said.

"Just like Kate," Mary Beth said. "Looks like you two have something in common."

I saw Kate blush out of the corner of my eye.

Mary Beth poured coffee into three of the cups, handed two of the cups to Kate and me, and took the third one for herself. She put the plate of cookies on the glass coffee table, and sat down in one of the leather armchairs.

Mary Beth said, "Kate asked me to research the backgrounds of our twelve dead Ohio drone sub engineering project managers. I looked into their educational and work histories, their families, and any clubs or organizations to which they might have belonged. The purpose of the research was to see if there were any common threads that might have caused the engineering project managers to have been marked for death. Other than their job descriptions, of course."

"Did you find a common thread?" I said.

"No," Mary Beth said. "The dead seem indistinguishable from the eighteen drone sub engineering project managers who were not killed."

Mary Beth shifted in her chair and her skirt rode up her magnificent thighs. I didn't want Kate to catch me staring again, so I forced myself to turn away.

"That's good to know," I said. "I would, however, like to make sure we've covered every conceivable base, so I have a couple of questions. Is that okay?"

"Of course," Mary Beth said.

"First off, I understand that each of the individual NASAD drone submarine project areas would need its own engineering project manager," I said. "I also understand that each of those thirty project areas would have to work seamlessly together to create a fully functioning drone submarine. My question is, is there any reason to believe the project areas the twelve dead project managers were working on might have intertwined more closely with each other than with the projects of the eighteen living managers?"

"We looked at that very carefully," Mary Beth said. "I'm confident the answer is 'no.'"

"Did you by any chance also investigate the make-up of all the team members that worked for each of the dead engineering project managers?" I said.

"You think the managers' deaths might have something to do with the people working below them?" Mary Beth said.

"Right now I don't know what I think, Mary Beth," I said. "Other than that I don't think the dead engineers' names were picked out of a hat, or that their deaths were just due to bad luck."

"Which means you believe there's a connection, but we just haven't found it yet?" Mary Beth said.

"That's what my gut says," I said.

Mary Beth took a sip of coffee.

"I bet your gut is usually pretty good about these things," Mary Beth said.

"I don't know about that," I said. "But if I don't listen to it, I get in trouble more often than not."

"Understood," Mary Beth said. "Right now I can't give you an analysis of each individual team member, but if you'd like, I can give you a general overview of the teams. Should I do that?"

"Yes, please," I said.

Outside, one of the NASAD stealth drones flew up close to Kate's office window. It hovered there for a few seconds, then quickly disappeared. While the drone's presence had been a bit disconcerting to me, neither Mary Beth nor Kate seemed disturbed by the drone's activity. Mary Beth looked like she was going to tell me about the teams, but I interrupted her.

"You two aren't bothered by drones flying by your window?" I said.

Kate and Mary Beth laughed.

Kate said, "At first I was, but since they do it all the time, I've gotten used to it. What about you, Mary Beth?"

"I'm at the point where I don't even know they're there," Mary Beth said.

I said, "From outside the building, the windows didn't appear reflective enough to block the drones from looking inside your office."

Kate said, "They probably aren't. But at least as far as I'm concerned there's not much for anyone to see."

Mary Beth smiled.

"Me either," Mary Beth said. She paused. "You think they're spying on us, General?"

"It seems possible, doesn't it?" I said.

Kate said, "This office is fully soundproof and routinely checked for bugs. I'm sure our conversation is completely private."

"Good, that makes my paranoid soul feel better," I said. "Now, Mary Beth, before I so rudely interrupted you, I believe you were going to tell me about the drone sub project teams?"

"Right," Mary Beth said. "Usually, a NASAD engineering project manager will oversee a team of about three hundred people. The thirty teams on the Ohio drone sub project have their own separate areas of expertise. The teams are responsible for things like weapons systems, communication systems, propulsion systems, and life support systems - the life support systems are needed, as even though the size of the drone submarines' crews are vastly reduced compared to the size of the regular submarines' crews, there will still be humans aboard the drones. Broadly defined systems such as the ones I mentioned depend on many discrete, smaller systems to support their functioning. The discrete, smaller systems also have their own engineering teams assigned to them. Those additional teams handle things like the designs for the smaller systems' computer hardware, computer software, and mechanical components. The mechanical components include items such as the control mechanisms that turn rudders, raise and lower diving flaps, or speed up or slow down motors. And then there is a whole team that just makes sure everything works together."

"That's a lot of teams," I said.

"It's a complicated process, no doubt about it," Mary Beth said. "Any particular team's focus sound like it is more likely to hold an answer for us?"

"Unfortunately, no," I said.

As soon as I'd said 'no', however, I got a nagging feeling in the back of my mind that I had spoken too soon, that one NASAD team, and only one, actually held the key to what was happening at NASAD in regard to the murders and the Chinese insurmountable edge. I had the uncanny feeling that the identity of that team was written in invisible letters then dancing in a dark corner of my mind, and that, if only I had the right light, I could read what they were spelling out. But at that moment I could find no such light, and whatever meaning the letters possessed remained unknown to me.

"I guess I had better start running crosschecks on all the employees within each team, similar to the crosschecks I ran on the project engineers then, hadn't I?" Mary Beth said.

"I know it seems like a burden...," I said.

"It's not, General," Mary Beth interrupted. "We'll get right on it."

I tried again to illumine those invisible letters in the dark regions of my mind, but again failed. Kate, who had been nibbling on a cookie, seemed to be struck by a sudden thought.

Kate said, "Something just occurred to me, Mary Beth. Maybe you already looked into it, but then again, maybe you didn't."

"What is it, Kate?" Mary Beth said.

"Each of the murdered engineers was replaced by someone new, weren't they?" Kate said. "I mean, we had the eighteen living ones, but you still needed to replace the twelve who died, didn't you?"

Mary Beth looked at Kate for a moment, then somewhat firmly banged her right fist against her chin.

Hmm.

That was interesting.

Hadn't I just recently done something similar to myself on the drive down from my ranch and also in the morgue parking lot?

Was it possible that I wasn't the only one who did such seemingly crazy things to themselves?

Then again, couldn't I have just imagined Mary Beth had hit herself?

I needed to check it out.

I said to Kate, "Did Mary Beth just hit herself?"

Kate nodded.

"She does that when she's disappointed by her performance," Kate said.

Which I took as confirmation that I actually wasn't the only crazy person in the world doing crazy things to themselves.

Still, it seemed like there might be other choices a person could make.

"I'm not sure that's a great idea, Mary Beth," I said.

Mary Beth said, "I know. It's a bad habit."

"And here I was thinking you were perfect," I said.

"Ah, well, I guess the cat's out of the bag," Mary Beth said, smiling. "Getting back to your question, Kate, I'm sorry but I didn't look for a common thread among the replacements like I looked for a common thread among the dead engineers. We lost three of the engineers just last week, so we've only replaced nine engineers so far, but we'll get started looking at those nine replacements immediately."

Kate said, "Thank you."

Another drone flew up close to the window. It got so close it actually banged up against the window before it flew away.

I said, "Along a similar vein, I assume the drone sub engineering project managers who replaced the managers that were killed were carefully vetted? I ask because I want to be sure the replacements were all people who were deserving of NASAD's trust, and who would also be loyal to NASAD."

A look of concern came over Mary Beth's face.

"You don't think whoever killed the drone sub engineering project managers did so in order to replace the managers with people who might sabotage the drone subs, do you?" Mary Beth said.

"It would be nice if we could rule out that possibility," I said.

"I don't see how it's possible," Mary Beth said. "All the engineers who replaced the engineers who were killed have been with NASAD over fifteen years. Our security did a full review of their personal and financial history with the assistance of the Department of Defense before they were promoted."

"Good enough for me," I said.

Mary Beth seemed to think for a moment.

"General, do you believe there's any chance the current twenty-seven drone sub engineering project managers could be in danger right now?"

"You're worried the added security that has been put in place around them isn't good enough?" I said.

"I haven't been impressed with the FBI," Mary Beth said.

"You've met Burnette, I take it?" I said.

"And, God bless his heart, I'm sorry I did," Mary Beth said.

"There's a new FBI team managing security for both Kate and the project managers now," I said. "The team leader is very good at what he does."

"Does that mean you think the current managers are safe?" Mary Beth said.

"As safe as they can be," I said. "By the way, Kate, what would your dad have done with a guy like Burnette?"

Mary Beth said, "Do you mind if I answer that?"

Kate said, "Be my guest."

"Milt would have screamed bloody murder until the guy was replaced," Mary Beth said.

"Very true," Kate said.

I said, "But no one's screaming now?"

"Other than me, no," Kate said.

Mary Beth said, "A lot of things are different at NASAD without your dad, aren't they Kate?"

Kate nodded.

I said, "And not for the better, I presume?"

Mary Beth said, "Lord, no, not for the better. Milt was an incredible man. The biggest thing I miss about him is not being around someone who loves our employees like he loved them. He was loyal to them, too, and they were loyal to him in return."

"But now?" I said.

Mary Beth looked at Kate as if she was asking for Kate's permission to answer my question.

Kate said, "You're free to say whatever you want, Mary Beth."

"Kate does her best to try to keep things as they were," Mary Beth said, "but Freddy really is in charge of NASAD's day-to-day operations, and he's not the man Milt was."

I said, "I can't think of any men who are."

Mary Beth took one of the cookies off the plate and took a small bite out of it. Her bright white teeth sliced exquisitely through the dough.

"You know, Milt really respected you," Mary Beth said.

"Me?" I said. "You remember something Milt said from over ten years ago?"

"I do," Mary Beth said. "Milt talked about how you were the kind of man he wished worked at NASAD. He thought you were the smartest and toughest soldier he had ever met. He wanted to make sure you, and men like you, had everything they needed to do their jobs. He wanted to give you the best technology NASAD could create, so that even though you and your men went into battle essentially alone, you were never really alone."

"That's pretty much how it always turned out," I said. "Whether they know it or not, every U.S. serviceman and woman owes a debt of gratitude to Milt." I paused. "Mary Beth, I apologize for this, but there's something I need to discuss with Kate privately for a moment."

"Do you want me to leave the room?" Mary Beth said.

"Thank you for offering," I said. "But that won't be necessary."

I leaned in close to Kate and whispered in her ear.

"I think we need to bring Mary Beth into our little two-person circle regarding Dr. Nemo," I said. "I have a hunch there's a good chance she'll be able to at least give us some clues as to how to find him."

Kate whispered, "We can trust her. Go ahead."

I turned to Mary Beth.

"Mary Beth, there's one last matter we need to discuss," I said. "Kate is the only person at NASAD who knows about it."

"A secret, huh?" Mary Beth said. "I'm good with secrets."

"This one could get you killed," I said.

"You serious?" Mary Beth said.

"Yes," I said.

Mary Beth studied me for a moment.

"I know Kate is the kind of person that would never put anyone else at risk unless she believed it was absolutely necessary," Mary Beth said. "I assume you're the same kind of person?"

Two more drones appeared outside Kate's office windows. Kate and Mary Beth again seemed unperturbed by their presence. The drones hovered a few more seconds, and flew away.

"I'd like to think so," I said. "The problem is that if I tell you, there's no going back. I can't un-tell you."

"Understood," Mary Beth said. "By telling me, will it potentially help you to avenge the deaths of NASAD's engineers? I ask, General, because I need them avenged. Not only for their own lives, but for the ones they left behind. Their children, grandchildren, husbands, wives, domestic partners, mothers, fathers, and friends. It's not right what happened to any of those people. And I also can't abide what was done to Paul Lennon's two little children in the desert."

"I can't abide it either," I said. "And yes, I believe by telling you, you may be able to help me find the people responsible for all the murders. If I find them, vengeance will follow."

"Are you willing to guarantee that?" Mary Beth said.

"The vengeance?" I said.

"Yes," Mary Beth said.

"Yes," I said.

"Is it a personal guarantee?" Mary Beth said.

"If by that you mean will I do it in person, then yes," I said.

"Tell me the secret," Mary Beth said.

"The name might sound funny," I said, "but someone using the name 'Dr. Nemo' left Kate a message about a potential catastrophe involving NASAD. I have every reason to believe that person is telling the truth."

"Dr. Nemo like in Jules Verne's 'Twenty Thousand Leagues Under the Sea'?" Mary Beth said. "No...wait...that was Captain Nemo wasn't it?"

"It was," I said. "Be that as it may, I believe the person using Dr. Nemo as a code name is most likely a NASAD employee."

"That's not hard for me to believe," Mary Beth said. "We have a lot of minds at NASAD that could come up with a name like that. But 'Dr. Nemo' sounds like a pretty odd code name, and odd code names are generally the province of one specific group around here."

"Which group?" I said.

"Programmers," Mary Beth said. "Hands down, programmers use the oddest names."

"The team I work with came up with the same idea by profiling the message the person left," I said. "They believe Nemo is a male programmer under the age of thirty-two."

"NASAD's got fifteen hundred of those," Mary Beth said.

"My team said that too," I said. "I need you to help me find a way to narrow it down."

Mary Beth shook her head.

"I'm not sure I would know how to do that," Mary Beth said. "The code name alone doesn't seem like enough to go on."

Kate put down the cookie she had been nibbling on.

Kate said, "Jack and I were playing with the idea that 'Dr. Nemo' could be an anagram for something else like 'Omen Road', 'Ned Mor', or 'M Drone'. Any of those strike a bell?"

"Not immediately, no," Mary Beth said. "But I can certainly run some searches through our personnel files."

"Please do that," Kate said. "There's another thing too."

"What?" Mary Beth said.

"Nemo sent a second message," Kate said. "The message was left on a cell phone in my bedroom under my pillow."

Mary Beth seemed taken aback.

"How could he have gotten into your house?" Mary Beth said. "And even if he did, how could he possibly know what bedroom was yours?"

I said, "I think the fact that the message was left under the pillow means that Nemo is someone who's been to the Lennon house before. I think he knows his way around inside it. So the question is, what NASAD male programmers have been to the Lennon house?"

Mary Beth's eyes suddenly went wide and she punched her chin again.

"Did she just hit herself again?" I said to Kate.

Kate nodded.

Mary Beth said, "Forget about my chin. I can't believe I didn't put two and two together as soon as you mentioned the pillow."

"What are you thinking?" I said.

"The dark programmers," Mary Beth said.

CHAPTER 63

Immediately upon hearing Mary Beth say, 'The dark programmers', that nagging feeling I'd had in the back of my mind a few moments earlier about one group at NASAD - and one group only - holding the key to the murders and the insurmountable edge came back. Only the feeling then was more than nagging. It was a pounding jackhammer.

Was it possible that I'd just been alerted to the existence of the team of NASAD employees that nagging feeling had seemed to foretell?

Were the dark programmers the key to the insurmountable edge?

The letters in the corner of my mind certainly thought so. They were then no longer invisible, but fully lit and dancing. They spelled out 'Dark Programmers'.

But, since I'd never heard the phrase 'Dark Programmer' before, how was it possible those letters had even been in my mind in the first place?

Or had I heard the phrase before?

Had Milt Feynman said something to me about them many years ago and I had simply forgotten?

Between the jackhammer and the letters, I felt like I was bordering on the thin edge of sanity. I reeled myself in and forced myself to proceed in as logical a fashion as I could. Which meant first things first.

"What's a dark programmer?" I said.

"About thirty of our male programmers - and close to thirty of our female programmers - are off-book employees, and are known as the dark programmers," Mary Beth said. "Their work, which mainly concerns keeping all the products NASAD makes invulnerable to cyber attacks, is top secret. The identities of the dark programmers are also top secret. The secrecy is felt to be necessary to keep the dark programmers safe from whoever might threaten or harm them in order to learn what they know. We pay the dark programmers, but we have no records of who they are."

I turned to Kate.

"Did you know about the dark programmers?" I said.

Kate nodded.

"I know about the dark programmers and what they do," Kate said. "But I never realized we didn't have records of who they were. Mary Beth, how is that possible? And if you don't have the records, who does?"

"The vice president of dark programming," Mary Beth said. "The vice president is the executive in charge of the dark programming division and the dark programming division is his only responsibility. All communications between the dark programming division and the rest of NASAD are handled only by him. Other than the vice president, the other employees in the dark programming division, Milt, and then later Paul, no one has ever known the dark programmers' identities. Their location is off-books too."

"I was aware the dark programmers were a very secret division, but I'm amazed I never knew they were *that* secretive," Kate said.

"I'm not amazed you didn't know," Mary Beth said. "We have nearly one hundred different divisions at NASAD, each with their own vice president. It would be natural for you to focus on what the divisions do, and not on the details of how each division is structured. Besides, your father's goal was always to call as little attention to the dark programming division as possible. Their safety was always his primary concern."

I said, "Mary Beth, do you know the name of the vice president?"

"I don't," Mary Beth said. "The first vice president of dark programming was selected by Milt thirty years ago and then the vice president's personal records were completely deleted from NASAD's books. Milt never told anyone who it was. Even I, the employee who was closest to Milt, had no clue who the vice president was, other than that Milt told me it was a man. The vice president was given the irrevocable, perpetual, and sole authority to replace him or herself when, and if, the time came to retire. No one has any idea if we are on our first or our tenth vice president. The vice president communicates in encrypted and coded messages to our offices here and our offices respond back in kind. The vice president then assigns and supervises all projects undertaken by the dark programmers and controls the bank account from which the programmers are paid."

Three drones in a very tight wing-to-wing formation flew up close to the office window. The drones executed a synchronized barrel roll and flew off.

"I assume the bank accounts are all highly secret as well?" I said.

"They are," Mary Beth said. "The bank account used to fund the payroll is used for one payroll period and then is changed. All monies that go to that funding account are always routed through ten different accounts at ten different banks and those are only used once as well and then changed. The whole payroll payment system is therefore completely untraceable. The dark programmers' identities are masked throughout their entire professional lives at NASAD. Even their initial employee orientations are completed by the dark programming division itself. Indeed, the only time HR ever hears anything about the dark programmers is when a new one is hired, or one of them leaves the company, so that we can adjust the amount of the payroll transfers."

"Sounds pretty impregnable," I said.

"It is," Mary Beth said.

"I assume that most, if not all, of the dark programmers' work is being done for projects directly involving, or at least directly affecting, the U.S. government?" I said.

"That's correct," Mary Beth said.

"The U.S. government doesn't insist on knowing who the vice president of dark programming is, or who the dark programmers are, or on having the ability to contact any of them?" I said.

"When the dark programming division first started up the government of course wanted to know everyone's identities and to be able to contact them," Mary Beth said. "But Milt blocked all of that. Milt said it was his way or the highway. Again, the vice president and dark programmers' safety was Milt's primary concern. And nothing has changed to this day."

"I don't see how the government could possibly permit that," I said. "I'm sure that everyone working in the dark programming division, including the vice president, would at the very least need high level security clearances."

Mary Beth took another sip of coffee and smiled.

"General, would you like to take a guess at the name of the company that has a contract to perform the vast majority of the U.S. government's security clearances?" Mary Beth said.

"You're saying the government allowed NASAD to do the security clearances for its own employees?" I said.

Mary Beth nodded.

"But that's such an obvious conflict of interest," I said.

"I don't know what else to say other than that the very fact the dark programming division exists in the manner it does speaks volumes as to the government's respect for Milt," Mary Beth said.

"It certainly looks that way," I said. "I suppose it also speaks volumes as to how desperately the government wanted the work of the dark programming division to proceed."

Mary Beth smiled again.

"That too," Mary Beth said.

"So, to this day not even the U.S. government knows the identity of the vice president or the dark programmers?" I said.

"Correct," Mary Beth said.

"That's probably pretty wise," I said. "It's been my experience that there are a lot of people in the government that leak like a sieve." I paused. "If for some reason I wanted to contact the vice president via the encrypted messaging system he uses, could I do that?"

"I've never done it, and contact with him is very strictly controlled," Mary Beth said. "My understanding is that, except for the highly routinized communications he has with NASAD regarding the dark programmers' projects, their payroll, and the rare hirings or terminations of employees within the dark programming division, the vice president never has any other contact with NASAD personnel. I think reaching him would be like trying to break in to Fort Knox. That's not to say we couldn't give it a go if it was something you wanted to do."

If my hunch about the dark programmers and the insurmountable edge developed into something more solid than a hunch, then contacting the vice president of dark programming seemed like something I would absolutely have to do. But it was way too early for any contact. Not only could I embarrass myself if my hunch was completely off base, but I would also have to try to gather as much information as I could about the vice president before I communicated with him. There was, after all, a chance he was on the side of the bad guys and could not be trusted. Since no one at NASAD even knew his identity, it was even possible that the enemy had inserted one of their own into his position. Still, if he was that hard to reach, there was no reason not to get the ball rolling. If Mary Beth was able to schedule some form of encrypted communication with the vice president of dark programming, and I later decided that communication could compromise my mission, I would just cancel the communication.

"Thanks," I said. "Please try to set up a method by which I can communicate with him." I paused. "There's still something missing in what you've told us, however. Why did you remember all of this when I mentioned that someone had been at Kate's house?"

Mary Beth punched herself on the chin again.

Kate and I shared a look.

Kate said, "Like I said, there's no way to stop her."

Mary Beth said, "Kate's right, there isn't any way to stop me. People have tried, but they've all failed. I guess deep down I must like it. In regard to your question, however, you're right - I *did* immediately think of the dark programmers when you told me some unknown visitor had been at Kate's house. And I apologize. Given what you just told me about Dr. Nemo, the first thing out of my mouth in regard to the dark programmers should have been *why* that mysterious house visitor made me think of the dark programmers. The reason why is there was a NASAD program that started up about six years ago. It was meant to help the youngest computer programmers who were slated to become dark programmers get some background as to what their life at NASAD would be like. They met with Paul Lennon as part of that program."

"At Kate and Paul's house?" I said.

"Yes," Mary Beth said. "Doing so at their house, and not at the NASAD campus, helped retain the secrecy that was, and is, so important to the dark programming division."

I turned to Kate.

"Did you know anything about this?" I said.

"No," Kate said. "But it's perfectly understandable how I wouldn't. My kids weren't born yet, and I was working full time as a physician back then. I got pregnant very quickly after we were married, but I was out of the house most of the day even though I was pregnant. If Paul and my dad felt it best to keep the program secret, they most likely wouldn't have mentioned it, even to me."

"How old were the programmers when they met with Paul?" I asked Mary Beth.

"Some of them were as young as thirteen when they started working with us," Mary Beth said.

"Thirteen?" I said.

"Yes," Mary Beth said. "They were geniuses. NASAD has a recruiting system that scours top colleges and universities for the specialized talents we need. The dark programming division plucks its programmers from the pool of talent that system creates. Of course, no one outside the dark programming division ever knows who the division hires, or even considered hiring."

"The thirteen-year-olds were already in college?" I said.

"Actually, they had all graduated college by the time we contacted them," Mary Beth said. "Most of them even had Ph.D.'s. Their parents didn't know what to do with them. They were happy their teenage kids could get a very high-paying job."

"It sounds stupid even as I say it, but aren't there laws against child labor?" I said.

Mary Beth lifted her coffee cup off the table and took another sip.

"You of all people should know how that went," Mary Beth said. "No one gets in the way of the government of the good ol' USA when it wants something. We got waivers."

"I guess I could see that happening," I said. "These kids were so young, though. They couldn't have lived on their own, could they?"

Mary Beth laughed.

"No, such a thing was never even considered," Mary Beth said. "When kids that young join the dark programmer division, they live with all the other dark programmers who are still under eighteen years old in a house with adult supervision. But don't ask me where the house is, or who the adults supervising them are, as all of that is, again, top secret."

The nagging feeling that had earlier become like a jackhammer pounding in my head, then progressed even further, and became a giant fireworks display in my mind. The fireworks display had all the concussive bangs and dazzling explosions such displays usually entail. The message all that cacophony and effulgence seemed to be conveying to me was, 'Listen up you idiot! It's clear as day now! Dr. Nemo is one of those kids who met with Paul Lennon before he became a dark programmer!'

That message, despite the somewhat rude manner in which it had been communicated, made sense, didn't it? As a dark programmer, Nemo would have had access to all the software controlling NASAD's products and could easily be involved with a product at NASAD that could put the U.S. at grave risk in the event of war, a product to which he had most likely been referring in his voicemail warning to Kate. And even if Mary Beth had no way to find out the identities of the dark programmers, wasn't that something MOM might be able to pull off? I would have to get in touch with Haley as soon as possible, but, at that moment, I had to shut out the lights and sounds and do my best to gather anything I could to help confirm the truth or falsity of the fireworks' message.

"Is there any chance there are records of Paul's meetings with the young geniuses?" I said.

"If Paul kept any, which I doubt he did, they would have all been destroyed," Mary Beth said. "Top secret is top secret, General."

"You said the NASAD program that included Paul's meetings - the program that was put in place to help the young geniuses get acclimated to their new lives at NASAD - was started about six years ago," I said. "When did it stop?"

"When Paul died," Mary Beth said.

"But that would mean it continued even after Kate had her children," I said. "Why wouldn't she have seen the dark programmers when she was home with them?"

"I'm pretty sure Paul moved the meetings to another site when his and Kate's kids were born," Mary Beth said.

Suddenly, the building began to shake, its windows began to rattle, and the sky was filled with a primordial roar. I recognized the roar as that of an approaching helicopter. From how quickly the roar was increasing in volume, I could tell the helicopter was moving extremely fast. The roar, and its intimation of speed, instantly flooded my mind with memories, both good and bad. The bad memories involved dangerous moments of combat when the approaching choppers were enemy airships raining cannon and rocket fire down upon my men and me. The good memories involved equally dangerous moments, but the choppers were U.S. military helicopters being piloted by my pals, and the rocket and cannon fire was being used to provide cover for my team and me to escape hot zones that had gotten far too hot.

I cleared my mind of those memories and looked at Mary Beth and Kate. Both women had astonished expressions on their faces. Clearly such rattling and shaking was not a normal occurrence at NASAD. The three of us then seemed to arrive at the same thought. Without saying a word to each other, Mary Beth, Kate, and I all ran to the window.

A Bell 206L helicopter - which is just like the 206 model favored by police departments, only the 'L' model has more seats - swooped low over the NASAD campus heading for the heliport. It was traveling at a brutally high speed, even faster than I first imagined, and one more appropriate to the killing fields of the world, than a tony Southern California neighborhood. The drones scattered in all directions.

Kate said, "That's the NASAD corporate helicopter Freddy uses. It must have picked him up shortly after we left the house."

I said, "Is Freddy normally in such a big rush?"

"No," Kate said. "I've never seen anything like this."

The Bell skimmed only inches above the helipad's surface, banked sharply left to slow itself down, and without hovering for even a millisecond, slammed its left landing skid on the ground with such force that it caused a shower of sparks to shoot up into the air. The force of the maneuver then also caused the right skid to smack down onto the ground as well. The whole process from flight to touchdown took less than two seconds.

"That's an Apache war chopper move," I said. "I've never seen a Bell do anything like that. In fact, I've only seen one pilot who could do it in an Apache as fast as that Bell just did."

"Freddy's pilot is an Afghanistan War veteran," Kate said.

"Is his name Donnie Kurstinger?" I said.

Both Kate and Mary Beth turned to look at me, their eyes as big as silver dollars.

"What did you say?" Kate said.

"I asked if the pilot was Donnie Kurtsinger," I said. "He's the only guy I ever saw make that move."

Mary Beth said, "The pilot *is* Donnie Kurtsinger. Freddy hired Donnie after Donnie retired from the military. The fact you could figure that out from the way he landed the helicopter is amazing."

"What can I say?" I said. "When you're good, you're good."

Both women rolled their eyes.

The helicopter's side hatch swung open. Four men exited and dashed under the whirling blades. The first two men immediately headed for the thirty-story building that was east of the building we were in, but the third man and the fourth man held back for the moment. It was hard for me to be sure, gazing down as I was from the high-up window of Kate's office, but the discombobulated walk and the short yet hefty size of the first man made me think the man was Freddy.

"Is that first man Freddy?" I said to Kate.

"Yes," Kate said. "The man next to him is Carter Bowdoin."

Mary Beth said, "Do you know who Carter Bowdoin is, General?"

"I do," I said. "He's the son of the immediately previous president of the United States and the chairman of Pennsylvania Avenue Partners. Kate also told me yesterday that PAP is the largest outside shareholder of NASAD."

Kate said, "I wonder why they're in such a rush?"

Mary Beth said, "Wellington's not."

I said, "Wellington, as in Bryce Wellington, the general?"

"Yes," Mary Beth said. "General Wellington is retired now and works for PAP. I think he's been with PAP for about two years. General Wellington is the one being ministered to."

Bryce Wellington - the man who had been the third man out of the helicopter - was positioned about ten yards from the chopper's doors. The ministering Mary Beth had referred to was in regard to the fact that the fourth man to exit the helicopter was standing behind Wellington and helping him into a suit jacket. The motions of the two men were such that they reminded me of a czar being dressed by one of his royal court dressers. After the fourth man had finished getting the suit jacket on Wellington, the man hustled around to Wellington's front to button one of Wellington's jacket buttons, and then took out a brush and began to tidy up the jacket's lapels and shoulders. Once the brushing was completed, both men set off after Freddy and Carter Bowdoin.

"Who's the guy that was doing the brushing?" I said.

"Wellington's valet," Mary Beth said. "It looks like the valet is probably a new one, since the last one was a woman."

The fact that Bryce Wellington had a valet didn't surprise me. I knew

Bryce when he was a general in the U.S. Army, and since he had been a pretentious asshole back then, I saw no reason he hadn't remained a pretentious asshole after shifting to the private sector.

General Bryce Wellington also just happened to be the general who, two and a half years ago, had requested Jeff and his team go on an emergency mission. That mission turned out to be Jeff's last mission, as it led directly to Jeff coming down with PTSD. I had reviewed the thought processes Wellington had employed in deciding to request that Jeff go out on the mission, and I had found those thought processes to have been, at best, highly questionable. Which was why I thought of Wellington not only as an asshole, but an idiot as well.

Kate said, "I don't know about you two, but I'm curious as hell about what the four of them are up to."

"Took the words right out of my mouth," I said. "Let's go check it out."

I turned to Mary Beth.

"It's been indescribably wonderful," I said.

"The feeling is mutual," Mary Beth said.

Kate said, "I'll fill you in later on whatever we learn, Mary Beth."

"Thank you," Mary Beth said. "I'm sure it will be quite interesting. In the meantime, I'm going to work on finding Dr. Nemo. The shields surrounding the dark programmers' identities and whereabouts are supposed to be impenetrable, but that's not going to stop me from trying. Maybe I can even dredge up a list of the kids that might have visited your home. I'll also try to arrange a way for you to communicate with the vice president of dark programming. If I can do that, or if I find out anything about Nemo or the dark programmers, you two will be the first to know."

"We'll be forever in your debt," I said.

Kate and I ran out of her office and raced each other down the corridor toward the elevator bank.

CHAPTER 64

Kate and I, still running, exited her building's lobby and set off towards the office tower we had seen Freddy, Carter Bowdoin, Bryce Wellington, and Wellington's valet heading for. To get to that office tower, Kate and I had to go through the little park with the man-made lake that sat between all three NASAD office towers. It was almost 10:30 a.m., and we had to maneuver between hundreds of employees fleeing the towers on their midmorning break. There were a number of older and middle-aged employees, but overall, the age range was definitely skewed toward the youthful side, and the dress code was overwhelmingly casual - jeans, shorts, summery dresses, t-shirts, sandals, and running shoes. I saw no one dressed in the traditional type of business attire such as what Kate and Mary Beth were wearing that day.

The breeze had picked up, and a dozen of the employees, six men and six women, were cheering four model sailboats that were racing towards a finish line demarcated by two small buoys at one end of the lake. The sailboats were about three feet long and were employing rather sophisticated tactics - they were raising and lowering their jibs, taking advantage of subtle wind shifts with sudden course corrections, stealing the wind from other boats' sails, and jibing - in their attempts to be the first one across the line. Each boat had what looked like laser remote sensing systems mounted atop their small decks. Miniature radar domes and stereo cameras also protruded from their hulls.

I recognized the sailboats' domes, cameras, and lasers as devices that, when coupled with an onboard computer, would allow the boats to be self-piloted. The software piloting the model sailboats was probably similar in many respects to the software used in self-driving cars. However, since the boats' software was generating commands that allowed the boats to execute intricate, competitive racing maneuvers, it was clear the boats' systems were much more complicated than the systems that merely drove cars from one point to another. In fact, since the boats' computers had obviously been programmed to find complex winning strategies, the sailboats' software was probably much more akin to the highly advanced artificial intelligence systems utilized, for example, by the chess playing computers whose digital brains had long ago beaten human grandmasters. The boats' artificial minds, however, seemed to have much less genteel rules of engagement than their chess playing counterparts. It had quickly become apparent to me that ramming and attempting to capsize an opposing boat were fair game.

"Those sailboats are making pretty spirited maneuvers," I said to Kate, my breath coming in rapid ins and outs from the exertion of our running.

"They're part of NASAD's artificial intelligence program," Kate said, her breathing perhaps slightly more labored than mine.

"Does NASAD have AI systems running anything bigger than a model sailboat?" I said.

"You mean like tanks or something?" Kate said.

"Yes," I said.

"Not that I know of," Kate said. "But it wouldn't surprise me if we did."

Kate and I came to the end of the lake and hustled up a path that led to the office tower to which Freddy, Carter Bowdoin, Bryce Wellington, and Wellington's valet had been headed. We had taken only a few steps up the path when I suddenly got the feeling I was being watched. I turned my head, scanning the crowds of people that were then surrounding Kate and me. One young man - who was sitting on a grassy knoll on the opposite side of the lake from us, and wearing sunglasses, a big billed, blue Yankees cap, a white t-shirt, and blue jeans - seemed to be looking right at Kate and me. He instantly turned away the moment my gaze landed on him. There was something odd in the way he turned that I couldn't quite put my finger on - perhaps it was its rapidity, perhaps something else - but in any event, I didn't make too much of his actions at the time. In retrospect, I wished I'd paid much more attention to the young man than I did. Things might have turned out quite differently if I had.

Kate and I ran up the front steps of the office tower. We passed between fifteen-foot-high glass doors - the doors were exact duplicates of the lobby doors of Kate's building - and found ourselves inside the tower's lobby. The lobby, like the doors, was a carbon copy of the lobby we had just left - exactly the same green glass, marble floors, and red mahogany walls. The security desk was the same too, and the guards manning it looked almost identical to the ones manning the desk in the other lobby as well. Kate and I leaned forward in front of the desk with our hands on our knees and caught our breath.

"Good morning, William," Kate said to one of the guards. "Might you be able to tell me where my brother was headed?"

"Tenth floor, Dr. Lennon," the guard, William, said. "Cyber Defense Hall."

"Thank you, William," Kate said.

"You're welcome, ma'am," William said. "Oh, and ma'am, your brother was also quite out of breath, but much more than you. Were you having a race or something?"

"Not really, William," Kate said.

"Honestly, I was extremely worried about how your brother looked," William said. "I was just about to call for a medic."

"That won't be necessary, William," Kate said. "If he croaks I'll revive him myself."

William laughed. "I'm sure you will, ma'am."

Kate and I took the elevator to the tenth floor. We exited the elevator and took the floor's corridor until we came to a set of double doors manned by two Uzi-toting NASAD security guards. A plaque on the wall to the right of the doors said 'NASAD Cyber Defense Hall'. The guards smiled at us and each one opened one of the doors. Kate and I walked into the room and the guards closed the doors behind us.

I took a moment to get my bearings. I hadn't expected to find anything like this room in the NASAD office towers. It was one of the most enormous rooms I had ever seen. It was three stories high and as massive as an airplane hangar. It reminded me of nothing so much as the mission control room NASA used for manned space launches. Only this room was bigger.

A thirty-foot-tall, fifty-foot-wide, electronic screen lined one wall. The screen was divided into twelve sections and each section flashed with its own pattern of multicolored lights and rapidly changing number strings that looked like they were hundreds of digits long. As I studied the sections more closely, it appeared to me that the flashing lights were actually displaying a series of mazes, and that each maze had a clearly demarcated center. A red dot of light was moving along the paths of each maze, seemingly searching for the maze's center. As the red dots got closer to the center, they either exploded in bright bursts of blue light, or the walls of the mazes' paths almost magically shifted and the red dots were forced to start over again.

Most of the room was taken up with long, semicircular seating rows that were facing the electronic screen and stacked one on top of the other, amphitheatre style. Each row had a continuous wood desktop with seats behind the desktop at regular intervals. Approximately one hundred young men and women, dressed in the same casual style as the men and women in the park - t-shirts, jeans, running shoes, and sandals - with most of the men having long hair, and some with beards, sat behind computer stations mounted on the desktop. The men and women occasionally made rapid keystrokes on their keyboards, apparently responding to what they were seeing on both their own computer monitors and the electronic wall screen.

I didn't see Wellington's valet anywhere, but Freddy, Carter Bowdoin, and Bryce Wellington were fifty feet away from where Kate and I had entered. Sweat was pouring off Freddy's face and his shoulders were heaving as he seemed to be trying to catch his breath. None of the three men appeared to have noticed Kate and me, as they were absorbed in a hushed conversation with a tall, thin man. The thin man exuded a casual, yet confident and focused demeanor - a demeanor that suggested to me he was in charge of the work being done in the NASAD Cyber Defense Hall.

"You going to tell me what's going on in here," I whispered to Kate, "or do you want me to guess?"

"I think I'd like you to guess," Kate said.

"Well, from the name on the door, I assume this is where NASAD runs its cybersecurity," I said.

"Correct," Kate said.

"I'd also say from the looks of the light show on that wigged out Jumbotron on the wall over there, that you're being hacked," I said.

Kate stiffened.

"Shhh," Kate said. "Don't let anyone hear you."

I looked around. No one seemed to be paying any attention to us.

"What?" I said. "Is that some kind of insult?"

"We're not being hacked," Kate said.

"Sure looks that way to me," I said.

"Someone is *attempting* to hack us," Kate said. "It's a big difference."

I rolled my eyes.

"If you say so," I said.

"These people take a lot of pride in their work," Kate said.

I studied the faces of the young men and women for a moment. There was a frenetic energy radiating from them, and they looked like they knew what they were doing, but I couldn't say they looked especially prideful. Maybe they looked prideful in private.

"Aren't there attempted hacks of NASAD all the time?" I said.

"There are," Kate said.

"So what's Freddy so lathered up about?" I said.

"I don't know," Kate said.

It was at that moment that Freddy finally spotted us. He appeared to become apoplectic with rage. His face turned bright red and his eyes looked like they might pop out of his head. Without saying a word to Carter Bowdoin or Bryce Wellington, Freddy spun on his heels - almost losing his balance in the process - and lumbered/waddled over to us, again seemingly as fast as his little feet would carry him. Freddy's movements caused his belly to swing back and forth in rhythm with the flapping of the shirttail that still hung out of his pants.

"What is he doing here?" Freddy said in a hiss as he drew up next to us. Up close, I could then see that Freddy's shirt collar was sopping wet and that there were sweat stains on the portions of his suit jacket under his armpits.

"Chill, Freddy," Kate said.

"We're being attacked, Kate," Freddy said. "It's none of his business."

"Let's just say you and I agree to disagree on this subject Freddy," Kate said.

Over Freddy's shoulder I could see Carter Bowdoin, Bryce Wellington, and the tall, thin man who looked like he was in charge, watching us. Wellington said something to the man, and all three started walking toward us. Freddy must have caught my gaze, as he turned around to see what I was looking at. Having done so, Freddy instantly clutched the sides of his head with both hands and squeezed hard.

"No, no, no, no," Freddy wailed. "I can't believe this is happening."

I said, "You're making me feel like some kind of pariah, Freddy."

Freddy turned back to face me.

"You are a pariah!" Freddy said. "You're worse than a pariah!"

"Freddy, I swear from the bottom of my heart I want to be healed," I said. "I want to be like other men, not this outcast nobody wants."

Freddy studied me for a moment. His eyes looked suspicious.

"Who said that?" Freddy said. "I know you didn't just make that up."

"You tell me," I said. "You went to Yale."

"Screw you," Freddy said.

Bowdoin, Wellington, and the tall, thin man arrived at our little group. Three-Star U.S. Army General, Retired, Bryce Wellington brushed past Freddy and grabbed me in a bear hug. Wellington at six foot, four inches tall was an inch taller than me, but his sixty-seven year old body was a bony skeleton and I could feel his bony ribs and knees jabbing into me at various spots on my body. The touch of his long bony fingers on my back made me shudder. Wellington's face was so close to mine I could feel the slight stubble on his cheeks and smell what I guessed to be his extremely expensive cologne. The cologne, however, couldn't hide a musty smell about him, an odor that reminded me of nothing so much as the stench of a big city sewer.

Wellington pushed back a little ways from me and placed his hands on my shoulders.

"So good to see you Jack," Bryce Wellington said in his deep gravelly voice. "Let me get a good look at you."

Unfortunately, while Wellington was getting a good look at me, I got a good look at him. Nothing much had changed from the last time I had seen him over four years ago. Same rheumy grey eyes, high sloping forehead, overly chiseled, cleft chin, hawk-like nose, yellow tobacco stained teeth, and pasty skin.

Wellington's hair and clothes were the only things that I could see that were different from our previous encounter. His crew cut was dyed a lighter red, but it still had the unnatural, washed out, other-worldly appearance I remembered. He was wearing a suit made of blue silk with tailoring that appeared to have come out of London's Saville Row - the last time I had seen him he was in full military dress at the funeral for a fallen special ops colonel we both knew.

I don't think anyone at the colonel's funeral wanted Wellington to be there other than Wellington himself. Wellington had always been the kind of man who had a much higher opinion of his abilities than those around him, and that went quintuple for his soldiering abilities. Wellington also had on a gold Rolex watch, red silk tie, white silk shirt, and black leather shoes that had been polished to a spit shine. I knew Wellington would never stoop so low as to polish his own shoes, so I assumed his valet had done it.

"Good to see you, Bryce," I lied. I gently moved out from under his grip.

The look on Freddy's face had now progressed from one of agitated disbelief to nearly hysterical disbelief.

"You know this guy, Bryce?" Freddy said, his voice almost a screech.

"Of course I know him, Freddy," Bryce Wellington said. "General Wilder is the most decorated soldier in the history of the United States Armed Forces."

"Him?" Freddy said.

"Is there something wrong, Freddy?" Wellington said.

"No, no, nothing wrong," Freddy said. "I just didn't realize, I mean, it's kinda hard to believe isn't it?"

I said, "Thanks, Freddy. Actually, Bryce, General Jeffrey Bradshaw is the most decorated soldier in the history of the United States Armed Forces."

Wellington said, "I suppose he is, isn't he?" He gave me a manly punch on the shoulder. "Well, being number two isn't so bad is it, Jack?"

I didn't say anything.

"As long as we're on the subject, how is Jeff, Jack?" Wellington said.

"Jeff's recuperating well," I said, and then silently thought, 'No thanks to you, asshole.'

"Where is he these days?" Wellington said.

"He's staying with me on my ranch," I said.

"That must be grand for him," Wellington said. "I gotta hand it to Jeff. He is one tough hombre to have lived through what he lived through."

"Indeed he is," I said.

"Is there any way Jeff is well enough to travel?" Wellington said.

"Travel, Bryce?" I said.

"It would be great to have Jeff here with us right now," Wellington said. "I'm sure he could be a big help on this nasty drone sub problem that's developed at NASAD."

Though I was tempted not to say anything about the fact Jeff at that moment was already on the road and on his way to Kate's house, there was no way I was going to be able to keep Jeff's presence a secret once he arrived.

"Actually, Jeff is on his way down here right now," I said. "I'm sure he'll be happy to see you."

The happy to see Wellington part was, of course, a lie, but I felt lying fit right in with the smarmy mode I was in. As soon as I said it, I also saw Wellington's eyes twitch slightly. Was that twitch because Jeff was on his way, or because Wellington found it hard to believe Jeff would be happy to see him? Or was it something else entirely? I had no idea, but I figured I'd get a better read on that issue if and when Bryce Wellington and Jeff ever crossed paths again.

"Fantastic," Wellington said. "It's great both of you are on board."

Freddy pushed his way between Wellington and me and put his mouth very close to Wellington's ear.

"On board? Who said we want either of them on board?" Freddy whispered loud enough for anyone within ten feet to hear. "I really don't think them being on board is a good idea, Bryce."

"Of course it is, Freddy," Wellington said loudly, showing no respect for Freddy's seeming need for secrecy. "We're lucky to have him. General Jack Wilder is the best in the business. Ain't that so, Jack?"

Wellington reached around Freddy to slap me on the back. The reach around moved Wellington's head away from Freddy's mouth, but that didn't keep Freddy from continuing to say what he must have felt needed to be said.

"Shouldn't we talk this over, Bryce?" Freddy said. "This is a top secret project we're working on."

"Top secret, top schmeecret," Wellington said. "Jack and Jeff have a higher clearance than anyone in this room."

Freddy appeared not to know what to say to that. He looked a bit sulky. I was just starting to think about how the lines of power seemed a little odd at NASAD - it appeared to me like Freddy, NASAD's chairman and CEO, was taking orders from Wellington, though it seemed in the normal order of things it would be the other way around - when Carter Bowdoin cleared his throat in a bid for attention.

"General, aren't you going to introduce us?" Bowdoin said to Wellington.

"Sorry, Carter," Wellington said. "Jack, this is Carter Bowdoin. Carter is the managing director of Pennsylvania Avenue Partners. You may not know this, but PAP is a major investor in NASAD."

Bowdoin extended his hand and I shook it. Carter's handshake was firm and strong. The skin of his hand was dry, not all wet and fishy like Freddy's.

Carter Bowdoin said, "Always a pleasure to meet a true hero, General."

I said, "Thank you, Carter." Then, just to prove to myself I could be as smarmy as the next guy when I needed to be, I added, "The pleasure is all mine."

Carter Bowdoin appeared to be in his mid to late thirties, was six feet tall, athletically built, and had a boyishly handsome face with very pale blue and very sharp eyes - perhaps too sharp, I thought. He also had a wide politician's smile that flashed shiny, orthodontically perfect teeth, and dark brown hair that was an exact match for Little Lord Fauntleroy's - bangs in front, long in back and on the sides, with the back nearly touching his shoulders, and the sides covering his ears. He was dressed in a blue Zegna blazer, a pink shirt, a carefully knotted tie with dark blue and light blue horizontal stripes that had little gold panthers flecked on the stripes in a random pattern, tan slacks, and brown Ferragamo loafers with no socks.

A diamond and sapphire Yale class ring was on his right ring finger and a platinum watch with a blue face that said 'Greubel Forsey Art Piece 1' was on Carter's left wrist. I remembered reading somewhere that an Art Piece 1 watch was worth over a million and a half dollars. Watches were on my mind because of what Bobby and Timmy had said about the party bus driver's watch, so I of course checked carefully to see if Bowdoin's watch had the multiple dials of the sporting watch that Bobby and Timmy had described. Bowdoin's watch didn't have such dials.

Freddy said, "Carter's father used to be president of the United States."

"Thanks again, Freddy," I said. "I didn't know that."

"You didn't?" Freddy said. "Everybody knows that."

"I was kidding Freddy," I said. "Of course I knew that."

"Next time, don't lie," Freddy said.

Kate, who had so far had been silently watching the proceedings with a somewhat annoyed expression on her face, loudly said, "Freddy, please."

Freddy scowled at her, then appeared to fall into a funk.

Bowdoin's cell phone buzzed in his jacket pocket. He took it out and checked the incoming number.

"Excuse me everyone, but General Wellington, Freddy, and I have to take this call," Bowdoin said. "There's a PAP board meeting in progress and we have to brief them on the current state of affairs here." Bowdoin answered the phone, said, "Hold on," and then addressed the tall, thin man I thought was in charge of the Cyber Defense Hall. "I'm sorry, Raj. No one's introduced you to the general yet, have they?"

"It's no problem, sir," Raj said. He had a refined Indian accent and looked to be in his mid-forties. He also had deeply intelligent eyes that were like polished obsidian, a warm smile, closely cropped black hair, and skin the color of fine bronze. He was wearing khaki pants, a loose fitting white peasant shirt, and sandals.

"You're too kind, Raj," Bowdoin said. "Raj Divedi, General Wilder. General Wilder, Raj Divedi. Raj is the head of cybersecurity and cyber warfare software at NASAD. Raj makes sure that not only are our own internal computer systems at NASAD safe from outside intruders, but that the software systems NASAD provides to the U.S. military are completely bulletproof and function flawlessly - something I am sure you can appreciate, General."

Carter Bowdoin smiled, then winked at me. I'm not much of a winker, but thinking it was the smarmy thing to do, I winked back.

"Yes, I certainly can appreciate that Carter," I said.

Raj and I shook hands. Raj's handshake was also firm, strong, and dry.

"Raj, why don't you tell the general what's happening here right now while we take the call with PAP's board," Bowdoin said.

Bowdoin's words roused Freddy out of his funk.

"With all due respect to Bryce's obvious confidence in General Wilder, I think that's a very bad idea, Carter," Freddy said. "From what

I've heard, the general is a train wreck waiting to happen."

"Who told you that, Freddy?" Bowdoin said.

"Burnette," Freddy said.

"Well, Agent Burnette is a fine man, but I'm sure he's way off base on that one," Bowdoin said. "Now, let's get out of here. We're going to need a room where we can talk in private."

Freddy, Carter Bowdoin, and Bryce Wellington headed towards the door through which Kate and I had entered the Cyber Defense Hall. Bowdoin acknowledged friendly goodbye waves from a large number of the programmers. Just before the three men reached the door, Wellington's valet appeared seemingly out of nowhere and joined them. Watching all of them exit, I thought the lines of power at NASAD had grown even more blurry for me. First Bryce Wellington, then Carter Bowdoin, had given Freddy orders. Who was really in charge around here?

I was also beginning to feel sorry for Freddy. It didn't seem like anyone liked him. Maybe he had a dog at home. Maybe it liked him. I made a mental note to ask Kate about the power lines and dog later.

Kate gestured towards the giant screen and its flashing lights and seemingly infinitely long numbers, and said, "Raj, Freddy said we are under an actual attack."

"That is correct, Dr. Lennon," Raj said.

I said, "Do you know where it's coming from?"

"We are fairly confident it is from China," Raj said. "The attack has a similar signature to previous Chinese attacks on NASAD."

"Datong Road?" I said.

"Ah, you know about Datong Road," Raj said. "But a man of your stature and responsibilities would, wouldn't he?"

"You're too kind," I said.

"Thank you, sir," Raj said. "Yes, we believe the attack is coming from the eleventh floor of the twelve-story building operated by Unit 61398 of the People's Liberation Army on Datong Road in the Pudong area of Shanghai. The building is in the midst of bars, cheap restaurants, and seedy massage parlors, but the goings-on inside the building are extremely sophisticated. The group running today's attack is an offshoot of the 'Comment Group', otherwise known as 'Byzantine Candor'. We call them the 'Nasty Pandas.'"

"Doesn't quite seem fair to pandas to link them up to such unsavory sorts, does it?" I said.

Raj seemed to consider this.

"Hmm, perhaps you are right," Raj said. "We may have to rethink that. In any event, the Nasty Pandas have moved around quite a lot. They started in Shanghai, went to Beijing for a while, then to Chengdu..."

"Hence the panda reference," I said.

"You know a lot, General," Raj said.

Kate said, "Excuse me gentlemen, but this talk about the panda reference has lost me."

"Sorry, Dr. Lennon," Raj said, "We were referring to the fact the official Chinese Research Base of Giant Panda Breeding is located outside of the city of Chengdu. It is rather famous as visitors can see the pandas in their natural habitat."

"Sorry I asked," Kate said. "Please go on, Raj."

"Certainly," Raj said. "From Chengdu, the Nasty Pandas returned to Shanghai, where they are now."

I said, "How do you track the Nasty Pandas' location?"

"They use hacking tools that are highly specific to their group, such as complex variations on the ASPXTool, which allows them to use a web shell to gain access to a company's servers, and an 'OwaAuth' credential tool to attack certain Microsoft software," Raj said. "If we see any of the specific tool variations in use, then we know the Nasty Pandas are behind it."

I looked back at the screen and tried to follow one of the moving lights.

"The red dots of light on the screen," I said. "Do they represent the attacker's entry attempts?"

"Very astute, General," Raj said. "Each dot symbolizes an individual hacker's activities and follows the progress - hopefully, the lack of progress - of the hacker's attempts to breach our firewalls."

"The firewalls appear to keep shifting," I said.

"Also very astute," Raj said. "Once the system senses that the entry is unauthorized, it will let the hacker believe he or she has been successful and allow access to another level. The levels ultimately lead nowhere, so it only appears to the hacker that progress is being made."

I watched the lines demarcating the mazes' walls on the screens as they continued to shift and reform.

"Must make an invader waste a lot of time," I said. "Bet it pisses them off."

"I believe it does General," Raj said. "I hope it is a most exquisite pissed off."

I followed the dots on the screen for another moment and watched the walls of the mazes' paths shift and re-shift some more. An idea came to me.

"I assume at various levels you give the attackers some false, but seemingly important, data so they think they're getting something of value?" I said.

Raj, who until that point had been keeping a good poker face, showed a little crack in his armor.

"What makes you say that, General?" Raj said.

"Basic battlefield tactics," I said. "Keep the enemy occupied with decoys so that the real mission is disguised. Think D-Day."

"I was hoping we were not so obvious," Raj said.

"I don't think it's that obvious," I said. "I assume you put a lot of time and effort into making the fake stuff look quite real?"

"This is true," Raj said. "The better the quality of the fake, the more time they waste before they determine it is not, as the saying goes, the 'real deal.'"

"So what are they hitting on now?" I said.

Raj was confused.

"Sir?" Raj said.

Kate said, "I believe the general is making a fishing allusion, Raj. Fishermen try all sorts of bait - lures, worms, grasshoppers, flies, whatever - until they get the fish to bite or 'hit on' what they are being offered."

I said to Kate, "You fish?"

"I do," Kate said.

"Hmm," I said.

"What's that supposed to mean?" Kate said.

"I don't know," I said. "I guess I think women fisherpersons are kind of sexy."

Kate rolled her eyes. Raj blushed.

"Sorry, Raj," I said. "I take it you're not a fisherman?"

"No, sir," Raj said. "I hope to become a fisherman someday though. I am very intrigued by fly fishing."

"Good," I said. "You're right to be intrigued. I've got some nice rainbow trout on my ranch. Maybe you can come up and visit me and I can teach you how to fish."

"I would like that very much," Raj said.

Kate said, "Can we get back to business, please, gentlemen?"

"Certainly, Dr. Lennon," Raj said. "I apologize for the interruption."

"No need for you to apologize, Raj," Kate said. "The general is the one who should apologize."

I said, "For what?"

"You know for what," Kate said. "Please Raj, go on."

Raj said, "Certainly. I do understand the allusion now. The hacker fish seem to like schematics very much. They are hitting on them like a baby on candy. Indeed, the hacker fish are filling their bellies."

I said, "Schematics of what?"

"Drone controls," Raj said.

Kate said, "What kind of drones?"

"Ohio class drone submarines," Raj said. "This is the first time they have made such an attack."

I said, "The first time?"

"Yes," Raj said. "In the past they have also gone after drone files, but always just fixed-wing aircraft, helicopters, or tanks."

Kate said, "You're absolutely sure about that, Raj? It is definitely the first time?"

"Yes, ma'am," Raj said.

There it was then. Kate's and my question about what had gotten Freddy, Carter Bowdoin, and Bryce Wellington so lathered up that they had hightailed it over to NASAD in Donnie Kurtsinger's helicopter had been answered. Information regarding NASAD's Ohio class drone subs had suffered its first ever hacking attempt.

I looked out at the sea of programmers typing furiously away as they watched the big screen and their own monitors. An idea was forming in the back of my mind.

"You train for this kind of thing, don't you Raj?" I said. "I mean you would never just throw a rookie crew in against a real attack from a group like the Nasty Pandas, would you?"

"Yes, we practice," Raj said. "It is part of our war game program. The war games help us to learn how to fend off groups like the Nasty Pandas, and also develop and test strategies that the U.S. military can use when operating NASAD's weapons. The games also help us to spot and fix any potential weaknesses in NASAD's weapons and weapons systems that an enemy might exploit. We certainly wouldn't want an enemy breaching our products' software systems and taking control of something like a jet fighter or missile in mid-flight would we?"

"No, that wouldn't be a happy thing, would it?" I said. "I assume your team tests the computer and software issues here, and the testing of the mechanical issues are handled elsewhere?"

"Yes," Raj said. "Mechanical testing is handled within the factories where the products are made."

I gestured towards the team of programmers sitting at the desks surrounding the Jumbotron.

"The crew in here represent the defensive team during your war games?" I said.

Raj appeared taken aback. He hesitated for a moment before responding.

"Yes, that is correct," Raj said. "But why do you say this?"

"They have the aura," I said. "They seem calm. They appear to patiently wait to see what will happen next, while at the same time calculating their next moves."

"Yes, you are right," Raj said. "This is the type of person we look for."

"Whereas offensive guys have a glint in their eye," I said. "They always look hungry."

"That would make sense, I suppose," Raj said.

"Why do you say suppose?" I said.

"I have never seen NASAD's offensive war games team," Raj said.

Which was what I expected him to say. I also thought I knew the answer to the next question, but I asked it anyway.

"Never seen them?" I said. "Why not?"

"They are offsite," Raj said. "No one at NASAD, other than the offensive team members themselves, have any idea who the members of the offensive team are. Their identities are top secret."

"Is the team part of the dark programmers' division?" I said.

Raj looked at Kate, as if questioning her whether or not he could talk to me about the dark programmers. Kate nodded.

"Yes, the offensive team in the war games is made up of programmers in the dark programmers' division," Raj said.

"And the war games are not just against agreed upon hacking scenarios, I assume?" I said. "The dark programmers are probably encouraged to use some creativity in trying to breach the command and control systems operating NASAD's weapons?"

"Yes," Raj said. "The dark programmers are definitely encouraged to use their creativity. The dark programmers' attempts at breaching our systems are the best way the systems can be properly tested so that we can be sure the systems are impregnable. The next war game is scheduled to be a very comprehensive battle. The rumors are that the dark programmers have something especially devious up their sleeves."

Upon hearing Raj say especially devious, I, of course, immediately thought again of the Chinese insurmountable edge. What else would an insurmountable edge have to be, after all, other than especially devious?

"Are some of the systems you're going to be testing as part of the war games already up and running on Global Command and Control?" I said.

Global Command and Control is the system linking all information systems in the United States military. The idea behind the linkage is that the Army, Navy, Air Force, and Marines are all connected together using the same hardware and software so that our forces can be rapidly, intelligently, and cooperatively deployed.

"The systems we will be testing during the war games are the newest, most up-to-date versions of the U.S. Global Command and Control's computer systems, and, indeed, of all the U.S. military's computer systems," Ray said. "The new versions contain functions the previous versions do not contain, and also have been modified to improve the older versions' performance. The new versions, however, are not running yet. All systems currently running on the U.S. military's computer were tested during previous war games before the systems went live."

"I assume you and the programmers in the Cyber Defense Hall have already worked on the new versions and tried to make them as bulletproof as possible?" I said.

"Yes," Raj said. "We will see how the new versions hold up to the dark programmers' war games attack. If any weaknesses are discovered during the attack, we'll fix them before the systems can go live in the U.S. military's computers."

"Do the dark programmers get to study your new, theoretically bulletproof versions of the military's systems before the war games commence so they can work out a plan of attack?" I said.

"Yes," Raj said. "They have been given a copy of the newest versions so that they can study them."

I was momentarily distracted by a burst of increased activity on the Jumbotron. The number strings seemed to grow even more infinite and dozens of red and blue lights erupted in a simultaneous convulsion of color. The mazes formed and reformed much more rapidly than they had before. A few seconds later the activity level, for no reason I could discern, dropped back to what it had been.

"During the war games is your defensive team fighting off whatever attacks the dark programmers are using, not just keeping track of any weaknesses the attacks reveal?" I said.

"Fighting is what the war games are all about," Raj said. "The tactics we use in real-time to fend off the dark programmers will help us determine the best methods to shore up any weaknesses the dark programmers' attack may bring to light."

I thought for a moment about what Raj had just told me.

"There's no way that the defensive team in the Cyber Defense Hall could be available in real-time during an actual war to fend off enemy attacks that might be occurring on millions of individual military computers is there?" I said.

"We can provide guidance during a war on how to fend off any such attack, but no, we cannot be available in real-time to protect the military's computers," Raj said. "That is why we need to develop products that are as perfect as we can make them before they are put into service."

"When were the last war games completed that allowed you to certify the newest versions of the military's computer systems had passed muster and could be put into service?" I said.

"The most recent war game testing was completed about sixty days ago," Raj said. "I'm not sure exactly when it would have happened, but the U.S. military's computer system software should have already been updated with any changes that we determined were necessary after the results of those war games came in. As NASAD is responsible not only for many of the weapons used by the U.S. military, but also for all cyber-security on the Global Command and Control System, the upcoming war games will provide a very broad ranging test of NASAD's products. I hope my team here in the Cyber Defense Hall holds up well. Would you like to come watch?"

"When are the next war games going to be?" I said.

"A week from Friday," Raj said.

"Ten days from now?" I said.

"Yes," Raj said.

The fireworks that had first gone off in my mind in Mary Beth's office when I'd had the inkling that Dr. Nemo might be a dark programmer reignited. Hadn't Hart said his intel was predicting war with China would commence in ten days? Could it be a mere coincidence that both the NASAD war games and the actual war with China might start on the same day?

The fireworks in my head were saying it wasn't a coincidence at all.

There had to be a good chance the upcoming NASAD war games and the Chinese insurmountable edge were related.

The good news was that I would have some time before war broke out to learn about the war games and their possible relationship to the insurmountable edge. The bad news was, that if I relied on watching the war games with Raj in order to learn about any possible connection between the insurmountable edge and the war games, and the day I watched the war games with him was the same day as the war with China was supposed to break out, then even if the edge and the war games actually did turn out to be related somehow, any knowledge I gained would probably come much too late to thwart the edge and stop the war. Which meant that my only option was to learn as much as I could about the war games well in advance of their commencement date. Still, there was no reason to be rude to Raj.

"Sure," I said. "I'd love to watch."

Just as I said that, the fireworks in my mind erupted in an even greater frenzy, their lights blinding, their sounds deafening. I shut them down quickly, however, as I didn't need fireworks to herald the realization that was dawning on me.

A realization about Dr. Nemo...

Wasn't it likely that Nemo was not only a dark programmer, but also a member of the dark programmers' offensive war games team?

Wasn't it also likely that Nemo and the dark programmers had built a software program to disrupt or destroy the systems NASAD was testing during the war games?

And wasn't it possible the dark programmers' war game software had been given to the Chinese, who planned to use it as their insurmountable edge?

Admittedly, I had little proof to go on to support my 'realization' about Nemo, the dark programmers, and the edge. Truth be told, it really wasn't much more than a guess. But the main point, as far as I was concerned, was that that guess was my best guess at the moment. Whenever I have little to go on, but I absolutely must go on, following my best guess has always been my best option.

And so, my mission plan then expanded to include not only searching for Nemo and Dragon Man, but an investigation into the dark programmers' software for the upcoming war games, with the hope the dark programmers' software, and the insurmountable edge, might turn out to be one and the same.

I could have asked Raj about the dark programmers' plans for the war games. But I didn't ask for two reasons. One, I thought it highly unlikely Raj would be privy to what the dark programmers were up to. The dark programmers were in a war against Raj's defensive team and I saw no reason for the dark programmers to make their plans known to Raj or his team. And two, I was still sticking to my strict 'need to know' policy. I couldn't afford any leaks that would alert my enemy about my concerns regarding the dark programmers' war game software, and, having just met Raj, I had no idea whether he was capable of being discreet, let alone his level of trustworthiness.

I thought again of my request to Mary Beth that she help me contact the vice president of dark programming. Whether or not the vice president could be trusted continued to be a point of concern - perhaps of even greater concern than the question of whether or not Raj could be trusted - given the vice president's intimate involvement with the dark programmers. Still, it seemed like it would be best to contact the vice president sooner rather than later. Perhaps Haley had a way to determine who the current NASAD vice president of dark programming was, and if he was someone we could trust. I made a mental note to text Haley when I got the chance.

I shifted my attention back to the red dots on the giant electronic screen. Raj and Kate watched with me as the red dots continued to either burst like ruptured balloons or be forced deeper into the mazes. I thought some more about what was happening on the screen in terms of battlefield tactics. I came up with additional questions I needed Raj to answer.

"Raj, what if the attacking enemy has learned of your system and what we're seeing is just a show the enemy is putting on for us?" I said.

"You mean the enemy is pretending to be fooled?" Raj said.

"Yes," I said. "They are taking your bait, but also, in a way you cannot see, have actually infiltrated your system and are taking the real Ohio drone sub schematics."

"The only way that could be done is if we had been betrayed by one of our own employees," Raj said.

"You don't think that's possible?" I said.

"We have fail-safes and very sophisticated systems to prevent that," Raj said. "All work must be done onsite and is monitored by video and digital surveillance. The digital surveillance is drilled down even to the keystroke level. There are repeated, ongoing, rigorous security checks on the monitoring system. I helped build the systems and they will also alert us if any of the real files suffer the smallest hack from inside or outside NASAD. So, no, I do not believe it is possible."

"So no one could have created some kind of undetectable back door?" I said.

"Absolutely not," Raj said. He paused. "Do you know something I do not, General?"

"No, not at all," I said. "I just like to ask questions."

"Good," Raj said. "I do not fear questions."

The next questions I wanted to ask Raj involved Dr. Nemo, but they were risky and I wasn't sure if I should ask the questions or not. I felt that the risk of asking Raj about Nemo was qualitatively different than asking Raj about the dark programmers' software. This was mainly because, unlike my theory that the NASAD dark programmers' war game software was what the Chinese considered to be their insurmountable edge - a theory the enemy couldn't possibly know I had since I had just formulated it - I was fairly certain the enemy not only already knew about Dr. Nemo, but also that the enemy knew that Kate knew about Nemo. Since the enemy already knew about Nemo, even if Raj mentioned Nemo's name to anyone, I believed such mentioning couldn't put Nemo in any greater danger than he was already in. That analysis, along with other reasons that I later explained to Kate, was why I went ahead and asked Raj about Nemo.

"It's nice to hear you don't fear questions, Raj," I said, "because I have another one for you. You ever read 'Twenty Thousand Leagues Under the Sea'?"

"Jules Verne," Raj said. "I like the book very much. You ask because of the drone submarines?"

"Yes, because of the drone submarines," I said. "You know of anyone on your team, or elsewhere within NASAD, that goes go by the name Dr. Nemo?"

Kate seemed a bit uncomfortable with my mention of Nemo, but said nothing.

"Dr. Nemo?" Raj said. "It was Captain Nemo, was it not?"

"It was," I said.

"No, I have never heard this name," Raj said. "Are you looking for this person?"

"Yes," I said.

"Is he a bad person?" Raj said.

"I don't think so," I said.

"If I come across him, I will tell you," Raj said.

"Thanks," I said. "I think we've taken enough of your time, Raj. Kate, anything on your mind?"

"No," Kate said. "Thank you so much, Raj."

"You are both very welcome," Raj said. "General, I sincerely hope you make it for the war games we are having a week from Friday. I believe Carter Bowdoin will be here as well."

"He will?" I said.

"He likes to bet on the outcome of the war games," Raj said. "We have a very large betting pool on this particular game coming up, and Mr. Bowdoin is a very big gambler. He plays in the Worldwide Challenge Poker event in Las Vegas every year. I think he once won a bracelet."

"Do you know which Worldwide Challenge event he won?" I said.

"It wasn't the main event, but it was big enough," Raj said. "I think he won close to eight million dollars."

"Not a bad haul," I said. "Which way is Mr. Bowdoin betting in your war game pool?"

Raj looked hurt.

"On my team of course," Raj said.

"The defense," I said.

Raj smiled.

CHAPTER 65

Kate and I took the elevator from NASAD's Cyber Defense Hall down to the lobby, exited the lobby's tall green glass doors, and made our way back across the park towards Kate's office tower. The wind had dropped down as the sun had climbed higher in the sky and the ripples on the lake were smaller and less frequent. The employees' midmorning break was over and the park was nearly deserted. The sailboats were gone.

I felt something nagging at the corners of my consciousness, but I couldn't quite put my finger on what that something was. I was nearly certain, however, that it was something I had missed, some basic question I'd failed to consider, in regard to the potential connection between the Chinese insurmountable edge and the NASAD dark programmers' war games software. I tried and tried to grab hold of that missed thing, but it kept slipping away. It slipped away entirely, and seemingly irretrievably, when the sound of Kate's voice interrupted my thoughts.

"Please don't do that again," Kate said.

"Do what again?" I said.

"You know what I'm talking about," Kate said.

"I do?" I said.

Kate grabbed my left elbow and forced me to a halt. She stepped in close to me so we were face to face, and appeared to study my eyes.

"You really don't know, do you?" Kate said.

"If we're talking about what I'm not supposed to do again, then no," I said. "Mainly because I don't know what I did."

"You don't remember making a comment about women fisherpersons?" Kate said.

"I said they were sexy," I said. "So what?"

"There was a clear implication that *I* was sexy," Kate said.

"There was?" I said.

"Don't play games with me, Jack," Kate said.

She dug her finger into the ulnar nerve at the back of my elbow. It hurt like hell. It was the same nerve Jeff had crushed the day before.

"Ow!" I said.

"Admit it and I'll let go," Kate said.

"Okay fine," I said. "I admit it. I implied you were sexy."

Kate let go of my elbow and I immediately started rubbing it.

"You sure are strong for a woman fisherperson," I said.

"It's embarrassing, Jack," Kate said. "You can't talk like that in front of the employees."

"What?" I said. "The employees aren't allowed to think of you as sexy? Because if that's the case, I'm sorry, but those beans are spilled, and that train has left the station."

"They can think whatever they want," Kate said. "It just makes me uncomfortable if you say things like that out loud."

"Alright," I said. "I get it. I'm sorry. I won't do it again. Can we go fishing in the lake?"

"There are no fish in the lake," Kate said.

"Can we pretend fish?" I said.

"You want to watch me fish that bad, huh?" Kate said.

"Actually, yes," I said.

"I promise I'll fish for you one day," Kate said. "Just not today."

"I could swear you said something almost exactly like that last night," I said.

"Deal with it," Kate said.

She started walking again towards her office building.

"Hold on," I said. "Do we have time before our next appointment to say hello to Donnie Kurtsinger and his helicopter?"

Kate stopped and looked at her watch.

"It's eleven now," Kate said. "We have an hour. Let's go see Donnie."

We detoured towards the helicopter which was still sitting on the helipad.

"You know, you haven't told me what our next appointment actually is," I said.

"We're meeting with Harold Sinclair," Kate said. "Mr. Sinclair is the executive who oversees NASAD's entire drone submarine project. Seeing how the Chinese hackers were just after our drone submarine schematics, it seems more clear than ever that all of our problems at NASAD are directly related to the drone sub program. The timing of our meeting couldn't be better."

The only way that meeting could be productive would be if the attacks on the drone sub program, including the murders of the NASAD drone sub engineers, turned out not to be a diversion. But I still hadn't changed my opinion on that matter, and remained convinced they were a diversion. The hacking attack we had just witnessed only strengthened my belief that my thinking was correct. Any commander in the Chinese military worth his or her salt would know damn well that the hacking attempt by the Nasty Pandas wouldn't have escaped detection. That commander would thus not have risked calling attention to anything having to do with the drone subs if he or she really intended to use them as part of his war plan. Whoever was behind the hacking attempt wanted us to be looking at the drone subs when the true insurmountable edge lay elsewhere.

I did decide, however, that I would take the meeting with Harold Sinclair. If I didn't take it, Kate would want to know why, and I couldn't come up with any reasons she would accept other than telling her the truth. And the truth would not do. With only ten days left before war broke out, I had almost no time to find whatever it was at NASAD the Chinese thought ensured them a victory. Again, telling Kate about my diversion theory meant risking Kate accidentally leaking my feelings to Hart or someone else. A leak to Hart was my biggest worry, however, as I remained afraid of Hart's infatuation with the drone subs and his propensity for micromanagement. I still couldn't afford to have Hart slow me down and potentially ruin my investigation by ordering me to travel down a path I knew was a dead end. Hart, along with my 'need to know' policy, also kept me from telling Kate about my theory that the dark programmers' war game software and the insurmountable edge might be one and the same.

Up ahead, I could see that the drone aircraft, which had scattered away from the helipad when the NASAD Bell helicopter had landed, were now back in force. The drones were flying circles around the chopper, diving at it like miniature bombers, then rising up and diving again.

"Donnie must love that," I said.

"Lucky for the drones the NASAD helicopter isn't outfitted with cannons," Kate said.

"It's not?" I said incredulously.

"Gimme a break," Kate said. "By the way, weren't you taking a pretty big gamble when you asked Raj about Nemo?"

"It seems to be a law of nature, inflexible and inexorable, that those who cannot risk cannot win," I said.

"Who said that, Bugs Bunny?" Kate said.

"John Paul Jones," I said. I knew it was John Paul Jones since one of my ancestors had scribbled the famous Revolutionary War naval commander's words in the little book that was on the shelf of my library back at home. "And you're just making fun of it since you didn't know who said it."

"True," Kate said.

"Anyway, I thought asking Raj was worth the risk, since it was a small risk in my estimation," I said.

"Would you care to share how you came to that conclusion?" Kate said.

"Two things would have to be true for my asking of Raj about Nemo to have put Nemo in more danger than he already was in," I said. "The first thing that had to be true was that our enemy doesn't already know, or suspect, that Dr. Nemo exists and represents a possible threat to them."

"But you believe the enemy already *does* know of Nemo's existence, otherwise the enemy wouldn't have had the Kazakhs try to kidnap me in order to find out what, if anything, Nemo had told me?" Kate said.

"Correct," I said.

"But if you're wrong, and the enemy didn't already know about Nemo, then you've outed Nemo to Raj, which could put Nemo's life at risk," Kate said.

"No," I said. "Nemo's life would still be safe as long as the second thing wasn't also true."

"Which was?" Kate said

"Raj would have to be on the side of the enemy," I said.

Kate thought about this.

"Because if Raj wasn't on the side of the enemy," Kate said, "there's no one he could tell about Nemo that could hurt Nemo?"

"Hurt maybe," I said. "But not kill."

"What do you mean by that?" Kate said.

"Well, from Nemo's original message, I believe it's clear Nemo is concerned that our own side may have a serious claim against him for some kind of security breach," I said. "Therefore, if Raj told someone on our own side about Nemo, Nemo could be at risk for a nasty journey through the federal criminal justice system, but I don't think such telling by Raj would create a threat to Nemo's life."

"The enemy will kill him," Kate said, "but the good ol' U.S.A. would just lock him up."

"Exactly," I said.

"Well, it's impossible for me to believe Raj is on the side of the enemy," Kate said. "I've known him for ten years. Raj is highly dedicated to NASAD and his work here."

"Which I sensed," I said.

"You gambled on your sense?" Kate said.

"No," I said. "I was going off the third thing."

"You said there were two things," Kate said.

"Three is kind of a thing on its own," I said. "It negated the need for one and two."

"What's the third thing?" Kate said.

"We're almost out of time," I said. "We only have ten days until the Chinese start a war. But it's not just the war. We're probably running out of time to save Nemo's life too. If we're right that Nemo is being hunted, then he is being hunted by a very sophisticated enemy. That enemy will kill Nemo if they find him, and they could easily find him in a lot less than ten days. With so little time left, if Raj did know who Nemo was, and we didn't ask him, then we might have lost one of our best chances of finding Nemo and saving his life."

"So it was a bigger risk not asking Raj than asking him?" Kate said.

"Well put," I said. "Now, while we're on the subject of risk taking, what did you think of the fact that Carter Bowdoin is betting on the outcome of the war games?"

Another dozen or so drones joined the ones dive bombing Donnie Kurtsinger's helicopter. I wondered how long it would be before Donnie decided to retaliate.

"Carter always bets on the war games," Kate said.

"Always?" I said.

"Carter started up the war game betting pools when Pennsylvania Avenue Partners first became associated with NASAD a little over two years ago," Kate said. "Carter said it would spice things up and make the war games more fun. Carter also said the thrill of potentially winning a bet can get some people to push themselves just a little bit harder, and even find a whole new gear in their brains."

"Is that what happened?" I said.

"Seems so," Kate said. "Raj told me some time ago that while both the offensive and defensive teams have always come up with new and ingenious ideas to support their war game play, the number of those ideas increased drastically once the teams started betting against each other."

"Wait a second," I said. "The dark programmers are the offensive team. Nobody knows who they are. How can they bet?"

"We figured out a way so they could," Kate said. "The vice president of dark programming takes their bets and transfers the money to the betting pool account. If the dark programmers win, their winnings go back to an account also controlled by the vice president. He, or she, then distributes the winnings to the dark programmers in the same way the dark programmers get their paychecks distributed."

"All the accounts for betting use the same untraceable system used for the payroll account?" I said.

"Yes," Kate said.

The drones continued to dive bomb the helicopter. I heard the helicopter's engines fire up and, a moment later, the rotor blades began to whir. The blades whacked one of the dive-bombing drones out of the air and it crashed to the ground. The other drones scattered in a dozen different directions like pheasants following a shotgun blast. The engines shut down and the rotors stopped. I guess Donnie had made his point.

"I'm not sure I like what I'm seeing there," Kate said. "Those drones are expensive."

"You should tell them not to mess with Donnie, then," I said.

The downed drone sputtered to life, limped into the air, and flew away.

"I guess it wasn't hurt too bad," Kate said.

"It'll live," I said. "So, in your opinion the betting's been a good idea for all the programmers, both offensive and defensive?"

"Yes," Kate said.

"Anyone else at the company other than the programmers in the Cyber Defense Hall, Carter, and the dark programmers allowed to bet on the war games?" I said.

"You mean do we let another seventy-five thousand employees into the pool?" Kate said.

"Yes," I said.

"No," Kate said. "We decided it just might be a teensy-weensy bit bad for our public image if NASAD were perceived as a giant, degenerate gambling den."

"Teensy-weensy is probably an understatement," I said. "Might not go over too well with the people at the Department of Defense who hand out national security clearances either. They're a pretty conservative bunch and degenerate gambling doesn't sound like their cup of tea. I assume the defensive and offensive programmers are only allowed to bet on their own team?"

"Wouldn't it be a pretty big conflict of interest to do otherwise?" Kate said.

"Certainly could be," I said. "Jockeys have been known to fix a horse race or two. College basketball players have been caught shaving points. Hell, someone even fixed the World Series in 1919. Unless your programmers are all angels sent from heaven, it's easy to imagine they might be tempted to do whatever the equivalent would be of race fixing or point shaving in the programming world. NASAD's war games are just games, not real war, after all."

"Lead us not into temptation, but deliver us from evil," Kate said. "Or, as I like to say, I generally avoid temptation unless I can't resist it."

"Somehow, I didn't take you for the Mae West type," I said.

"Shows how little you know about me," Kate said.

"And whose fault is that?" I said.

Kate rolled her eyes.

"How big are the betting pools for each war game?" I said.

"A few thousand dollars," Kate said.

"Who usually wins?" I said.

"The overall matches are pretty even," Kate said. "But the Cyber Defense Hall team has made more money."

"Why is that?" I said.

"Carter always bets on the defensive team in the Cyber Defense Hall," Kate said. "When Carter wins, he always gives part of his winnings to the defensive team members. No one other than the dark programmers themselves bets on the dark programmers. The dark programmers, even when they win, make less money than the defensive programmers since there is no one sharing his or her additional winnings with them."

"I wondered why the programmers in the Cyber Defense Hall were so friendly to Carter," I said. "I guess that's my answer."

"They do seem to like Carter a lot," Kate said.

I suddenly got an uncomfortable feeling at the base of my skull. It felt like anger mixed with nausea. There was something wrong with the picture that Kate had just painted about NASAD's betting pools, but I couldn't put my finger on what it was. I suppose one could say it was bad enough that the betting pools may have given the dark programmers - and Nemo, if he was among them - the extra motivation that drove them to build a war game weapon that ultimately, and hopefully unwittingly, might have become the Chinese insurmountable edge. But I sensed there was something even worse going on. Try as I might to give a name to that something, it still eluded me, and my anger and nausea grew stronger. So strong in fact, that they began to overwhelm my sense of balance, and I felt like I might topple over. I grabbed on to Kate's shoulder in order to stay upright.

"Jack, you're white as a sheet," Kate said. "What's going on?"

I felt that if I spoke, I would throw up. I held a finger up, as if to say 'give me a moment, please' and took some deep breaths. The breaths slowly caused the anger and nausea to dissipate and my balance returned. I took my hand off Kate's shoulder and stood on my own.

"Phew, that was bad for a moment," I said. "I must be more over-tired than I thought."

"That's the third time I've seen you pass out or almost pass out since I met you," Kate said. "Actually the fourth, if I include the news video showing you going down onto your knees at the stoning site. I understand how hard it's been for you with Jeff and the sniper rifle, the Kazakhs, the elephant tranquilizer, and Bobby and Timmy and the biker gang, but are you sure there isn't something else going on? Maybe we should get you checked out?"

"I'm fine now," I said.

"If it happens again, I'm taking you to see a doctor," Kate said. "No ifs, ands, or buts."

"You're a doctor," I said.

"Yes, I am," Kate said. "But we need someone who can take some blood and run some tests on you."

"Fine," I said. "Deal."

Kate and I resumed our walk towards Donnie and the NASAD chopper. The drones that had retreated at the time of their compatriot's whacking were then moving in again on the chopper. If I were those drones, I would have been very careful. Donnie had plenty of tricks up his sleeve.

"They shouldn't keep doing that," Kate said. "They're going to get smacked again."

"Hopefully this time they'll stay far enough away to avoid that," I said. "Now, I've been wondering about something."

"What?" Kate said.

"Does anybody like Freddy?" I said.

Kate smiled.

"Good question," Kate said. "I think Freddy's wife likes him."

"What's his wife like?" I said.

"Incredibly obnoxious," Kate said. "Her name is Victoria and she bought a Rembrandt for their house. Victoria says it's because she wants the kids to grow up around art."

"What a great idea," I said. "Why doesn't everybody do that?"

"Maybe because it would cost them fifteen million dollars?" Kate said.

"I'll buy that," I said. "What about Freddy's kids? They like him?"

"The oldest is two and the youngest is a newborn," Kate said. "I don't think they know who Freddy is."

"Probably for the best," I said. "Does Freddy's dog like him?"

"Freddy had a dog but he had to give it away," Kate said.

"Why?" I said.

"It kept biting him," Kate said.

"Smart dog," I said.

"Genius dog," Kate said.

The drones seemed to be getting dangerously close to the chopper once again. It appeared to be only a matter of time before one or more of them got thumped.

"As long as we're on the subject of Freddy," I said, "I'd like to know who's really in charge of NASAD."

"Is that a trick question?" Kate said.

"I noticed that Freddy seemed to take orders from Carter Bowdoin and Bryce Wellington," I said.

"That's true," Kate said. "Freddy does. And I hate it. Carter, via Freddy, does his best to try to control NASAD's board. When Freddy and Carter put forth ideas that I especially dislike, I try hard as hell to convince the board to vote against them. But I rarely win."

"Why does Freddy abdicate all that power to Carter and PAP?" I said.

"Freddy idolizes Carter Bowdoin," Kate said. "They went to Yale together. Freddy was a freshman when Carter was a senior. Carter got Freddy into the Skull and Bones."

"Lovely group," I said. "Not."

"Not is right," Kate said.

"I can see why he would bow down to Carter then," I said, "but what about Wellington?"

"I think Freddy sees General Wellington as an extension of Carter," Kate said.

"Makes sense, I guess," I said. "Is Freddy's undying devotion to Carter the only lever Pennsylvania Avenue Partners has? Does PAP have any legal right to call the shots?"

"No way," Kate said. "PAP only owns ten percent of NASAD."

"And I think you said PAP didn't have any ownership interest whatsoever until after your father died?" I said.

"You mean after he was murdered," Kate said.

"After he was murdered, yes," I said

"My father wouldn't let PAP near us," Kate said.

"Has PAP done any good for you?" I said. "Other than Carter's betting pools that is?"

"Depends on what you say is good," Kate said. "They secured the financing to build Taj Mafreddy."

"Something your father Milt would never have allowed," I said.

"Never," Kate said. "He would have thought Taj Mafreddy was a disgusting waste."

We were still about fifty yards from the helipad, but closing in. The drones had grown courageous once more and were dive bombing within a foot of the chopper. Donnie suddenly fired up the engines again, and in a move I had never seen before, somehow threw the rear of the chopper almost straight up in the air. Thwap! Thwap! Two drones were knocked to the ground and the others scattered once again. The chopper's engines shut down as quickly as they had started up.

"Those two look like they might be more seriously injured than the first one that went down," I said.

"The drone pilots shouldn't keep testing Donnie," Kate said. "I'm going to call their boss."

Kate took out her cell phone, but just as soon as she did, another fleet of six drones appeared directly over our heads. Kate made a sharp upward gesture with her right arm and right thumb. She reminded me of an umpire calling a batter out on strikes.

"Scram!" Kate said.

The drones hightailed it out of our vicinity.

"They can hear you?" I said.

"I don't know how well they can hear, but they can see fine," Kate said. "Those pilots knew exactly what I meant."

"Pilots know not to mess around with you, huh?" I said.

"Yep," Kate said.

"You still going to call their boss?" I said.

"No need," Kate said. "Looks like they got the message loud and clear."

"You must watch a lot of movies from the '30's," I said.

"You're referring to my use of 'scram'?" Kate said.

I nodded.

"I watch some," Kate said. "But I got it from my dad. He thought scram was a funny word. He'd say it to me whenever he had an excuse to use it."

"Did he ever say 'scram' to Freddy?" I said.

"Never," Kate said. "My father was very protective of Freddy's feelings. He knew Freddy might cry if he told him to scram."

"I was wondering about that too," I said.

"If Freddy cried a lot?" Kate said.

"No," I said. "If your father was protective of him."

"Very," Kate said. "Obviously both Freddy and I took it very hard when my father died, but Freddy took it worse than me."

"Damn," I said. "I'm actually feeling a little sympathy for the guy."

"Freddy is obnoxious, but deep down he's got a good heart," Kate said.

"Very deep down," I said.

"I can go with 'very,'" Kate said.

"Did you know 'scram' also means to shut down a nuclear reactor in an emergency?" I said.

"You know a lot of strange things, Jack," Kate said.

"You mean worthless things," I said.

"I was trying to be polite," Kate said. "Which reminds me. Who really said that stuff about not wanting to be an outcast nobody wants."

"It's from 'Maurice' by E. M. Forster," I said. "I read the book when Jeff and I took a tanker from Hong Kong to Haiphong. It was the only book on board."

"Good book?" Kate said.

"Actually it was," I said. "Shoot, I just remembered something."

"What?" Kate said.

"We should have asked Mary Beth and Raj if they knew of any employees who like to run around in dragon masks," I said.

"You think it's safe to do that?" Kate said. "If Dragon Man finds out we're looking for him, wouldn't he take extra precautions to make sure we don't find him?"

"That's good thinking," I said. "But since we both trust Mary Beth and Raj, I think the risk-benefit ratio is in our favor."

"You mean that since it's unlikely they would tell anyone that we're looking for Dragon Man, there is little risk," Kate said, "but if they do know him, we will get a huge immediate benefit?"

"Yes," I said.

"I'll text Mary Beth and Raj right now and ask them to tell us if they know of any employees who wear dragon masks," Kate said.

"Be sure to tell Mary Beth and Raj not to tell anyone you asked them that question," I said.

"Do I look like an idiot?" Kate said. "Of course I'll do that."

Kate sent the text.

We arrived at the NASAD helicopter where it lay parked on the helipad.

CHAPTER 66

It had been nearly an hour since the NASAD helicopter had landed and deposited Carter Bowdoin, Freddy, Bryce Wellington, and Wellington's valet on the helipad's tarmac. Since landing the whirlybird, Donnie Kurtsinger had started up the engines twice in order to whack the drones, so the engines were still radiant with heat, and the pungent odor of exhaust fumes lingered in the air.

I walked up around the back of the helicopter so Donnie couldn't see me coming, and made my way along the helicopter's left side until I was just behind the door next to the pilot's seat. Through the door's window, I could see Donnie sitting in the pilot's seat and studying some flight charts in his lap.

Donnie looked his normal tough guy self - square jaw, hawklike eyes, and a well-conditioned two hundred and sixty pound body on a six foot, two inch frame. He had on a black flight helmet, a khaki shirt, and pants. The shirt had a NASAD patch on its left sleeve. The helmet had a microphone attached to it via a mini-boom, and presumably built-in earphones as well.

I rapped on Donnie's window.

"You're in a no parking zone, flyboy," I said. "You got thirty seconds to get this pile of junk outta here or I'm gonna have it towed."

Donnie turned. He looked mightily annoyed. But then his expression quickly changed to surprise and he broke out in a big smile. He opened his door, jumped out of the chopper onto the helipad, grabbed me in a big bear hug, and lifted me off the ground.

"Jack!" Donnie said. "What the hell you doing here?"

He was crushing my ribs so hard I could hardly breathe.

"Canth brith," I eked out.

"What was that?" Donnie said.

Kate said, "I think he said he can't breathe."

Donnie turned his head toward Kate.

"Oh hi, Dr. Lennon," Donnie said. "Sorry, I didn't see you there."

Donnie let me down. I took in a deep breath.

"You're still strong, Donnie," I said. "The Hulk's got nothing on you."

"Coming from a pussy such as yourself, I'm not sure if that means anything," Donnie said.

"I'm the pussy, huh?" I said. "Last time we rode together I seem to remember it was you who made a screaming U-turn at Tora Bora."

Kate said, "Tora Bora? You guys weren't after Bin Laden were you?"

"Who else would we be after?" I said. "Donnie here doesn't turn his chopper around, my team gets that asshole years before the Seals do."

Donnie said, "You make it sound like it's my fault, Jack."

"Just bustin' your balls, Donnie," I said.

"You better be," Donnie said. "Goddamn generals sittin' in some bunker in Florida gave those abort orders without having a clue what's goin' on on the ground. Goddamn generals don't know a goddamn thing." Donnie gave a quick tap to his helmet and gestured to Kate. "Excuse my language, ma'am."

Kate said, "I've heard far worse, Donnie."

I said, "You have something against generals, Donnie?"

Donnie stared at me for a moment.

"Sorry, Jack," Donnie said. "I forgot you're a general."

"What's that supposed to mean?" I said.

"Well, I know you deserve to be one and all, but dude, you ain't general material," Donnie said. "Bryce Wellington, now that's general material. Prime grade A, jackass, know nothin', general material."

Kate said, "Looks like neither of you guys like Wellington very much."

I said, "'You guys'? Did I say anything?"

"It's not what you said, Jack," Kate said, "I hope I'm not speaking out of turn, but back in the Cyber Defense Hall I got the sense you didn't particularly care for Bryce Wellington."

Donnie said, "Of course Jack doesn't care for him. Jack hates Bryce Wellington."

I said, "Hate's a strong word."

"Come off it, Jack," Donnie said. "After what happened in the Sudan, anybody would hate Wellington."

Kate said, "What happened in the Sudan?"

"She doesn't know?" Donnie said to me.

I said, "No, but I guess she's about to, isn't she?"

Donnie got red in the face.

"It's fine, Donnie," I said. "Go ahead. Tell her."

"You sure?" Donnie said.

"I'm sure," I said.

Donnie hesitated.

Kate said, "Donnie, you don't really think you can keep anything from me, do you?"

I said, "I doubt there's a person alive who can keep anything from you, Dr. Lennon."

"I believe I was talking to Donnie, Jack," Kate said.

I heard some commotion coming from behind me. I turned around and saw one of the newscasters hoisting himself over the top of the exterior wall guarding the NASAD complex. He quickly disappeared back to where he had come from, however, apparently having been pulled down from behind by either the FBI agents or the NASAD security guards on duty outside the wall.

"Indeed you were," I said. "Sorry for the interruption. Donnie, would you be so kind as to answer the good doctor?"

Donnie didn't immediately respond. He was staring at Kate and me as if we were some kind of complicated math problem he couldn't quite figure out.

"Donnie, you still with us?" I said.

"Uh, yeah, I'm still with you," Donnie said. "I hope you don't mind my asking, but how long have you two known each other?"

"Too long," Kate said.

"A little over twenty-eight hours would be more precise," I said. "Why do you ask?"

Donnie said, "The way you two are behaving, it's just..."

"Just what?" I said.

"Forget it," Donnie said. "Ain't none of my business. Anyway ma'am, what happened is General Bryce Wellington is the asshole responsible for the deaths of seven of the bravest, toughest special ops guys I ever knew. Wellington also screwed up General Jeff Bradshaw something fierce. Jeff Bradshaw, along with this man right here in front of us, are probably the greatest soldiers this country has ever known."

I said, "So you remembered Jeff is a general, but not me?"

"I only remembered about Jeff since you just reminded me that you were one," Donnie said.

"Nice save," I said.

"It's the truth," Donnie said. "No offense, Jack, but Jeff being a general makes even less sense than you being a general."

"Why?" I said. "Because he's less of an asshole than me?"

"You said it, not me," Donnie said. "By the way, do you know how Jeff's doing?"

"Jeff has been staying with me on my ranch," I said. "His recovery seems to be progressing well lately."

"Damn, that's good to hear," Donnie said. "Give him my best will you?"

"I will," I said.

Kate said, "What did Bryce Wellington do to get General Bradshaw so badly injured and all those other men killed, Donnie?"

Donnie said, "First off ma'am, you gotta understand that General Bryce Wellington don't know his ass from a hole in the ground. Only reason he got his stars is 'cause his pappy was a general, and the only reason his pappy got his job was because his father was a genuine American hero."

Kate looked questioningly at me.

I said, "It's all true. Neither Bryce Wellington nor his father know their ass from a hole in the ground. Wellington's grandfather, however, was a good man. He served under Pershing in World War I. General Grandpa Wellington personally led a division of the American Expeditionary Force at Argonne. The Expeditionary Force's victories are what pretty much finally brought the Germans to their knees."

Donnie said, "And the Wellington male line's gone to hell ever since. Bryce Wellington's dad is known as 'first putz' and Wellington himself is known as 'second putz.'"

"Or some variation thereof," I said.

"Variations thereof include 'shit for brains one' and 'shit for brains two,'" Donnie said.

Kate said, "But what actually happened to Jeff and the men?"

"Not all the guys in charge of the U.S. Army are idiots, and some of them were smart enough to shove Bryce Wellington where he couldn't do any harm," Donnie said. "They made him assistant deputy chairman of the NATO Military Committee, which sounds badass, but the committee's main job is procurement - you know, they make sure everyone has enough jello and toilet paper and shit. Anyway, the commanding general of the 101st Airborne gets shot up in Afghanistan and Wellington just happens to be in Kabul at the time. Some idiot commences to undo all the good work done by the guys who weren't idiots and puts Wellington temporarily in charge of the 101st. Over the next thirty days, the 101st proceeds to suffer its greatest number of casualties on a percentage basis for any thirty day period in Airborne history."

Two drones suddenly appeared overhead. Kate spotted them. She gave them a dirty look and shook her fist at them. The drones quickly flew away.

"Why didn't they just replace Wellington?" Kate said.

"By the time the casualty reports filter up to the top brass, the original commanding general of the 101st is already healed up and on his way back to Afghanistan," Donnie said. "Only the general doesn't get back fast enough to save Jeff Bradshaw and his squad from Wellington."

"The seven men were part of Jeff's squad?" Kate said.

"Yes," Donnie said. "The whole thing started because Wellington got a panicked call from a guy who said he was in charge of the 101st Airborne's training missions in Egypt. He tells Wellington a 101st Airborne transport plane suffered a mechanical failure and went down in the Sudan in an area controlled by mega crazy Islamic terrorists. Guy in charge of the training mission says his team doesn't have the resources to mount a rescue operation, and sends Wellington documents that include very detailed info on the crew of the plane that went down, the plane itself, the flight plan, and maps of the area. He even sends satellite photos of a twenty-man strong squad of Islamists closing in on the downed aircraft. Wellington doesn't have any idea what to do, but of course doesn't say that to the guy on the phone. Wellington talks to his subordinates in Afghanistan who tell him they won't be able to get anything organized for at least twenty-four hours. Wellington goes into a panic. He calls Washington, and some fool at the Pentagon, who has no idea who Wellington is, somehow finds out Jeff Bradshaw and his team are in Libya and requests they immediately go to the Sudan."

"You weren't with Jeff and the team?" Kate said to me.

I said, "I was in the hospital recuperating from my knee surgery. A fact for which I don't think I'll ever forgive myself."

"But that's not your fault," Kate said.

"It's not," I said. "But I can still wish things didn't happen the way they did, can't I?"

"If you like torturing yourself, I suppose you can do whatever you want," Kate said. "But why didn't Jeff have an inkling something was off? I mean, the request did come from Bryce Wellington."

"Jeff didn't know it originated from Wellington," I said. "The 'fool at the Pentagon' Donnie referred to was a major who was an aide to a very respected four-star general. Jeff thought the request was coming from the four-star, only the aide didn't even check with the four-star, just took it upon himself to handle the situation without consulting his boss. The whole thing was just a shit show from start to finish."

"What wound up happening once Jeff got there?" Kate said to Donnie.

Donnie said, "Turns out the whole thing was a hoax, and Jeff and his team proceeded to fall into the biggest ambush anyone has ever seen. Two hundred hostiles with Humvees, RPG's, and even helicopter support, surrounded Jeff and his team and they got slaughtered."

It was a lot worse than just a slaughter, but I didn't want to burden Kate with the details just then. Other than Jeff, Hart, me, and some others at MOM, no one else knew those details, which is why Donnie couldn't share them either.

"So you're saying Wellington got tricked?" Kate said.

"Enemy took advantage of his inexperience or stupidity or both," Donnie said. "Guy who called for help and said he was head of the training missions wasn't who he said he was, and Wellington was so panicked he never stopped to check it out."

"Donnie, I hope you won't take this the wrong way," Kate said, "but how do you know all this stuff?"

Four more drones appeared overhead. They were circling us, but keeping a good distance from us. Kate looked up at them, but apparently decided they were too far away to bother with.

I said, "I'll answer that. Something as bad as what happened to Jeff and his squad goes down, every special op guy in the world, even the retired ones, is going to know about it within hours of it happening. Donnie's job in the military was to ferry those ops guys into and out of hot zones anywhere on the planet. To put it as simply as possible, ops guys like to talk."

Donnie said, "General is telling it like it is, Dr. Lennon."

Kate said, "I apologize that I haven't been around Wellington long enough to know much about him. But now that I do, I'm confused why Pennsylvania Avenue Partners would have him working for them."

"It's because of his incredible kickass expertise in an area in which any real soldier would have been ashamed to admit they spent their entire goddamn career," Donnie said.

"You're talking about procurement, I take it?" Kate said.

"Yes, ma'am," Donnie said. "I kind of exaggerated. It wasn't all toilet paper and jello. Bryce Wellington's procurement responsibilities also had him rubbing elbows with all the generals who made the decisions to buy the bigger shit too - you know, stuff like Humvees, missiles, planes, tanks, whatever. Most of those generals Wellington rubbed elbows with wound up becoming buddies with him. So now that Wellington has retired from the Army and is making his way in the outside world as a Pennsylvania Avenue Partners employee, it's a piece of cake for Bryce to call on his old cronies in the Pentagon's procurement departments and sell them PAP's own special brand of bigger shit items. I'm sure PAP and all the defense companies they own are making vast sums of dough now that General Bryce Wellington is heading up their sales division."

Kate looked at me. She seemed to want confirmation of what Donnie had said.

I said, "It is pretty much of a revolving door. Most generals who retire from the Army quickly start a new career with a defense contractor. The generals, like Wellington, usually take a position in sales where they can use their Army relationships to market their new employers' products."

Donnie said, "Like Avon."

"Yeah, like Avon," I said, then added to Kate, "I would've thought you'd be pretty well versed in the subject, no?"

Kate said, "I didn't know it was most generals. It's not the kind of hire my dad ever made."

"Milt Feynman was the exception," I said. "Not the rule."

Donnie said, "How much you want to bet that some of those generals buying from Wellington also wind up working for PAP when they retire?"

Kate said, "That's not a pretty thought."

"Maybe you can get a piece of that action too, Jack," Donnie said. "Just think of all the big bucks that could be waiting out there for you."

"Yeah, just think of it," I said. "It would be a nightmare come true."

The communication gear within Donnie's helmet crackled. He turned away from us, listened intently, then pulled the microphone down in front of his mouth.

"Yes, got it," Donnie said into the microphone.

He turned back to us.

"Dr. Lennon, Jack, sorry but they're in a big hurry again," Donnie said. He gestured with his head behind us back towards the tower that housed NASAD's Cyber Defense Hall. "I gotta go."

I turned around to look where Donnie had gestured as Donnie climbed into the chopper's pilot seat. Carter Bowdoin, Bryce Wellington, Freddy, and Wellington's valet were running towards us. Freddy's arms were shooting off at odd angles as he again seemed to have a hard time keeping his balance when moving at high speed.

"From what that security guard said, I take it Freddy isn't the kind of guy who does too much running?" I said to Kate.

"Twice in one day," Kate said. "It's unheard of."

"Hope he doesn't have a heart attack," I said.

"If he does you're the one who's going to give him mouth to mouth," Kate said.

"You told the guard in the lobby you would do it," I said.

"I changed my mind," Kate said.

"I don't know about that," I said. "Mouth to mouth on Freddy doesn't sound too hot. Besides, what makes you think I know how?"

"Wasn't that you at the rest stop yesterday bragging about your medic training?" Kate said.

"I think that was Mosi," I said. "Or Manu. It's hard to tell them apart."

Kate shook her head.

"It was you, dear," Kate said.

Carter Bowdoin, Freddy, Bryce Wellington, and Wellington's valet arrived at the helicopter. The four men were on the helicopter's right side, which was the side opposite from where Kate and I were standing next to the pilot's door. Kate and I ran around the helicopter's nose and we got to the chopper's right side just as Bowdoin and Freddy were climbing into the passenger cabin.

Wellington hadn't boarded yet, however. The valet was helping him out of his suit jacket. The valet produced a clothes hanger seemingly out of thin air and carefully hung the jacket on it. I could then see that the valet was just a kid - he looked barely more than eighteen years old. He was about five foot ten and a hundred and forty pounds if he was lucky. He had clean-cut facial features, blue eyes, straight black hair that was short and neatly combed, and was wearing a spotless, scrupulously pressed blue suit that, unlike Wellington's Saville Row costume, appeared to have been purchased with the utmost care off a rack at J.C. Penney or Macy's. His red tie was perfectly knotted, his white cotton dress shirt was wrinkle free, and his black leather wingtips were so meticulously shined you could almost see your reflection in them.

Bryce Wellington noticed Kate and me and turned to us.

"Dr. Lennon. Jack. I'm glad you're here. We were looking for you," Bryce Wellington said. "One of NASAD's manufacturing facilities was just attacked by terrorists. We've suffered casualties. It'd be best if you both come with us."

Kate said, "How bad are the injuries? Was anyone killed?"

"I'm sorry, ma'am," Wellington said. "We don't know yet."

"Which plant?" Kate said.

"Antelope Valley, ma'am," Bryce Wellington said.

Whoa, I thought to myself.

These two needed to slow down.

Casualties?

And Wellington didn't know how bad they were?

Did he really expect me to allow Kate to visit a battle zone?

I said, "Hold on there one second, Bryce. I'm not sure that sounds like the kind of situation we should be exposing Dr. Lennon to."

"The perpetrators have all fled and the area has been secured by the FBI," Wellington said.

"Who is the FBI agent in charge at the site?" I said.

"Burnette," Wellington said. "He's a good man."

I looked over at Kate's and my black Suburban FBI escort that was still parked in front of the tower that held Kate's office. Though I couldn't see them, I knew Carpenter and his men were behind the vehicle's tinted windows.

"We should probably bring along Dr. Lennon's personal security detail," I said.

"We can't wait for them, and besides, there's not enough room in the chopper," Wellington said.

"I'm sure we could squeeze at least two of them in the helicopter with us," I said.

"Where are they going to sit, Jack, on your lap?" Wellington said. "We have to go. You coming or not?"

I didn't say anything. I was thinking instead.

Wellington shrugged and boarded the helicopter. His valet followed him in.

Kate said, "Come on, Jack. Let's go. You heard Wellington say the attackers were gone. It'll be fine."

I said, "I don't know about that, Kate. Have you ever been to this plant before?"

"Yes. Once," Kate said. "It's perfectly safe. It has barbed wire all around it."

"Barbed wire, huh?" I said. "Unless all we're worried about is being attacked by cows, horses, and pigs, barbed wire's not going to provide much in the way of protection."

"Well, I'm going," Kate said.

She started to climb the helicopter's boarding ladder. I grabbed her arm.

"What are you doing, Jack?" Kate said. "Let go of my arm."

I didn't let go of her arm.

"I don't think it's a good idea," I said.

"Why not?" Kate said.

"What if Wellington's wrong?" I said. "What if the attackers really haven't left the area? What if Burnette didn't properly secure the compound? Hell, knowing Burnette, I'm sure he *didn't* properly secure the compound."

"Then we'll leave," Kate said.

"Leave?" I said.

"Donnie is flying us in," Kate said. "He can fly us right out if there is a problem."

"It's not that simple," I said.

Donnie's voice boomed loudly out of the open helicopter door.

"Dr. Lennon, I'm sorry, but we have to go," Donnie said. "Either come on board or please get down off the ladder, because we're takin' off."

Kate said, "Ten seconds, Donnie." Then to me, she added, "I'm a grown woman, Jack. I want to see what happened at that plant. I'm going. Now, please, let go of my arm."

"What about our appointment with whatshisname?" I said.

"You mean Harold Sinclair, the head of the drone sub project?" Kate said.

"Yeah," I said. "Good old Harold. You don't want to be rude do you?"

"It's not a problem," Kate said. "If you'll let go of me, I can call Mary Beth and cancel right now."

I didn't know what to do. If Wellington's information was inaccurate, our visit to the plant could turn very bad, very fast. But I knew there was no way I could get Kate to change her mind. Which meant, if I was to stop Kate, my only option was to tackle her to the ground and pin her there until the helicopter took off. Call me a coward, but I didn't think that was a good idea.

"You promise to stay by my side the whole time we're at the plant?" I said.

"I promise," Kate said.

I let go of her arm. Kate turned her head toward the helicopter's open door.

"Five more seconds, Donnie," Kate shouted.

Kate pulled her cell phone out of her suit jacket pocket, tapped the screen, and put it to her ear.

"Mary Beth, sorry, I've got an emergency," Kate said into her phone. "Please cancel the meeting with Harold. I'll explain later."

Kate tapped the phone's screen and put it back in her pocket. She climbed the rest of the boarding ladder's stairs and disappeared into the helicopter's cabin.

I looked over again at Kate's and my black Suburban escort. Agent Roy Carpenter was getting out of the passenger seat. I hunched my shoulders and spread my arms with my palms up in the universal gesture which meant, "Sorry, there's nothing I could do." I then took out my iPhone with my left hand and drummed on it with the fingers on my right, hoping Carpenter would understand that I was trying to say I would text him.

My signaling seemed to work.

Carpenter gave me a thumbs up.

I waved, turned, climbed the ladder, and entered the chopper.

CHAPTER 67

The helicopter's passenger cabin was luxurious. It had two rows of plush, blue leather seats, three seats to a row. The three front row seats were all then facing backward, but were mounted on swivels and could be adjusted to face any way the passenger desired. The three seats in the back row only faced forward.

A thick plexiglass wall separated the front row of seats from the pilot's cabin. There was also a partition that separated the front and back rows of the passenger cabin seats from each other. The partition's bottom half was teak wood and the top half was plexiglass. The top half raised and lowered for privacy - just like the partition in the Maybach - and was at that moment retracted into the bottom half of the wall.

Red velvet-sheathed shelves had been mounted on the lower portion of the plexiglass wall behind the pilot and were reachable from the front row of passenger seats. Similar shelves were mounted on the back of the teak wall and could be reached from the back row of seats. Crystal shot glasses, wine glasses, a dozen crystal decanters filled with various amber liquors, and bottles of red and white wine lined both sets of shelves.

From left to right, the front seats were taken up by Carter Bowdoin, Freddy, and General Bryce Wellington. Kate and the valet sat in the rear seats that were next to each side window. There was an empty seat between Kate and the valet for me. Since the three front seats were then turned backwards on their swivels, Bowdoin, Freddy, and Wellington were facing Kate and the valet.

By the time I entered the cabin, everyone had already buckled up and was wearing headsets with earphones and a microphone. The headsets were all connected to a central communication system that allowed everyone to speak with everyone else in the helicopter. The headsets also protected the wearer's ears from being damaged by the extremely loud sound the helicopter's engines made at full throttle.

Donnie craned around from the pilot seat, opened a small window in the plexiglass wall behind him, and shouted at me.

"Move it, Jack!" Donnie said. "And shut that damn door!"

Donnie quickly closed the little window, spun back around, and snatched the chopper's joystick.

I reached for the cabin door, but before I had it barely halfway shut, Donnie gunned the engines and the chopper shot into the air, the fuselage shuddering under the stress. Somehow I managed to stay upright and I used the momentum of the already moving door to get it closed. Since I didn't yet have my headset on, the thunderous 'thwacka thwacka' of the rotors nearly exploded my eardrums. The brutally rapid increase in fuel consumption caused the engine fumes to enter the cabin. The fumes stung my nostrils as I stumbled into my seat, buckled up, and threw on the headset that had been dangling over the seat back.

Donnie was facing forward and studying the sky in front of him. He spoke into his headset microphone and I heard his voice come through my earphones

"Just like old times, huh, Jack?" Donnie said.

"Yeah, Donnie, just like old times," I said into my microphone. "You're still the worst chop jockey on the planet."

"Ain't that the truth," Donnie said. "All we need now is a SAM on our tail."

Donnie accelerated to full forward speed. A moment later he violently banked the chopper left. I had expected Bowdoin, Freddy, and Wellington to be slammed together, but apparently they were well versed in Donnie's tactics and had already braced themselves in their seats. The valet had done likewise. Kate, however, had not expected the maneuver and whacked her head against the window.

"You okay?" I said to Kate.

"Yeah," Kate said into her microphone. "Donnie, you never flew like this any other time I've been with you."

"Never been in this big a rush with you before, ma'am," Donnie said.

The helicopter hit an air pocket and fell about thirty feet. No one was prepared for that, and all of our heads other than Donnie's - who had strapped himself to his seat much more tightly than any of us had - nearly hit the ceiling as we went into zero gravity.

Freddy, looking like he was going to be sick, clutched his head in his hands and put his elbows on his knees. Carter Bowdoin seemed annoyed, as if falling through an air pocket was not the kind of thing that was supposed to happen to him. Bryce Wellington smiled, as if to say 'wasn't that fun?', though the green pallor of his skin said quite the opposite. The valet seemed unfazed, and Kate was frightened. She grabbed my thigh. It felt like a giant lobster had my leg in its pincers. I liked the feeling.

I pulled Kate's earphones aside so that the others wouldn't hear what I had to say and whispered into her ear.

"Nothing to worry about, Kate," I said. "Donnie knows what he's doing."

My words apparently weren't as soothing as I had hoped, since Kate, instead of relaxing her grip, increased it. Increased it, that is, until she noticed all the other males in the cabin staring at her hand, at which point she immediately let go. I was disappointed, to say the least.

I turned to face Bryce Wellington.

"Where we headed, Bryce?" I said.

"Fifty to sixty miles northeast of here," Wellington said. "Near Lake Hughes."

I did a quick calculation in my head. At the Bell's top speed of 150 miles per hour we would be there in about twenty-five minutes.

"That's where the NASAD manufacturing plant is?" I said.

"Yes," Wellington said. "It's a top secret installation. We have about four hundred employees squirreled away there working on Ohio class drone subs."

"Does NASAD have any other plants like it?" I said.

"A few," Wellington said. "I'll brief you on them later. But right now we've got to focus on the attack on this plant and the immediate issues the attack has created for us."

"And those are?" I said.

"First off," Wellington said, "we have to make sure that if the attack did indeed inflict any serious harm on the drone sub program, the sequelae from that harm in no way impinge on the security of our fighting men and women."

"Which you have to do quickly," I said, "since war with China is about to break out any day now."

"Very quickly," Wellington said. "And second, we need to do some damage control so that the attack doesn't cause NASAD's reputation to suffer."

"What's more important to you, Bryce? NASAD's reputation or the safety of our fighting men and women?" I said.

Kate jammed her elbow into my ribs.

Freddy glared at me, then covered his mouth as if he was about to throw up.

Carter Bowdoin, who had been staring out the window and seeming to take no interest in Bryce's and my conversation, apparently had been paying attention after all.

"I know you're joking, General," Bowdoin said. "But we take this situation very seriously. It is not just NASAD and its responsibilities to our military men and women we're worried about, but we're also worried about Pennsylvania Avenue Partners' own employees as well."

"You're speaking of your employees on the ground in Saudi Arabia?" I said.

"Saudi Arabia, Qatar, Kuwait, the entire Middle East," Bowdoin said. "PAP's engineering and construction company, American Oil Energy Corp., is the largest of its kind in the world. It is bigger than Fluor, KBR, and Bechtel combined. We have over 30,000 people working in the Middle East on everything from pipeline and oil field construction, to road building and water desalinization and reclamation projects. We're also in the midst of a major renovation of the oil port facility at Yanbu on the Red Sea."

"Are you evacuating your employees due to the threat of war?" I said.

"As we speak," Bowdoin said. "We're expecting another call from the PAP board on that subject any minute."

I thought about what Bowdoin had said. Bowdoin's words seemed quite reasonable, and I wasn't sure why - maybe it had something to do with his gambling with the NASAD Cyber Defense Hall team - but I was getting an odd feeling about the man. I decided to keep him talking if for no reason than just to hear him speak.

"If there is a war with China, and the U.S. and Saudi Arabia lose that war, will your employees in Saudi Arabia lose their jobs?" I said.

"I don't expect us to lose the war," Bowdoin said. "Do you?"

"No, I don't expect us to lose," I said.

"Good. You had me worried for a moment," Bowdoin said. "In answer to your question, however, if we do lose the war, PAP will do its best to place those employees on other projects. China has its own construction and energy companies, so it's unlikely PAP will have any place in a China-controlled Saudi Arabia."

The helicopter passed over Simi Valley. From the air, the valley appeared to be a pleasant bedroom community with thousands of tract homes, most with pools in their backyards. Simi Valley, however, like Lancaster, also had its own sections of abandoned housing developments with half-constructed homes surrounded by acres of barren ground.

"So you're saying there's little chance the Chinese would hire PAP to help rebuild the country after the war?" I said.

Bowdoin gave a short, bitter laugh.

"Sorry, General, but probably due to some unconscious wishful thinking on my part, I believe I understated the situation," Bowdoin said. "What I should have said is that it is impossible PAP will have any place in a China-controlled Saudi Arabia. The giant Chinese engineering and construction conglomerates are well connected with the Chinese government."

"Kinda like PAP with our own government," I said.

Bowdoin smiled.

"Yes, kind of like that," Bowdoin said.

When Bowdoin said that, I then realized what one of the things was that had been bothering me about the gambling going on at NASAD. Gamblers hate to lose, even if the stakes are relatively small, and Carter Bowdoin was a gambler. According to Kate, the war game matches between the NASAD offensive and defensive war game teams were pretty even. Bowdoin, however, always bet on the defensive team. Which meant Bowdoin was probably losing at least half the time. Bowdoin couldn't be happy about that, could he? It might easily turn out to be a trivial point, but still, it didn't add up. Rather than pondering that question further just then, I tabled it for future consideration. I didn't know when I would again have such close access to Carter Bowdoin and thought my time would be better spent continuing to keep him talking.

"You ever wonder what China will do with the Saudi royal family if they win?" I said to Bowdoin.

Bryce Wellington jumped into the conversation.

"You serious, Jack?" Wellington said. "What do you care about the Saudi royal family? They're just a bunch of backstabbing sons of bitches."

"They're paying PAP's bills, aren't they?" I said.

"What's your point?" Wellington said.

"Aren't you pretty much biting the hand that feeds you?" I said.

"The Saudis fund Al-Qaeda for chrissake," Wellington said. "It's not like they have a divine right to all that oil they happened to stumble upon."

"Divine right?" I said.

"The House of Saud is self-anointed," Wellington said. "They've been in power all of what, eighty years? Maybe it's time for someone else to come along and call themselves king."

Carter Bowdoin gave Wellington a sharp look, then turned to me.

"I know you were just teasing Bryce, but you make a good point General," Bowdoin said. "It might appear Bryce's comments are, as you say, biting the hand that feeds us, but surely you're aware that business can get very complicated when you play it on a worldwide scale. And if we sometimes deal with people we perhaps don't adore, well, it might sound trite, but if we don't do it, someone else will, won't they? In the end, I'd rather see the jobs go to Americans. Wouldn't you?"

Bowdoin's cell phone rang. He looked down at the phone's screen.

"Sorry General, there's that call we've been expecting coming in from the PAP board now," Bowdoin said. "Donnie, please patch this call in via my cell's Bluetooth."

"Yes, sir," Donnie said.

"The helicopter has the latest in technology thanks to one of PAP'S communication companies, General," Bowdoin said. "We can assign this call to just Bryce's, Freddy's, and my headsets so the rest of you can be free to chat while we take it. We will talk again soon."

Bowdoin, Wellington, and Freddy swiveled their seats around so that they were all facing forward. Bowdoin pushed a button on the side of his seat and the soundproof plexiglass partition between our row and theirs went up. Bowdoin then tapped on his cell phone and it appeared that the conversation with the Pennsylvania Avenue Partners board had begun. Freddy and Wellington seemed to be listening intently. I couldn't hear a word of their conversation.

"Hey Donnie," I said into my headset.

"Yes, Jack?" Donnie said.

"I can't hear them," I said. "Can they hear us?"

"Nope," Donnie said. "System was built so the head honchos could carry on private conversations whenever they wanted. The three of them are in their own little world now and we're in ours."

"Interesting," I said.

I turned to Kate.

"I guess Bryce Wellington doesn't much like the House of Saud," I said.

Kate leaned in close to me, pushed my earphone aside, and whispered into my ear.

"Uh, Jack, the three of them up front can't hear what you're saying," Kate said, "but he can."

She pointed with her finger at Wellington's valet, her movement so small as to be barely perceptible.

"Oh, right," I said. I turned to the valet and extended my hand. "No one has introduced us yet. This is Dr. Lennon and I'm Jack Wilder. What's your name?"

"Martin Papadopolous, sir," the valet said, shaking my hand. "Please call me Martin."

"Thank you, Martin," I said. "What do you think about the House of Saud?"

Kate said, "Jack!"

"Shh," I said. "Let him speak."

Donnie said, "Yeah, I want to hear what the kid has to say."

Martin said, "Well, I don't think my opinion counts for much, sir. But please don't worry about speaking freely in front of me. I won't tell my uncle. Frankly, he's a bit of a blowhard."

"Bryce is your uncle?" I said.

"Yes, sir," Martin said.

Martin seemed nice enough. It was impossible for me to believe he was from the Wellington male line, or for that matter, had any Wellington blood in him at all.

"By marriage, I bet," I said.

"Yes, sir," Martin said. "General Wellington's wife is my mother's sister. How did you know?"

"Lucky guess," I said.

The helicopter was continuing its northeasterly journey. We were being buffeted by mild winds, but had thankfully not found any more air pockets. The landscape below was covered with old grey ash and blackened tree stumps where once fire had attacked the earth.

"I would like to add, sir, it is a pleasure to meet such eminent figures as Dr. Lennon and yourself," Martin said. "I know of your unparalleled combat record and hope to emulate it one day, sir."

"You do?" I said.

"Yes," Martin said. "This is my gap year. I am entering West Point a year from this September. Uncle Bryce got me this job and my security clearance as well. I will be working with him for the next twelve months."

Donnie said, "Do yourself a favor, kid. Don't let anyone at West Point know Wellington is your uncle."

"Thank you, Captain Donnie," Martin said. "I had already decided upon that course of action, but it is good to have it validated by such an illustrious warrior as yourself."

I said, "What's better, eminent or illustrious?"

Donnie said, "Don't answer that, Martin."

Martin said, "Eminent, sir."

"What'd I just say, Martin?" Donnie said.

I said, "Leave the kid alone, Donnie."

Martin said, "May I comment on your discussion with Mr. Bowdoin and my uncle, sir?"

"Go right ahead, Martin," I said.

"While Mr. Carter Bowdoin and my uncle expressed to you their concerns about the possible upcoming war with China, I don't believe they shared all their feelings," Martin said.

"What was it they left out?" I said.

"They believe there is a bright side to the war," Martin said.

"Do they?" I said.

"They like the idea that if the U.S. wins," Martin said, "PAP gets to rebuild Saudi Arabia all over again."

Martin's statement appeared to make Kate uncomfortable.

Kate said, "I wouldn't make too much out of that, Martin. They probably were just making a bad joke."

Donnie said, "Joke, huh? Maybe yes, maybe no."

Donnie could think what he wanted, but I was pretty much on Kate's side. I imagined most defense company executives might, in an unguarded moment, say something like Bowdoin and Wellington had said. I didn't take it at all seriously.

"Come on, Donnie," Kate said. "Don't fill this nice young man's head full of nonsense. There are enough skeptics out there who think defense companies are evil, when all we are really trying to do is create products to defend what we believe is a great nation."

Martin said, "I understand, ma'am. But I still don't trust Mr. Bowdoin and my uncle."

I said, "Why not?"

"Well, Dr. Lennon's brother is a nice enough man, but I do not believe Mr. Bowdoin and my uncle are patriots," Martin said.

Kate said, "Martin, Carter Bowdoin's father was president of the United States!"

"Sometimes the apple falls far from the tree," Martin said.

Donnie said, "How old did you say you were, kid?"

"I didn't say," Martin said. "But I'm eighteen."

"Kid's got a lot of smarts for eighteen, doesn't he Jack?" Donnie said.

I said, "Certainly seems that way. I especially liked his views on the difference between eminent and illustrious."

"Aw, Jesus," Donnie said.

Kate said, "You do seem like a bright young man, Martin, but I'm not so sure it's a good idea to start questioning people's patriotism."

Donnie, Kate, and Martin all kept chattering along, but at that point I reached up and turned off my headset and left the conversation. I figured their discussion was going to get more and more political, and politics are not my forte. Besides, I had important work to do. I needed to get Haley up to speed with all that I had learned that morning and have her team start researching a few things for me.

I don't know why - perhaps it was the fact I was thinking about Haley doing research for me - but it suddenly came to me what the something was that had nagged at the corners of my mind back when I'd exited the NASAD office building shortly after leaving the Cyber

Defense Hall. The something was a very basic question that needed answering. It was such a basic and obvious question that I kicked myself for not considering it - at least not consciously considering it - earlier. The fact I hadn't considered asking the question until that moment also made me once again face up to just how rusty spending the last two years cooped up on my ranch had made me.

The basic and obvious question that needed answering was, if the Chinese insurmountable edge and Dr. Nemo's and the NASAD dark programmers' war games software were actually one and the same, was that software already active and currently producing any noticeable deleterious effects on the military's live computer systems?

I had a hunch as to the answer to that question.

My hunch was that if the insurmountable edge and the war games software were one and the same, the edge wouldn't yet be active. It seemed to me that the most likely scenario was that the edge wouldn't activate until ten days from now, as that was when the NASAD war games and the Chinese war were both set to commence.

And even though it was a hunch, it hadn't come completely out of thin air.

The hunch was supported by three things -

One. Jeff's and my conversations of the day before. Jeff had spoken with CENTCOM, I had spoken with CENTCOM, and I had also spoken with General Hart. It seemed to me that if anything even remotely qualifying as the Chinese insurmountable edge was already active and affecting any of the U.S. military's capabilities or functions, then CENTCOM and Hart would have known about it and advised both Jeff and me of that activity. But neither CENTCOM nor Hart had advised us of any such thing. Indeed, CENTCOM seemed to have no good ideas about what the edge was, and Hart only had his notion that the edge had something to do with the NASAD drone subs - a notion of which I was extremely skeptical.

Two. Surprise. Surprise is a key tactic of war. The Chinese would do everything in their power to keep the U.S. military from knowing what the insurmountable edge was until they surprised us with the edge when they started their war. If the Chinese had already activated the insurmountable edge, they would potentially allow the U.S. to identify what the edge was before the war began, and the U.S. could thus prepare for the edge. But if the insurmountable edge was still inactive, then the Chinese had a better chance of keeping the U.S. military unprepared for the edge's capabilities, and it was much more likely the initial Chinese attacks on the U.S. forces would inflict tremendously more damage on those forces than if our military had been prepared.

Three. The goals of the NASAD dark programmers for their upcoming war games. It seemed to me that Dr. Nemo and the NASAD dark programmers would have written their war games software to turn on and begin its attack on the NASAD defensive war games team precisely at the scheduled start date and time of the NASAD war games. If the insurmountable edge and the NASAD war games software were one and the same, wouldn't the insurmountable edge most likely be using the same date and time that had been written into the dark programmers' war games software? Wouldn't the insurmountable edge also then remain inactivated until the start date and time of the NASAD war games?

In any event, I needed to know whether or not the U.S. military's computer systems were functioning normally. Haley was the best person to provide the answer to that question. It was time to ask Haley that question, along with all the other questions I had been storing up for her. It was also time to get Haley up to speed on my current thoughts about our mission.

I texted her -

-Haley, since we last communicated has anyone come up with a better determination of what the Chinese insurmountable edge is? Even if the answer to that is no, is there any evidence that any threat that could qualify as the insurmountable edge is already affecting the functioning of the U.S. Armed Forces? I am especially curious as to whether the U.S. military computers are working normally?

-Search for Dr. Nemo remains a top priority. I believe he may be a NASAD employee who is between eighteen and twenty-one years old and might have visited the Lennon estate on more than one occasion about six years ago.

-I also believe Dr. Nemo may be a member of a top secret group of about sixty computer programmers at NASAD known as the dark programmers. Their identities and location are completely unknown and they are involved in conducting war games that test the integrity of the computer systems that NASAD provides to the U.S. military. The dark programmers are paid by wire transfers from NASAD to multiple shifting accounts. Suggest you look for evidence of amounts equal to about $375,000 going out of NASAD twice a month - I figure this equals the payroll for sixty people earning about $150,000 yearly??? - and then trace the money as it gets split into many streams. The money trace might help us find Nemo. However, I would also like to talk to any other dark programmer you find.

-Contact with the dark programmers is allowed for authorized persons only. I have a hunch that an unauthorized person somehow managed to contact them. As the security surrounding the dark programmers is very tight, this would mean that security was breached. I think the most likely way that breach would have occurred is that someone with inside knowledge broke protocol. My gut says that someone could be a NASAD computer programmer who started out as a dark programmer, but later transferred to the team of programmers working in the NASAD Cyber Defense Hall. Please see if you can find any evidence for the existence of this hypothesized person. I will work on this from my end as well.

-Mary Beth Lankowski, the head of HR at NASAD, may be able to help me contact the NASAD executive who oversees the dark programming division. The executive is known as the vice president of dark programming. I cannot discuss our situation openly with him, however, unless we are sure we can trust him. Please do whatever you can to discover his identity and get your best read on whether we can trust him or not.

-Raj Divedi, the head of NASAD's cybersecurity, says there's no chance a back door exists into NASAD's system. What do MOM's people think?

-General Bryce Wellington has reappeared in our lives. Please find out who the NASAD Army liaison was three years ago and if Wellington had any connection to him or her.

-Give me anything you can on Carter Bowdoin's gambling habits. Especially interested in the bracelet he won at the Worldwide Challenge Poker event.

-Any news on the plane that brought the Kazakh mercenaries into the U.S.? The decoding of Nemo's message?

-Thanks, Jack.

I wrote another short text to Carpenter to tell him where Kate and I were headed, sent it as well, and put the cell phone away.

The chopper's path then took us over an amusement park. There were a large number of huge, elaborately designed roller coasters. The roller coasters' cars slowly climbed up tracks that were supported by giant steel columns, and then, after reaching the top of their climb, rapidly descended back to earth. During their descent the coaster cars catapulted through dozens of sharp, tight curves that subjected them to brutal centrifugal force.

The roller coasters made me think of my wife Grace. Grace loved the terrifying thrill of riding roller coasters. Careening through space in the coasters' cars, Grace would scream with fright, seemingly never quite believing she was not in any real danger.

Whenever I brought up to Grace the fact that I didn't understand how she could be so terrified by a ride where the danger was so carefully contained and controlled that she could not possibly get hurt, Grace would counter me by saying, "Perhaps it would be better to ask yourself why you keep throwing yourself into situations where the danger is neither contained nor controlled, but absolutely deadly, and yet you do so with such an absence of terror, that a normal person like myself would be completely justified in questioning your sanity."

I probably should have done what Grace had suggested and asked myself that question, but I never quite got around to doing so. Partly, because deep down I suspected there was no good answer, but also because thinking about Grace's question seemed to get in the way of whatever I had to do, whenever and wherever I had to do it.

I didn't think about the answer at that moment either, because just then my cell phone began to ring. It was Haley calling on FaceTime.

CHAPTER 68

The NASAD chopper passed over a series of housing developments and a golf course. The developments seemed much more upscale than the ones in Simi Valley or Lancaster, and there appeared to be far fewer abandoned homes. One of the developments was next to a cemetery. I could make out a line of cars and dozens of mourners next to a gravesite. A funeral was in progress.

The lack of privacy in the passenger cabin tempted me to message Haley that I would have to call her back. But with time so short before war was to break out with China, and the fact it was unlikely that Haley would be calling me unless she had something important to say, I felt it would be unwise not to take her call. I didn't want Kate or Martin the valet to see what was on my screen, so I pushed my headset's microphone away from my mouth and slipped my cell phone in between the headset's earphone and my ear.

"Jack Wilder speaking," I said.

"What kind of greeting is that?" Haley said. "I know it's you, you idiot. And why can't I see you?"

"Thanks for asking," I said. "I'm in a helicopter with six other people."

"That's why you aren't using FaceTime and are speaking so mysteriously?" Haley said.

"The answer to that would be yes and yes," I said. "You got my text?"

"Yes," Haley said. "I'm working on it. I can tell you right now, however, that we aren't any closer to determining what the insurmountable edge is. I can also tell you that all U.S. military systems, including all computer systems, are functioning normally." Haley paused. "I assume that since you asked me questions about the NASAD dark programmers, and also about a potential 'back door' into NASAD's computer systems, that you believe the Chinese insurmountable edge might have something to do with the computer systems NASAD provides to the U.S. military?"

"Smart girl," I said.

"I also assume that you believe that if Dr. Nemo turns out to be a member of the NASAD dark programmers, then he would have worked on those computer systems?" Haley said. "And that if Dr. Nemo did indeed work on those systems, and also on the dark programmers' war games software, then his work may have resulted, however unwittingly, in the creation of the insurmountable edge? The insurmountable edge in turn being the grave risk Dr. Nemo is warning us about?"

"I'm definitely considering it," I said. "Right now it's just a hunch."

"Your hunches are usually pretty good," Haley said.

"We'll see," I said. "When you get me the answers to the other questions I asked, I'll have a much better idea if I'm headed in the right direction or not."

"Understood," Haley said. "In regard to my own hunches, however, it seems that getting you a dark programmer to speak to would probably be the most effective thing I can do for you. I also agree with your assessment that out of all the dark programmers you could talk to, talking to Dr. Nemo would probably benefit us the most, as we're at least assured Nemo wants to tell us about what he's deemed a grave risk. It would be great to find Dr. Nemo so we can stop worrying about cracking his code, too."

"Agreed," I said.

"Dr. Nemo could also wind up being the easiest to find of the bunch because we've already got some information on him, whereas we have nothing on the other dark programmers," Haley said. "Hell, if Nemo really wanted to be nice, he'll tell us where to find him whenever he gets around to sending that message he promised to send to Dr. Lennon."

"That would be very nice of him," I said.

"Next topic," Haley said. "There's something I want to show you."

"Can't you just tell me?" I said.

"It's better if I show you," Haley said.

I thought for a moment.

"Alright, hold on," I said.

I pulled my headset's microphone back down over my mouth.

"Donnie, I just got a cell phone call," I said. "I need to patch it into my headphones."

"Our conversation isn't good enough for you?" Donnie said.

Kate and Martin turned to look at me. I gave them my most sheepish grin.

"Sorry, everyone," I said. "But it's important."

Kate said, "No need to apologize. Go ahead and take the call."

I saw Donnie reach down and flip a switch in the cockpit.

"Line six is open for you," Donnie said. "Connect to it with your Bluetooth."

"Thanks," I said. "Is it private?"

"What kind of question is that?" Donnie said.

"Sorry," I said.

I connected my phone to line six, unbuckled my seat belt, and got out of my seat. I turned around, gripped one of the cabin partition's shelves to brace myself, and hoped we wouldn't hit any air pockets any time soon. I then looked down at my iPhone screen so that I was eye to eye with the beautiful Major Haley. Since Freddy, Bowdoin, and Wellington were facing away from me, and Kate and Martin were facing toward me, none of them could see my phone's screen.

"What you got?" I said.

"We found the guy," Haley said.

I couldn't say 'What guy?', because if I did I'd lose Haley's and my little mind reading game. So I thought it over. I was sure Haley would have already told me if she had found either Nemo or the identity of my hypothesized dark programmer who had switched over to the defensive team in the NASAD Cyber Defense Hall. Which meant she had to be talking about someone else. Who could that be? A moment later I had figured it out.

"You mean the guy whose fingerprints were lifted from the van the Kazakhs had driven to the Coso Junction rest stop?" I said.

"Goddammit," Haley said. "I didn't think you'd get that one."

"Ye of little faith," I said

"Guy's name is Casper Felix," Haley said.

"He's named after two cartoon characters?" I said.

"That's one way to look at it," Haley said.

"Did the Kazakhs buy the van or expropriate it?" I said.

"Expropriate," Haley said. "Take a look at this picture."

A photograph appeared on my iPhone screen. The photograph showed a very gaunt man who looked to be in his early thirties and maybe five feet, seven inches tall. The skin on his face had the yellowish, grey tinge of a chronic alcoholic. He also had a mohawk haircut, a beak-like nose, rotted teeth, a big Adam's apple, and was wearing a ratty gas station attendant's coverall with the name 'Cas' written inside a blue ringed oval patch above the left chest pocket. Both the coverall and Casper's face were smeared with dirt and grease. In the center of Casper's forehead was a nice, neat, black hole with a raised purple rim.

"Hole made by a 9mm Parabellum?" I said.

"Correct," Haley said.

"Ballistics match it up with one of the guns I took off the Kazakhs?" I said.

"Ding ding ding ding ding," Haley said. "Three for three."

"That was five dings," I said.

"Five dings sounds better than three dings," Haley said.

I silently tried three dings in my head.

"What are you doing?" Haley said.

"I was trying it out," I said. "You're right. Five dings is better. When did they find him?"

"Last night," Haley said. "He'd been dead about twenty-four hours."

"Where was he?" I said.

"In a ditch by the side of a rural road near Pixley," Haley said.

"The Pixley between Bakersfield and Fresno that's about two and a half hours by car to the rest stop at Coso Junction?" I said.

"I'm impressed," Haley said.

"I've driven through Pixley," I said. "I once stopped for a hamburger there. Casper Felix have any previous relation to the Kazakhs?"

"Doubtful," Haley said. "Felix's fingerprints were on file since he'd been arrested for dealing a small amount of pot ten years ago. He spent most of his life as a garage mechanic working at gas stations within ten miles of Pixley. Other than the pot arrest, he never got in any other trouble."

"So Felix just got unlucky he had a vehicle the Kazakhs wanted," I said.

"Looks that way," Haley said.

"I assume then you're okay going forward with our working theory being that the Kazakhs killed Felix, stole his van, outfitted it with their tracking computer and kidnap paraphernalia, and drove to Coso Junction?" I said.

"It's a good theory," Haley said.

The chopper hit an air pocket. Turned out gripping the partition shelf didn't work too well. My hand snapped free, my feet left the floor, and I banged my head on the top of the cabin. When I came back down, I smashed into the floor and my left knee screamed in agony. Kate and Martin had concerned looks on their faces. I smiled and gave them a thumbs up.

"You alright?" Haley said.

"No," I said.

"You need to hold on tighter," Haley said.

"Easier said than done with Donnie Kurtsinger at the controls," I said.

"Donnie's the pilot?!" Haley said.

"Yes," I said.

"I take back what I said," Haley said. "You better bolt yourself to something."

"I'll take that under advisement," I said. "Now, the big question then is how did the Kazakhs get to Pixley?"

"We don't know," Haley said.

"You mean you don't know yet," I said.

"Yet. Yes," Haley said. "Sorry, I misspoke."

"You're forgiven," I said. "My guess is the Kazakhs entered the country somewhere close to where they stole Casper's van."

"We've cast a bigger net than that," Haley said. "We took photos of the faces of the dead Kazakhs at the Coso Junction rest stop and we're using facial recognition to check every U.S. inbound flight that could have originated in Afghanistan or Kazakhstan, or connected out of those places, in the last seventy-two hours. So far, none of the Kazakhs were on those flights though."

"Seventy-two hours?" I said. "You just pull that number out of your hat?"

"I hate to say it, but I've grown to like your pork rind wrapper theory," Haley said. "I agree with you that the pork rinds were probably an airline snack, and most people wouldn't keep an empty wrapper in their pocket for long."

"Hmm...," I said.

"Hmm, what?" Haley said.

"I think you're keeping something from me," I said. "I'm sure you wouldn't do all that work just based on my theory and your 'agreement' with it. What else did you find out?"

Haley sighed.

"Don't let it go to your head, but the only company making those snacks is the Bissengaliyev Snack Company in Almaty, Kazakhstan," Haley said. "They only sell them in Kazakhstan too."

"How could I not let that go to my head?" I said.

Haley rolled her eyes.

"So you'll keep checking all the flights and call me when you find the right one?" I said.

"You'll be the first to know," Haley said.

"And speaking of flights, please send me a copy of the video of Milt Feynman and Paul Lennon's Otter from takeoff until it crashed into the sea," I said. "I may want to study it some more."

"Will do," Haley said.

The screen on my iPhone flashed and the phone made a beeping noise. My boss/surrogate father General Jim Hart was sending a FaceTime request to me.

"When it rains, it pours," I said to Haley. "Hart's trying to FaceTime with me."

"Take it," Haley said. "We're done here anyway. I'll contact you when I find anything new."

Haley clicked off and I answered Hart's call.

"General," I said. "Good to see you, sir."

"Good to see you too, son," Hart said.

Hart was standing on the deck of an aircraft carrier that was violently rolling on very high seas. I assumed the carrier was the George Washington since the day before Hart had said he was headed to the Washington to talk to Admiral Bagley about taking NASAD's Ohio drone submarines offline. The ocean wind blowing across the carrier's deck was battering an American flag mounted on a pole next to the bridge. The wind was so strong it seemed to be fluttering the hairs on Hart's closely cropped head. Hart's cheekbones looked a little sunburned and perhaps slightly greenish as well. His grey eyes, while quite fierce, may have looked a tad bit tired. He appeared to be wearing the same tan shirt I had seen him in when he was cruising in the Humvee across the African plains.

"How are your balls, sir?" I said. "Have they lowered back to their normal position in your scrotal sack?"

"I appreciate your heartfelt concern, son," Hart said. "The carrier landing actually wasn't too bad. It's these damn waves that are getting to me."

"A little seasick are we, sir?" I said.

"Yes," Hart said. "But I'm feeling better ever since I barfed up my dinner. By the way, that was excellent work you did in proving Feynman and Lennon were murdered."

"Thank you, sir," I said. "I apologize, however, if this new information caused you any pain. I know how close you were to Milt."

"You're going to catch the bastards who did it, aren't you?" Hart said.

"I am, sir," I said.

"And after you catch them, you're going to make sure they rue the day they were born, correct?" Hart said.

"Absolutely," I said. "Without a doubt, sir."

"Then don't worry about it," Hart said.

"Understood, sir," I said. "Any luck with Admiral Bagley taking the NASAD drone subs offline, sir?"

"The old coot is refusing to cooperate," Hart said. "Says he has to think about it."

"Think about it, sir?" I said.

"He actually makes some good points," Hart said. "Chief among them being that it wouldn't set a good precedent to back down militarily without more proof the drone subs are really a potential liability."

"So the drone sub engineers' deaths are not enough for him to take the subs out of service?" I said.

"Bagley says if we do, where will it stop?" Hart said. "Are we going to take tanks offline if someone starts killing tank engineers, or F-16's if someone starts killing F-16 engineers, or...well you get the picture."

"I do, sir," I said.

"So what I need is more evidence," Hart said.

"Evidence?" I said.

"Yeah, evidence the insurmountable edge is related to the drone subs," Hart said. "My gut tells me the drones are where we're vulnerable, so you're just going to have to get something that will convince Bagley."

Since I believed the drone subs were a diversion and not a real threat, I answered with as much fake enthusiasm as I could muster.

"I'm on it, sir," I said.

Hart studied my face.

"You playing me, son?" Hart said.

"What makes you say that?" I said.

"I've known you long enough to be able to tell when your heart is not really in something," Hart said.

I was tempted to tell Hart what I really thought, but I knew that would only cause him to dig his heels in deeper about the drone subs. Which also might cause him to start micromanaging me and prevent me from actually getting some real work done.

"Not sure why you say that, sir," I said. "Drones are all I think about. Here a drone, there a drone, everywhere a drone, drone."

"What is that, some goddamn nursery song?" Hart said.

"'Old MacDonald', sir," I said.

"Don't be bullshitting me, son," Hart said.

"I'm not, sir," I said. "I'll get you your evidence."

"I need it as fast as you can get it," Hart said. "The Chinese just put another 50,000 troops on the Saudi Arabian border."

The view behind Hart suddenly shifted. The American flag behind him disappeared and his face became silhouetted by blue sky. I guessed Hart must have bent over. He looked even more greenish than before.

"Damn," Hart said. "I gotta go throw up again. Take care of yourself."

Hart clicked off.

50,000 more Chinese troops on the Saudi border? Things were getting even more serious, weren't they? I stumbled back to my seat and belted myself in just as the chopper hit another air pocket. My hips felt the strain, but my head and knee avoided any further damage.

The helicopter kept flying north and east. At the twenty-fourth minute of our flight I saw plumes of smoke rising in the distance. A minute later, I could see the plumes were coming from a large industrial site situated on the ground below. I assumed the site was the one belonging to NASAD.

CHAPTER 69

As expected, Donnie Kurtsinger piloted the helicopter through a final approach to the NASAD site that was fast, steep, and seemingly dangerously out of control. While my co-passengers appeared to be trying to deal with their own varied levels of terror, I, having been through Donnie's drill dozens of times before, was able to keep whatever little wits I had about me and get a gander at the site during the helicopter's descent. It encompassed about three hundred acres, clearcut in a forest of lush, green trees. The barbed wire fence Kate had mentioned encircled the entire perimeter. Armed FBI agents and NASAD security staff roamed the area. Some of the FBI agents patrolled with dogs on leashes. Since the dogs were obsessively sniffing the ground, I assumed it likely they were bomb-sniffing dogs and that they and their handlers were looking for explosives.

Two large hangars were on the north side of the site. The hangars were an old, wood-style military design from the 1940's. As I saw no other structures that were even close in size to the hangers, I assumed all the site's manufacturing took place within the hangars.

Two hundred yards south of the hangars lay ten barracks. The barracks looked to be of the same vintage as the hangars. Faces of NASAD employees peered out of the barracks' windows. A big grassy field, swimming pool, and tennis courts lay between the barracks and the hangars. An FBI helicopter was parked in the middle of the grassy field. I presumed the helicopter was the one that had transported Burnette to the site.

Plumes of smoke rose from patches of brush that must have caught fire in whatever attack had just occurred. Men in yellow fire helmets, turnout jackets, and pants were standing atop two bright red fire trucks emblazoned with NASAD insignias. The men were spraying the burning patches with water from high pressure fire hoses.

Donnie, after making a screaming, high speed, brutally banked turn just inches above the grassy field, broke the helicopter's momentum by slamming the landing skids down on the grass in the sharp left skid, right skid progression I had seen him use in landing at NASAD headquarters and also countless times before. The brutal thump of the landing - which left us parked about fifty feet from the FBI helicopter - jarred all my bones and internal organs, the shock waves so intense my body felt like it was vibrating. By the looks on the faces of my seatmates, it appeared their bones and organs were experiencing the same thing. While the rest of us tried to regain our equilibrium, Donnie, seemingly unfazed, shut down the engines, wriggled free of his seat belt, opened his door, hopped to the ground, ran around the front of the chopper, opened the right side passenger compartment door, and pulled down the landing steps.

As if from out of nowhere, Burnette, with a coterie of six other FBI agents, each armed with MP5 submachine guns, appeared outside the open chopper doors. Carter Bowdoin, Freddy, Bryce Wellington, Martin the valet, Kate, and I slowly climbed down the steps to meet them. The temperature was in the nineties, more than twenty degrees warmer than what it had been at Taj MaFreddy.

Kate leaned in close to me as soon as we both were standing on solid ground.

"Mary Beth and Raj answered my texts," Kate whispered.

"And?" I whispered back.

"Neither of them know any employees who wear dragon masks," Kate whispered. "Or any masks for that matter."

"Was worth a try anyway," I whispered. "Nothing ventured, nothing gained."

Kate nodded.

Burnette, whose scalp was dripping with perspiration beneath his porkpie hat, and whose pale skin had been turned lobster red by the sun, seemed to be having trouble breathing in the smoke and heat. He had abandoned his suit jacket but retained the tie and dress shirt, both of which were stained with pools of sweat. Burnette's gold-plated, pearl handled Glock was in a holster on his hip, but his big yellow bullhorn was nowhere in sight. I was surprised Burnette didn't have the bullhorn since I thought he would have felt naked without it. The idea of Burnette naked made me so queasy, however, that I quickly ceased any further meditations on the matter.

Everyone gathered in a semicircle around Burnette and his team. I recognized all the agents on the team as having been at our little get-together at the Coso Junction rest stop the previous day. I even remembered two of the team members' names - Conklin and Finlayson. I smiled at them and they smiled back. Burnette then scowled at Conklin and Finlayson, however, and that was the end of that.

I scanned the surrounding area for anything that might represent a threat. Normally with such a large contingent of FBI agents present, I wouldn't have expected to find anything of concern, but these agents were under Burnette's command, and I felt it was better to be careful than dead. Carter Bowdoin seemed to feel the same way - I could see him taking furtive peeks at the barracks and the hangars. From my point of view, everything looked fine at that moment.

Bryce Wellington stepped forward from our semicircle, grabbed Burnette's hand, and shook it.

"Agent Burnette, I can't tell you how comfortable we feel with you in command," Wellington said. "We truly appreciate your service to NASAD."

Burnette's piggy eyes beamed, and his floppy jowls, blubbery lips, and chubby cheeks all coalesced into a disturbingly wide smile. Burnette the hard-ass had turned into a kiss-ass.

"We are always happy to be of service, General Wellington," Burnette said. "And I'm proud to say that our security arrangements worked perfectly. By the time I arrived, the attackers had been driven off and the site had been secured by our agents on-site and NASAD's own men."

"No serious casualties?" Wellington said.

"A few flesh wounds, but that's all," Burnette said.

"Have you determined the reason for the attack?" Wellington said.

"We have an idea," Burnette said. "Please follow me."

Burnette started walking towards one of the large hangars. Donnie Kurtsinger stayed behind with the helicopter, but Wellington, Bowdoin, Freddy, Martin the valet, Kate, and I fell in behind Burnette as his agents formed a protective circle around us. I bent my head close to Kate's ear and spoke to her in a whisper.

"Remember," I said, "stay next to me. Never more than a foot away."

"Burnette just said they drove off the attackers," Kate said to me in an equally hushed tone.

"There's no way anybody could know that for sure," I said. "And until *I'm* sure, please, just do as I ask."

"Yes, mein führer," Kate said. "I would never think of disobeying a direct order."

"Somehow I find that hard to believe," I said.

"That's because you know me too well," Kate said.

"Is that a good thing?" I said.

"I believe so," Kate said.

We arrived at the hangar. It was about one hundred yards wide, three hundred yards long, and a hundred and fifty feet high. The front of the hangar had two huge sliding wooden doors, each one about one hundred feet high and one hundred feet wide. Both doors were closed.

Three FBI forensic technicians kneeled on the ground in front of the sliding doors examining a green canvas knapsack. Arrayed around the knapsack were plastic explosives and detonators. The explosives appeared to be Semtex. A fourth technician was taking plaster casts of footprints that were next to the knapsack. I recognized the shoe treads at the bottom of the footprints as coming from the same type of boots the Kazakhs at the rest stop had worn.

Freddy stared wide-eyed at the explosives.

"Are those bombs?" Freddy said.

"Yes, Mr. Feynman," Burnette said.

"Are you sure it's safe to be here?" Freddy said.

"Yes," Burnette said. "The plastic can't explode unless the detonators are inserted and triggered."

Freddy looked at me.

"Is that true General Wilder?" Freddy said.

I was momentarily taken aback. I think it was the first time Freddy had ever spoken to me with anything close to respect. It appeared to be a classic case of fear doing strange things to men's minds.

"It's true, Freddy," I said. "The explosives you see on the ground can't hurt us."

"Thank you," Freddy said, seemingly relaxing a bit.

"That doesn't mean there aren't other potentially dangerous explosive devices that the techs haven't found yet, though," I said.

Freddy's eyes went wide again.

Burnette said, "Mr. Feynman, I can assure you we have combed the area with superbly trained bomb-sniffing dogs and very sophisticated explosive detection equipment. There are no other bombs or explosives."

Freddy looked at me.

I said, "The dogs look like they know what they're doing and the equipment used to identify any chemical traces left by explosives is pretty reliable and easy to use. Even Agent Burnette probably couldn't screw up a search that employed such fine animals and equipment, Freddy."

Burnette's piggy eyes narrowed.

"Ho, ho, ho. How clever, Mr. Wilder," Burnette said to me. Then to Freddy, he added, "Mr. Feynman, Mr. Wilder is correct about the detection equipment. It's so incredibly easy to use, even *he* might be able operate it."

Martin the valet said, "Excuse me, Agent Burnette, but as General Wilder is a general in the U.S. Army, I believe you would be best advised to follow Mr. Feynman's lead and address him as General Wilder, which is his proper title."

Burnette was taken aback. Wellington glared at Martin.

I said, "Thanks, Martin."

Wellington said, "Agent Burnette, I'm sorry, my nephew at times doesn't know when to keep his mouth shut. I'm sure you won't be saying another word, will you, Martin?"

Martin said nothing.

"Martin, I just asked you a question," Wellington said.

"I'm sorry, sir," Martin said. "But I see no reason to let this buffoon insult a decorated combat hero."

"That is quite enough, young man," Wellington said. "Go wait in the helicopter. I will deal with you later."

Martin shrugged and calmly walked away.

I called after him, "You're a good man, Martin."

Martin gave me two thumbs up and kept walking.

Wellington said, "Please forgive him, Agent Burnette. I'm sure you were young and impetuous once yourself."

Somehow, I found that impossible to believe.

Burnette said, "Of course, sir."

"I assume this hangar was the target of the attack?" Wellington said.

"Yes, as best as we can determine the hangar was the target," Burnette said. "The hangar houses the project that NASAD is working on here. We believe the attackers' goal was sabotage."

"Do you have any idea who the attackers were?" Wellington said.

"Indeed we do, sir," Burnette said. "There is no doubt in my mind they were Islamic terrorists. They were shouting 'Allahu Akbar.'"

I said, "Very compelling. Did they throw Korans as well?"

"We believe the terrorists are part of a sleeper cell," Burnette said, ignoring me. "They appear to be part of the same sleeper cell that attacked Dr. Lennon at Coso Junction yesterday. The bootprints on the ground match the boots we found on the dead men there."

At least Burnette got the boot part right, I thought to myself. But terrorists? No. Not unless there was such a thing as Islamic terrorists who ate pork and tattooed crucifixes on their necks. Of course, there was no reason to say anything to Burnette about that. The longer Burnette remained focused on his terrorist wild goose chase, the less likely there was a chance he would somehow muck up my own investigation.

Carter Bowdoin said, "Agent Burnette, what do you think the terrorists' motive was?"

"We have picked up internet chatter that seems to imply the cell's goal is to destroy NASAD as payback for the fact that NASAD supplies so many of the weapons that are used against their brethren in the war on terror," Burnette said.

"Do you know what particular terror organization the sleeper cell is associated with?" Bowdoin said.

"No, but we will soon," Burnette said. "We always get our man."

I said, "I'm sorry, Burnette. I'm confused. I thought you were with the FBI."

"Your point being?" Burnette said.

"That's the Mounties' motto you just quoted," I said.

Burnette shook his head in disgust. Kate kicked my shin.

Bryce Wellington said, "Tell us about the attack."

Burnette said, "The fires you see were caused by incendiary and smoke grenades. A number of our agents moved to assess the fires, but being highly trained, they quickly realized the fires were probably diversions and looked elsewhere. The agents spotted four suspicious men by the hangar, who, upon seeing our agents, made a dash for the perimeter fence. The agents got shots off, but the men escaped through a hole in the fence which we believe is also the same hole they came in through. The green knapsack and explosives were left behind by the four men."

I said, "Sounds like the four men didn't put up much of a fight."

"We think the attacking force had underestimated the number of men we have here," Burnette said. "I'm sure they were scared off by our overwhelming force."

"That must be it," I said.

Burnette took a deep breath, then spit on the ground.

"Does the illustrious Mr. Wilder have another explanation?" Burnette said.

"If Martin were here, he could back me up on this," I said. "But the correct phraseology is actually the *'eminent* General Wilder.'"

"I don't care what the hell you call yourself," Burnette said.

Wellington said, "Please gentlemen. I know we're all under a lot of stress, but let's keep this civil. Agent Burnette, you said all four terrorists escaped through a hole in the perimeter fence. Didn't your men continue to give chase?"

"We did, sir," Burnette said. "The terrorists had motorcycles hidden in the trees. The terrorists had already ridden off on the motorcycles by the time our agents reached the spot where the motorcycles had been hidden. The agents could not give chase, as they were on foot. No one heard the motorcycles approach, so we believe they were probably dropped off by a truck or some other large vehicle. We found four motorcycles by the side of the road about two miles away, so we assume that the same truck that originally dropped off the terrorists and the motorcycles probably picked up the terrorists and drove them to safety."

"So the terrorists are still at large?" Wellington said.

"Unfortunately, yes," Burnette said. "We are continuing to search for them."

I said, "And since you always get your man..."

Kate elbowed me in my ribs.

Wellington said, "Agent Burnette, I think it's time we took a look inside the hangar, don't you?"

"Yes, sir," Burnette said.

Burnette removed a cell phone from his back pocket, dialed a number, and said something I couldn't hear into the phone. A moment later, the large wooden hangar doors began to slide slowly open. As they did so, an equally large set of doors made of blast-hardened steel, and the front wall of a concrete warehouse of very modern design - both of which had been hidden behind the wooden doors - came into view. The warehouse's walls looked to be least three feet thick. It was hard to imagine the Semtex Burnette's terrorists had brought with them could do much damage to any portion of the newly revealed structure before me.

The wooden doors took a full minute to completely open. Once they had locked into their open position, a small door - one that was at the bottom of the steel door on the left, and that I hadn't noticed before - was opened from the inside by an armed FBI agent. The agent stood in the doorway, his body silhouetted by bright light coming from the inside of the warehouse. Over the agent's shoulder I could see just a tiny fraction of the warehouse's contents, but what I saw filled me with awe.

CHAPTER 70

Carter Bowdoin, Freddy Feynman, Bryce Wellington, Burnette, Kate, and I entered the hangar's small open door and found ourselves standing on a metal catwalk. The construction of the giant hangar must have entailed a massive excavation, as the catwalk was at ground level but the hangar's floor was fifty feet below us. The floor itself was vast. It was bigger than six football fields and the space above it was entirely open and completely free of both support beams and girders all the way up to the top of the building's two hundred foot high ceiling - another marvel of engineering from Milt Feynman's mind I was sure. The air inside the hangar was cold and as odorless as any air I had ever breathed. The only sounds I could hear were muffled human voices coming from the hangar floor below.

Hundreds of overhead spotlights lit every inch of the floor, so that the hangar's warehouse interior was completely without shadows. All that light gave me an eerie feeling, as if I had entered a land where there was no day, no night, and time was standing still. But the eerie feeling was no match for my growing sense of awe, an awe that had started outside the hangar with my first glimpse of the huge object then in front of me, and had continued to increase the closer I got to that object. The object looked as if it had materialized from a place and time in a far distant future and had been created by a civilization much more advanced than our own.

The object was a submarine, but a submarine unlike any I had ever seen before. The design of the sub's sail, overall shape, and diving planes, suggested the sub had been birthed from boats of the Ohio class, but it had evolved so far beyond those ancestors that it bore as much resemblance to an Ohio as a man does to an ape. The submarine was over 700 feet long and the exterior of its hull was raised, ribbed, and curved in such a way as to make the sub seem a living creature. Not a friendly living creature like a fluffy bunny, however, but a bloodthirsty, rapacious predator, like something out of the imagination of H. R. Giger. I almost expected the sub to leap out and attack me, propelling itself with the undulating, serpentine motions of a monster eel.

I had heard rumors that the next generations of submarines would be built with space age composite materials that could cloak the subs in such a way that they would be undetectable by sonar, much in the same way stealth bombers had used those materials to avoid radar detection. I assumed the raises, ridges, and curves represented that rumored cloaking, and so was fairly certain I was looking at just such a sub at that moment. Let loose under the open seas, the sub would be as dangerous a killing machine as man had ever invented.

As much as the submarine's design impressed me and stimulated my imagination, I knew the submarine would never see the world outside the warehouse. It wasn't a working version, but a model that had been built for study and testing. The sub was raised a few feet off the warehouse floor, but firmly rooted to it - wide steel columns sunk deep into the concrete floor had been welded to the sub's bottom hull - and its thick outer shell had been cut away on one side to reveal its inner workings. The cutting away reminded me of a movie set where, while the rooms appear real through the lens of a carefully placed camera, the rooms actually have only three walls instead of four. Contained within the sub's walls were four decks, each deck with its own set of unique compartments. Some of the compartments held crew berths, engines, life support equipment, nuclear reactors, and torpedoes, while others were tasked for command and control, a commissary, and an infirmary. Stairwells and passageways were visible as well. The compartments were color coded in yellow, blue, red, or green to make them easily distinguishable from each other. The periscope was extended.

Two forklifts laden with wooden crates crisscrossed each other as they passed under the nose of the sub. Overhead, a crane suspended from rails that traversed the entire length of the ceiling departed from the far end of the hangar and slowly slid towards us.

A few dozen men and women in white lab coats and red hard hats were performing various tasks throughout the hangar. Some were adjusting machinery and equipment inside the sub. Others sat at desks on raised platforms surrounding the sub, typing on computer keyboards and studying the changing monitors in front of them. I watched them work as Burnette led Bowdoin, Freddy, Wellington, Kate, and me down a steel staircase to the floor below.

A tall, beautiful African American woman carrying a clipboard approached as we reached the bottom of the staircase's steps. Her eyes were a deep, dark brown and her lips were painted a glistening scarlet red. She was long-legged and the portion of her legs that showed beneath the knee-high hem of her lab coat were strong and toned. She wore very tasteful gold earrings and a matching gold bracelet. The way she carried herself made both her drab hardhat and even drabber lab coat seem fashionable.

Wellington stepped forward and shook her hand.

"It's good to see you again, Monique," Wellington said.

"And you, General," Monique said.

"Monique, everyone else you know, but I'd like to introduce you to General Wilder," Wellington said. "General, Ms. Kerbet oversees all testing of our Ohio class drone submarines' systems."

Monique and I shook hands. She turned her attention back to Wellington.

"General Wellington, is it true the Navy is considering pulling back the three drone subs we have operating in the Persian Gulf?" Monique said.

"You just survived a terrorist attack and that's what you're worried about?" Wellington said.

"Is it true or not?" Monique said.

Carter Bowdoin said, "The Navy is concerned about what they see as breaches in NASAD's security, Monique. But the subs are still online. They haven't decided what the appropriate response is yet."

"The subs have multiple fail-safes built into them," Monique said. "It's impossible for an enemy to gain control of any of those subs."

Kate said, "Are you absolutely sure about that, Monique?"

"Absolutely, Dr. Lennon," Monique said.

Multiple fail-safes sounded like a fine idea to me, and was pretty much the way I thought the drone submarines would have been engineered. It wouldn't be a good thing if one of these new class of underwater robo-beasts fell into enemy hands, but I highly doubted that could happen.

Nothing I had seen so far had made me change my mind that the subs were unlikely to be the Chinese insurmountable edge. Again, the Chinese had their own nukes - nukes that could be launched from air, land, and over and under the sea - so what would the Chinese need our nukes for? I decided, however, that as long as I had Monique in front of me, there was no harm in finding out as much as I could about the killing machines, not only to make doubly sure the drone subs couldn't be the insurmountable edge, but also to make good on my promise to Hart to investigate the drone subs. The subs' fail-safes were as good as any place to start.

I said, "I don't doubt what you say, Monique, but no system is completely fail-safe."

"True," Monique said. "But the fail-safe systems we're using are the most sophisticated we have ever built. I assume you have some background in military command and control communications, General Wilder?"

Kate said, "May I answer that, General?"

"Go right ahead, Dr. Lennon," I said.

"Monique, General Wilder worked with my father when he was developing some of the fourth generation encryption systems including crypto ignition keys," Kate said. "The general, in addition to giving his input, field tested the devices."

Monique's eyebrows made a barely perceptible upward movement and her scarlet lips smiled. I assumed that meant that Monique was impressed by what Kate had said. Impressing beautiful women, especially ones that appear not to impress easily, is usually not a bad thing. And it probably wouldn't have been that time either, except I made the mistake of smiling back at Monique, a smile which Kate caught and seemed none too pleased about.

Monique said, "Our encryption systems are on the sixth generation now and use a dual key design, General. Each character within the keys is encrypted by its own algorithm. Unless you have the key for the key, you cannot unlock the system. The enemy is not going to be able to communicate with, let alone control, an Ohio Class drone."

MOM was already on eighth generation encryption, but I didn't want to rain on Monique's parade. The only reason MOM was so far advanced was because we used our own cryptographers and programmers. Sixth generation was the highest encryption available to the rest of the military, Navy included, as the rest of the military used private contractors. NASAD was the best of those contractors. If Milt Feynman had still been alive, NASAD would probably have been on ninth generation encryption by now, but as it was, NASAD was still stuck on a sixth generation product. Sixth generation was good, but not perfect. There were ways to break it.

I said, "You're not saying the nature of the key is your only fail-safe are you?"

"Not good enough for you, General?" Monique said.

"Is it good enough for you?" I said.

She smiled.

"No, of course not," Monique said. "The drones carry a crew of seven as opposed to the normal crew of one hundred and forty. The crew itself is one of our fail-safes. If they suspect the drone control systems have been tampered with, or there is any unauthorized communication coming in from the outside world, any one of the crew members is capable of turning off the communication systems that link the sub to the land-based pilots. The nuclear weapons' firing mechanisms are all controlled by an encryption system which will cause the firing mechanisms to self-destruct if the wrong decoding sequence is entered. The firing mechanisms also have a unique design that matches each firing mechanism to one individual warhead. The firing mechanism is thus irreplaceable, and its disabling also permanently disables the warhead itself. Which of course means the warhead not only can't be launched from the sub, but also couldn't be used if it is somehow removed from the sub."

"The warhead is actually *permanently* disabled?" I said. "I would think that once the warhead is returned to the factory and the encryption sequences are unlocked, then a new firing mechanism could be installed?"

"You're correct," Monique said. "I should have said the nukes are disabled until they are returned to the factory."

"Good," I said. "That makes more sense. I assume the officers on board the sub can't launch the missiles on their own?"

"No," said Monique. "The high ranking naval officers who supervise the drone pilots have the firing codes and decide if, and when, a launch is to be made."

"So Denzel Washington and Gene Hackman wouldn't have had to fight over whether to initiate World War III in 'Crimson Tide'?" I said.

"Exactly," Monique said. "You don't happen to know Denzel, do you?"

"I don't," I said. "But if I ever meet him I'll send him right over to you."

"Thank you," Monique said.

"It does appear to me, however," I said, "that due to the presence of the crew, the subs aren't really true drones?"

Bryce Wellington said, "Even though all the drone sub pilots are ensconced at the naval air station in Jacksonville and under the direct control of the Navy, the Navy isn't quite ready to entirely give up on the idea of sailors aboard their boats, Jack. They will one day, though. Besides, the crew is really only there for an emergency."

Monique said, "I believe it is also valuable to note that the boats can stay undersea a lot longer than a non-drone sub due to the life support systems only having to serve seven sailors instead of one hundred and forty. Which also means there are far fewer lives at risk as well."

Overhead, the crane moving on the ceiling rails stopped at the middle of the hangar. The crane's cable had a hook on the end of it. The crane slowly lowered the hook towards a large control panel sitting on the warehouse floor below.

I said, "I assume the crew has been highly trained and can take over control of the sub in the event of an emergency?"

"Yes," Monique said.

"Who decides when such control would be handed off to the crew - the drone pilots and their commanding officers, or the officers on board the sub itself?" I said.

"Protocol demands it be a discussion between the sub's officers and the land-based pilot team," Monique said.

"Assuming the communication channels are still operative," I said.

"If they aren't, then the commander on board the sub would make that call," Monique said.

"My experience has been that engineers seem to pay a lot more attention to designing protocols to protect command and control of high-tech weaponry than in guarding seemingly simple systems such as voice communications," I said. "I would think that'd go double for a drone sub where the ultimate plan calls for there being no humans on board at all."

"What are you getting at, General?" Monique said.

"It seems to me that an enemy trying to commandeer one of the drones would do so by using the least complicated method they can come up with," I said. "Breaking the encryption systems protecting the drone controls and becoming proficient in operating the highly complex software that runs the drone's systems are exceedingly difficult tasks. I think an enemy would look for an easier way to accomplish their goals."

"I suppose you already have an idea what that easier way is?" Monique said.

"My best guess is that the enemy would just try to defeat the systems protecting the sub's voice communications," I said. "Once that was done, the enemy could trick the crew into believing they were receiving orders from their commanders, when in actuality it was the enemy telling the crew what to do. I understand there are fail-safes built into the nuclear warheads' firing mechanisms, but it seems to me that if an enemy actually took control of the sub, they would have the luxury of time to try to defeat those mechanisms. And, theoretically, given enough time any encryption can be defeated."

Monique seemed to think this over.

"So," Monique said, "you're saying that an enemy could gain control of the drone sub via interference with voice communications between the drone sub personnel and the drone sub's land-based command unit, and once the enemy had control of the sub, they would have the time they needed to then gain control of the nuclear weapons on board?"

"Yes," I said. "It certainly would be a lot easier for an enemy to get one of the highly trained humans on board to do its bidding, rather than the enemy learning how to control the sub itself."

"Wouldn't the same problem apply for a non-drone Ohio, though?" Monique said. "Couldn't an enemy trick that crew as well?"

"They could," I said. "My gut says, however, that an Ohio drone sub with seven crew members is much easier to commandeer than a regular Ohio sub with 140 crew members. One against six is much better odds than one against 139."

"I can see that," Monique said. "Still, an enemy would have to steal the passwords for verbal communication in order to accomplish what you are suggesting."

"Passwords get stolen all the time," I said.

Monique didn't say anything.

"In fact it happens way too often for any of us to ever feel comfortable it won't happen again," I said. "A prime example is what happened to General Bryce Wellington when he was in command of our forces in Afghanistan. General Wellington was duped by an enemy into responding to a false emergency in the Sudan because the enemy was using a stolen password." The false emergency I was alluding to was, obviously, the one that had so badly injured Jeff. I turned to Bryce Wellington and added, "I'm correct in that, aren't I, Bryce?"

Wellington said, "That was a long time ago, Jack. And it didn't involve nuclear weapons."

"But the theory is the same, isn't it?" I said.

Wellington did not respond. Monique seemed about to speak, but stopped herself. She looked hard at me, her earlier smile a distant memory. Kate, who had been silently taking everything in, seemed to perfectly understand my point and appeared to be worried. Freddy stared at me, his face slowly turning red and his breathing coming in and out in what sounded like a loud nasal wheeze. I guessed he didn't like what he was hearing and was perhaps worried I had brought up a scenario that might hurt his business interests if the wrong entity got wind of it - say, for example, the Congressional Defense Appropriations Committee. Carter Bowdoin didn't say anything. His face was unreadable.

Monique took in a deep breath, and let it out.

"You might be overstating your case, General," Monique said. "It's true voice communication systems are a lower priority during the development of drone weapons. But they are far from having been ignored. And voice communications still are protected by sixth level encryption systems."

"Have the voice systems been a personal priority of yours?" I said. "Or have you passed it on to one of your subordinates?"

Monique took in another deep breath, and let it out.

"You clearly have a knack for cutting to the heart of an issue, don't you, General?" Monique said. "I'm ashamed to admit it, but I really haven't paid much attention to the voice systems at all."

Freddy Feynman's wheezes transformed into threatening snorts. He looked like a bull getting ready to charge me.

"General, with all due respect," Freddy said, his voice seething with contempt, "if the enemy had discovered a method by which they could defeat our voice encryption systems, why would they attempt to blow up this hangar? What good does that do them?"

"Think about it for a moment, Freddy," I said.

"I have thought about it and it's ridiculous," Freddy said.

"Think more," I said. "Use some of that old Yale Boola Boola. Carter can probably help you with that."

I smiled at Carter Bowdoin. He frowned. I got the impression Bowdoin may not have been too happy with the point I had been making either.

"I've thought about it as much as I'm going to think about it," Freddy said. "I would thank you to keep your opinions to yourself and not circulate them outside this room."

"Who would I tell them to, Freddy?" I said.

"You know exactly what I'm saying," Freddy said.

"If you're worried about your funding from the U.S. government, I'm not going to tell anyone," I said. "Besides, there may not even be a problem with how secure drone subs' voice communication systems are. And in the unlikely event there is a problem, I have every confidence that Monique and the other teams at NASAD working on this project will find it and fix it."

Monique said, "Our review will begin immediately. But please, General, while I respect and acknowledge Mr. Feynman's questioning why the terrorists would attack our site today, if the problem is indeed within the voice communication systems, I would very much appreciate it if you would apprise us of your own thoughts concerning the terrorists' motivation."

What motivated the terrorists was, of course, an interesting question, especially since I believed the terrorists were not terrorists, but most likely either Kazakh or Afghan mercenaries in the employ of the enemy I was hunting. I also believed the mercenaries' attack on the site was part of the enemy's ongoing diversion, a diversion whose goal was to keep us focused on the drone subs, and away from the true source of the insurmountable edge.

So far that diversion had been made up of a series of actions, and those actions had been consistent with the diversion's own internal logic - that is, whatever actions the enemy perpetrating the diversion had planned and carried out, those actions had made people believe that a hostile entity truly was attacking the NASAD drone sub division in order to hobble, if not outright destroy, the division. I certainly wasn't going to tell my then current audience that I thought the attacks on the site that day were a diversion.

Having been put on the spot by Monique, however, I felt I'd look foolish if I didn't at least say something. Following my view of the diversion's internal logic, I came up with an answer for Monique that seemed to me to be motivation aplenty for terrorists to attack the site, even though, again, I was sure no such terrorists existed.

"What do you think the purpose could be, Monique?" I said.

"I'm sorry, but if we take as a given that the best, in fact, only, route for an enemy to gain control of the subs is the one you outlined, then I can't come up with a motivation for the terrorists either," Monique said.

"Well, I could be wrong," I said. "But I think it's possible the terrorists might just want everything to stay the same."

Monique considered this.

"As in they might be happy with their ability to exploit our systems now, but if we make any improvements, not so happy?" Monique said.

"Correct," I said. "And if they blow up your plant here, they probably believe those improvements won't be happening anytime soon."

"Perhaps you would like a job with us, General?" Monique said.

"Thank you, Monique," I said. "But I'm not really cut out for this kind of work. If I'm not killing someone, I tend to feel empty inside."

Monique laughed.

"Besides, I'm quite confident you can handle everything without my help," I said. "Wouldn't you agree, General Wellington?"

Wellington, who seemed to have been pouting ever since I brought up the Sudan, somehow managed to keep his response surprisingly cordial.

"Yes, I agree, Jack," Wellington said. "And now is probably a good time to leave and let Monique and her team get back to work."

"It's been a pleasure," I said to Monique.

"The pleasure was all mine," Monique said.

Burnette gestured for everyone to follow him as he turned and headed back towards the stairway that led up to the catwalk. Carter

Bowdoin, Freddy, and Bryce Wellington pulled in right behind him. I grabbed Kate's hand, maneuvered us in front of Bowdoin, Freddy, and Wellington, and made a beeline for Burnette.

"What are you doing?" Kate said to me.

"Shh," I said. "I want to ask the big cheese a few questions."

We got up close to Burnette and I tapped him on the shoulder. Burnette kept walking, but swiveled his head towards me. He grimaced when he realized it was me.

"What do *you* want?" Burnette said.

"I watched an attack on NASAD's computer system this morning," I said. "It was done by Chinese hackers going after the drone sub's schematics."

"I know all about the attack," Burnette said huffily.

"Good," I said. "I'm curious what you think the relationship is between the terrorist attacks here at the plant and the Chinese attack on the computer systems."

We reached the foot of the stairs and started climbing up to the catwalk.

"You really are a moron, aren't you Wilder?" Burnette said. "The answer is so obvious a two-year-old could come up with it."

"Humor me," I said.

"It wasn't the Chinese who attacked the NASAD computer systems," Burnette said.

"No?" I said.

"It was terrorists, same as here," Burnette said. "Same terrorists at Coso Junction. Same terrorists that stoned the kids in Lancaster and killed their mother and grandparents. Same terrorists that murdered the twelve NASAD engineers."

"NASAD's head of cybersecurity said it was the Chinese who did the hacking," I said.

"I know Raj Divedi," Burnette said. "He's almost as stupid as you are."

Kate seemed about to say something. I waved her off.

"Aha," I said.

"What Raj saw was terrorists pretending to be Chinese," Burnette said.

"And you know this how?" I said.

"I got cyber terrorism experts on my team, Wilder," Burnette said.

"You mean back at the FBI home office in D.C.?" I said.

"The D.C. guys are worthless," Burnette said. "I'm talking about my personal experts. They travel with me. That's probably too hard for you to grasp though, isn't it?"

"No," I said. "Actually, everything makes complete sense now."

"What's that supposed to mean?" Burnette said.

It means you're one of the biggest idiots I have ever met, I said to myself.

"It means I understand how you know so much," I said.

"You got that right," Burnette said.

Burnette, Kate, and I continued to climb the stairs. Freddy, Carter Bowdoin, and Bryce Wellington followed close behind us. Burnette and Kate reached the catwalk at the top of the stairway just ahead of me. I was just taking my first step onto the catwalk, when the hairs on the back of my neck went up. The hairs on the back of my neck are an early warning system and they generally don't go up unless there's some kind of threat in my vicinity. I stopped in my tracks. Kate, apparently not noticing I had stopped, kept walking towards the hangar's exit with Burnette.

I surveyed the area in front of me. I found nothing of concern. I craned my head around. Bowdoin, Freddy, and Wellington were finishing their own climb up the steps. All three of them ignored me as they passed right by me on the way to the exit.

I turned away from them and stared out at the vast warehouse space. Monique and the NASAD technicians were going about their business on the floor below. The crane on the ceiling rails that was carrying the control panel stopped above the sub and started lowering the control panel into one of the sub's rooms. None of that activity seemed to pose any obvious threat, but I began to feel something was off about the scene in front of me. And, though I couldn't quite put my finger on exactly what it was that was off, I knew it was not just slightly off, but deeply off.

I watched the control panel's descent and tried to figure out what was off about the scene. A moment passed, and I slowly realized what it was. What was off was that what I had witnessed within the hangar, and perhaps even everything I had seen since the helicopter had set me down on NASAD's site, was not real. Though I might never be able to prove it to anyone other than myself, I was convinced that everything

I had seen had been arranged for me. It was all part of a show. I didn't know what the purpose of the show was, or if it had been intended for an audience of more than just me, but it was a show.

Just as soon as I came to that conclusion, I heard Kate's voice. It seemed to be coming from a very distant place.

"Jack," Kate said. "Are you coming?"

I turned around to where I thought Kate's voice had come from, but it felt like it took a very, very long time to do so, as if my body was moving through thick molasses. Kate, Carter Bowdoin, Freddy, Bryce Wellington, and Burnette were standing next to the exit door and they were all staring at me.

"Just a minute," I said. "There's one last thing I want to see."

My voice sounded distorted to me, like my words had been recorded and were being played back in slow motion. The eyes, mouths, and jaws of Bowdoin, Freddy, Wellington, Burnette, and Kate all appeared to be moving in slow motion as well. From the expressions that gradually formed on their faces, I took it that they were all annoyed with me.

"I'll be there in a moment," I said, my words still sounding drawn out and slurred to me. "Don't worry."

All five of them appeared to be reacting in their own way to what I had just said, but those reactions seemed to take an infinite amount of time, as if every one of us was standing at the moment the Big Bang occurred, and time was just about to start for the entire universe. The whole situation spooked me.

I slowly turned back to look at the floor of the warehouse and instantly the intensity of the feeling that I was watching a show became overwhelming. I tried to shake the feeling by telling myself I was being paranoid, but it wouldn't go away.

And then, a new, even more distressing feeling came over me.

I began to feel that something bad was going to happen, and that that bad something was going to happen soon. I had no idea what the bad something was, but, somehow, deep down inside of me, I knew the bad something had something to do with my feeling that everything that had happened at the site so far had been a show.

Suddenly, I felt a hand grabbing my right elbow. I looked down and saw that it was Kate's hand. I stared at her hand and an eternity seemed to pass. Then, for reasons I have never been able to explain, my strange reverie instantly ceased and I snapped back to reality. I felt Kate's lips close against my ear.

"You're having another spell, aren't you?" Kate whispered.

My mind was still a little foggy from what I had just experienced, but it wasn't so foggy that I didn't remember that Kate had warned me that if I had another 'spell' she was going to drag me to a doctor to get me checked out. I didn't want that. I put on my best 'I'm fine' face, turned to her, and smiled. Kate's eyes narrowed. She didn't appear to be buying my face at all.

"I'm not having a spell," I said. "Whatever made you think that?"

I gently freed myself from her grip and turned to look at Bowdoin, Freddy, Wellington, and Burnette.

"Sorry, gentlemen," I said. Then, gesturing at the drone sub below, I continued, "I had such a good time here, and am so absolutely amazed by NASAD's stunning technological marvel, that I couldn't bear to leave without taking one last look. I thank you for your patience. Shall we go?"

Burnette said, "As long as you're sure you're ready, Wilder. I can't speak for everyone else, but I'd be happy to stay here all day and stare at the back of your goddamned head."

Bryce Wellington said, "Agent Burnette, please remember what I said about remaining civil."

Burnette seemed taken aback by the reprimand.

"Yes, sir," Burnette said sheepishly.

I said, "Bryce, I think what you need to understand is that that is civil for Agent Burnette."

Burnette appeared to instantly boil over.

"Go to hell, Wilder!" Burnette said.

Wellington said, "Agent Burnette!"

"Sorry, sir," Burnette said.

Burnette turned on his heel, and walked briskly out the warehouse's exit door. Carter Bowdoin, Freddy, and Bryce Wellington followed him. I took Kate's hand, protectively moved her very close to me, and together we headed for the door as well. As we walked, I could feel Kate's eyes boring into the side of my head, but all I was thinking about was that something bad was about to happen, and I had better figure out what it was before it did.

CHAPTER 71

Outside the drone sub hangar, the day had grown brighter and hotter as the sun had traversed the sky. The fires had all been extinguished and reduced to nothing more than smoldering black patches. The smell of smoke still lingered, but the smoke itself had been completely dissipated by the gentle breeze that moved through the site. The fire trucks were parked between the barracks and the grassy field, and the firemen were stowing their hoses. The bomb-sniffing dogs had completed their duties and were lounging in the shade of the barracks. Bowls of water were at the dogs' sides. Employees had left the protection of the barracks and were milling about in small groups, most likely sharing whatever gossip could be gleaned about the attacks.

Freddy, Carter Bowdoin, Bryce Wellington, Burnette, Kate, and I had been met at the drone sub hangar door by our coterie of a half dozen FBI agents. The six agents - Conklin and Finlayson still among them - surrounded us, and together we walked back towards the grassy field and NASAD's waiting Bell helicopter. I was able to just make out Donnie in the helicopter pilot's seat and Martin the valet sitting on the floor of the open rear passenger compartment, his legs dangling outside the sill of the chopper's door. I had decided that the only way I was truly going to feel safe was to get Kate and me away from the site as quickly as possible, and the best way to do that was to board the chopper and have Donnie get us airborne. We were then about four hundred yards from the chopper, a distance I thought we could cover in about five minutes, which seemed like an eternity to me.

Everyone else in our little group seemed relaxed as we walked toward the helicopter, but my mind was in a spin, and I continually scanned the area for threats. I became concerned that maybe I'd made a mistake, that perhaps Kate and I would have been safer if we'd stayed inside the hangar until I could sort out what bad thing might be about to happen. But then I decided that, since I had no idea what that bad thing was, there was no reason to believe we would be safer in the hangar than outside of it.

I kept going back to my belief that everything that had happened to

Kate and me so far at the site had been a show. But what was the purpose of the show? Was the show at the site just another component of the diversion that also included the murders of the NASAD drone engineers over the last two years and the hacking attempt earlier that day on the drone sub program? The ongoing diversion could be part of the reason for the show, but it seemed like there was more to it. Otherwise, why was I continuing to have such intense feelings of foreboding? Those bad feelings made me focus even harder on trying to identify exactly what types of potential threats I might have to face, and from what locations in the site those threats might come.

I wasn't too worried about a bomb. It looked like the bomb-sniffing dogs were well trained, and their work, coupled with the efforts of the bomb detection technicians, made it unlikely anything had been missed.

There could have been a close quarters assassin mixed in among the FBI agents or NASAD's own security, but there was no one giving even the slightest vibe that suggested any such hostile intent.

I didn't think a helicopter was about to swoop down with guns ablaze. A chopper attack could have occurred either back at NASAD headquarters or during our flight to the site, so there was no reason to believe it would take place just then.

I came to the conclusion that the most likely attack would be a sniper attack. Either the FBI's sweep of the area had missed some Kazakhs who had stayed behind, or the Kazakhs might once again come out of the trees in the forest surrounding the site's fence. With that in mind, I scanned for snipers everywhere they were most likely to be. I started with the barracks - which were then about fifty yards away and to our left - focusing first on the barracks' roofs and windows, then moving to the drone sub hangars' roofs and the tree line beyond the site's perimeter fence.

All was clear.

I continued to scan the area as Freddy, Carter Bowdoin, Bryce Wellington, Burnette, Kate, I, and our coterie of agents crossed the halfway point in our journey between the drone sub hangar and the helicopter. It was at that point that I saw Carter Bowdoin give a hurried, searching look towards the barracks. I assumed he was probably thinking like I was, and followed his gaze. I saw nothing that appeared out of the ordinary, just empty windows in the barracks' outer walls.

Bryce Wellington, who up until then had been quietly walking along with the rest of us, apparently decided it was time to strike up a conversation.

"Jack, I really appreciate your input on the potential flaws you noticed in the drone subs," Bryce Wellington said.

"Thank you, Bryce," I said.

Freddy said, "Yeah, well I didn't appreciate it at all."

"This might come as a surprise to you, Freddy," I said, "but you already made that pretty clear."

"Here's something else you should get clear on," Freddy said. "I can't stop my sister if she wants you along for whatever, but just stay out of our business."

Kate's face instantly reddened.

"Jesus, Freddy," Kate said. "What's wrong with you?"

"Nothing wrong with me," Freddy said. "You're the one who brought an outsider into this."

"Because we needed help," Kate said.

"We were doing just fine without him," Freddy said.

"Twelve dead employees is not fine," Kate said. "Someone murdering my father and husband is not fine."

Freddy stopped in his tracks, which caused our entire entourage to stop as well. Burnette appeared not to have heard what Kate just said. I was pretty sure Carter Bowdoin and Bryce Wellington had heard her, however, as the two men exchanged a brief look. The look was so brief though, that I felt it was impossible to read anything into it.

"What are you talking about?" Freddy said. "Who said they were murdered? Have you lost your mind?"

I squeezed Kate's hand hard. Kate looked up at me. I kept my face blank. I hoped she would get the message. I didn't want any of those assembled asking Kate or me anything about the Alaskan plane crash that had killed Feynman and Lennon, especially how we knew it wasn't an accident. Hart, MOM, and I were breaking all sorts of federal laws by being involved with an operation on U.S. soil and I didn't want Burnette having any excuse to raise holy hell and mess up my investigation. Also, though I didn't think it was likely, it was possible one or more of the people in the group surrounding us might have somehow been involved in the murders. The last thing I'd want to do was tip off any of those people that Kate and I were on to the fact the crash had been a meticulously planned, sophisticated murder. All that would do is get them scrambling to cover tracks they had to have believed they'd completely buried long ago. But my overwhelming goal in hushing Kate was to get us going again so we could get to the chopper as quickly as possible.

Kate said, "Forget it, Freddy. You wouldn't understand anyway."

"Don't go around saying crazy things," Freddy said. "Because people are going to think you're crazy if you do."

Kate said nothing.

I said, "Does anyone mind if we keep moving? This little excursion took me away from my lunch and I'm really hungry."

Freddy said, "Are you serious? Don't you understand we came here because of a terrorist attack?"

"And they're gone and I wanna eat, so let's go," I said.

"You're just as nuts as she is," Freddy said.

"Probably," I said.

I put my arm around Kate's shoulders and resumed walking towards the helicopter. The agents surrounding us moved with Kate and me, which meant everyone else had no choice but to start moving as well. We still had another two hundred yards to go. Maybe two or three minutes.

I scanned the area again. Still nothing. No backpacks, boxes, packages, or anything else that might conceal a bomb. No one in the security detail acting funny. No approaching helicopters. No snipers. But I couldn't shake my feeling of impending disaster either. Since that feeling was so interconnected with my belief that everything at the site was part of a show, I thought about the show again.

I replayed in my mind what had happened since we had arrived at the NASAD drone sub site. I gained no further insight. I went back further. To just before Kate and I had boarded the helicopter.

Back then, Kate had wanted to go to the site. Freddy, Bowdoin, and Wellington had also all wanted to go to the site, and indeed, had boarded the helicopter before Kate and I had. I didn't know if Donnie and Martin the valet had wanted to go to the site, but it really didn't matter since they had no choice - it was their job to go. In fact, as I had remembered it, everyone but me was essentially fine with going to the site. I hadn't wanted to go because I thought the site might be too dangerous for Kate. But I had capitulated. Because Kate had insisted on going.

Because Kate had *insisted*...

Insisted...

Insisted...

Insisted...

I realized then how stupid I had been.

The show was for Kate, not me.

Kate had been baited into coming to the site.

The Kazakhs had come to the site for Kate, just like they had come to the Coso Junction rest stop for her.

I had to get Kate off the site as fast as I could.

I pulled Kate even closer and picked up my pace, dragging her along with me. Kate looked up at me. I shook my head slightly and whispered, "No time for questions. We have to get out of here." Kate seemed to sense how deep my concern was. She said nothing, picked up her pace to match mine so that I was no longer dragging her. At that moment Kate and I had been just behind Burnette, but I maneuvered the two of us around him so that we were right up on the heels of the two FBI agents who were in the front part of the circle of agents that was escorting us.

"Dr. Lennon is not feeling well," I said to the two agents. "I'd like to get her back to the NASAD helicopter as soon as possible."

Both agents nodded and matched their walking speed to Kate's and mine. Kate, I, and the two agents quickly distanced ourselves from Bowdoin, Freddy, Wellington, Burnette, and the other four agents surrounding them. Kate, I, and our two agents still had about one hundred yards to go to get to the NASAD helicopter, when the hairs on the back of my neck went up once again.

I turned my head around to look behind me. I saw that Carter Bowdoin was looking intently in the direction of the middle barracks. I followed Carter's gaze. I tried to determine exactly what Carter was focusing in on, but could not.

I checked to see if there was something that might be a threat on the barracks' roof. There was nothing. The windows appeared clear as well. So did the ground in front of the windows.

But then...

I saw a glint.

And the glint was moving.

On the top floor of the middle barracks.

The third room from the left end of the building.

The glint was against the room's far wall, the wall that most likely separated the room from the barracks' interior corridor.

From the angle of the light coming off the glint, the glint had to be located just inside, and to the right, of the window.

I focused on the right edge of the window frame.

The barrel of a rifle equipped with a sniper scope slowly came around the frame and rotated to point in our direction.

"Gun!" I shouted.

The two FBI agents in our coterie came to an abrupt halt as I spun Kate around and put my body between Kate and the barracks. I encircled Kate's torso with my arms so that her back was against my chest and my back was to the barracks, then slammed both of us sideways and to the ground, cushioning our fall with my arms, and covering Kate's entire body with my own.

A bullet hit right behind where Kate had been standing, making a 'pfft' sound and kicking up clods of dirt as it tore into the earth.

"Middle barracks, top floor, third room on the left!" I yelled to the agents.

Kate's and my dive to the ground had changed the sight lines between us and the sniper in the window. The two FBI agents who had separated along with Kate and me from Burnette's group were then blocking those sight lines and both of them were reaching for the MP5 submachine guns on their shoulders.

But the two agents never got their weapons unslung.

Their heads vaporized in a cloud of pink mist that was accompanied by the sound of a soft 'thwap'. The agents' bodies fell with a thud to the ground.

More shots hit the earth around Kate and me, but I saw none hitting anywhere near anyone else in our group. It was clear Kate was the only target.

Still covering Kate's body with my own, I craned my head around towards the barracks.

Three more sniper rifles appeared in the windows of the three barracks rooms that were adjacent to the first room, so that there were then a total of four rifles aimed at Kate and me. Behind each gun was a Kazakh, who, in size, build, bowl haircut, and by being clothed in a green windbreaker, closely resembled the commandos who had tried to kidnap Kate at the rest stop.

The four FBI agents - two of whom were Conklin and Finlayson - that had stayed with Freddy, Carter Bowdoin, Bryce Wellington, and Burnette when Kate and I had split off, quickly formed a shield between the four men and the barracks. Having also un-shouldered their MP5's, the four agents shot at the four Kazakhs in the windows. The Kazakhs, forced to defend themselves, turned their attention away from Kate and me, and shot at the agents. Dozens of rounds were fired from the agents' automatic weapons in the space of a few seconds. The air rapidly filled with both an ear-piercing din and the acrid smell of gun smoke.

I had expected Conklin and Finlayson and the other two FBI agents to quickly move Freddy and the others to safety, but that's not what happened. With Conklin in the lead, the four agents, firing their weapons all the time, started to move their group toward Kate and me in what looked like an attempt to get us within their shield as well.

Burnette screamed, "What are you doing?!"

"Dr. Lennon and the general, sir," Conklin said. "We've got to help them. They're sitting ducks."

"We'll never get to them in time!" Burnette said. He pointed to a fire truck that was thirty yards away from them. "We need to take cover behind that fire truck!"

"With all due respect, sir, we just can't leave the doctor and the general out in the open," Conklin said. "They'll be slaughtered."

"Do as I say Agent Conklin," Burnette said. "Or your career is toast."

Conklin ignored Burnette and kept moving the other agents and the entire shielded group towards Kate and me.

"Goddamnit, Conklin!" Burnette said.

But Conklin never got a chance to respond. His head exploded. And then Finlayson's head did the same thing. Both men gone in a flying fountain of bone, brain, and blood.

"Get us out of here!" Burnette said to the two FBI agents who remained alive in his guard.

The two FBI agents looked at Kate and me, then Burnette, then back to Kate and me. I hadn't gotten the impression the two agents were as big of assholes as Burnette, so I assumed those looks meant they were at least giving Kate and me the courtesy of trying to decide whether or not to leave us for dead. Their courtesy was nice, but in the end they must have concluded that Kate's and my situation was so hopeless that it would be best to cut their losses - they quickly changed course and steered Bowdoin, Freddy, Wellington, and Burnette towards the cover of the fire truck. It wasn't a decision I would have made, but I wasn't what you could call a fully objective observer at that moment either.

My eye was attracted to movement in the distance off of my left side. Other FBI agents who had been at a far corner of the site were running towards us. Reinforcements were always a good thing but these reinforcements were still a long, long way away. Unless the two agents in Freddy and Burnette's group were able to keep the Kazakh gunmen fully occupied, and prevent the Kazakhs from turning their attention to Kate and me, everything was going to be over for Kate and me well before the FBI reinforcements got into position to help us. Since it was then four Kazakhs against two FBI agents, I didn't like Kate's and my odds.

I needed a gun.

Ten feet away from us and to our right lay the lifeless body of the FBI agent who had been closest to Kate and me when he was killed. The dead agent's MP5 was still slung over his shoulder.

"We're going to have to slide about ten feet to our right," I said to Kate. "Can you handle it?"

I could feel Kate's body trembling beneath mine, but I could also feel her try to steady herself.

"I think so," Kate said.

With Kate still face down on the ground and me on top of her, we coordinated our movements, our fingers and toes seeking purchase in the grass beneath us, and started clawing our way towards the dead agent.

"The snipers are being kept at bay by two of the FBI agents that are escorting Freddy and his group," I said. "Which means the bad guys have the good guys outnumbered four to two. Which isn't good. We have maybe about twenty more seconds before the gunmen are able to turn their attention back to us."

"Okay," Kate said.

"It'll be hard for the gunmen to kill you through my body," I said. "Therefore, if they kill me, your best option will be to remain under me. Hopefully the reinforcements will get here in time to be able to get you to safety."

"Don't say things like that," Kate said.

"Like what?" I said.

"About anybody killing you," Kate said. "It's an awful thought."

"But it could happen," I said.

"Don't let it," Kate said.

"I'll do my best," I said. "But if they do, and it doesn't look like the reinforcements will be able to help you, you might have to go to option two."

"Which is?"

"You'll have to make a run for it," I said

"Where to?" Kate said.

"The fire truck," I said. "Same place your brother and the others are headed to. It's good cover."

"I understand," Kate said.

I continued to keep Kate's body completely covered with mine and the two of us kept crawling. We made it to within three feet of the dead agent, which was close enough for me to reach out my arm and grab his MP5.

"I can get the gun now," I said to Kate. "Hold still."

Kate stopped moving her arms and legs but her body continued to tremble.

I snatched the shoulder strap of the dead agent's MP5 submachine gun and wrestled it off his arm. I drew the weapon in close to me and grabbed it with two hands. Just as I did that, I saw the heads of the two remaining agents guarding Freddy and the others explode in a flash of pink vapor. The agents' headless bodies then went limp and crumpled to the ground.

The Kazakh gunmen shifted their focus to Kate and me.

Bullets strafed in front and on either side of us, spitting up turf as they rammed into the earth.

One bullet flew so closely over my head I could hear its 'whoosh' as it went by.

There was no way the Kazakhs would keep missing.

"Cover your ears and close your eyes," I said to Kate.

Kate did as she was told.

Keeping Kate's body beneath me, I raised up on my elbows. My goal was to kill all the Kazakhs as quickly as possible, as that was the only hope for Kate's and my survival. The best way to quickly kill them was to shoot the MP5 while rapidly and continuously sweeping it across all four gunmen, starting first with one on one end, and finishing with the fourth and last one on the other end. I quickly scanned all four Kazakh gunmen and their locations within the barracks' windows, then imaged the gunmen in my mind's eye. Holding all four images steady, I laid the MP5's sights on the Kazakh farthest to my right. I had chosen the Kazakh on the right as my first target because I'm right handed and it's easier for me to sweep from right to left.

I was just about to squeeze off my first round when one of the Kazakhs' bullets grazed my right arm and knocked me off target.

Another bullet whizzed over my head.

I heard the bullet hit metal and a millisecond later there was the sound of a huge explosion. I assumed the explosion had come from the NASAD helicopter. For a split second the faces of Donnie and Martin came to me and I worried about whether they'd be able to make it out of the chopper before the flames overtook them. If I could have gone to them I would have, but there was no way I could do that until I cleared the Kazakhs and got Kate to safety.

More bullets hit in front of and behind Kate and me, missing us by the barest of inches. Kate's hands were clenched to her ears. It felt to me like she was holding her breath as well.

I pushed aside the pain in my bleeding right arm, resighted on the rightmost Kazakh's head, and squeezed the MP5's trigger. I didn't take the time to see if my bullets had had any effect, just swept the submachine gun to the left, firing off a round every time I saw another Kazakh's head. Three more heads. Three more rounds.

The entire sequence took me under a second.

After I fired the last shot I swept the submachine gun's sights back rightward and stopped where the rightmost Kazakh had been. He looked just like the FBI agents guarding us had looked after their skulls had been pierced by one of the Kazakhs' bullets - no head.

I swept and sighted back to the left, stopping for a millisecond at each window that had contained a Kazakh, just long enough to confirm their occupants were headless as well.

They were.

The top frame of the window where the leftmost Kazakh had stood was being splattered by a fountain of arterial blood shooting out of the black void where the Kazakh's neck had been. The Kazakh's body tottered for a moment, then, still gushing blood, fell out of the window and to the ground. Almost on cue, the bodies of the other three Kazakhs crumpled and fell out of their own windows to the ground as well.

The combat zone, which had been filled with the nightmarish roar of automatic weapon fire, had suddenly gone almost completely silent. The only sounds I could hear were those of my own beating heart and the hiss of the burning gasoline flames behind me.

I sighted down the MP5 and swept all three barracks, window to window, and floor to floor, to be sure they were clear, then rolled my head around to look at the NASAD helicopter. It was a blazing inferno. Donnie was slumped in the pilot's seat but Martin the valet was nowhere to be seen. The helicopter's main tanks hadn't yet exploded but they could at any second. I jumped to my feet and grabbed Kate's hand and pulled her off the ground.

"Donnie's still in the helicopter," I said. "Martin might be too. I've got to get you to safety and then go help them."

"Forget safety," Kate said. "I'll go with you to Donnie and Martin."

"The hell you will," I said. "If the chopper explodes your kids will be orphans."

"Not your decision," Kate said.

"Yeah, it is," I said.

I slung the MP5 over my right shoulder, then grabbed Kate around her waist, threw her over my left shoulder so that her head was behind me, and ran towards the fire truck behind which Freddy, Bowdoin, Wellington, and Burnette had taken refuge. The fire truck was about fifty yards away. The helicopter was also fifty yards away but in the opposite direction from the fire truck.

"Goddamnit, let me down!" Kate said.

"As soon as you're safe," I said.

"No," Kate said. "Now. Go save Donnie and Martin."

"You first, then them," I said.

Kate pounded on my back.

"Stop that, please," I said, still running.

"Let me down then," Kate said.

"Nope," I said.

Kate thrashed her legs and got her feet up in my face.

"I can't see where I'm going," I said.

"That's the idea," Kate said.

Afraid I was going to trip, I came to a stop.

"If I put you down, will you do exactly as I say?" I said.

"I will," Kate said.

"Promise?" I said.

"Yes," Kate said. "Just do it."

"You ever slid into home plate head first?" I said.

"Yes," Kate said.

"Really?" I said. "You were a player?"

"Softball," Kate said.

I spun Kate off my shoulder and she landed her on her feet.

"The fire truck Freddy and the others are hiding behind is home plate," I said. "Go!"

Kate sprinted toward the fire truck which was still thirty yards away. When Kate was within ten feet of the truck, I shouted, "Slide now!"

Kate dove forward, her hands outstretched in front of her head and her body knifed through the air. Her chest landed hard on the ground and her momentum carried her behind the cab of the fire truck. A great slide. Not as great as Lou Brock, Rickey Henderson, or Billy Hamilton, but still great.

I turned around and ran for the NASAD helicopter which was then about seventy yards away from me. The flames were moving from the rear of the helicopter and bearing down on the passenger compartment. The closer I got to the chopper, the more and more unbearable the heat from the flames became. I felt like I'd walked into a blast furnace.

Donnie was in the pilot's seat, unconscious. Martin the valet was in the rear passenger compartment, lying against the back of the pilot compartment partition, also unconscious. I'd last seen Martin sitting on the edge of the open doorway, so he must have been blown inward by the blast. I jumped inside the passenger compartment, grabbed Martin under both shoulders, hauled him out of the compartment, dragged him ten yards away, and laid him on the ground. I didn't know if it would be far enough away to keep him safe if the chopper exploded, but I couldn't risk leaving Donnie in the helicopter another moment.

I sprinted back to the helicopter. I tried to open the pilot's door. It was stuck. I grabbed the handle with both hands, put both feet up on the side of the door and yanked with all my strength. It didn't budge. I ran around to the other side of the chopper and tried to open the copilot's door. It was stuck too. I yanked on it just like I had yanked on the pilot's door. Nothing happened.

There was only one thing left to do.

I ran to the front of the chopper, unslung the MP5 submachine gun from my shoulder, pointed it at the chopper's front window, angled it well away from Donnie Kurtsinger, and fired a long burst. The window shattered into a million plastic shards that flew in all directions. I jumped into the pilot's compartment, put my arms under Donnie's arms, and straining against his rather considerable weight, hauled him out of his seat, and dropped him to the ground through the front window as gently as I could - which, in truth wasn't very gently at all.

I leapt out after Donnie, picked him up by the back of his shirt collar and ran, dragging him as fast as I could away from the helicopter. I hadn't gotten far when a blast wave knocked me into the air. As I was flying through the air, I heard the sound of the explosion that had created the blast wave - the blast always comes before the sound since blast waves are faster than the speed of sound - and I thought to myself, 'I guess the main tank ignited'.

Then everything went black.

CHAPTER 72

The blackness remained. Grace was kissing me. Her lips were warm and soft and wet. I tried to kiss her back but was unable to. I liked Grace's kisses, but they were a little strange. Instead of just kissing me, Grace was also blowing into my mouth very hard, so hard I could feel my chest expanding. I also found it kind of odd that Grace wasn't just kissing me, but was pushing on my chest as well. She didn't do both at the same time, though. She would kiss me twice, then stop and push down on my chest. The chest pushing wasn't very fun. It felt like Grace was trying to crack my ribs. And Grace would push down on my chest about thirty times before she would kiss me again. I only tolerated the chest pushing since I knew she would kiss me again. After about the tenth set of thirty chest compressions, I tried to reach up to grab Grace, planning to hold on to her forever. But my arms wouldn't move.

"You give up too easily," a voice said.

I looked in the direction of the voice and found that that damn coyote from the Agua Dulce freeway exit had returned. He was staring at me.

"Give up?" I said. "Who said I've given up?"

"What else would you call this?" the coyote said.

"Let me not to the marriage of true minds admit impediments," I said.

"Love is not love which alters when it alteration finds," the coyote said.

"So you understand," I said.

"I understand your wife Grace is dead," the coyote said.

"Four years now," I said. "But it's a minor impediment."

"They're not going to keep doing this forever," the coyote said.

"You don't know that," I said.

"The hell I don't," the coyote said.

He stepped back a few feet from me.

"All clear!" the coyote shouted.

"All cle...?" I said.

But I never got the last word out.

Because my body suddenly stiffened. I felt like someone had plugged both my hands into an electrical outlet and a million volts was shooting through me. Then, just as quickly as it had started, the voltage vanished.

"What the hell was that?" I said.

"Flatline," the coyote said.

"Flatline?" I said.

"All clear!" the coyote shouted again.

That time the shock was worse. It was like a giant thunderbolt was coursing through my body. I not only stiffened, but twitched until the current stopped again. Which thankfully, it did.

"Flatline," the coyote said. "You've got to help them."

"I'm not helping them," I said.

"You don't, you're dead," the coyote said.

"Parting is such sweet sorrow," I said.

"Bad time for an awful non sequitur," the coyote said.

"It's not a non sequitur," I said. "Not if I die by too much cherishing."

"If you die right now you'll never satisfy your curiosity about Carter Bowdoin," the coyote said.

"I have no idea what you're talking about," I said.

"Yes you do," the coyote said.

"If you're referring to the fact that Bowdoin was looking at a window that just happened to have a sniper in it, I couldn't care less," I said.

"I told you you knew what I was talking about," the coyote said.

"There's lots of things that could explain why Bowdoin was looking where he was," I said.

"Name more than one," the coyote said.

"I'm not playing this game," I said. "You're keeping me from my wife Grace. Just like those assholes out there making like Nikola Tesla."

"Not your time," the coyote said. "This also isn't just about you, you know. If something happens to you, Kate and Dr. Nemo are as good as dead. And I haven't even mentioned all those servicemen and women who will die in the upcoming war with China. All clear!"

"Stop saying tha...," I said.

Bam. A billion volts that time. My back arched in an excruciating reverse C and my body flew off the ground and smashed back down. The current turned off again.

"Hold on," another voice said. "We might be getting something."

The coyote turned and started trotting away.

"Hey, where you going?" I said.

"My job is done," the coyote said.

"But I've got questions," I said.

"Good for you," the coyote said.

"What about the keyholes in numbered doors?" I said.

"You'll figure it out," the coyote said.

"What about Green Day?" I said.

"Not my department," the coyote said. "Ask Dr. Nemo."

The coyote disappeared.

"Normal sinus," the other voice said.

The blackness lightened and I drew in a deep, long, violent breath. It seemed the kind of breath a drowning man would take after having finally breached the water's surface at the end of one, last, desperate, upward swim.

I had not realized my eyes were closed, but they must have been.

Because simultaneously with that breath, my eyes snapped open.

The sun was shining, a breeze was blowing, and I was flat on my back in the middle of the NASAD site's grassy field.

There were a lot of people surrounding me and staring down at me. The people made me feel like I was the Wizard of Oz's Dorothy waking up in Kansas after her long, strange dream.

Burnette was there. Freddy, Carter Bowdoin, and Bryce Wellington too. There were two paramedics as well.

But the person closest to me was Kate.

She was kneeling beside my chest and she had a cardiac defibrillator paddle in each hand. Kate appeared to breathe a deep sigh of relief. Behind her one of the paramedics was looking at my EKG on the screen of the defibrillator machine to which the paddles were attached. There were wires stuck on my chest that were connected to the machine. Someone had placed a tight bandage on my right arm where the bullet had grazed me. There was blood on the bandage, but not much.

"Stable rhythm, Dr. Lennon," the paramedic said.

I said, "I must have fallen asleep."

"You were more than asleep," Kate said.

"Was that you kissing me?" I said.

"If you want to think of it that way," Kate said.

Freddy said, "She was giving you mouth-to-mouth resuscitation, you idiot."

"How kind of her," I said.

"Your heart stopped," Freddy said.

"Damn," I said. "I was hoping those paddles were for a spanking."

"You're sick," Freddy said. "Why couldn't you just stay dead?"

"Freddy!" Kate said.

"I wasn't dead Freddy," I said. "My heart was just taking a vacation."

One of the paramedics crouched down next to me and took the wires off my chest. I started to get up.

Kate put a hand on my chest and pushed me back down.

"Where do you think you're going?" Kate said.

"Back to work," I said.

"No chance," Kate said. "There's an ambulance on the way. You're going to a hospital."

"You think you're the only person to ever shock me back to life?" I said. "Happens all the time. Occupational hazard."

"I'm sure it does," Kate said. "You're still going to a hospital, however."

I rolled my eyes.

"Whatever," I said.

I then suddenly realized that of all the faces surrounding me, Donnie and Martin the valet were not among them. I shuddered.

"Kate, where are Donnie and Martin?" I said.

"Over there," Kate said, pointing behind me and to my left. "Both alive thanks to you."

I craned my head around.

Donnie was sitting on his ass about ten yards away from the top of my head. His knees were spread, his chest rested between them, and he had an ice pack on his neck. Martin the valet was sitting next to him. Martin was also sitting on his ass and had an oxygen mask covering his mouth and nose. His hair was singed and one side of his face looked like it had been burned. Another fifty yards behind Donnie and Martin NASAD fire trucks were spraying large streams of firefighting foam over the flames that had consumed the NASAD helicopter. The flames were rapidly diminishing. The FBI helicopter appeared unscathed.

"You two look pretty good for a couple of clowns who should be dead," I shouted to Donnie and Martin.

"So do you," Donnie yelled back.

Martin the valet gave me a thumbs up.

My cell phone rang. I rolled a bit on my left side to take it out of my back pocket. I looked at the screen. It was Jeff who was calling.

"Sorry," I said to Kate. "Gotta take this. Unless you got some rule against me talking on the phone as well, that is."

"Go ahead," Kate said. "Just don't rile yourself up."

I answered the phone.

Jeff's voice said, "We here."

"Dr. Lennon's house in Malibu?" I said.

"Yep. Gonna catch some waves," Jeff said. "What you doing?"

"Getting defibrillated," I said.

"You see a little white bright light?" Jeff said.

"Didn't get that far," I said.

"Who try to kill you this time?" Jeff said.

"Can't talk right now," I said.

"You got company?" Jeff said.

"You could say that," I said.

"Coming back here anytime soon?" Jeff said.

"Hope so," I said.

"I be the African American on the surfboard when you do," Jeff said.

"Should be easy to spot," I said.

"Damn straight," Jeff said.

"I have to warn you about something, though," I said.

"Ain't afraid of sharks," Jeff said.

"Not sharks," I said. "There's a Coast Guard cutter patrolling outside the break."

"Think they're gonna shoot me?" Jeff said.

"It's within the realm of possibility," I said.

"Ray already took care of that," Jeff said.

"You met Agent Carpenter?" I said.

"Nice guy," Jeff said.

"Competent too," I said. "Later, buddy."

"Later," Jeff said.

He hung up.

Kate said, "Was that Jeff?"

"Yes," I said. "He's at your house."

"Is Adelaide with him?" Kate said.

"He said 'We here', so I assume so," I said.

"Good," Kate said. "We can all keep you company in the hospital."

Bryce Wellington stepped forward.

"Do you mind if I speak to your patient, Dr. Lennon?" Wellington said.

"That depends on what you're going to say," Kate said.

"What I was going to say, is that General Wilder's actions today were one of the greatest displays of heroism I have ever witnessed," Wellington said. "His reputation as one of the finest soldiers our military has ever produced is well deserved."

"I'm not sure you're qualified to judge that, General Wellington," Kate said.

"Excuse me?" Wellington said.

"You're a goddamned, coward, General," Kate said. "You're a disgrace to the uniform you once wore."

"Now, now, Kate," Wellington said. "You've had a very stressful day. Let's not go saying things you'll regret later."

"I'm not going to regret a thing. You and that pig in the porkpie hat," Kate said, jerking a thumb toward Burnette, "are two of the biggest assholes I have ever met in my life."

Burnette said, "With all due respect, Dr. Lennon, you're being very inappropriate. We made a calculated, professional decision and acted appropriately."

"A person needs a brain to make calculated, professional decisions, Mr. Burnette," Kate said.

Freddy's face was crimson.

"Kate, you need to shut up because you're way out of line," Freddy said. "These two men saved my life."

"And left Jack and me for dead while all of you ran for cover," Kate said.

"Well, you have to admit your situation looked pretty hopeless," Freddy said.

"Luckily for me, Jack didn't think so," Kate said.

Martin the valet, who must have had pretty good hearing, shouted,

"Luckily for Donnie and me too!"

Wellington scowled at Martin. Carter Bowdoin seemed to want no part of the conversation. He appeared to be shrinking into himself, trying not to be noticed.

But Kate noticed.

Kate said, "What about you Carter? What do you think about all of this?"

"Frankly, Kate, I was so scared I was about to shit my pants," Bowdoin said. "I wasn't doing too much thinking."

"At least you're honest," Kate said.

Freddy said, "Are you saying I'm not?"

"I don't know what you are, Freddy," Kate said.

"What's that supposed to mean?" Freddy said.

"I'm your sister," Kate said. "You should have tried to get them to help us."

"But I was going to shit my pants too!" Freddy said. He instantly looked horrified, as if the words had slipped out and he hadn't intended to say what he did.

"Did you?" Kate said.

"Did I what?" Freddy said.

"Shit your pants," Kate said.

"Screw you," Freddy said.

I noticed a van driving across the grassy field and headed towards the barracks. It was an FBI forensics van. Up until that moment, I had been lying on the ground calmly waiting for the ambulance and thoroughly enjoying the tongue-lashing Kate was handing out, but I realized it would be a mistake to keep doing what I was doing.

I had to examine the snipers' bodies before the forensic techs spent any time with them.

There were things I had to see.

I tried to get up again.

Kate instantly pushed me back onto the ground.

"Please lie down," Kate said.

I shook my head.

"Help me up," I said, and extended my arm to her.

"Not a good idea," Kate said.

"I'm getting up whether you help me or not," I said. "There's something I have to do."

"You were flatline for seven minutes," Kate said.

"So in theory I'm already brain dead," I said. "How much worse can I get?"

Kate studied me.

"What is it you have to do?" Kate said.

I gestured for her to lean in close. She did.

"I can't let those FBI forensic techs examine the bodies of the snipers before I do," I whispered.

"Why not?" Kate whispered back.

"Don't make me explain right now," I said. "If you do, it'll just waste time and the techs will beat me to the punch."

Kate studied me again.

"Is it mission critical?" Kate said.

"You know what mission critical means?" I said.

"I wouldn't use the words if I didn't know what they meant," Kate said.

"Of course you wouldn't," I said. "And, yes, it is."

Kate sighed, and taking hold of my wrist, helped me to my feet. My head started pounding, my stomach felt like it was going to come up out of my mouth, and my knee felt like someone was battering it with a jackhammer. A cold sweat broke out on my forehead and my hands felt clammy.

"You still sure you want to do this?" Kate said, continuing to whisper in my ear.

"I'm fine," I said, swallowing hard to keep from throwing up.

"How come you look like you're going to die then?" Kate said.

"I'm a good actor," I said.

"You're asking me to believe the sweat running off your face, your thready pulse, and your pale skin are an act?" Kate said.

"Yes," I said.

"If it's an act, it's a pretty good one," Kate said.

"Thanks," I said.

"Do you mind if I ask why?" Kate said.

"Why I'm acting like I am going to die?" I said.

"Yes," Kate said.

"I'm making a play for your sympathy," I said.

"You already have my sympathy," Kate said. "You can stop acting."

"Okay," I said.

A wave of nausea hit me and I felt very woozy. I almost fell over. Kate held me up.

"Is that your idea of stopping?" Kate said.

"Sometimes when you fully immerse yourself in a role, the role takes on a life of its own," I said.

"I see," Kate said. "So it might take a while for you to be just Jack again."

"Yes," I said.

"How convenient," Kate said.

"Isn't it though?" I said.

I put my left arm around Kate's shoulder, and with her propping me up, we set off towards the barracks.

Burnette ran up behind us, grabbed my free right arm, and spun me around.

"Where the hell do you think you're going, Wilder?" Burnette said.

"To do some investigating," I said. "I'd like to know who was trying to kill me."

"We do the investigating around here," Burnette said.

"Are your investigation skills as good as your protection skills?" I said.

Burnette didn't say anything.

"I didn't think so," I said.

I ripped my arm from his grasp.

Burnette pulled out his gold-plated, pearl handled Glock and pointed it at my chest.

"Don't move," Burnette said.

Before I could stop her, or even had an inkling of what she was about to do, Kate jumped between Burnette and me.

"Put that goddamn gun down, Burnette, or I'll goddamn tear your heart out," Kate said.

I said, "This is not a good idea, Kate. Agent Burnette is at point-blank range, and even he might not miss at that distance."

"Be quiet please, Jack," Kate said. "I'm handling this."

"Okay," I said.

Burnette said, "With all due respect, Dr. Lennon, you are in way over your head."

Wellington said, "Agent Burnette, isn't it possible you are overreacting just a tad?"

"General Wilder is a member of the Armed Forces," Burnette said. "He is not allowed to take any action on U.S. soil."

Kate said, "I'm going to count to three, Agent Burnette. If that gun is not back in its holster by then, you're a dead man. One..."

"Dr. Lennon, interfering with a federal officer in the performance of his duties is a serious crime," Burnette said.

"Two...," Kate said.

Freddy said, "Kate, have you lost your mind? Get out of his way right now!"

"Shut the hell up, Freddy, or I'll tear your heart out next," Kate said.

Burnette said, "You could be facing a very long prison sentence, Dr. Lennon."

The muscles in Kate's shoulders bunched up and she slightly bent her knees. I assumed that meant she was getting ready to strike. I didn't think Burnette had it in him to shoot, but if Kate got to three, I was going to have to take some quick action. Throwing Kate down on the ground and covering her with my body again was probably my best option.

Carter Bowdoin said, "Agent Burnette, are you seriously going to shoot a NASAD board member?"

Bryce Wellington said, "Burnette, Mr. Bowdoin is correct. You can't possibly believe this is the best way to handle this matter, can you?"

Burnette looked over at Bowdoin and Wellington. As he did so, his gun wandered in their direction. Bowdoin and Wellington looked horrified.

Kate leapt through the air and grabbed Burnette around the neck. The force of her leap knocked her and Burnette down to the ground where Kate wound up on top of him. She started choking him.

"Three!" Kate snarled.

Damn.

I had thought for sure she was going to at least finish the count before she would do anything.

I stepped forward, leaned down, bent the wrist of Burnette's gun hand backwards almost to the point of breaking it, then snatched the pearl handled, gold-plated gun out of his hand. I shoved the gun in my waistband.

Kate's fingernails had drawn blood on the skin of Burnette's neck and Burnette's eyes were bulging out of his head. He appeared to be having trouble breathing.

"That was a bit of a dangerous move, Kate," I said.

Kate stopped choking Burnette and instead started pummeling his face with her fists. Burnette, probably too stunned to believe what was happening to him, put up only a flimsy defense.

"He's a goddamned coward. Just like Wellington," Kate said. "I knew he wouldn't shoot."

"Clearly your assessment was accurate," I said. "But still risky."

Kate kept pummeling him.

"I'm not sure this is going to lead to anything good," I said. I gently grabbed one of Kate's elbows. "Come on, I think he's learned his lesson."

Kate stopped hitting Burnette.

"You think so?" Kate said.

"I do," I said.

"Okay," Kate said. "But just to be sure..."

She punched Burnette hard in the right eye.

"Stay down there unless you want more of the same, asshole," Kate said to Burnette. She then crawled off him, and got to her feet, and added to me, "You understand, right? I mean he almost got me killed."

"Perfectly," I said.

Burnette rolled to his hands and knees. He struggled to catch his breath.

"Give me my gun back, Wilder," Burnette said.

"Just as soon as I'm done with my investigation," I said.

"You mess up that crime scene, a whole world of shit is going to rain down on you," Burnette said.

"You afraid you won't figure out who shot the Kazakhs?" I said. "Well, I got news for you. It was me. I killed all four of them while you were hiding behind the fire truck."

Kate and I once again set off for the barracks.

Martin the valet called out, "Way to go Dr. Lennon!"

Donnie Kurtsinger said, "Nice work, Doc!"

Kate gave them a thumbs up. We kept walking.

"I didn't know you had that in you," I said.

"I didn't either," Kate said.

"Impressive," I said.

"Thanks," Kate said. "Jesus, what the hell is wrong with that guy anyway?

"Burnette?" I said.

"Yeah, Burnette," Kate said.

"He's a power mad idiot with poor impulse control who doesn't like people invading his turf," I said. "Plus he also lacks the intelligence to consider the broader consequences of his actions."

"That's a hell of a good spur of the moment analysis," Kate said.

"Thank you," I said. "But it wasn't that difficult to make. I've met a lot of guys like Burnette."

"You think Burnette will arrest me for beating him up?" Kate said.

I looked over my shoulder. Bryce Wellington and Carter Bowdoin were standing over Burnette's kneeling form. The two men appeared to be having some heated words with him.

"That depends," I said. "How bad would it be for Pennsylvania Avenue Partners' stock price if he did?"

"Stock price?" Kate said.

"Take a look," I said.

Kate turned her head around.

"You think that's what Bryce and Carter are talking to Burnette about?" Kate said.

"Hard to imagine those two would be so passionate about anything else," I said.

"Good point," Kate said.

We both turned back around.

"So," I said, "Was I really down for seven minutes?"

"Yes," Kate said.

"You must be a good resuscitator," I said.

"Pediatric cardiac surgeons are like that," Kate said. "We don't like to lose any kids."

"Understandable," I said.

We arrived at the body of the first dead Kazakh. The FBI forensic techs were still unloading their equipment from the van. One of the techs saw us.

"Hey!" the tech said. "Stay away from that body. This is a crime scene."

"Burnette said it was fine," I said.

"Burnette didn't say anything to me about that," the tech said.

"No?" I said. "Why don't you go talk to him yourself? He's right over there. He's the one on his hands and knees."

The tech looked over at Burnette.

"I'll do just that," the tech said.

He stomped off. I kneeled down next to the body and carefully looked it over.

Kate said, "What are you looking for?"

"I have a hunch," I said.

"What is it?" Kate said.

"I don't want to say," I said.

"You don't want to be embarrassed in case you're wrong?" Kate said.

"Something like that," I said.

The truth was I didn't really know what I was looking for. I couldn't say why, but I had a feeling there was something important the dead snipers would reveal to me. Since that sounded odd even to myself, I didn't say anything about my feeling to Kate.

I checked the soles of the dead sniper's boots. The tread on the soles matched the footprints near the knapsack containing the explosives at the drone sub hangar, and also the boots of the Kazakhs at the Coso Junction rest stop. I patted down the corpse's legs. There was nothing hidden under the pants. I checked the pants pockets. I found a Koran. I took it out and rifled the pages. Nothing had been hidden between the pages. I put the Koran back in the pants pocket.

I worked my way towards the body's shoulders. I stopped at the chest pocket. A cord with a set of small earphones on the end of it was dangling out of the pocket. I reached in and found a cell phone connected to the cord. My suspicion had been that the snipers had probably been communicating with each other via cell phone. The earphones seemed to confirm that suspicion.

The cell phone's screen was on the lock screen. On the lock screen was a photo of the Ascencion Cathedral in Almaty, Kazakhstan. The cathedral's blue, green, red, and white checkered domes had gold crosses mounted on top of them. Strange lock screen choice for an Islamic terrorist, I thought.

I tried to get past the lock screen, but it was password protected. I was confident I would find cell phones on the three other snipers as well. Ideally I would send all four cell phones to Haley to see what, if any, information she could get off of them. But I had already decided I would take only one of the phones. Taking more than one would risk making Burnette and the forensic techs suspicious that I had stolen a phone from the scene. Those suspicions could turn into accusations, which would mean I might once more have to spend time fending off attacks from Burnette. Fending off Burnette was for me a form of sport, but I felt like I had much more important things to do. I didn't, however, want to decide which one of the cell phones I would take until I had seen all of them, so I put the one I had in my hand back in the body's chest pocket.

I peeled the collar of the headless Kazakh away from what remained of his neck just in case some of the skin behind the ear was still present. There wasn't any skin, so no crucifix and cobra tattoo either.

The dead sniper's gun was lying next to him a few feet away. I took a quick look at it. It was, as I had thought it would be, a Spetsnaz AN-94 assault rifle.

I got up.

"Let's check out the other bodies," I said to Kate.

Body number two was exactly like the first one, only the picture on its cell phone lock screen was of a beautiful dark-haired young woman. She wasn't wearing a hijab, but she did have a crucifix around her neck. How many Islamic terrorists dated Christian girls? Not a whole lot, I thought.

Headless body number three's cell phone lock screen had a picture of a mountain meadow with a stream running through it. I was pretty sure it was one that came standard with the phone. The body also had a bit of skin still remaining at the top of its neck just below the ear. There was a crucifix and cobra tattoo there. Which effectively erased any possible doubt that these four men could be anything other than members of the same crew that had attacked us at the Coso Junction rest stop.

Body number four was where things got interesting.

The screen of the cell phone belonging to body number four was different from the screens on the cell phones belonging to the other three bodies.

Much different.

The cell phone itself was in the body's chest pocket. The cell phone's camera was just peeking out and over the rim of the pocket. The cell phone's screen was cracked and the image on the screen was the one that must have been there when the body hit the ground.

"Hmm," I said as I examined the phone.

"Find what you were looking for?" Kate said.

"I believe so," I said.

"What is it?" Kate said.

"It's a bit complicated, but I promise to explain later," I said. "Right now, would you please do me a favor and move to your right so you're blocking Burnette's view of me?"

"You don't want him to see what you're doing?" Kate said.

"Correct," I said.

"You going to take the phone?" Kate said.

"Smart woman," I said. "I'm then going to have Haley crack it open and see what she can find."

"Good idea," Kate said.

Kate moved into position to block Burnette.

I took one last look at the phone before I put it in my pocket.

The screen had two apps open.

One app had two photos displayed side by side. The photos were head shots of Kate and me. Kate's photo was labeled 'Odin' and mine was labeled 'Dva'. I knew enough Russian to know those were the words for 'One' and 'Two'. Which I assumed meant 'Target One' and 'Target Two'.

I had been added to our enemy's hit list.

Which was fine with me.

I had expected it sooner or later.

The second app confirmed my hunch that I would find something important on the snipers' bodies.

The second app was an app whose name I couldn't decipher as it was written in Chinese. But the app clearly did the same thing as FaceTime -

it allowed two way video communication between the sniper's cell phone and someone else's cell phone or computer.

The face of the someone who was using the cell phone or computer that was communicating to the sniper's phone via the FaceTime-like app was still on the screen.

I knew who that someone was.

He was wearing a mask.

But, still, I knew him.

Because the mask was a dragon mask, and deep down, I had known the man behind the mask couldn't resist watching the assassination attempt on Kate's and my lives.

He was Bobby and Timmy's Dragon Man.

CHAPTER 73

A NASAD helicopter, a near duplicate of Donnie Kurtsinger's chopper, picked up Freddy, Carter Bowdoin, Bryce Wellington, Kate, and me at the site for the flight back to Freddy and Kate's Malibu compound. Donnie and Martin the valet were taken to a nearby hospital for further observation. Burnette stayed behind at the site to perform whatever the dumbass thing in his skull that was trying to pass itself off as a brain had determined a forensic investigation of a 'terrorist attack' should entail. I'm almost ashamed to admit it, but I had given Burnette back his gun before boarding the chopper.

Bowdoin, Freddy, and Wellington huddled in the chopper's front passenger seats during the flight to the compound. The plexiglass privacy partition was in place and I heard not a word of their conversation. Kate fell asleep next to me. I had a pretty bad headache, which would have made sleep impossible if sleep was what I had wanted. But what I wanted to do was think.

I spent the first part of the flight carefully reviewing everything that had happened at the NASAD site and trying to determine what it all meant to my mission going forward. I was convinced that Dragon Man had set up what I had sensed was a 'show' at the site - a show whose only purpose was to lure Kate to the site so that she and I could be murdered. I didn't yet know what to make of the fact I'd also seen Carter Bowdoin zero in on the sniper's window well before the sniper had appeared. Bowdoin's actions could have been coincidental, but I was highly suspicious they weren't, and I decided to redouble my investigation into Bowdoin's possible involvement in all things bad at NASAD. There was also the issue of what Freddy, Bryce Wellington, and Burnette - all being close cohorts of Bowdoin - knew as well. The problem was, no matter how hard I thought, I made no progress. My mind was so fuzzy - which wasn't surprising considering I'd been flatline for so long - and my head hurt so bad, I accomplished nothing at all and I had to table the thinking for later.

I sent a quick text to Haley summarizing what had occurred at the NASAD site then spent most of the rest of the flight watching the sleeping Kate. Perhaps her dreams were terrifying her at that very moment, but all I could see was a beautiful woman who seemed at peace. I hadn't told Kate about the cell phone with the picture of Dragon Man on it, or Bowdoin's seeming prescience about the impending sniper attack, and I wasn't sure when, or if, I would. 'Need to know' had been a lifelong obsession with me and varying that approach had nearly always caused me problems. I trusted Kate, and I'd already told her about what Bobby and Timmy had said about Dragon Man, but her slip about her father's and husband's murders gave me pause about what I could share with her going forward.

The helicopter cleared the ridge of the coastal foothills above Malibu at about the twenty-fifth minute of the flight. Freddy and Kate's compound and the Pacific Ocean came into view. The sun shimmered off the sea. The water's surface alternated between areas that were either as smooth as a mirror or rippled in fiercely swirling spirals.

Three hang gliders were about a thousand feet above the beach. The hang glider pilots must have launched the gliders from one of the coastal mountain peaks a few miles east of the coastline. The hang gliders' frames appeared to be made of aluminum, and the wings were covered with a bright scarlet fabric. The aluminum glinted in the sun, and the scarlet fabric of the wings billowed in the wind. The scarlet color of the wings also made the hang gliders easy to track, as the scarlet sharply contrasted with the blue of the sky.

The NASAD chopper landed in the middle of the Malibu compound. Bowdoin, Freddy, and Wellington immediately headed to Freddy's pink palace, and Kate and I started walking to her house. The walking increased my heart rate and blood pressure, which caused my head to throb even more.

Kate said, "I would have thought Adelaide and Jeff would have been here to greet us."

"I didn't tell Jeff exactly what time we'd get back," I said. "They're probably at the beach."

"There's no lifeguards down there," Kate said. "Are they both good swimmers?"

"Good question," I said.

Kate studied my face.

"You're kidding, right?" Kate said.

"Yeah," I said. "Jeff's a surfer and Adelaide was a champion swimmer in high school before she decided she'd rather spend her time learning how to kill people."

"To thine own self be true," Kate said.

"And then it must follow," I said, "as the night the day, thou canst not then be false to any man."

"Polonius was such a goddamn blowhard," Kate said.

"Yes," I said. "At least he got what he deserved."

"Death," Kate said.

"All that lives must die," I said. "Passing through nature to eternity."

"That from Hamlet too?" Kate said.

"Think so," I said.

Kate and I reached the FBI mobile command post. Agent Ray Carpenter, still in his black SWAT helmet and body armor, exited the post and joined us. I noticed that the snipers on the roof of Kate's house seemed to be keeping a careful watch on the hang gliders, which were then high in the sky and about a quarter mile west of the estate. I thought to myself that whoever the hang glider pilots were, they better be careful to keep their distance from the estate, otherwise they might get themselves shot.

Carpenter said, "Heard you all had quite a scare, Dr. Lennon. Are you okay, ma'am?"

"I'm fine," Kate said. "Hero boy over here says he's also fine, but given the fact he was clinically dead for seven minutes that's highly unlikely."

Carpenter looked me over.

"Doctor's right," Carpenter said. "You don't look so good General."

"Shooters look worse," I said.

"Just the same, maybe we should take you to a hospital in town, get you checked out," Carpenter said.

Kate said, "Save your breath Agent Carpenter. I've been fighting that battle and it's already lost."

I said to Kate, "What do I need a hospital for? You're observing me."

"You need a hospital," Kate said.

"You think I'd be better off with strangers?" I said.

Kate frowned.

"You're the most stubborn person I ever met," Kate said.

Carpenter said, "Excuse me for interrupting, ma'am. But in the military, we call that perseverance."

"Then I guess the general's going to persevere himself into an early grave," Kate said.

I said, "Sounds good to me."

"I'm sure it does," Kate said. "And for the record, I'm not observing you anymore. I need to spend some time with my kids. Make sure you're always in someone's sight."

I gestured to the snipers on the roofs of Freddy's and Kate's houses.

"Hard not to be," I said.

"Those snipers are a little too far away to adequately judge your status," Kate said. "Agent Carpenter, will you please ask your men to occasionally take a close look at the general? Face to face would be best."

"Will do, ma'am," Carpenter said.

"Please alert the Coast Guard too," Kate said. "I think this knucklehead intends on going to meet his friends, Adelaide and Jeff, whom he believes are down on the beach."

"Yes, ma'am," Carpenter said. "Actually, I can confirm that the beach is exactly where Adelaide and Jeff are. They went there almost as soon as they arrived at the compound."

"Thank you," Kate said. "I'll see you later, gentlemen."

Kate headed off for her house.

I said, "Hold on a second please, Kate."

Kate stopped and turned around.

"Yes, Jack?" Kate said.

"Nemo said he would contact you today," I said.

"You'll be the first to know if he does," Kate said.

She turned and strode away.

Carpenter said, "Dr. Nemo is planning on contacting Dr. Lennon?"

I thought that moment was as good as any to bring Carpenter up to speed on what I'd recently learned about Dr. Nemo, Paul Lennon, and the dark programmers, so that is what I did. I also told him that Nemo had left a message saying he would contact Kate, but that I wasn't going to get my hopes up. Sticking with my 'need to know' protocols, I said nothing to Carpenter about the possible connection of Nemo and the dark programmers to the insurmountable edge. When I was finished, Carpenter said, "If anything arises where you need my help with Nemo, don't hesitate to ask."

"I won't," I said.

"You know, seven minutes is a long time to be dead," Carpenter said.

"Seven is nothing," I said. "My record's twelve."

"Congratulations," Carpenter said. "Just the same, please be careful. You die, I'm sure someone will find a way to blame me."

"We certainly wouldn't want that," I said. "You up to speed on what happened at the NASAD site?"

"Yes," Carpenter said. "FBI lost a lot of good agents today."

Two of the hang gliders appeared to be heading inland towards hills above the coast. The third one seemed to be lingering behind, however, perhaps even going a bit out to sea.

"It was pretty bad, Ray," I said. "You're aware it was only Dr. Lennon they were after?"

Carpenter gave me a questioning look.

"Agents were just in the way," I said. "She was the target."

"You think she was lured out there?" Carpenter said.

"Had to be," I said.

"Coso Junction rest stop yesterday and the NASAD site today," Carpenter said. "Should we try again to move her to a safe house?"

"She'll never go for it," I said.

"How about confining her to the estate?" Carpenter said.

"Dr. Lennon will probably argue about that too, but it's something we should probably consider discussing with her," I said.

I reached into my pocket and pulled out the Kazakh's cell phone that had the pictures of Kate, me, and the masked Dragon Man frozen on its screen. I snapped a photo of the screen with my iPhone, then handed the Kazakh's phone to Carpenter.

"Got this off one of the dead snipers at the NASAD site," I said. "I need you to please get it to Haley as soon as possible."

Carpenter looked at the cell phone's screen.

"Both you and Dr. Lennon are on here," Carpenter said. "I thought you said she was the only target."

"She's the only target I'm concerned about," I said.

"With an attitude like that you really are going to get yourself killed, and then I really am going to get blamed," Carpenter said.

"Just tell everyone you told me to be careful, but that I refused to listen to you," I said.

"I'm sure that'll work just swell," Carpenter said. "Who's behind the mask?"

"I believe he's the guy who ordered the killings of Sam and Lizzy, their mother and grandparents, and also the kidnapping and hit attempts on Dr. Lennon," I said. "I don't know his identity, but I'm hoping Haley can find out."

"I'll make sure Haley gets the phone by no later than the end of the day," Carpenter said.

"Thanks," I said. "And please keep in mind that no one knows about what's on that phone right now other than you and me."

"My lips are sealed, sir," Carpenter said.

"Good," I said. "How do I get to the beach?"

Carpenter pointed westward along the road on which we were then standing.

"Across that grassy area at the end of this driveway, a path goes between Dr. Lennon's and her brother's houses," Carpenter said. "Behind Dr. Lennon's house, the path turns right and leads to the top of a staircase. The staircase will take you down to the beach."

"Later," I said.

I turned and started walking in the direction Carpenter had pointed.

"Sorry, General," Carpenter said. "One last thing."

I stopped and turned.

"Yes, Ray?" I said.

"Is it true Dr. Lennon beat the crap out of Agent Burnette?" Carpenter said.

"Yes," I said. "It was a joy to behold."

"Wish I'd been there," Carpenter said.

"There's always the chance they'll go a second round," I said.

"You gotta promise to call me if they do," Carpenter said.

"I will," I said.

I turned and started walking toward the beach. The walking again caused my headache to grow worse. I felt like my skull might explode. When I reached the grassy area Carpenter had directed me to, however, the cool breeze blowing in from the Pacific picked up, and the breeze, coupled with the sponginess of the green Poa grass beneath my feet, the brilliant blue sky, and the smell of salt air mingling with the estate's flowers, made me feel a little better. I spotted a pod of dolphins diving in and out of the water about a quarter mile from shore. The two hang gliders that had been heading towards the hills were then at a much lower altitude. I assumed they were coming in for a landing. The third hang glider was circling higher in the sky and farther out to sea.

My cell phone rang. General Hart was calling again on FaceTime. I stopped walking and answered his call. Hart appeared to still be out to sea on the USS George Washington aircraft supercarrier and he didn't look happy. I assumed his seasickness hadn't abated.

"Good day, General," I said. I gave Hart my most charming smile, hoping it might cheer him up.

"What the hell did you do, Jack?" Hart said.

"Sir?" I said.

"Why'd you tell that Monique Kerbert woman at NASAD how to fix those drone sub issues she didn't even know she had?" Hart said.

"Just doing my duty, sir," I said.

"Well you screwed up everything I've been working on," Hart said.

"I did?" I said.

"Yes, you did," Hart said. "NASAD already made some of your changes and now Admiral Bagley feels he's safe. He says he's definitely not going to take the Ohio drone subs offline. We have only ten days left until we have a full scale war on our hands and right now it looks like our whole mission has been shot to hell. Those drone subs have to be the Chinese insurmountable edge, which means they're going to nuke us with our own missiles thanks to you."

"I hope not, sir," I said.

"That's all you have to say?" Hart said. "'You hope not'?"

"Sorry, sir, I just have this awful headache," I said.

"Yeah, I heard about that chopper blowing up," Hart said. "You just gotta suck it up, son."

"Honestly, sir, I wasn't doing too bad a job of that until you called," I said.

"Is that you being funny?" Hart said.

"Sort of, sir," I said. "But I actually do feel like crap."

"How do you think I feel?" Hart said.

I didn't say anything.

"Look, just don't help NASAD out with their drones anymore, okay?" Hart said.

"I won't, sir," I said.

"Did you find that damn Nemo asshole yet?" Hart said.

"Not yet," I said. "You'll be the first to know if I do."

"Good," Hart said. "I gotta go work on Bagley some more."

Hart's face turned green.

"Aw shit," Hart said. "I think I'm gonna throw up again."

Hart suddenly bent over and my cell phone screen went blank.

I started back on my journey to the beach. I couldn't see the Coast Guard cutter beneath the bluff, but I could hear the roar of its engines amid the sounds of crashing waves. A moment later, another sound was added to the mix. My cell phone was ringing. I looked at the screen.

I was getting a FaceTime call.

But not from Hart this time.

It was from Haley.

I stopped walking again and answered the phone. Major Marian Haley's deep brown eyes, silky brown hair, perpetual red-lipped smile full of flawless white teeth, and tight uniform blouse filled the screen. It looked like she was still somewhere deep in NORAD's cave.

"You're making me paranoid," I said.

"How's that?" Haley said.

"Last time I was talking to you, Hart called," I said. "And now you call two seconds after I just got off the phone with him. It feels like a conspiracy to me."

"It's not a conspiracy," Haley said. "It's a coincidence."

"I don't believe in coincidences," I said.

"That's because you're paranoid," Haley said.

"Alright, you win," I said. "I stepped into that one. I do have a question for you, though."

"What is it?" Haley said.

"How much longer did the plane the Kazakhs and Afghans took to Pixley take to get to its final destination than its original flight plan called for?" I said.

"What?" Haley said.

"That's part of what you were supposed to be working on the last time we talked, wasn't it?" I said.

"Yes," Haley said. "But how did you know about the delay?"

"I've been thinking a lot about how all those mercenaries could have been offloaded into the U.S. without detection," I said. "I think their bosses are probably the same assholes who took down Feynman and Lennon's Otter in Alaska, so I figured those bosses would try a variation of what worked so well for them in that situation."

"You mean worked so well until we saw what happened on the satellite tapes," Haley said.

"Correct," I said.

"Well, it looks like you made a good guess," Haley said. "It appears the mercenaries may have used NASAD's radar mislocating technology to hide their drop off location. Have you also been thinking about how they got in the country in the first place?"

"I'm pretty sure they landed in Texas after a long flight from Kazakhstan," I said.

"Jesus!" Haley said. "How'd you know that?"

I looked up at the sky again. I hoped whoever was in the third hang glider knew what they were doing, as the glider seemed dangerously high and far out to sea.

"Which part?" I said. "The Kazakhstan or the Texas?"

"Both," Haley said.

"Since Kazakhstan is closer to the U.S. than Afghanistan, I figured they'd pick up the Afghans first, then stop and get the Kazakhs," I said. "After that I knew they would probably have to refuel, maybe in Thailand or Hong Kong. But the question I had to answer for myself was where would they go after they refueled? Odds were against it being California, since that was where they were ultimately headed and they'd most likely think that landing in California would make it too easy for someone to trace them. Oregon and Washington were also unlikely, as those states would be the next states we'd check for planes arriving from Asia. So that left somewhere in the middle of the country. Kansas or Oklahoma could have worked, but Texas would be less conspicuous - the flight would blend in with a lot of other flights."

"That's amazing," Haley said. "Sometimes I wonder what you even need me for."

"Oh, I definitely need you, darling," I said.

"I hope so," Haley said. "Do you mind if I ask what city in Texas they landed in?"

"I wanna say Houston," I said. "No...strike that. Dallas."

"You know, I was just starting to believe you were telling the truth when you said you need me, but now you ruined it," Haley said.

"I ruined it?" I said.

"Yes," Haley said. "By patronizing me, you asshole. You were never going to say Houston. It doesn't have as many international flights."

"I'm sorry," I said. "You're right, I shouldn't have done that. I was never going to say Houston."

"Where'd they go from Dallas?" Haley said.

"You mean according to the flight plan that was filed?" I said.

"Yes," Haley said.

"San Francisco," I said.

"Goddamnit!" Haley said. "You really don't need me!"

"Haley that was easy and you know it," I said. "These guys are all about diversion and subterfuge. The Kazakhs were dropped off in Pixley, which is in the California Central Valley. From there they wouldn't go to Los Angeles International, as Los Angeles International is very close to NASAD headquarters, and that would be one of the first places we'd think to look for the plane. San Francisco International is the other major airport that's closest to Pixley, and San Francisco International has the advantage of being hundreds of miles away from NASAD headquarters."

"Okay, I guess that was pretty easy," Haley said.

I once again heard the roar of the Coast Guard cutter's engines. The intensity of the roar didn't seem to have changed much, so I assumed the cutter had not moved toward or away from me and was still circling close to shore.

"It wasn't *that* easy," I said.

"Aw, did I hurt General Wilder's little ego?" Haley said.

"You did actually," I said.

"You deserved it," Haley said. "So, you ready for the details?"

I nodded.

"A Gulfstream 550 landed at Dallas/Fort Worth International Airport two days ago," Haley said. "The flight originated in Herat, Afghanistan, then stopped at Almaty International in Kazakhstan, and refueled in Hong Kong on its way here. The Gulfstream is registered to a charity called 'Doctors of Mercy'. The charity sends doctors anywhere in the world they are needed, generally to third world countries in time of war. Thirty men cleared customs in Dallas. They were listed as Afghan and Kazakh doctors who had come to get specialized training in the U.S."

"Any of them stay in Dallas?" I said.

"Just one," Haley said. "A Dr. Nursultan Aitmukhambetov."

"Is he real?" I said.

"Yes," Haley said. "He's attending an ophthalmology conference in Dallas."

"What'd he say about the others?" I said.

"Who said anyone talked to him about the others?" Haley said.

I rolled my eyes.

"Alright, sorry," Haley said. "Aitmukhambetov said he didn't know any of the others. He said they were pretty much equally split between Afghans and Kazakhs. Dr. Aitmukhambetov also said none of the others really looked like doctors, but that whenever he tried to talk to them to see if his suspicions were correct, they just gave him the cold shoulder."

"Thirty men on the plane, and one real doctor gets off in Dallas," I said. "That means there were twenty-nine mercenaries. I killed seven of them over the last day or so, which leaves twenty-two still running around."

"Hold on," Haley said. "I'm getting my calculator out to check your math."

"Funny," I said.

"I thought so," Haley said.

"Of course, that's twenty-two assuming there were no other planes," I said.

"Haven't found any yet," Haley said. "But we'll keep looking."

"What about the flight plan from Dallas to San Francisco?" I said

"Scheduled departure time was 10:00 p.m. Central and arrival time was midnight Pacific," Haley said. "But it took four hours and thirty minutes. Pilot reported he was having some issues with turbulence and had to change his routing."

The hang glider was climbing ever higher and farther away from the beach. I wondered how the pilot would get back to shore if the wind shifted and started coming off the mountains instead of from over the ocean.

"And radar showed the Gulfstream nowhere near Pixley?" I said.

"Correct," Haley said. "We did however find multiple reports of a 'UFO' landing in a field outside of Pixley right around midnight. Midnight is the time the Gulfstream would have arrived in Pixley if it made a beeline to Pixley straight from Dallas. Witnesses said the UFO appeared to land and then almost immediately take off back in the direction from which it came."

"The route deviation, plus the landing and takeoff in Pixley, add up to about thirty minutes?" I said.

"Very close," Haley said.

"Which brings us back to the idea that the mercenaries' bosses used the same NASAD radar mislocating system to falsify the Gulfstream's location that they used when they took down Feynman and Lennon's Otter in Alaska," I said.

"Looks that way," Haley said.

"How many people got off the Gulfstream when it finally landed in San Francisco?" I said.

"Just the pilots and two flight attendants," Haley said.

"No one else?" I said.

"Nope," Haley said. "Plane is still parked on the tarmac in San Francisco. We reviewed all the airport's videotapes since it arrived. No one has gotten on or off since."

"And you checked inside the plane itself?" I said.

"Who do you think you're talking to?" Haley said.

"Sorry," I said. "I assume the plane was empty?"

"Correct," Haley said.

"Which means that little field in Pixley was the landing zone for a twenty-nine man invasion force," I said.

"A reasonable conclusion given the facts," Haley said.

"You got anything else for me?" I said.

"I do, but first I have to ask you something," Haley said.

"Okay," I said.

"How come you haven't asked me yet if I know who the donors are behind Doctors of Mercy?" Haley said.

"Good question," I said. "Maybe because I just got up from being dead for seven minutes?"

"Seven minutes?" Haley said. "That sounds like it might be a record."

"My record is twelve, but I'm glad you're so concerned about me," I said.

"Oh, sorry," Haley said. "Are you okay?"

"Yes," I said. "Thanks for asking. Do you mind if I ask you a question, now?"

"Shoot," Haley said.

"Who are the donors behind Doctors of Mercy?" I said.

Haley smiled.

"Don't know yet," Haley said. "But I'll tell you when I do."

"I'm sure you will," I said.

"As for your 'anything else,'" Haley said, "as far as we can tell there's no back door for NASAD's computer system, but we will keep looking for it. We haven't yet been able to identify Dr. Nemo, any of the other dark programmers, the NASAD vice president of dark programming, or determine the dark programmers' location. Tracing the dark programmers' payroll transfers was a good idea, but, as one would expect from NASAD, the system used to keep those transfers hidden from the outside world is so sophisticated that it seems like it's going to be a wild goose chase. I don't want to waste any more precious resources on that angle at this time. There may be some interesting information on Bryce Wellington's relationship to the colonel who was the NASAD defense department liaison three years ago, and there is definitely something fishy about the way Carter Bowdoin came by his Worldwide Challenge Poker bracelet, but I'm waiting for confirmation on each of those items."

"I assume there's also no progress on cracking Dr. Nemo's code?" I said.

"It's a tough one, Jack," Haley said. "I think it will take a miracle to get it done before war breaks out."

"Not great news," I said. "But also not unexpected. Did you find anything to support my theory that a dark programmer might have switched over to the defensive team in the Cyber Defense Hall?"

"Nothing on that yet either," Haley said. "What are you doing next?"

"Joining up with Adelaide and Jeff," I said.

"They're down there in Malibu with you?" Haley said.

"Yep," I said.

"The 'A' team," Haley said.

"Maybe in an alternate universe," I said.

"Good luck," Haley said.

"Same to you, my love," I said. "Oh, wait."

"Yes?" Haley said.

"Carpenter's sending you a cell phone I took off one of the snipers at the NASAD site," I said.

"A cell phone?" Haley said. "You didn't mention a cell phone in the text you sent me."

"Sorry, I'm not running on all cylinders," I said.

"Oh, right, I forgot," Haley said. "You were dead for seven minutes."

"I hope that's it," I said.

"What's on the phone?" Haley said.

"The screen is cracked and frozen, but it shows a picture of Dragon Man," I said. "I believe he was using a Chinese FaceTime-like app to watch the attempted assassination of Kate at the site. I'm hoping you can determine what his location was at the time of the attempt by tracking the cell phone's signal."

"We 'll certainly give it a try," Haley said. "I'll call you if we find out where he was."

We both clicked off.

I walked on until I found the path at the end of the grassy patch that Carpenter had told me about. I followed the path between Freddy's and Kate's houses toward the beach. Kate's house had been blocking my view of the cliff's edge and when I passed her house I saw not only the edge, but Manu and Mosi standing next to it.

The giant Samoan twins were dressed in shiny cobalt colored suits, white shirts, and blue ties. The brothers had binoculars they were training up at the sky. Following the angle of their gaze, I saw what they were probably looking at - the third hang glider, which was then at least fifteen hundred feet high and moving farther out to sea.

I approached Manu and Mosi. They must have been very interested in the hang glider's progress, as they never took their eyes off it, even when I got right up next to them.

"Looks like you boys really love hang gliding, huh?" I said.

The twins startled and dropped their binoculars, the binoculars bouncing at the end of the lanyards the twins wore around their necks. The Samoans' massive bodies may even have twitched a bit, which was not exactly a pretty sight in three hundred and fifty pound men.

Mosi appeared to regain his composure the quicker of the two.

"Hi, General," Mosi said. "You're back sooner than we expected."

"Is that a good or a bad thing?" I said.

"Uh...," Mosi stammered.

"Interesting," I said. "Is there some kind of problem I'm not aware of?"

Manu said, "No sir, of course not, sir. We're happy to see you, sir."

"Good," I said. "You had me worried there for a moment."

"Nothing to worry about, sir," Manu said.

"Except for the 'sir' part," I said.

"Sir?" Manu said.

"Remember we talked about not calling me 'sir'?" I said.

"Yes, sir," Manu said. "I'm sorry, sir, I..."

"Enough. You're just making it worse," I said. "I'm going down to meet Jeff and Adelaide at the beach. Did you say hello to them when they got here?"

Manu and Mosi looked at each other. They might have twitched again. The twitch wasn't any more attractive the second time. Neither one spoke.

"Sorry, I guess that question must have been harder than I thought it was," I said.

Mosi stammered again, "No, it was not hard. We did say hello to them."

"Good," I said. "I thought perhaps Jeff might take this opportunity to teach Adelaide how to surf. Is that what they're doing?"

The twins shook their heads.

"They just went for a swim then?" I said.

They shook their heads again.

"Do you know what they did?" I said.

The twins looked at each other again. They seemed to share a tele-pathic moment. Manu gestured with his eyes at Mosi in a manner that seemed to say, 'You tell him.' Mosi shook his head. Manu glared at him. Mosi shook his head again. Manu sighed, and said in a barely audible mumble, "Adelaide said not to tell you."

"Said not to tell me what?" I said.

Both men in unison sheepishly raised their right arms, extended their index fingers, and pointed at the sky. I followed their fingers. They were pointing at the hang glider.

"What?!" I screamed.

I grabbed the binoculars from around Mosi's head and focused on the hang glider. It had risen another few hundred feet and was then almost two thousand feet above me. It was definitely Adelaide hanging from the harness.

Mosi said, "Adelaide said she was an expert hang glider."

"Adelaide's never been on a hang glider in her life!" I said.

CHAPTER 74

Adelaide's hang glider rose higher into the sky and flew farther out to sea.

Mosi said, "How were we supposed to know that?"

Manu said, "She said you said it was okay."

Keeping the binoculars locked on Adelaide, I said, "Where'd she get it?"

"The hang glider?" Manu said.

"Yes, the hang glider," I said. "What else could I possibly mean?"

"You can rent them in the Malibu Village Mall," Manu said.

"They just rent to anybody?" I said. "They don't demand some kind of certificate of training?"

Mosi said, "Adelaide had one."

"Adelaide had a certificate of training?" I said.

"Yes," Mosi said. "She had a United States Hang Gliding and Paragliding Association certificate that said she was an H5."

"What's an H5?" I said.

"A master hang glider," Mosi said.

I lowered the binoculars from my face and stared at the twins. An idea came to me that would explain how Adelaide had become an 'H5'.

"Did Adelaide have her computer with her when she got here?" I said.

"Yes," Mosi said.

"She didn't happen to ask to borrow a printer, did she?" I said.

"We let her use one in the library," Mosi said.

Manu said, "She wanted to print her certificate."

I said, "How long did it take her to print it?"

"About fifteen minutes," Manu said.

"That didn't strike you as odd?" I said.

Mosi said, "It did seem like kind of a long time."

"Do you want me to tell you why it took so long?" I said.

Both twins nodded.

"Adelaide has excellent computer skills," I said. "She was forging the certificate."

The twins looked confused.

Manu said, "You mean she's not an 'H5'?"

"She's a zero!" I said.

Mosi said, "Uh oh."

"'Uh oh' is right," I said.

I looked back up at Adelaide. Her flight path was taking her closer and closer to the estate. I checked on the FBI rooftop snipers. They were still tracking her.

"You two told the FBI it's Adelaide on the hang glider, right?" I said to Manu and Mosi.

I didn't get a response.

"You told them, right?" I repeated.

They both looked shamefaced.

"For chrissakes!" I said.

It was over three hundred yards back to Kate's house. I sprinted towards the house, my head spinning and knee in agony. When I finally reached it, my lungs were burning and heaving. I bent over with my hands on my knees and tried to force myself to both breathe and speak at the same time as my face craned upward at FBI snipers on the roof. The snipers looked at me as if I'd gone crazy.

"Don't shoot!" I yelled.

One of the snipers came to the roof's edge. The other two kept a bead on Adelaide.

"We'd only shoot you if we thought you were some kind of threat, General," the FBI sniper at the edge of the roof said. "Are you some kind of threat?"

I thought I detected a smirk. I ignored it.

"Not me," I said. "Her!"

"Her?" the FBI sniper said.

"The girl in the hang glider," I said.

"You know the target?" the sniper said.

"Don't call her that!" I said.

Overhead, Adelaide was rapidly approaching the eastern border of the estate.

"No one's allowed in the airspace over the compound," the sniper said.

"She's a friendly," I said. "She's my ward."

"Seems like your ward could use a little discipline," the sniper said.

"This is no time for jokes," I said.

"Snipers aren't allowed to have a sense of humor?" the sniper said.

I didn't respond. The other two FBI snipers lowered their rifles and joined the first sniper at the roof's edge.

The second sniper to arrive said, "Don't worry, sir, we would never shoot the ward of a former Delta commander."

"You were Delta, Agent?" I said.

"The three of us up here were Marines, sir," the second sniper said.

"Damn," I said. "I've just been wasting my breath haven't I?"

"Sir?" the second sniper said.

"All three of you would have missed anyway," I said.

The snipers laughed. The second sniper took out his walkie talkie.

"You want me to call the guys on the other roof and the commander of the Coast Guard cutter?" the second sniper said.

"If you would be so kind," I said.

I waved goodbye to the snipers and walked towards the cliff. I was in far worse physical shape than I was before I'd started my sprint back to Kate's house. My head felt like someone was taking a jackhammer to it, my knee felt like there was a molten dagger in it, and I wanted to throw up.

When I reached the cliff, Manu and Mosi were again watching Adelaide. She was well above 2,000 feet and had drifted over the estate. I didn't think there was much that I could do except keep an eye on her and hope she landed safely. The wind was blowing inland and, as long as it continued to do so, I assumed Adelaide wouldn't be in too much danger. If the wind shifted and started blowing Adelaide even farther out to sea, however...well, I didn't want to think about that.

I gave Manu and Mosi a cursory nod and looked out over the edge of the cliff. Jeff was down below. He was wearing neon green Hurley board shorts, and surfing the waves on a bright yellow surfboard. Jeff and I had learned how to surf when we were on R&R in the Mentawai Islands of Indonesia. Jeff was a better surfer than me, and even though neither of us had surfed in more than five years, Jeff didn't look rusty at all. He was carving in and out of the curls, hanging ten, and wheeling 360's.

I had heard the local Malibu surfers could be very territorial and would do almost anything - up to, and including, physical assault - to drive off interlopers. I scanned the waves, but saw no other surfers within a quarter mile. Which wasn't surprising considering the Coast Guard was patrolling the area and had probably kept any unwanted visitors at bay. I sort of hoped there had been some local surfers in the immediate vicinity, however, because it would have been very entertaining to see a local, or better yet, a gang of locals, try to drive off General Jeff Bradshaw.

A rickety wood stairwell led to the beach below. The stairwell's wood was weathered, and deeply grooved from years of salt spray, sun, and wind. The stairwell hugged the cliff and jogged back and forth in three places on its way to the bottom. Plants sporting red and yellow flowers grew in clumps in the dirt of the cliff. My head throbbing and knee burning, I stepped very gingerly down the stairs, slowly taking them one by one, and clinging to the railing much more fixedly than I care to admit. I reached the bottom stair, stepped onto the sand, sat down, and took my shoes and socks off. It had been years since I had been on a beach, and I enjoyed the feeling of the sand between my toes as much as my headache and nausea allowed.

The beach was crescent shaped. It was bounded on one side by the base of the cliff where the cliff jutted out to sea, and on the other side by a huge rock. A three hundred pound sea lion sunning himself on the rock barked when he saw me. Some seagulls cawed as they hovered above the beach. A pod of a dozen or so pelicans flew in a line as they headed south over the ocean about a quarter mile from shore. The pelicans moved in a sine wave pattern, rising and falling, rising and falling, their wings seeming to almost touch the surface of the sea at the low point of their flight.

Jeff was just outside the surf break, his legs straddling the board. The Coast Guard cutter rocked in the waves about fifty yards farther out to sea. Two coast guardsmen had their binoculars trained on Adelaide. The guardsmen were smiling, which led me to believe they weren't about to shoot down Adelaide anytime soon.

"Hi," a voice said from somewhere behind me.

I turned around.

A slim, tan, long-legged, gorgeous red-headed woman was sitting on a towel behind me. She looked to be in her early twenties and had incredibly large breasts that were barely covered by a tiny yellow bikini top. Her yellow bikini bottom was so small it barely covered anything at all. Jeff's running shoes and his Shoemaker t-shirt were on the sand next to her. I had missed seeing the woman until she called out to me because she had tucked herself away in a cave-like alcove at the bottom of the cliff. I didn't see anyone else nearby, however, and I assumed the Coast Guard, for eminently understandable reasons, had probably made an exception for the woman and allowed her access within their security perimeter.

"Hi," I said.

"My name's Christa," the woman said. "What's yours?"

"Jack," I said.

Christa pointed at Jeff.

"Jeff a friend of yours?" Christa said.

It seemed Jeff hadn't wasted any time acquainting himself with the natives.

"How'd you know?" I said.

Christa smiled a wide smile that was both welcoming and wicked at the same time.

"You've both got the same aura," Christa said.

"What kind of aura is that, Christa?" I said.

"You look like you both could be movie stars," Christa said, "but you'd rather kill people instead."

"You always been this perceptive?" I said.

Christa laughed a deep throaty laugh.

"It helped that Jeff told me he was a general," Christa said. "Are you a general too, Jack?"

"Yes," I said.

"I'm having a party tonight at my house," Christa said.

She pointed at a very large, modern house on the beach about a quarter mile south of us.

"Nice house," I said.

"My daddy gave it to me," Christa said.

"Nice daddy," I said.

Christa laughed again.

"The party is for generals only," Christa said. "Want to come?"

"Maybe I better clear that with Jeff first," I said.

"Okay," Christa said. "Are you going to ask him now?"

"Good idea," I said.

I turned around and walked down to the surf line. I rolled up my pant legs and entered the water, stopping when the high point of the waves came up to my calves. When the water receded, it left little liquid-filled gorges next to my feet. I watched as sand crabs hurriedly burrowed into the sand, leaving bubbles and tiny pinholes in their wake.

I waved to Jeff.

"I heard there was a meeting here of the Malibu African American Surfing Club," I shouted over the roar of the breaking waves.

"You got an invitation?" Jeff yelled back.

I searched in my pockets.

"Must've left it at home," I said.

"You African American?" Jeff said.

"No," I said. "But I have a friend who is."

"How good of friends are you?" Jeff said.

"Pretty good," I said.

"Alright," Jeff said. "You can join."

"How many other members does the club have?" I said.

"Now you in, we got two," Jeff said.

Jeff caught a wave and rode it all the way to the beach. He grabbed his surfboard and headed for dry sand. I followed him.

"Rad waves," I said.

"Too bad that ranch of yours ain't worth a lot more money," Jeff said.

"Why is that?" I said.

"If it was, we could sell it and buy a place down here," Jeff said.

"Thought you liked the Sierras," I said.

"Just saying," Jeff said.

"We got seagulls in the Sierras," I said. "Same ones as here."

"Oh yeah, forgot," Jeff said. "Guess that makes your place cool then."

Christa walked up next to us. She gave Jeff a peck on the cheek.

"Gotta go," Christa said. "My yoga instructor is waiting for me at the house. See you boys tonight."

Christa set off for the house she had earlier pointed out to me. The view of Christa from behind was as spectacular as from the front. Especially the back of her bikini. I had never seen anything quite like it before. It was made out of just a few thin strips of yellow fringe.

"Nice girl," I said.

"Daddy's a billionaire," Jeff said.

"I figured that was the case," I said.

"He owns a bunch of soccer teams in Europe," Jeff said. "You coming to her party?"

"I wouldn't want to intrude on whatever the two of you have planned," I said.

"Yeah," Jeff said. "New missus probably wouldn't like it either."

"The new missus?" I said.

"That angel lady who looks just like Grace," Jeff said.

"Dr. Lennon?" I said.

"Um-hmm," Jeff said.

"Aren't you being a bit premature?" I said.

"Not according to what those snipers told me," Jeff said.

"You always believe everything a sniper tells you?" I said.

"I do if they telling the truth," Jeff said.

I sat down on the sand facing the sea and drew up my knees in front of me. Jeff put the surfboard down, and laid next to me, resting the back of his head on the sand. Small beads of water ran off his chest and legs onto the sand. We both looked up at Adelaide cruising the sky on her hang glider.

"You think that's as dangerous as it looks?" I said.

"Been watching her," Jeff said. "Adelaide knows what she's doing."

"Can't tell you how reassuring that is coming from a man with zero hang gliding experience," I said.

"It don't look that hard," Jeff said.

"What if the wind shifts, blows her out to sea?" I said.

"Hasn't shifted yet," Jeff said.

I rolled over on my stomach and propped myself up on my elbows. I figured I'd probably feel better if I couldn't see Adelaide.

Jeff said, "So, you solve the mystery yet?"

"I was just going to ask you the same thing," I said.

"You the one down here stumbling onto all the clues," Jeff said.

"Lot has happened since I talked to you yesterday," I said.

"You gonna tell me about it?" Jeff said.

"Yes," I said.

I told Jeff how I'd discovered that Milt Feynman and Paul Lennon's plane crash in Alaska had been made to look like an accident, but had actually been a meticulously planned murder. I told him about the Kazakh and Afghan mercenaries landing in Pixley on the Doctors of Mercy plane, and how the same radar mislocating technology was probably used to disguise that plane's flight path as had been used to mislead the searchers looking for Feynman and Lennon's Otter. I apprised him of the fact that we had yet to find any connection among the twelve murdered NASAD engineering project managers other than that the managers were all working on the drone sub project. I told him about Carter Bowdoin and the gambling on the outcome of the NASAD war games going on between NASAD's dark programmers and the programmers in the Cyber Defense Hall, how Dr. Nemo was probably a dark programmer, and that the next NASAD war games were slated to commence a week from Friday, which was the same day Hart believed China would start their war in the Middle East. I told him that I had a hunch that Nemo and the NASAD dark programmers had developed a war games software that could be used to conduct an attack on the U.S. military's computer systems, that that software might actually turn out to be the Chinese insurmountable edge, and that while Nemo was our top priority, Haley was also searching for any other dark programmer to talk to about the edge. I advised him about what Mary Beth had said to me regarding NASAD's young genius program and Paul Lennon's involvement with it. I also told him there was a chance that Mary Beth might be able to arrange for me to communicate with the NASAD vice president of dark programming - who was the executive in charge of the dark programming division - but only if Mary Beth could somehow get by the security protocols that kept nearly everyone at NASAD from contacting that executive, and that I would only communicate with the vice president if he could be deemed worthy of our trust. I said that if indeed the dark programmers' war games software turned out to be the insurmountable edge, it didn't appear to have activated yet, as the military's computer systems were all functioning normally. I described the Kazakh sniper attack at the NASAD drone sub manufacturing site and my suspicions that Carter Bowdoin may have known about the attack in advance. I showed him the photo stored on my iPhone depicting the frozen image of Dragon Man that had been on the cracked screen of the cell phone belonging to one of the dead Kazakh snipers at the NASAD site. Lastly, I explained to Jeff how I'd sent Haley that same Kazakh's damaged cell phone to see if Haley could find out where Dragon Man had been located while he was using the Chinese FaceTime-like app with the Kazakh sniper during the attack at the drone sub site.

When I was finished, Jeff said, "How many computers you think the U.S. military got?"

"Millions," I said.

"Sounds right," Jeff said. "All them computers operating on a lot of different networks aren't they?"

"I'm sure they are," I said.

"Military also got computers inside tens of thousands, if not hundreds of thousands, of different devices, don't they?" Jeff said.

"You mean like in missiles, planes, satellites, tanks, and warships?" I said.

"Yeah," Jeff said.

"Your questions are good ones," I said. "They also appear to suggest we're both wondering about the same thing."

"As in how Dr. Nemo, even though he be a genius and all, design a software weapon that's going to make a successful attack on all those millions of computers at once? Jeff said.

"Yes," I said. "Doesn't it seem like it would be a nearly impossible task to build a weapon that could simultaneously attack not only every computer we have on every network, but also every computer in every one of our missiles, planes, satellites, tanks, and warships? Especially considering that at the time of that attack those missiles, planes, satellites, tanks, and warships could be almost anywhere on land or sea, in the air, or orbiting the earth?"

"Impossible be putting it mildly," Jeff said. "On the other hand, if Nemo's software weapon really can do all that simultaneous attackin', then it truly be insurmountable."

"Agreed," I said, "Still, it seems implausible."

"Except for one very serious mitigating factor, of course," Jeff said.

"The Chinese?" I said.

"Um-hmm," Jeff said. "Chinese look like they be building their whole war plan around Nemo and the dark programmers' war games weapon, so somehow the Chinese absolutely convinced it works."

A great blue heron, seemingly coming from out of nowhere, dive-bombed through the sky and shot beneath the sea. A moment later it reappeared on the water's surface with a fish clutched in its beak.

"Maybe it isn't so implausible, then?" I said. "Maybe the main problem is our imaginations can't encompass it yet?"

"If that be the case, we better fix our imaginations quick," Jeff said.

"Otherwise, hundreds of thousands of our troops are going to die," I said.

"Not on our watch," Jeff said.

"Perhaps now would be a good time to give some thought as to how Nemo's war games weapon might be able to accomplish such a seemingly impossible task?" I said.

"No time like the present," Jeff said.

"A thousand unforeseen circumstances may interrupt you at a future time," I said.

"Didn't know you knew that how that go," Jeff said.

"Clearly I did," I said.

We were both quiet. A few minutes went by.

"You come up with anything?" I said.

"Nope," Jeff said.

"Probably has to marinate in our minds," I said.

"Yeah," Jeff said. "Let's give it some time. Next subject then. Hand me your cell phone."

I gave Jeff my phone. He studied the photo I had taken of Dragon Man on the Kazakh sniper's cracked cell phone screen.

"This photo cut off," Jeff said. "It don't show the dragon mask's feet and claws. You ever be asking Bobby and Timmy how many claws the dragon mask has?"

"Sorry," I said. "I forgot you asked me to do that."

"That because you be dead for seven minutes?" Jeff said.

"Probably," I said. "I'll text Vandross right now and ask him to set up a call with Bobby and Timmy."

I wrote the text to Vandross and hit the arrow to send it. It didn't go through.

"Huh," I said. "The text won't send."

"Maybe we in a texting dead zone," Jeff said.

"Yeah," I said. "Could be the cliff is in the way. I'll send it later."

I deleted the text.

"You don't need to delete it," Jeff said. "It will send itself next time the signal is good."

"It should," I said. "But sometimes it doesn't. Safer if I text him next time we're up on the estate."

"Don't forget again," Jeff said.

"I won't," I said. "By the way, what makes you so sure the mask has feet and claws?"

"This kind of mask always has feet and claws on the bottom of it," Jeff said. "You know how you never see the Sphinx without its feet? This be the same thing."

A wave rolled up and over our own feet. Something about the air around us suddenly seemed to change. I couldn't quite put my finger on what the change was, but it gave me a chill down my spine.

"Why are the number of claws so important?" I said.

"I told you before it better if you don't know," Jeff said. "I don't want you influencing Bobby and Timmy when you talk to them."

"Come on," I said. "I'm not going to influence them. Besides, it's better if you tell me so we're both on the same page about this. What if I've seen something that could be related to how many claws there are, but didn't know it was important since you didn't tell me what I should be looking for?"

Jeff stared at me for a moment.

"You never seen that mask other than in this picture, right?" Jeff said.

"Right," I said.

"And they aren't any claws in the picture, right?" Jeff said.

"Right," I said.

"So where the hell you gonna be seeing anything else related to how many claws the mask has?" Jeff said.

"I don't know," I said. "But I could have."

"You full on crazy," Jeff said.

"You know it's possible," I said.

Jeff rolled his eyes.

"I'm sure I'm going to regret this, since I know what you're saying is complete and utter bullshit," Jeff said. "But I don't think I can take a chance you're right, even though that chance probably be one in a quadrillion."

"Exactly," I said. "Because if you don't tell me, and I'm right, I'll never let you forget it."

"I know you wouldn't," Jeff said. "What's important about the number of claws is whether it be four or five."

"Could it be another number?" I said. "Like three or six?"

"Nope," Jeff said. "Chinese dragon mask only got feet with either four or five claws. Four claws be for commoners."

"Who is five for?" I said.

"The emperor," Jeff said.

"Only for the emperor?" I said.

"Yep," Jeff said.

"Emperor would be interesting," I said. "Emperor of what, though?"

"I don't know," Jeff said. "China. World."

"How about Saudi Arabia?" I said.

"That fit," Jeff said. "Saudi Arabia got kings. Maybe Dragon Man think they need an emperor instead."

My iPhone rang. It was Hart requesting FaceTime again.

"It's Hart," I said to Jeff. "He just called ten minutes ago."

"Never seen Hart call that fast after he just hung up," Jeff said.

"Usually a day, half a day minimum," I said.

"Must be important," Jeff said.

"One would think so," I said.

"You gonna answer it?" Jeff said.

"Probably should," I said.

I pushed the answer button. It appeared that Hart had moved off the landing deck of the USS Washington and onto its tower instead. The wind was ravaging his hair and his skin looked even more green.

"General," I said to the screen.

"What took you so long to answer?" Hart said.

Jeff said, "It's because we were wondering why you be calling back so soon."

"Is that Jeff?" Hart said.

I turned the iPhone camera at Jeff.

"Good day, General Hart, sir," Jeff said.

"Great to see you, Jeff," Hart said. "You on board with this mission now?"

"Yes, sir," Jeff said.

"You sure you're up to it?" Hart said.

"Never been more sure of anything in my life, sir," Jeff said.

"Good to hear," Hart said. "You look like you've been surfing."

"Indeed I do," Jeff said.

Hart seemed a little confused by that answer, but apparently decided to let it slide.

I positioned the iPhone so that we could all see each other.

"What's up, General?" I said to Hart.

"The Chinese keep upping the ante," Hart said. "Three more Chinese aircraft carriers are steaming towards the Persian Gulf and seventy more Chinese fighter planes just landed at a Chinese airbase in Iraq."

Jeff said, "Looks like it's gonna be a pretty big conflagration, huh, General?"

Hart said, "That's one way to put it."

"Don't worry, General," Jeff said. "There ain't gonna be no war."

"I think I'd feel better about that statement if the two of you were actually doing something useful, rather than just sunning yourselves on the beach," Hart said

"This be where we do our best thinking," Jeff said.

"Is that so?" Hart said.

"It's so," Jeff said. "And it just so happens Jack and I were discussing the situation when you called. Everything's under control, sir."

I hit the mute button on my iPhone's microphone.

"Are you out of your mind?" I said to Jeff.

"You know I hate rhetorical questions," Jeff said.

Hart said, "I just talked to Jack a few minutes ago. He didn't say anything about being close to a solution."

Jeff pointed a finger at the cell. I took that to mean Jeff wanted me to unmute the microphone.

"No way," I said.

"Yes way," Jeff said.

Hart said, "I can't hear what you boys are saying. Can you hear me?"

Another wave crashed on the shore and rolled up and over our feet.

Jeff said to me, "Unmute that sucker. Hart just gonna get suspicious when he sees us keep talking but doesn't hear anything."

I said, "I'll unmute it only if you promise to keep your mouth shut."

"I got this dude, trust me," Jeff said.

I gave Jeff a hard look.

"I got it," Jeff said. "Now chill."

Did I really want Jeff to talk to Hart? No. But I didn't want to talk to Hart either. And since it was Jeff who had put his foot in his mouth, shouldn't he be the one to take it out again?

"Good luck," I said to Jeff. "It's your funeral."

I unmuted the phone.

Jeff said, "Think we lost the audio connection there for a minute, General. Where were we?"

"I was saying that Jack hadn't said anything about things being under control," Hart said.

"That's because Jack hadn't talked with me yet," Jeff said. "We figured out who behind everything, now we just gotta nail his ass."

"You know who it is?" Hart said.

"Yes, sir, we do," Jeff said. "He's a little Asian dude in a dragon mask."

"What?!?!" I screamed as loud as I could. I kept my mouth closed, however, so the sound came out my nose.

Jeff put his right index finger to his lips.

"Shhh," Jeff said.

Hart said, "Did you say something Jack?"

"I just sneezed, sir," I said.

"Bless you," Hart said. "Do you know the little Asian dude's name, Jeff?"

"Haley working on it for us right now," Jeff said.

"Is that true, Jack?" Hart said.

I glared at Jeff. Jeff gave me his 'don't you let me down now asshole' look.

I said, "It will be true very soon, sir."

"What the hell does that mean?" Hart said.

The sea lion on the rock gave a loud bark. He then jumped off the rock, slid effortlessly beneath the ocean waves, and disappeared.

"I just sent Haley a cell phone," I said. "It's a cell phone that the Asian man in the dragon mask was connected to during the attack at the NASAD drone sub site. The man in the mask appears to have been directing the attack. Once Haley gets the phone and helps us locate this man, we should be able to quickly wrap this up."

"Quick is right," Hart said. "We have less than ten days left."

"Believe me, no one is more aware of that than I am, sir," I said.

Hart suddenly appeared to take his attention off of us and focus lower down on his cell phone screen instead.

"Shit," Hart said.

"Sir?" I said.

"The president is calling me," Hart said. "You two solid on this man in the dragon mask thing?"

Jeff said, "We're solid, sir."

"Good," Hart said. "I'll tell the president about it. He'll be happy we're making progress. Gotta go."

Hart clicked off.

I turned to Jeff.

"Great work, dickwad," I said.

"You ain't worried about the president are you?" Jeff said.

The pelicans that had been flying south in a sine wave pattern low over the ocean a little while before, had circled back and were then flying north in the same pattern about fifty yards out to sea from us.

"No, of course not," I said. "Why would I be worried about you putting our asses on the line with the president of the United States with some bullshit story about some little Asian dude?"

"Had to tell Hart something," Jeff said. "He looked all stressed out and green and everything. I didn't want him to have a heart attack."

"Hart's just seasick," I said.

"You a doctor now?" Jeff said.

"What if it's not an Asian dude?" I said.

"Didn't Timmy say guy at the stoning site was wearing a Chinese dragon mask?" Jeff said.

"He did," I said.

"Timmy also said guy in mask spoke with a Chinese accent, right?" Jeff said.

"Timmy said that, yes," I said.

"Wouldn't you agree it highly doubtful whoever been doing all of this regard himself as a commoner?" Jeff said. "That it much more likely he believes he destined to be an emperor?"

"I could see that," I said.

"Trust me, if this guy wearin' a Chinese dragon mask, speakin' with a Chinese accent, and wants to be emperor, he Asian," Jeff said.

The Coast Guard cutter pulled in close to us and came to a stop just outside the wave break. The crests of the waves surrounding the cutter were being blown back towards the sea and the ripples on the sea's surface were also moving away from the shore. With a sinking feeling I realized what it was that had changed earlier about the air and given me that chill down my spine. The wind had changed direction, and instead of blowing inland, was blowing out to sea.

A coast guardsman on the cutter holding a bullhorn maneuvered his way along the deck until he was looking directly at Jeff and me. Seeing he had our attention, the guardsman shouted through the bullhorn, "General Wilder, I think you better take a look at this." He then jabbed a finger at the sky.

I followed the line of his jab and found Adelaide and the hang glider at the end of it. Adelaide and the glider had been blown more than three miles out to sea and were descending in a corkscrew spiral to the ocean below.

CHAPTER 75

"We're going to pick up your girl," the guardsman said through the bullhorn. "You gentlemen want to come along?"

"We'll be right there," I said.

Jeff grabbed his surfboard and ran into the waves. I stripped off my shirt, dashed off right behind him, and sprinted through the first ten yards of low water. I was about to dive under a breaking wave when I suddenly remembered I had my MOM iPhone in my pants pocket and put on the brakes. MOM iPhones are supposed to be waterproof but they're souped-up to the tune of a hundred thousand smackers over the ones normal citizens can buy and I didn't think it was worth the risk of swimming with it. I also couldn't risk leaving it on the beach where it could get stolen.

"Hey, Jeff," I yelled. "I need your board."

"What you mean you need my board?" Jeff said.

"I have my MOM phone in my pocket," I said.

"So swim with it holding your hand above your head," Jeff said.

"I'll never get to the cutter in time," I said.

"I got my MOM phone too," Jeff said. "One of us has to swim."

"Why does it have to be me?" I said.

"It's my board," Jeff said.

Which made sense.

But I still didn't have time to swim.

"Let me ride with you," I said.

"You serious?" Jeff said.

"What's wrong with that?" I said.

"Two dudes on a surfboard?" Jeff said. "That ain't cool, man."

"Who's gonna see?" I said.

"Those boys on the boat," Jeff said.

"When did you start giving a damn about what other people think?" I said.

"You got a point," Jeff said.

Jeff paddled back to me, and I jumped on the front of the surfboard and kneeled down. Jeff kneeled down on the back of the board and we both started paddling with our hands. We looked really uncool.

Two minutes later we were aside the cutter where a ladder had been lowered to the water. The guardsman who had called out to us reached down, gave us each a hand in turn, and hauled us aboard. The guardsman was a solidly built five foot ten, blue-eyed, had a blond crew cut beneath a black Coast Guard baseball style cap, and wore an orange life preserver over his royal blue shirt and pants. 'William Turner' was spelled out on his name tag and the two red stripes on the insignia on his sleeve marked him as a chief petty officer. There were five other similarly dressed men aboard, one of whom was manning a 50 caliber machine gun on the front deck.

As soon as we were aboard, Turner pulled up the ladder and the ship's pilot gunned the engines. The cutter took off towards Adelaide, the boat quickly accelerating into the faces of the oncoming waves. Turner handed both Jeff and me a towel and a life preserver.

"Sorry about the preservers, sir," Turner said. "Regulations. Can the girl swim?"

"Like a fish," I said.

"Good," Turner said. "She might need to. We're about ten minutes from her likely position at touchdown."

Jeff said, "Officer Turner, is it true they have great white sharks in the bay?"

I said, "What the hell, Jeff!"

"Just asking," Jeff said.

Turner said, "There are some, General Bradshaw. But your girl would have to get real unlucky to find a great white in the short amount of time it should take us to reach her once she hits the water. Of course, if we have to turn back before we reach her, the risk would go up."

I said, "Turn back?"

"We'd only do that if the FBI calls and tells us they need us," Turner said. "Protecting the estate, after all, is our primary operational objective."

I think Jeff sensed I was about to strangle Turner. He jumped between Turner and me, then shoved me aside.

Jeff said, "Officer Turner, I don't mean any disrespect, but you have two U.S. Army generals on this boat."

"I'm aware of that, sir," Turner said.

"I think we got a little better understanding of combat tactics than the FBI, don't you?" Jeff said.

"You won't get any argument from me on that, sir," Turner said.

"You see that cliff there, Turner?" Jeff said, pointing back at the cliff below Freddy and Kate's estate.

"Yes, sir," Turner said.

"I appreciate you patrolling the seas and all," Jeff said, "but anyone dumb enough to try and scale that cliff gonna get their head blown off by the FBI the moment they peek over the top of it."

"I can believe that, sir," Turner said.

"Plus I'm pretty sure that a U.S. Army general outrank the FBI," Jeff said.

"I don't doubt that, sir," Turner said.

"So you see my point," Jeff said.

Turner looked confused.

"Sorry, sir," Turner said. "I'm not sure I do."

"Maybe you'll understand this, then," Jeff said, and then, yelling at the top of his lungs, added, "They ain't no goddamned way in hell we are turning back without the girl! You got that?!"

Turner recoiled. He seemed quite frightened by Jeff's outburst. Which didn't surprise me, since I'd seen many a serviceman cower under Jeff's withering reprimands for behavior, that Jeff, to put it delicately, considered less than adequate. Turner, to his credit, seemed to quickly recover.

"Yes, sir," Turner said. "I'm sorry, sir. I've got it, sir. I'll go and tell the commander and make sure he understands as well, sir."

"You do that," Jeff said.

Turner left.

I said, "Thank you, General Bradshaw."

"You're welcome," Jeff said.

Jeff and I grabbed the rails and walked to the front of the boat. We sat down on top of the forward cabin about ten feet behind the gunner. The almost deafening whine of the engines, along with the boat's violent bouncing on the roiling sea, did nothing to improve my headache and nausea. I kept my eyes glued on Adelaide as we sped towards her. She was about five hundred feet above the ocean and continuing to spiral down.

"Thanks again for handling that," I said to Jeff.

"Actually, I'll be just as happy if Adelaide gets eaten by a great white," Jeff said. "But I figure that mess you up so bad, mission might suffer."

"True," I said.

"So, what's the plan?" Jeff said.

"We pick up Adelaide and bring her back to the beach," I said.

"I mean the big plan," Jeff said.

"To stop World War III?" I said.

"Uh huh," Jeff said.

I gestured with my chin at the gunner in front of us.

"He can't hear anything," Jeff said. "Hell, I can barely hear you over all those redlining engines and waves and shit."

"I'll buy that," I said. "The plan is to keep working on what I've been working on."

"Which be?" Jeff said.

"Looking for Dr. Nemo, or any other dark programmer, to talk to, trying to crack Nemo's code, and running down Dragon Man," I said.

"There's a problem with that," Jeff said.

"What's the problem?" I said.

"Intangibilityness," Jeff said. "Etherealitytiousness."

"Are those words?" I said.

"You know what I mean," Jeff said. "Never seen Nemo. Never seen no dark programmer. Nemo code invisible. All we got is a bad photo of Dragon Man."

"We have Bobby and Timmy's description," I said.

"Of a mask," Jeff said.

"What do you suggest we do then?" I said.

"Look at what we can see," Jeff said.

"Which is?" I said.

The boat went up the face of a huge wave. The bow went airborne then slammed down into the trough on the back side of the face. My brain hit the top of my skull on the upstroke and smacked into the base of my skull on the way down. It felt like someone was banging a sledgehammer inside my head. I saw stars.

"Bowdoin," Jeff said. "Lots of evidence pointing at him."

"All of it either vague or coincidental," I said. "We can't afford to waste time going down a wrong path."

"I don't think Bowdoin knowing where a sniper gonna shoot from coincidental," Jeff said.

My iPhone rang. I pulled it out of my pocket and looked at my screen. Haley was requesting FaceTime. I answered the call. Jeff peered over my shoulder at the screen.

"That woman always look fine," Jeff whispered into my ear.

Haley's big brown eyes got even bigger and her gorgeous lips turned up in a huge smile.

"My, my, my," Haley said. "Been a long time, handsome."

"Fifteen minutes," I said. "An eternity."

Jeff said, this time loud enough for Haley to hear, "I believe Major Haley be talking about me."

Haley said, "I most certainly was. Great to see you, Jeff."

"Great to see you, beautiful," Jeff said.

The cutter struck another huge wave. Jeff and I once again catapulted into the air and crashed back down.

"Where the hell are you two?" Haley said.

"At sea," Jeff said.

"World War III is set to commence in ten days and you boys are on a cruise?" Haley said.

I said, "Not exactly."

I pointed the iPhone camera at Adelaide and the hang glider spiraling down out of the sky.

"Is that a hang glider?" Haley said.

"Yes," I said. "And Adelaide's the pilot."

"Adelaide knows how to hang glide?" Haley said.

"No," I said.

Jeff said, "Adelaide making like Icarus. We're on a rescue mission."

Haley said, "Aren't there sharks in the Santa Monica Bay?"

"Great whites," Jeff said.

"Wow," Haley said. "Sounds dangerous."

I said, "It's not dangerous, since we're going to get to her before they do. And, as any further discussion on the topic of Adelaide and sharks is truly not going to be in any way helpful, I'll thank the two of you to cut it out." I turned the camera back around. "Now, what do you have for us, Haley?"

"Updates on Bowdoin and Wellington," Haley said. "Who do you want first?"

"Dealer's choice," I said.

"That's very apropos," Haley said.

"I thought it might be," I said.

"Carter Bowdoin then," Haley said. "Bowdoin is not the great card player he makes himself out to be. He won eight million dollars at the Worldwide Challenge Poker Championship, not due to his mastery of Texas Hold'em, but because he somehow managed to tap into the table camera feed that showed all the other players' cards for the television audience."

"I've seen that show," I said. "They've got tiny cameras mounted in the rim of the poker table, right?"

"Correct," Haley said. "It's more fun for the audience at home to see the cards since they can tell if the players are bluffing or actually holding good cards. The audience can also tell whether or not the players are making good decisions when they call, bet, or fold."

"One would think the camera feed system would have been protected by an incredible amount of security," I said.

"It's supposed to be," Haley said. "What the cameras show to the people at home is on a delay. Bowdoin had an accomplice who was able to intercept the video feed in real time and thus defeat the delay. The accomplice then communicated the information to Bowdoin by broadcasting pictures of Bowdoin's opponents' cards on the back of the lenses of sunglasses Bowdoin was wearing during the competition."

"How did you figure that out?" I said.

"There was a lot of internet chatter that something had significantly gone wrong with the competition, but no details," Haley said. "We started looking for those details and ultimately hacked copies of a secret settlement agreement between Bowdoin and the organizers of Worldwide Challenge Poker on their attorneys' servers."

"Bowdoin was caught, then?" I said.

"Yes," Haley said. "But the organizers thought it would be better for the game if they kept it secret. The fact Bowdoin also paid them thirty million to hush it up certainly helped as well."

"So Carter Bowdoin is a big time cheater," I said. "What about Bryce Wellington?"

"Your instinct Wellington had something to do with the NASAD military liaison at the time of Feynman's and Lennon's deaths three years ago was correct," Haley said.

The Coast Guard cutter slammed into an especially large roller and the jolt smashed my head against the cabin window. Spray from the collision ripped into my skin like needles.

"Who was the liaison?" I said.

"Colonel Riley Whitelock," Haley said.

"Never heard of him," I said.

"Whitelock, though this was never revealed in any of Whitelock's or Wellington's military records, was Wellington's godson," Haley said.

"Was?" I said. "How do you stop being a godson?"

"Die," Haley said.

"How'd he die?" I said.

"Car accident," Haley said.

"Come on," I said.

"I kid you not," Haley said. "One car accident. Whitelock was drunk and wrapped his car around a tree."

"When did this happen?" I said.

"When do you think it happened?" Haley said.

"Day after Feynman and Lennon's plane went down?" I said.

"Ta da!" Haley said. "Give the man a prize."

"That is seriously messed up," I said.

Jeff said, "For what it's worth, I never liked Bryce Wellington. He always been a candy-ass piece o' shit."

Haley said, "For the record, I never liked Wellington either. And after what Wellington did to you in the Sudan, Jeff, I can honestly say I hate him."

I said, "I don't think hate is quite a strong enough word."

"Loathe?" Haley said. "Despise?"

"What do you think, Jeff?" I said. "They strong enough?"

"They're okay," Jeff said. "Execrate probably best."

Haley said, "As in I execrate Bryce Wellington?"

"Uh huh," Jeff said.

"Execrate it is, then," Haley said. "I need to mention two more items."

I said, "Go ahead."

The cutter smashed into another roller. My head bounced off the cabin window again and more needle-like spray stung my skin.

"Item number one," Haley said. "Army files show that Wellington definitely got Whitelock the NASAD liaison job."

"Wellington probably assumed no one would ever find out Whitelock was his godson," I said.

Jeff said, "Tough luck for Wellington Major Marian Haley is the furthest thing from a no one there ever was."

Haley said, "Thank you, Jeff. Item number two. Whitelock was a teetotaler. He never drank alcohol in his life."

I said, "How did they explain that Whitelock was drunk when he crashed his car, then?"

"They never did," Haley said.

"Who handled the investigation?" I said.

"FBI," Haley said. "They were called in to investigate due to Colonel Whitelock's high-level national security clearance status. Guess who the lead FBI agent was?"

"No goddamn way," I said.

"Way," Haley said. "Burnette led it from start to finish."

"Have you found out how Burnette was assigned to the case?" I said.

"Not yet," Haley said. "But I will."

"Anything else?" I said.

"Nothing right now," Haley said.

"Thanks for your help," I said.

"Bye, boys," Haley said.

I looked up at the sky. Adelaide was still spiraling down. It looked to be about a fifty-fifty proposition that we would arrive at her most likely splashdown point before she did.

Jeff said, "Still think everything coincidental and vague in regard to Carter Bowdoin?"

I didn't say anything.

"Know what I think?" Jeff said. "I think you doubting yourself because you died today."

"Are you implying that would be a completely inappropriate response to death?" I said.

"Nope," Jeff said. "But it ain't germane. You seen what you seen."

A dolphin suddenly appeared on our starboard side. It was surfing the wake created by the cutter's bow. I had heard stories of dolphins protecting people from sharks. I hoped the dolphin would stay with us until we got to Adelaide, but it dove below the waves and disappeared.

"You're referring to Bowdoin looking where the sniper was at the site?" I said.

"Before sniper started shooting," Jeff said.

I said nothing.

"No matter whether you gonna share it or not, I know you got a pretty good theory already worked out in your head," Jeff said.

"Do you now?" I said.

"I do," Jeff said. "Because that's the way you are. Always theorizing. So, why don't you tell me what you think and let me decide if you dying made you come up with something stupid or not."

My skull suddenly felt like it might explode. I closed my eyes and breathed through the pain. The pain subsided a little.

"You really want to hear this?" I said.

"I just said I did," Jeff said.

Another stab of pain shot through my head. I took another deep breath.

"I suppose," I said, "if one is honest, Bowdoin does appear to be a nexus for all the weirdness."

"I like that word," Jeff said. "Nexus."

"I thought you would," I said.

"Tell me about the nexus," Jeff said.

"A lot of it is conjecture," I said.

"Conjecture okay under the circumstances," Jeff said.

"Alright," I said. "Carter Bowdoin. He runs Pennsylvania Avenue Partners. About four years ago, PAP makes overtures to NASAD. They want to be involved with the company. Milt Feynman vehemently opposes that involvement, and repeatedly rebuffs PAP for the next year. Then, about three years ago, Milt Feynman and Paul Lennon die in a plane accident..."

"Except it ain't no accident," Jeff said. "It was murder."

"Murder, yes," I said. "With Feynman dead, PAP finally gets an ownership share in NASAD about two years ago. At the same time PAP gets its share, PAP also hires Bryce Wellington..."

Jeff interrupted again, "Wellington only officially hired two years ago, but I bet they were paying him long before then."

"I wouldn't doubt that," I said. "We need to look into it. Continuing then, we now know that Colonel Riley Whitelock, the NASAD military liaison at the time of Feynman's and Lennon's deaths, was also Wellington's godson."

"Dead drunk guy who don't drink," Jeff said.

"Right," I said. "Whitelock would have known about NASAD's radar mislocating technology that can trick radar into believing Feynman and Lennon's Otter went down at a precise location in the Gulf of Alaska, when in reality, the Otter went down nowhere near that location."

"And Whitelock can make that technology accessible to Bowdoin, who then uses it to kill Feynman and Lennon," Jeff said.

"Yes, that's what I think happened," I said. "But I don't have any idea how Whitelock could have gotten it to Bowdoin."

"With Whitelock dead, we may never know," Jeff said.

"True," I said. "Which brings us back to what I said before. All I really have is a bunch of conjecture."

"We'll see about that," Jeff said. "Go on."

"After Carter Bowdoin and PAP purchase ten percent of NASAD, a purchase Kate's brother, Freddy Feynman, helps orchestrate, NASAD drone sub engineers start dying," I said.

"In phony accidents," Jeff said. "Like Feynman, Lennon, and Whitelock. Except..."

"Except what?" I said.

"Managers dying might be something else," Jeff said.

The dolphin reappeared off the cutter's bow. It stayed with us for only a few seconds, then disappeared beneath the waves again.

"What do you mean?" I said.

"There a pretty direct line from Whitelock to Wellington to Bowdoin for the deaths of Feynman and Lennon," Jeff said. "Nothing other than timing connects Bowdoin to the dead NASAD drone sub managers."

"My death-addled brain says the connection is there," I said. "We just haven't found it yet."

"I can go with that for now," Jeff said.

"Thank you," I said. "Bowdoin is linked to NASAD's dark programmers due to his war game gambling. Since we believe Nemo is likely a dark programmer, that would also link Bowdoin to Nemo. If Bowdoin also knew where the sniper would be at the NASAD site, that links him to Dragon Man. Dragon Man is linked to the Afghan and Kazakh mercenaries who came into the country pretending to be doctors sponsored by the organization Doctors of Mercy."

"Dragon Man linked to the Afghans and Kazakhs since Dragon Man was at the stoning site with the Afghans, and he also was using a Chinese FaceTime-like app with the Kazakhs when they were doing their sniping at the NASAD site," Jeff said.

"Correct," I said.

"Bowdoin not just any old nexus," Jeff said. "He's a super nexus."

"Certainly looks that way," I said. "So..."

I paused.

"Why you pausing?" Jeff said.

"The next place I gotta go to is one I don't like going to," I said.

"Lucille Ball," Jeff said.

I checked on Adelaide again. She was spiraling down more quickly. I thought the odds of getting to her before she splashed into the sea were getting worse. From fifty-fifty to maybe forty-sixty.

"Lucille Ball?" I said.

"'Where No Man Has Gone Before' was the second 'Star Trek' pilot," Jeff said. "Desilu producer of 'Star Trek'. Lucille Ball owned Desilu, and she was the one that pushed for second pilot after studio nixed the first one. Reason she pushed is that she liked Gene Roddenberry. Lucy doesn't get second pilot made, there never be no 'Star Trek'."

It took me a moment to understand what Jeff was talking about. I had to think extra hard to gain that understanding and the extra thinking made my head throb. My head hurt so much I couldn't speak.

"You knows it make sense," Jeff said.

I took a few deep breaths. The pain lessened.

"Unfortunately, it does," I mumbled.

"What's wrong with you?" Jeff said.

"I told you I have a headache," I said.

"Lucille Ball segue make it worse, huh?" Jeff said.

"It did," I said.

I took another deep breath. The pain lessened some more.

"You wanna go on, or wait awhile?" Jeff said.

"I can go on," I said. "My problem is actually the opposite of the 'Star Trek' pilot. Many people have gone where I'm going before, but the problem is those people are all too nutty for my taste. I would normally call them conspiracy freaks."

"Some of the craziest people we know be the most sane ones," Jeff said.

"True," I said.

"And some conspiracies be real," Jeff said.

"Also true," I said. "So, I'll just say it then. Bowdoin and Pennsylvania Avenue Partners, due to their defense company holdings, will make a shitload of money if we go to war with China, since they will be providing most of the U.S. military's weapons."

"Which go to motive," Jeff said.

Adelaide's descent had continued to accelerate. I figured we'd gone from forty-sixty that we'd get to her in time, to maybe two in ten. Not good. Not good at all.

"Which goes to motive," I said. "And there is another big shitload of money in rebuilding the infrastructure of Saudi Arabia - ports, oil wells, roads, you name it - after the war."

"And Carter Bowdoin's companies do that too," Jeff said. "Except if the Chinese win, they'll give those contracts to a Chinese company, not to PAP, if you know what I'm saying."

"I think Bowdoin solved that problem," I said.

Jeff stared at me. I could almost see the wheels spinning in his brain. Then the wheels seemed to stop spinning and a little light appeared to go off in Jeff's head.

"Shit, man," Jeff said. "You *are* crazy. But it's a good crazy."

"It fits, right?" I said.

"It fits," Jeff said. "Carter Bowdoin made himself a deal."

"With someone in China," I said. "Someone in the same business as Bowdoin is. Someone in the Chinese defense industry and the Chinese infrastructure rebuilding industry - maybe even China's version of Pennsylvania Avenue Partners. Bowdoin and the guy who runs the Chinese PAP agree to some kind of profit sharing arrangement, so it doesn't matter which side wins the war. Except..."

"Except?" Jeff said.

"Except it will be much better if China wins," I said.

"How come?" Jeff said.

"U.S. wins, deal maybe worth a few hundred billion dollars," I said. "China wins, it's ten trillion."

Jeff thought this over.

"Because Saudi Arabia sitting on top of ten trillion dollars in oil and now China owns it all," Jeff said.

"And Bowdoin's Chinese buddy becomes emperor," I said.

"Dragon Man, my little Asian dude," Jeff said.

"If Bowdoin's fee is even just twenty percent of that ten trillion, that comes out to two trillion dollars," I said. "I think two trillion dollars is enough money for a former U.S. president's son to sell out his country for, don't you?"

"For that much money, he sell out his mama," Jeff said.

"I believe what Bowdoin sold is the insurmountable edge," I said.

"If it truly insurmountable, China gonna win," Jeff said. "Bowdoin gonna get his two trillion instead of just a piece of a few hundred billion."

Almost as soon as Jeff said that, however, his face fell.

"You know man, that is a hell of a lot of crazy ass speculating, though," Jeff said. "I mean, I know I told you to go in that direction, but still."

"I just went with our standard operating procedure," I said. "When we're not sure..."

"We go with worst case scenario," Jeff said.

"It's definitely the worst case I can come up with," I said.

"We gotta get Haley working on all the companies in China that fit the profile of a Chinese PAP," Jeff said.

"And Haley has to see if any of those companies are owned by some-one that might have a personal grudge against Paul Lennon," I said.

"Grudge that making him mad enough to kill all of Lennon's relatives," Jeff said.

"We also need to talk with Bobby and Timmy and see how many

claws Dragon Man's mask had," I said.

"Better have five," Jeff said. "Or our whole thinking is in the toilet."

"I would have put that a little differently," I said.

"Like 'we screwed'?" Jeff said.

"World War III screwed," I said.

"'World War III screwed' be right," Jeff said.

The Coast Guard cutter rolled violently to the side as it took a wave at a bad angle. Jeff and I each grabbed a rail and hung on. I felt like my arm was going to tear out of its socket.

The cutter had barely re-righted itself when it flew over the top of another high wave and the bow went airborne, clearing the ocean's surface by about five feet. Jeff and I each raised our butts off the top of the cabin by bridging ourselves on our feet and hands. It helped ease the pain a little when the boat smashed back down.

"We could get good at this," Jeff said.

"Do we want to?" I said.

Jeff gestured to the coast guardsmen who appeared completely unfazed by the all the rocking and rolling.

"They seem to like it," Jeff said.

"Probably gotta pass some kinda aptitude test before they join up," I said.

"Like throwing them in a washing machine and see if they come out smiling after the spin cycle?" Jeff said.

"That would work," I said.

Adelaide's hang glider was spiraling down even faster now. She had only fifty feet and maybe twenty seconds before she would be in the water. We were still about a minute away from her.

I was close enough then to see that Adelaide was wearing only a very skimpy gold bikini, almost as skimpy as the one Christa had been wearing. She also appeared to be wearing her combat belt with her knife in its scabbard. I wasn't the only one who noticed Adelaide's attire, however. The guardsmen were also taking a close look. They seemed to be enjoying themselves. Which didn't make me happy, but there wasn't much I could do about it.

The guardsmen, Jeff, and I watched as Adelaide detached herself from the glider's harness, then grabbed and supported herself from the glider's metal cross strut. Adelaide looked like she was planning on jumping into the ocean before the glider hit the water. Which I thought would be a smart move since that way she would avoid getting tangled up in the glider and being pulled under with it when it sank.

"You think great white sharks are watching Adelaide?" Jeff said. "You know, calculating her entry point?"

"Jeff, this might be hard for you to understand," I said. "But if there is anything I don't want to think about right now, great white sharks would be it."

"I once saw a great white leap out of the water and snatch a baby seal in midair," Jeff said. "It was on the Discovery Channel."

"Fascinating," I said.

Adelaide sprang out and away from the glider when she was about twenty feet above the ocean and the cutter was still about thirty seconds away from her. She spun in the air, hit the water hands first in a perfect swan dive, and surfaced a few seconds later. The glider's descent slowed after Adelaide had jumped from it and the glider plopped into the water about ten yards from her.

Adelaide swam towards the glider and held on to it. She seemed to be trying to keep it from tugging her under, but was having a hard time doing so. She went beneath the waves and resurfaced three times while we were watching. The waves and the current kept moving Adelaide away from us.

"Adelaide, let go of that thing!" I shouted.

"Bet she put a deposit down," Jeff said. "She probably doesn't want to lose it."

"Deposit isn't worth her life," I said.

The cutter kept racing toward Adelaide. It took only about twenty seconds more to get to her, but it felt like an eternity. The boat pulled up close to Adelaide and idled. Adelaide had both hands on one of the glider's metal bars and was kicking with both feet trying to keep her head above water. She was tugged down beneath the waves by the glider again, but somehow managed to resurface.

One of the guardsmen tossed Adelaide a circular red and white life preserver that was tied to one end of a long braided rope. The braided rope's other end was secured to a cleat on the cutter's deck. The life preserver landed a few feet away from Adelaide. Adelaide was too busy struggling with the hang glider to notice the preserver.

"Come on Adelaide, let go of the glider!" I shouted.

"I'm not losing my deposit!" Adelaide said. She sunk beneath the surface, then bobbed back up and spit water out of her mouth.

Jeff said, "Told you it was about her deposit."

I ignored Jeff.

"It's not worth it," I said. "Grab the preserver and get on board."

A wave tore the hang glider from Adelaide's grasp and the glider disappeared beneath the ocean's surface. Adelaide dove down. She came back up, but didn't have the glider. Adelaide took a deep breath, dove down, and again came up empty-handed.

"I lost it," Adelaide said.

"Fine," I said. "Get on board."

"One last try," Adelaide said.

Adelaide dove down again. Jeff tapped my shoulder and pointed at something about twenty yards away from the boat. I looked. A large dorsal fin was cutting through the water.

"Is that a shark?" I said.

"Ain't no dolphin," Jeff said. "Dolphins have blowholes."

"Is it a great white?" I said.

"He's big enough to be," Jeff said.

A coast guardsman carrying a shotgun ran past Jeff and me. The guardsman stopped at the bow and took aim at the shark. He didn't fire, however.

I ran up beside the guardsman.

"That's a great white, isn't it?" I said.

"Yes, sir," the guardsman said.

"What are you waiting for, then?" I said. "Shoot it!"

"Don't really want to unless I have to, sir," the guardsman said.

"Unless you have to?" I said.

"Yes, sir," the guardsman said.

"How the hell are you going to decide when you have to?" I said.

"It's more of a feel than anything else, sir," the guardsman said.

"A feel?" I said.

"Sharks usually circle for a while before they attack," the guardsman said. "I get any sense he's being aggressive, I'll shoot him, sir."

Adelaide resurfaced.

"Damn, I think it's gone," Adelaide said.

"Get in here now!" I said.

Adelaide looked back down under the waves.

"Wait, I see it!" Adelaide said.

"You've got a shark at one o'clock, Adelaide," I said. "You need to get in now!"

Adelaide turned. She spotted the shark. Her right hand disappeared beneath the surface, and then reappeared holding her combat knife. Adelaide lifted the knife above her head and kept herself afloat by paddling with her free hand.

"Let him try something," Adelaide said.

"This is all your fault," I said to Jeff.

"You think I can magically conjure up sharks just by talking about them?" Jeff said.

"I wouldn't put it past you," I said.

The shark seemed to be moving closer to Adelaide.

I turned to the guardsman with the shotgun.

"That looks pretty aggressive to me," I said.

"He's still just circling, sir," the guardsman said.

I turned back to Adelaide.

"Get in here now!" I yelled.

"Okay, okay, calm down," Adelaide said.

Adelaide swam to the life preserver that was still floating nearby and grabbed hold of it. One of the guardsmen hauled her towards the boat. It seemed like the shark was following her.

"Shoot!" I yelled to the guardsman with the shotgun. "Shoot!"

"We're not quite at that point, sir," the guardsman with the shotgun said.

"Goddamnit!" I said.

"Patience, sir," the guardsman said. "Patience."

Adelaide finally reached the side of the boat and the guardsman hauling the life preserver's rope helped her in. Three more guardsmen, each holding a towel, came to her side. None of the three offered a towel to Adelaide, however, as they all appeared too focused on gawking at her scantily clad body.

"What the hell are you guys looking at?" I said.

The three of them startled and stared at me.

"Hand her your towels and get back to your goddamned stations!" I said.

The three guardsmen each gave Adelaide their towels and scampered away. Adelaide dried herself off with one of the towels.

Jeff said, "That was really a stupid move girl."

"That hang glider is expensive," Adelaide said.

"Not worth drowning for," Jeff said.

Adelaide smiled.

"Could you repeat that please, Jeff?" Adelaide said.

"I said hang glider wasn't worth drowning for," Jeff said.

"Boy, am I ever glad you said that," Adelaide said.

Jeff eyed her for a moment.

"What you mean by that?" Jeff said.

"Just what I said," Adelaide said. "I'm glad you said that."

"There something more going on here," Jeff said. "Why are you glad?"

"Because you agree with me the hang glider wasn't worth drowning over, so now I know you won't be mad," Adelaide said.

"Mad about what?" Jeff said.

"That I used your credit card for the deposit," Adelaide said.

Jeff flew at Adelaide. He tackled her so hard that his momentum took them both over the cutter's deck railing and into the sea.

CHAPTER 76

Adelaide and Jeff thrashed about in the water, each trying to drown the other, both of them apparently oblivious to the shark's presence. Admittedly, the shark had swum a good distance from the boat once Adelaide had been hauled aboard, but I still didn't like the idea of the two of them being in the water with a great white. Especially since the guardsman with the shotgun seemed to have such a reluctant trigger finger.

I knew there was only one way to get my two knuckle-headed companions back onto the cutter.

"I'll cover the deposit," I yelled to Adelaide and Jeff. "Get back on board."

Adelaide and Jeff stopped thrashing.

"You will?" Jeff said.

"What'd I just say?" I said.

Jeff and Adelaide looked at each other.

"You down with that?" Jeff said to Adelaide.

"Of course I'm down with that," Adelaide said.

Adelaide and Jeff swam to the ship's side. I reached over the cutter's gunwale and helped them aboard. They each picked up one of Adelaide's three towels, and dried themselves off. The cutter's pilot gunned the engines and we turned around and headed for shore.

Adelaide and Jeff sat down next to me.

"You want me to teach you how to surf, Adelaide?" Jeff said.

"Sure," Adelaide said.

I stared at both of them.

"You're kidding, right?" I said.

Jeff said, "Kidding?"

"Not two minutes ago you were at each other's throats," I said, "But now you're all lovey-dovey."

Adelaide said, "What's your point?"

"My point is," I said, "how do such things happen?"

Jeff said, "Such things happen because there be more things in heaven and earth, Horatio, than be dreamt of in your philosophy."

I said, "You just said the same thing yesterday in my dream."

"What you talking about?" Jeff said.

"In my dream," I said, "you were sitting next to me in the Maybach..." I suddenly realized how stupid my explanation would sound and stopped myself. "Forget it, I don't know what I was thinking."

"If you say so," Jeff said.

Adelaide said, "Who's Horatio?"

"He's a friend of Hamlet," Jeff said.

"Who's Hamlet?" Adelaide said.

"A prince," Jeff said.

"What kind of prince?" Adelaide said.

I felt like I'd entered the 'Twilight Zone'. My head started throbbing and I was sure it would burst if I listened to Jeff try to explain Hamlet to Adelaide. I covered my ears with my hands and started humming to myself. Neither Adelaide nor Jeff took any notice of me.

It was about 3:00 p.m., the sun still high in the sky, when the cutter dropped the three of us off fifty yards from shore. Jeff and I paddled on the surfboard back to the beach while Adelaide swam next to us. Adelaide's surfing lesson commenced as soon as we were on dry land.

Leaving Jeff and Adelaide behind, I made my way back up the wooden cliffside stairs. My head continued to throb, but, with the war deadline of a week from Friday fast approaching, I was far from ready to call it a day. I began to think about what my best next step would be.

I would have loved to have talked to Dr. Nemo, but unless he made contact with Kate and agreed to meet with us, that wasn't going to happen. It would be a complete waste of time for me to try to crack Nemo's code - its secrets would only be revealed by the man himself or if Haley and MOM's cryptologists somehow had a miraculous breakthrough.

I had no idea how to even begin to try to track down Dragon Man on my own. It seemed to me on that issue I needed to rely on Haley and MOM as well, and hope they might generate a useful lead. I had my doubts, but maybe even the cracked cell phone with the picture of Dragon Man that I had sent to Haley would provide some useful information.

As to Carter Bowdoin, my evidence against him was all circumstance and conjecture. I'd be raked over the coals if I hauled

Bowdoin in and tried to torture him into revealing what he knew about the insurmountable edge.

I reached the halfway point of my climb up the cliffside stairs. I realized there was only one good option for me to pursue at that moment. That option was to try to uncover the deal I believed Carter Bowdoin and Dragon Man had made with each other.

I had a crazy hunch about that deal.

My hunch was that it wasn't just a handshake deal. With billions, and maybe trillions of dollars at stake, my guess was that they wrote up a contract between themselves. A contract like that surely wouldn't be enforceable, but at least Carter and Dragon Man would know exactly what to expect from each other. My hunch extended to also believing I had a reasonably good notion where to start looking for that contract. Beginning my search for the contract, however, would be wholly dependent on the answer to a question I needed to ask Kate. I called her on my iPhone.

She answered on the first ring.

"Where are you?" Kate said.

"I'm walking up the stairs from the beach," I said. "Where are you?"

"Out by the pool with my kids," Kate said. "Did you see the Coast Guard rescue that crazy person on the hang glider?"

"You mean Adelaide?" I said.

"That was Adelaide?!" Kate said.

"Yes," I said. "Jeff and I were on the cutter when the Coast Guard picked her up."

"She's truly an amazing girl," Kate said.

"That's one way to look at it," I said. "I've got a question for you."

"Shoot," Kate said.

"When Carter Bowdoin and PAP came on board at NASAD, they didn't happen to put in a new chief financial officer, did they?" I said.

"How do you know these things?" Kate said.

"I don't," I said. "That's why I asked."

"His name is Roland Wachtel," Kate said.

"Is he at the Westlake campus?" I said.

"Yes," Kate said.

"I need to see him," I said.

"When?" Kate said.

"Now," I said.

"Right now?" Kate said.

"Right now," I said.

"I'll set it up," Kate said. "You going to tell me why you need to see him?"

"It's complicated," I said. "And it may turn out to be nothing."

"But if it doesn't?" Kate said.

"You'll be the first to know," I said.

"Would you like Manu and Mosi to drive you over there?" Kate said.

"Please," I said. "And Kate..."

"Yes?" Kate said.

"Promise me you'll stay on the estate so Carpenter can keep an eye on you while I'm gone," I said.

"I promise," Kate said.

CHAPTER 77

With Manu driving, Mosi riding shotgun, and me partaking of a few snacks from the backseat refrigerator, the Maybach transported us east over Kanan Dume Road, north along the 101, through the low foothills of Westlake, and past the NASAD security gates. Thirty minutes after leaving Freddy and Kate's estate, the Maybach stopped in front of Kate's office tower.

I exited the car. The temperature was in the nineties, at least fifteen degrees hotter than it had been at the beach, and there was no breeze at all. The drones were dogfighting above the helipad and the air was full of the smell of their burning fuel. All was quiet around the man-made lake and the remote-controlled sailboats were nowhere to be seen.

As I was walking up the stairs to Kate's office building, I realized that neither Jeff nor I had filled in Adelaide on the details of our mission yet. If Adelaide was to be of any use to us, she needed those details. I stopped on the stairs for a moment and texted Jeff to ask him to tell Adelaide everything we knew so far about Kate, the insurmountable edge, Dr. Nemo, the upcoming war with China, Dragon Man, the dark programmers and their war games software, the defensive war game programmers in the Cyber Defense Hall, Raj, the Afghan and Kazakh mercenaries, Freddy Feynman, Carter Bowdoin, General Bryce Wellington, Pennsylvania Avenue Partners, and the killings of Paul Lennon, Milt Feynman, Sam and Lizzy, Sam and Lizzy's mother and grandparents, and the NASAD drone sub engineers. I also reminded Jeff to be sure Adelaide understood the highly confidential nature of what was being revealed to her.

Texting Jeff stimulated me into further ruminations about the details of Nemo and the dark programmers' software weapon. How could they possibly have found a way to make a successful simultaneous attack on all of the U.S. military's millions of computers? Nothing that could work presented itself to me.

I entered the lobby of Kate's building and was given a new security badge. I went up the building's elevator, then into the anteroom of the office of NASAD's chief financial officer, Roland Wachtel.

Wachtel's office anteroom had dark mahogany walls, a mahogany desk, and a Persian rug covering the center of the mahogany floors. To the left of the desk was the only door in the anteroom other than the one I had come in through. I assumed it led to Roland's private office.

Roland's secretary was sitting at the desk. Her nameplate read 'Glenda Parnassus'. Glenda was big in every way and it wasn't because she was fit and muscular. She had large, helmet-like dyed blond hair, a large nose that appeared to have been constructed out of putty, large ears, large teeth, large shoulders, large arms, large hands, and a large belly. The only thing that was not large were her eyes. They were tiny. And ferret-like.

Glenda set aside the dainty quarter pound jelly doughnut from which she had just taken a bite and gave me an unfriendly look.

I smiled.

"May I help you?" Glenda said. Her voice was high-pitched and whiny.

"My name is Jack Wilder," I said. "I'm here to see Roland Wachtel."

"Mr. Wachtel is busy," Glenda said.

"I believe Dr. Lennon told you I was coming," I said.

"And I just told *you* Mr. Wachtel is busy," Glenda said.

"Is he with someone?" I said.

"I fail to see why that is any of your business," Glenda said.

"Perhaps I could show you," I said.

"Show me what?" Glenda said.

"Why it's my business," I said.

I walked past Glenda's desk towards the door to Roland's office.

"Where do you think you're going?!" Glenda said.

"Isn't it obvious?" I said.

I opened the door, entered Roland's office, shut the door behind me, and locked it.

Roland Wachtel, a burning, fat cigar in one hand, and a highball glass filled to the brim with amber liquid and ice cubes in the other, was leaning back in a wide, chrome-framed, black leather chair. Roland looked to be in his late sixties, was tall and thin, had longish grey hair, a tan, weathered, angular face, tired yellow eyes, and long, narrow fingers. One of those fingers wore a sapphire, diamond, and gold Yale class ring.

He was dressed in a brown wool suit too heavy for the time of year, a gold bow tie with blue polka dots, and brown wingtip shoes. There was nothing on Roland's ten foot long, three foot wide rosewood desk other than Roland's feet, an open bottle of twenty-five year old Macallan single malt scotch, an ice bucket, an ashtray, and a phone.

The office itself was a corner office and was at least forty feet long and twenty feet deep. Behind Roland was a stunning view of endless blue sky, and Westlake's green, rolling foothills. The coterie of buzzing drones could also be seen above the helipad. Large oil paintings of English countryside hunting scenes with red-coated riders, stout horses, and a pack of sleek dogs chasing a wily orange fox hung from the wood paneled walls. The carpet was deep braided wool and beige in color.

The intercom of Roland's desk phone came to life with Glenda's high-pitched whine.

"I'm sorry, sir," Glenda said. "He just barged in. Do you want me to call security?"

"Not unless you want whoever they send to get hurt," Roland said. "Please hold my calls."

Roland clicked off the intercom.

"I presume you're the war hero Kate asked me to see?" Roland said.

Though it appeared the drink in Roland's hand was not Roland's first, there was no slur to his words. Maybe he had already rotted away all the brain cells responsible for slurring. Maybe they were gone by the time he was twenty-five. I easily could have passed Roland off as an irredeemable alcoholic, but I didn't. I couldn't quite put my finger on why, but I think it was something I saw in Roland's eyes. Yes, his eyes were tired and worn and they were planted in a face that was also tired and worn - the skin sallow and wasting beneath his leathery tan - but there was a spark of life, even a hint of nobility, behind those eyes. Both the spark and the hint were very faint, however, and seemed close to dying. It could have been all my imagination, but I sensed something deep within Roland knew how close to death he and his eyes were, and that that something was fighting back desperately to keep both him and them alive.

What was killing off those precious parts of his being, I wondered? Was his physical body failing after years of abuse? Did he have some deep, dark secret gnawing away at him? Whatever it was, I found myself feeling sorry for Roland. He seemed like a lost man.

I said nothing about my feelings to Roland, however, and instead simply smiled, and reached out my hand towards him. Roland took my hand and firmly shook it.

"Jack Wilder," I said. "Nice to meet you. But I'm afraid Kate's being too kind."

"Oh, I doubt that," Roland said.

He gestured to the bottle of Macallan.

"Can I offer you a drink, war hero?" Roland said. "All I have is scotch, but it's a rather fine scotch."

Normally I wouldn't drink on the job, and it probably wasn't a good idea to drink given the fact I still had a pounding headache and my heart had stopped earlier in the day, but I had the very distinct sense that Roland was the kind of guy who would be much more likely to open up to me if I shared a drink with him. And the Macallan truly was a rather fine scotch.

"Certainly," I said. "Don't like watching a man drink alone."

"Well put," Roland said.

He reached into his desk drawer, pulled out another highball glass, filled it with ice and scotch, and handed it to me.

"Cheers," Roland said.

"Cheers," I said.

We clinked glasses. I took a sip. The scotch made a nice burn going down my throat and it had a soft smoky aftertaste.

"Cigar?" Roland said.

"Why not?" I said.

Roland reached into a different drawer and pulled out a box of Cohiba Behike cigars and a gold guillotine-style cigar cutter monogrammed with the initials 'RW'. He carefully clipped off the end of the cigar and handed it to me. Roland then took out a gold lighter, also monogrammed with the initials 'RW', from his inside jacket pocket, thumbed a flame, and extended the lighter to me. I put the cigar in my mouth, leaned forward so that the end of the cigar was in the flame, and inhaled a few times to get it going. Very tasty. Almost as good as the scotch. Roland put the lighter and the cutter back in his jacket.

"Good cigar," I said. "Thank you."

"You're welcome," Roland said. "Always happy to be of service to our men in uniform. What can I do for you hero?"

"We had a president of the United States named Niles W. Bowdoin," I said. "'W' stood for Wachtel, I believe."

"Indeed it did," Roland said.

Three drones appeared outside the window. They hovered there for a moment, then flew away.

"Any relation?" I said.

"Wachtel is the ex-prezzie's mother's maiden name," Roland said. "Niles's mother had a brother, Roland the first. Roland was my father, but has since passed. God rest his soul."

"I'm sorry for your loss," I said.

"No great loss," Roland said. "He was hardly ever home and when he was home he was drunk and beat me with a clothes hanger."

"Must have been rough," I said. "So if your father was Niles Bowdoin's mother's brother, that means President Bowdoin was your cousin?"

"Yes," Roland said.

"What does that make Carter Bowdoin then?" I said.

"An asshole," Roland said.

I laughed.

"I know that's not what you meant," Roland said. "I believe they call it first cousin once removed, but don't hold me to it. Carter Bowdoin is also my boss."

Roland downed his drink and refilled his glass from the bottle. He took a sip, put the glass down, and pulled a puff from the cigar. Roland was a very skilled puffer. I noticed the ash ring at the end of the cigar burned down exactly the same amount every time he puffed. My puff ash length, on the other hand, was very undisciplined. I felt a bit ashamed.

"Isn't Freddy your boss?" I said.

"General, please," Roland said. "You and I both know you're too smart to believe a thing like that."

"I didn't take you for a flatterer, Roland," I said.

"I'm not," Roland said.

Roland took another sip from his glass, then eyed me carefully for a moment.

"You're hiding something, aren't you, General?" Roland said.

"I am?" I said.

"You think I'm a lush, don't you?" Roland said.

I didn't say anything.

"Well, I might very well be a lush," Roland said. "But you should know that I normally don't start my cocktail hour until after I get home."

"Okay," I said.

"Would you like to know why I'm already three sheets to the wind this particular afternoon?" Roland said.

"If you'd like to tell me," I said.

"Because, I'm a coward, General, and this," Roland said pointing to his glass, "is liquid courage. I started downing it as soon as Kate told me you were on your way."

"Are you afraid of something, Roland?" I said.

"Good question," Roland said. "Let me put it this way. I've been expecting someone like you to show up. I was hoping it would be much, much sooner though."

"Better late than never," I said.

"Indeed," Roland said.

Roland picked up his glass and appeared to study it carefully. A minute passed and then he put the glass back down on his desk. He seemed to have made some kind of decision.

"I need to tell you something, General," Roland said. "It's something that has been on my chest for a long time."

"I'm listening," I said.

"It's difficult for me to talk about," Roland said. "You see, I'm quite torn."

"Torn?" I said.

"Yes," Roland said. "Between duty and self-preservation."

"Ah," I said.

"You must think about that at times, mustn't you General?" Roland said.

"Actually, I try not to think too much about the self-preservation part, Roland," I said.

"You don't?" Roland said.

"It tends to get in the way of doing my job when I do," I said.

"I could see that," Roland said.

Roland downed the rest of his drink, then stared at me for a moment.

"Screw it," Roland finally said. "Listen. Something is rotten in the state of Thousand Oaks, or Calabasas, or wherever the hell this is."

"Heaven will direct it," I said.

"They teach 'Hamlet' at West Point?" Roland said.

"High school," I said. "What is it that's rotten, Roland?"

Roland sighed.

"Shit," Roland said. "I want to say it, but I can't."

"Dueling loyalties," I said.

Roland nodded.

"I've got an idea," Roland said. "If you threaten me, then I'll have no choice but to tell you."

"You don't seem like a man who would be easily threatened," I said.

"May I make a suggestion with regards to that?" Roland said.

"Be my guest," I said.

"I saw a movie once," Roland said. "The hero, or maybe it was the villain, I don't know which, dangled someone by his ankles out a ten-story window until he talked."

"I've had a really rough day Roland," I said. "I'm afraid I might hurt my back."

"Damn," Roland said.

We both took another sip of scotch.

"Perhaps you can ease into it," I said.

"Ease into it?" Roland said.

"Start talking about what it is you feel you need to tell me, but approach it indirectly," I said. "Then you can see how you feel as you go along."

"Hmm," Roland said. "That might work."

Roland took a long puff on his cigar.

"I come from a long line of patriots," Roland said. "My great-great-great-grandfather rode with Paul Revere."

"That's very impressive," I said. "It's something to be proud of."

"Thank you," Roland said. "I've always believed I was a patriot, and I rue the day my family ever mated with the Bowdoins."

Roland poured himself another glass of scotch and quickly downed it. He stared at me for another long moment.

"What's the penalty for treason?" Roland said.

"Treason?" I said.

"Treason, sedition, high crimes against the state," Roland said.

"Last I heard it was death," I said. "I think there's a lot of flexibility in regard to the method however. Gas chamber, electrocution. Hanging is an option."

"In this day and age?" Roland said.

"I believe so," I said. "Why do you ask?"

"I think I may be guilty," Roland said.

"Of treason?" I said.

Roland nodded. I realized then that it was probably guilt that had been the cause of those dying pieces of Roland's soul I had earlier seen behind his eyes. Guilt he had been carrying around for a long time and waiting for someone like me to whom he could confess.

"Do you want to tell me why you think that way?" I said.

Roland was silent.

"You're afraid I'll tell someone and you'll be locked up?" I said.

"Or worse," Roland said.

"How about this," I said. "When special forces squads go on long missions, each of us has to perform multiple tasks. A sniper might be a medic. A radioman might be a cook. From time to time I have served duty as a field chaplain. Chaplains have the same responsibilities and privileges as priests. Anything you say to me is covered under penitent-clergy privilege and will remain confidential."

"But I'm not in the Army," Roland said.

"I'm still a chaplain," I said.

"I don't know," Roland said. "You're the furthest thing I've ever seen from a man of the cloth."

I thought about what Roland had said for a moment.

"You know what?" I said. "You're probably right about that."

Roland gave me what could be best described as a half-smile. He poured himself another drink and downed it in one gulp.

"I suppose this clergy privilege thing might work if you were actually ordained, however," Roland said. "Were you ordained, General?"

"Well, no," I said.

"Damn," Roland said.

"Let's forget about the privilege thing for a moment," I said, "and look at it in another way then."

"What way is that?" Roland said.

"Please don't be insulted, Roland," I said, "but I've got much bigger fish to fry than you. Whatever you've done, or think you've done, is of absolutely no interest to me as it pertains to you alone."

Roland appeared to consider this.

"I guess given everything that has been going on around here I can believe that," Roland said.

"Good," I said. "And you have my solemn promise, as one patriot to another, nothing you say here will leave this room."

Roland seemed to think this over as well.

"Screw it," Roland said. "You seem to be a man of your word. Let's do this."

He picked up the scotch bottle and extended it toward me.

"Can I freshen your drink?" Roland said.

I held out my glass to him and he topped it off. I took a sip.

"Do you want to take notes?" Roland said. "Or are you one of those fellows who can remember everything in your head?"

I smiled.

"I thought so," Roland said. "I can't remember a damn thing anymore."

Roland puffed on his cigar, tapped the ash into an ashtray, then rested the cigar in a slot in the tray.

"I started here shortly after Milton Feynman and Paul Lennon died in a plane crash," Roland said. "I replaced a fine man who had been here for over twenty years. I was okay with it. Business is business, after all."

"Carter Bowdoin probably needed someone he could trust," I said. "And who better than a first cousin once removed?"

A drone streaked across the window. A second later it was followed by two more hot on its tail.

"Who better," Roland said. "I knew before I started exactly who Carter was and what he was like. I was okay with the idea that many of the things his company Pennsylvania Avenue Partners does are legal, but should not be."

"Such as?" I said.

"Hiring the sons, daughters, nieces, nephews, and other assorted relatives of foreign presidents, prime ministers, and other like fools, to be junior associates of Pennsylvania Avenue Partners for one," Roland said.

"Must help PAP make lots of sales to those countries," I said.

"Tajikistan, Uzbekistan, Republic of the Congo, Venezuela, Sudan, the list goes on and on," Roland said.

"Paragons of human freedom and democracy," I said.

"Quite," Roland said. "But it's just legalized bribery. Bribery once removed."

"But not treason," I said.

"Neither is it treason to hire former United States government procurement directors, senators, and cabinet members," Roland said. "It is simply good business."

"I still don't see anything that's going to lead to a noose around your neck," I said.

"I'm getting there," Roland said.

He downed his drink in one big gulp, lifted the bottle, and refilled his glass. He skipped the ice this time.

"One of the first things I was asked to do when I was hired was to create a special class of stock in NASAD," Roland said. "I did it with the assistance of a very pricey outside law firm."

"As opposed to NASAD's in-house legal counsel," I said.

"You're a smart man, General," Roland said.

"I have my moments," I said.

"Yes, in-house counsel would have presented problems for Carter," Roland said. "Carter would have worried about others in NASAD learning things he did not want them to learn. Whereas, with a first cousin once removed and an outside law firm running the show, he had no such worries."

"What was special about the stock, Roland?" I said.

"Most stock transfers have to be registered in some fashion or another, but this stock is more like a bearer bond," Roland said. "The owner is whoever has it in their hands."

I thought about that for a moment.

"Interesting," I said. "Aren't there a lot of nasty little federal regulations concerning who may and may not own stock in defense companies that work with classified information?"

"There are," Roland said.

"The bearer bond nature of the stock might make it so those regulations could be bypassed, couldn't they?" I said.

"Which is why the stock itself was as illegal as hell right from the get-go," Roland said.

I took another sip of scotch and a puff on my cigar.

"I'm wondering, Roland, how such stock could be created in the first place?" I said. "Wouldn't NASAD have its own rules about such things?"

"Loophole in the company bylaws," Roland said. "The president of NASAD is allowed to conduct any transactions he or she deems necessary in his or her sole and absolute discretion."

"Even an illegal one?" I said.

"When the bylaws were written it was never contemplated that the president of NASAD would ever even consider anything illegal," Roland said.

"Because the NASAD president was Milt Feynman?" I said.

Roland puffed on his cigar.

"Yes," Roland said. "If Milt had any weakness, it was that he never adequately planned for succession."

"Many great men don't," I said.

"True," Roland said.

"So when Freddy took over as president from his father that rule was still in place?" I said.

"Sadly, yes," Roland said.

"Did Freddy, in his role as president, approve the creation of the special bearer-bond-like stock?" I said.

"He did," Roland said.

"The board wasn't notified?" I said.

"Only Freddy and Carter Bowdoin knew about it," Roland said. "No other members of the board, including Kate Lennon, had any knowledge of it."

"Freddy didn't question the legality of NASAD stock potentially being transferred to an owner that never underwent the approval process required by U.S. law?" I said.

"Freddy absolutely questioned it," Roland said.

I was a bit surprised by that. Maybe I'd underestimated Freddy.

"What did you tell him?" I said.

Two more drones flew by the window behind Roland. Both did a loop de loop, then dove out of sight.

"I didn't tell Freddy anything," Roland said. "Someone else did."

"Carter Bowdoin?" I said.

"Correct," Roland said. "There was a meeting between Carter, Freddy, and me. Carter did most of the talking."

"What did Carter say?" I said.

"Carter told Freddy that he needed a free hand if he was going to quickly raise the hundreds of millions of dollars Freddy was requesting to fund his expansion plans for NASAD," Roland said. "Carter said the Department of Defense regulations were bureaucratic bullshit and that complying with them would only slow down the process. Carter also said Pennsylvania Avenue Partners routinely ignored the regulations and had never had an issue."

"That was it?" I said. "That enough for Freddy to give the go-ahead?"

"Not quite," Roland said. "Carter also promised Freddy the stock would never wind up in the hands of any person or entity that had not already been approved by the Department of Defense in regard to the purchase of shares in companies similar to NASAD."

"And Freddy just took Carter at his word?" I said.

"Carter's word is gold in Freddy's eyes," Roland said. "Freddy idolizes Carter."

I remembered Kate had said the same thing. I took another sip of the Macallan and another puff of the cigar. I considered all that Roland had told me.

"I hope you're not disappointed, Roland," I said, "but nothing you've said so far sounds like treason to me."

"Unfortunately, there's more," Roland said.

Roland poured himself another shot, gulped it down, and took a long drag on his cigar.

"After Carter, Freddy, and I had concluded our meeting, Carter snatched the stock certificates...," Roland said.

"Snatched?" I interrupted. "I wouldn't have expected the Carter I've seen so far to be that indiscreet."

"He snatched them," Roland said. "Then he hightailed it out of the room. I watched from this window right behind me as he raced across the quad, boarded a waiting helicopter, and flew out of here."

"Did you know where Carter was headed?" I said.

"Carter likes to keep his business to himself," Roland said. "If he doesn't volunteer what he's up to, you don't ask."

"Did you try to find out on your own?" I said.

"Of course I did," Roland said. "The certificates, Carter dashing out of here...it was just too strange."

"Were you successful?" I said.

"I figured the helicopter was most likely going to the Van Nuys Airport," Roland said. "NASAD executives fly in and out of there on company jets all the time. I waited until I was sure plenty of time had elapsed for Carter to have taken off to wherever he was going and called the flight coordinator at the private airport terminal NASAD uses. I told her I had forgotten to give Carter some important documents and asked her about his flight plan. She told me he was flying on a Pennsylvania Avenue Partners' jet nonstop to Panama. I thanked her and told her that was all I needed since I knew where he stayed when he went there."

"That's Panama as in Panama the offshore banking haven for drug dealers, money launderers, terrorists, and other assorted dregs of the earth?" I said.

I took another sip of the Macallan.

"Yes," Roland said. "That Panama."

"You weren't afraid the flight coordinator might tip off Carter that you asked about him?" I said.

"As far as Carter is concerned, the flight coordinator is one of the 'little people,'" Roland said. "Carter wouldn't even know she was alive, let alone talk to her."

"I assume Carter visited a bank when he was in Panama?" I said.

"I thought there was a reasonable likelihood of being caught if I continued nosing around into Carter's affairs, so I didn't attempt to check," Roland said. "But Carter was back in Pennsylvania Avenue Partners' D.C. office within twenty-four hours after he left my office, so I don't think he was there for the beaches and the nightlife."

"Is there any particular bank PAP might use in Panama?" I said.

"There is," Roland said.

Roland opened one of his desk drawers, took out a piece of paper, wrote on it, and slid it across to me. I read what he had written. It said 'Banco Mundo de Panama'. I folded the paper and put it in my pants pocket.

"Thank you, Roland," I said. "Do you know if your special brand of bearer-bond stock was ever transferred to anyone?"

"Please don't call it mine," Roland said.

"No problem," I said.

"I know nothing about the stock other than what I've told you," Roland said.

I tapped some of my cigar's ash off in Roland's ashtray.

"Sorry, Roland," I said, "but I gotta say I still don't see a hangman anywhere in your future."

Roland poured himself another drink and gulped it down.

"There's one more piece of the story you don't know, General," Roland said. "The day after Carter returned to D.C. was the day the first NASAD drone submarine engineer met an untimely death."

I hadn't expected that. I hoped my surprise didn't show on my face. If it had, Roland didn't appear to notice.

"Are you sure?" I said.

"Quite sure," Roland said.

Hadn't Jeff just said, only a little over an hour ago, that the only thing we couldn't link to Bowdoin was the drone sub engineers' deaths? I don't believe in coincidences, so I was highly suspicious that the engineers' deaths and Bowdoin's trip to Panama were related. So related, in fact, that my mind was suddenly filled with an image of Carter Bowdoin standing on a train track as a freight train named 'Not a Coincidence' hurtled right for him, mere seconds away from squashing him.

Still, following my 'need to know' instincts, I didn't mention to Roland anything to do with the thoughts churning through my head.

Roland suddenly held out both his arms towards me, his palms up.

"What are you doing?" I said.

"Cuff me," Roland said.

"I'm not a cop, Roland," I said.

"Call one," Roland said.

"Come on," I said. "The timing of the deaths could all just be a co-incidence, couldn't it?"

"Do you think it's a coincidence?" Roland said.

"I don't know what I think, Roland," I said. "Have you ever found any actual evidence linking Carter Bowdoin to the drone sub engineers' deaths?"

"No," Roland said.

"Is that why you never brought this to anyone else's attention before?" I said.

"Partially," Roland said. "Also, I'm a coward."

"Why did you tell me then?" I said.

"I don't know," Roland said. "Maybe because I sensed you might believe me. Maybe because I thought you were someone who could, and would, do something about it. Maybe because I just can't live with the guilt any longer."

"Well, I'm glad you told me," I said. "Can I give you some advice on what I think you should do now?"

"What?" Roland said.

"First, put your arms down," I said.

Roland put his arms down.

"Second, never say a word of this to anyone," I said.

"But I'm guilty," Roland said.

"Of what?" I said.

"Treason," Roland said. "I betrayed my country. And I'm responsible for the murders of the NASAD drone sub engineers."

"The only thing you're guilty of is supervising an outside law firm that should have known better," I said.

"I should have known better," Roland said.

"Even in the incredibly unlikely event Carter is somehow responsible for those murders, if indeed, they truly turn out to be murders instead of accidents," I said, "you had no way of knowing that what you did in regard to those stock certificates could possibly lead to such mayhem, did you?"

"No, I didn't," Roland said.

"Then drop it," I said. "I'm not telling anyone and you're not telling anyone. "

"Okay," Roland said.

"But I do need you to do one thing for me," I said.

"What's that?" Roland said.

"Did you keep copies of the certificates?" I said.

"Yes," Roland said.

"May I see them, please?" I said.

Roland pushed his chair back and spun around to face a credenza beneath the window. He pulled a key out of his pants pocket, inserted it into a lock in one of the credenza drawers, and took out a large envelope that was sealed with a red string twisted around a small cardboard button. He unwrapped the string, took out a sheaf of papers, spun his chair back to his desk, and handed me the papers. I looked them over. They were the stock certificates and they said everything Roland had said they would say.

"You know what the long drop method is?" I said, continuing to study the certificates.

"No," Roland said.

"It's a method hangmen use," I said. "They measure the condemned person's weight and the distance of his or her neck from the ground, then calculate the length of rope needed from the 'Official Table of Drops' to ensure a quick death with as little suffering as possible."

"Why are you telling me this?" Roland said.

I looked up.

"Just screwing with you," I said.

Roland studied me.

"I just realized something," Roland said.

"What?" I said.

"You don't believe the drone sub engineers' deaths are any less a coincidence than I do," Roland said.

I didn't say anything.

"And you're not down here just to protect Dr. Lennon, are you?" Roland said. "You're here to figure out if Carter Bowdoin has something to do with the impending war with China."

"Roland, you're letting your imagination get the better of you," I said.

Roland said nothing.

"You don't mind if I take these certificates with me, do you?" I said.

"They're yours," Roland said. "I wish I'd never laid eyes on them."

I folded the certificates and put them in my pants pocket.

"Remember," I said. "Not a word to anyone."

Suddenly there was a tremendous roar and the windows in Roland's office rattled and shook. A NASAD helicopter flew by the window and made a wickedly banked turn. Roland and I both went to the window to get a better look. The helicopter banked again just inches from the ground and slammed down onto the NASAD helipad, first one skid then the other. It had to be Donnie Kurtsinger at the controls, but how did he get cleared to fly so soon after what had happened at the drone sub plant?

My iPhone rang. I took it out of my pocket and looked at the screen. It was Kate. I answered the phone.

"We're on the helipad," Kate said. "We need you down here right now please, Jack."

PART V

THE VALLEY

CHAPTER 78

It was about 5:00 p.m. when I quickly left Roland Wachtel's office, rode the elevator to the lobby, and sprinted to the helipad. The chopper waiting for me was an exact duplicate of the other two NASAD helicopters I had ridden in earlier that day and its rotors were still spinning. I ducked under the chopper's blades and climbed the ladder into the rear passenger compartment.

Both rows of the compartment's seats were filled. Adelaide, Kate, and Jeff sat in the forward row. Ray Carpenter, along with two other members of his FBI SWAT team, were in the back row. Ray and the SWAT team members were in full armored black regalia, toting MP5 submachine guns, and carrying Glocks in holsters at their sides. Everyone in the passenger compartment was wearing a flight headset with a microphone and earphones. Donnie Kurtsinger was up front in the pilot seat. The plexiglass cabin partition separated him from everyone in the passenger compartment.

Jeff was munching on potato chips from an oversize bag. He still wore his neon green Hurley board shorts, but since I'd last seen him at the beach he'd also put on his Willie Shoemaker t-shirt and running shoes. Adelaide's clothing was also different since I had last seen her. She was still in her gold thong bikini, but had added a pair of flip flops for her feet. Adelaide's camouflage belt was still around her waist and her SOG tactical combat knife was sheathed in the scabbard attached to her belt.

"I got down here as fast as I could," I said to Kate. "What's going on?"

Donnie yelled through the plexiglass partition, "What's going on is we have to get moving. I'll brief you en route. Now, take a seat."

Which I would have happily done, except there were no empty seats in the compartment.

"Donnie," I yelled back, "you realize there are no seats back here, don't you?"

Jeff said, "You can sit on my lap."

Jeff's lap was covered with greasy potato chip fragments.

"I think I'll pass," I said.

Adelaide said, "You're a macho dude, why don't you just hang onto the skids outside?"

"That's a great idea," I said. "Why didn't I think of that myself?"

Kate, indicating a spot on the floor between her knees, said, "There's room right here."

That had an understandable momentary attraction. However with Donnie Kurtsinger at the helicopter's controls, I knew I needed to find a place where I could strap myself in or risk grave bodily harm.

"Thanks," I said. "But with Donnie driving, I feel that might be particularly unwise."

"Unwise?" Kate said.

"Let's put it this way," I said. "I'd feel more comfortable with my very own seatbelt."

Donnie yelled, "Stop wasting time, asshole. You can sit up here with me."

I backed out of the passenger cabin and shut the door. Staying low beneath the spinning blades, I sidestepped over to the copilot's door of the front cabin. I opened the door, lowered my head, crawled in, and took the copilot's seat. Donnie handed me a headset just like the one everyone else was wearing and I put it on.

"Which switch controls the intercom so that you and I are the only ones that can hear each other?" I said.

Donnie pointed at a switch on the chopper's control panel. I flipped it, then said, "What's up?" into my microphone.

"Massive explosion," Donnie said. "NASAD is now an official war zone."

"You must feel right at home," I said.

"You betcha," Donnie said.

"What blew up?" I said.

Donnie flipped some switches on his instrument panel and appeared to be checking the gauges as well.

"Some kind of super top secret plant," Donnie said. "I still don't know what they did there, but it must've happened close to 3:00 p.m. Dr. Lennon saw her brother, Carter Bowdoin, Bryce Wellington, and Burnette hustle off in a chopper from her estate at around four o'clock. She called the NASAD transportation department to see where they were going."

"Neither Freddy or anyone in his crew told her themselves?" I said.

"Nope," Donnie said. "Dr. Lennon said the four of them were moving very fast and looked real worried, so she figured she better see what was up. Dr. Lennon's not the kind of woman who likes to be kept in the dark."

I studied Donnie's face. His eyes were sunken and his lower eyelids were black bags. His skin was pale and there was a fine sheen of sweat on it.

"They cleared you to fly with a concussion?" I said.

Donnie flipped some more switches on the instrument panel.

"No," Donnie said. "Dr. Lennon overrode NASAD transportation. She told them it was an emergency flight and she needed a pilot."

"Aha," I said.

"If I pass out, just take over," Donnie said.

"Jeff's the pilot, not me," I said.

"You'll just have to wing it then," Donnie said.

"Is that a pun?" I said.

"Yes," Donnie said. "A good one, too."

Donnie shoved the throttle all the way forward and the engines whined loudly. I was thrown back in my seat as the helicopter violently lifted off the ground. Donnie kept the throttle on full, pushed the chopper's nose down, and, hugging the low foothills to the east, we raced away from the NASAD campus.

I braced myself in my seat and pointed at another switch on the chopper's control panel.

"That one make it so that I can communicate with everyone on board?" I said.

Donnie nodded. I toggled the switch.

"Donnie says there was an explosion at a NASAD facility but he doesn't know what the facility was used for," I said into my headset.

Ray Carpenter said, "Correct. A NASAD building in the east San Fernando Valley blew up, but we still have no information regarding what kind of work was done there."

"Casualties?" I said.

"Maybe fifty or more," Carpenter said.

"Deaths?" I said.

"Unclear at this moment," Carpenter said. "Hopefully we'll find out when we get to the site. ETA is fifteen minutes."

Donnie sharply banked the chopper into a small canyon and my head was slammed into the cabin door. I saw stars and nausea swept through my body. I was glad I hadn't taken Kate up on her offer to sit between her knees. If I had, stars and nausea would have been the least of my problems - Donnie's last maneuver could easily have pitched me through a window and sent me plummeting to the ground.

My iPhone vibrated as a text arrived. It was from Jeff. It read, "FYI, Adelaide be up to speed on everything. She understand it confidential. She also say thanks for trusting her."

"Well I'll be," I texted. "An Adelaide thank you. A very rare beast indeed."

"Exceedingly rare," Jeff texted. "We should enjoy it while we can."

A few minutes later the chopper entered the airspace above the San Fernando Valley and made a beeline for its northeast corner. The valley was a huge basin bounded by low mountains on all sides. Dozens of east-west and north-south boulevards cut the entire valley surface into tiny chessboard squares of green and white and brown. Giant freeways exited and entered the valley through canyon passes to the east, west, north, and south.

A transparent orange and purple haze floated over the valley's basin, and, even inside the chopper, ozone burned my nostrils. Apartment buildings, factories, malls, and single-family homes shimmered beneath the haze while cars moved everywhere like confused ants. The helicopter temperature gauge showed the outside air had been heated to at least one hundred and five degrees. The San Fernando Valley might have been a pleasant enough - though perhaps somewhat challenging - area within which to live a few hundred years ago when it was an empty desert, but in its present condition it had the look of a hopeless place, walled-in and doomed.

My iPhone vibrated again as a new text arrived. This one was from Adelaide.

"You and Jeff didn't have to tell me to keep the mission secret," Adelaide texted. "I know secrecy is of vital importance in military operations."

"I know you do," I texted.

"Then why did you do it then?" Adelaide texted. "Wait. Don't answer. You probably think I don't know the difference between professional soldiering and taking Jeff's boots and using his credit card and running away to Carson City to enlist."

"I'm sure you know the difference," I texted. "So does Jeff. We never would have trusted you with mission critical information if we didn't. We both believe you are well beyond your years when it comes to being a professional soldier, and nothing in your training has ever led us to believe otherwise."

"Good, because I am," Adelaide texted.

"Of course, Jeff and I also believe some of your other behaviors leave a lot to be desired," I texted.

"Ugghh!" Adelaide texted. "Why didn't you just quit when you were ahead?"

I felt Adelaide had just made a good point, so I cut off the text conversation, and so did she for that matter. I also realized I needed to get my own text out to Haley. I wanted to get her working on the information I'd learned from the NASAD chief financial officer Roland Wachtel. I took out my iPhone and texted Haley the date of Carter Bowdoin's visit to Panama, the name of the bank he used, and a general description of the bearer-bond-like stock certificates that Roland had told me about. I asked Haley to use her unique talents to hack into the bank and find the agreement.

The reason I asked Haley to hack into the Panamanian bank to find the agreement was that I thought it was a good bet that Carter had met his Chinese counterpart at the bank, and that the bank would have been given the role of safekeeping whatever agreement had been made between the two of them. The odds were also good both Bowdoin and Bowdoin's Chinese counterpart had each used a Panamanian holding company, or its equivalent, to be the signatory on the agreement. If we learned the name of Bowdoin's Chinese counterpart's holding company, it might allow us to track back to the counterpart's identity. I was hoping that Bowdoin's counterpart and Dragon Man would turn out to be the same person, because if he was, I was confident, that armed with Dragon Man's true identity, MOM and I could hunt Dragon Man down. Of course, everything depended on my assumption being correct that there was an agreement between Carter and his Chinese counterpart. I had a very strong hunch, however, that there was a good chance that assumption was correct, and that I was on the right path.

The NASAD helicopter continued on towards the northeast corner of the San Fernando Valley. As we passed over the 405 Freeway a flock of birds suddenly appeared in front of us. I thought we would smash into the birds, but they parted to make way for the chopper like a river moving around a rock. A moment later, we hit a thermal and the chopper rose and fell fifteen feet in a matter of seconds. A moment after that, we crossed the Hollywood Freeway and it was then that I first saw our destination. A few miles ahead of us, a huge crater was sitting like a scar upon the earth.

My iPhone vibrated again indicating another text had come in. The text was from Kate this time. It read, "God I hope no one is dead at the site."

"I hope so too," I texted back.

"The reason I'm texting you instead of talking is because I have a question that is nobody else's business," Kate texted. "How did your meeting go with Roland Wachtel?"

I didn't answer Kate right away. I was still running my 'need to know' filters, and I didn't feel my conversation with Roland was something Kate absolutely needed to know at that moment. I decided my best course of action was to stall.

"The meeting with Roland was very interesting," I texted. "I'll fill you in when we get a moment alone."

"Okay," Kate texted.

"Were you the one that invited Adelaide and Jeff to come along?" I texted.

"Yes," Kate texted. "I asked Carpenter to call the Coast Guard and get them to send Jeff up from the beach. When Jeff arrived, Adelaide was with him. Jeff told me he had filled her in on our mission, so I asked her to come with us too. I'm glad they're on the team."

"Me too," I texted. "I think..."

"Nothing to think about," Kate texted. "They're great."

"You sure you're okay with Adelaide coming along?" I said.

"If you and Jeff trust her, I trust her," Kate said.

The closer we got to the crater, the more it reminded me of a newly extinguished volcano. Plumes of smoldering white smoke rose from its black, crusty, funnel-shaped walls. Charred chunks of exploded concrete and steel lay near the crater's edges and looked like nothing so much as the giant rocks that form when lava flows cool and that can be found strewn about most volcanic fields.

I'm not sure what it was – maybe it was the utter devastation surrounding the crater and its intimations of all out war – but right at that moment something finally clicked in my mind about how Dr. Nemo and the dark programmers might have constructed their war games weapon. I felt an urgent need to share my insight with Jeff.

"Donnie, do you have a way to patch Jeff's and my headsets together so that I can have a private conversation with him?" I said.

Donnie kept his head facing forward, and without saying a word, reached over and flipped two switches on the chopper's instrument panel.

"Thanks," I said.

Donnie gave me a thumbs up.

"Jeff, can you hear me?" I said into my headset's microphone.

"Loud and clear," came Jeff's response over my earphones. "What's up?"

"We've been looking at this whole thing the wrong way," I said.

"What thing?" Jeff said.

"Nemo and the dark programmers' war games software weapon," I said.

"That ain't surprising, since everything we come up with so far make it seem like the dark programmers' weapon got major deficiencies," Jeff said.

"That's because we've been thinking *on*, not *in*," I said.

"'*On*, not *in*'?" Jeff said. "What the hell you talkin' about?"

"We've been thinking it's an attack *on* the military's computers," I said. "But the only way I can see the weapon being foolproof is if it's already *in* the computers."

Jeff was quiet for a moment.

"That'd solve a lot of problems for the enemy, wouldn't it?" Jeff said. "No need to try to breach network firewalls or try to target a million computers that could be anywhere on God's green earth. How you'd come up with that?"

"I've been toying with the idea of how to make something the Chinese would consider an insurmountable edge," I said. "And I kept replaying in my mind what I'd watched on the Jumbotron as the defensive team in the Cyber Defense Hall fended off a hacking attack from the Nasty Pandas…"

"But that be a hacking attack coming from outside of NASAD," Jeff interrupted.

"Yes, outside," I said. "But then while I was replaying what happened, I remembered Raj said the war games would be conducted on software that, pending any modifications that might be needed based on the results of the war games, had already been approved for updating into the military's live computer systems. Raj also said that in order to prepare their war game attacks, the dark programmers had a copy of the software. So…"

"Being the devious person you is," Jeff interrupted again, "you said to yourself 'If I had a copy of the software, what's the nastiest thing I could do to it to give myself an insurmountable edge?'"

"I don't know if I'd call myself devious, but yes that's what I did," I said.

"And what you figured you could do was alter that copy so that the copy itself got a powerful weapon already in it, and then find a way to be sure the war games run on your altered copy, not on the copy Raj gave you to study," Jeff said. "Since the defensive team in the Cyber Defense Hall be waiting for an external attack to show up on their Jumbotron, they'd have no idea what hit them." Jeff paused. "Also come to think of it, they probably got no idea how to defend against something that already hardwired into the software."

"Now who's the devious one?" I said.

"You come up with it first," Jeff said.

"But you didn't need much leading to get there, did you?" I said.

"I guess we both devious then," Jeff said.

"Thank you," I said. "So, the next obvious logical step, of course, would be that an evil piece of shit gets hold of my altered copy…"

"Such piece of shit being in the employ of the Chinese," Jeff said.

"Absolutely, without a doubt," I said. "And while in the employ of the Chinese, such person finds a way to get that altered copy installed on all the U.S. military's computers."

"I bet they coulda' just made it look like a standard software update," Jeff said.

"How would they do that?" I said.

"I don't know," Jeff said. "But it seems like it could be done if you knew how the updating process worked."

"What do you think the alteration is?" I said.

"I got no clue," Jeff said.

"You'd agree with me, however, that if the Chinese think the alteration is insurmountable, it has to be bad enough to severely disrupt the fighting capacity of our entire armed forces?" I said.

"No question about that," Jeff said. He paused. "I think we definitely on the right track. Should we get Haley and MOM to start looking at the live military computer systems' software to see if they can find an alteration to the programming that could qualify as an insurmountable edge?"

"Even though we both believe we're on the right track," I said, "given that we pretty much just came up with this, that we don't have any hard evidence to back up our thinking, and that it probably would take up a lot of MOM's resources to conduct such a search…"

"It seems like a pretty big ask," Jeff said.

"It does," I said.

"Maybe we can do a little more thinking on this subject and have ourselves a full discussion after we figure out what's goin' on down at that crater," Jeff said. "We still believe we headin' in the right direction, then maybe we share it with Haley."

"Sounds like a plan to me," I said.

We continued to fly closer and closer to the crater. I could see that the crater was bordered on the north by a flood control basin, and to the south by a salvage yard's acres of wrecked cars. To the crater's east was what looked to be a huge parking lot covered with an endless sea of cracked concrete. The lot was surrounded by a high barbed wire fence. Hundreds of blue cargo shipping containers sat atop the concrete. To the crater's west lay row upon row of warehouses whose roofs and walls were made of rusting steel.

When we were half a mile away from the crater, I could make out dozens of big red fire trucks around the crater's rim. The fire trucks' water cannons were aimed at the center of the crater, though at that moment the cannons were inactive. The firemen must have felt their job was done.

The ring of fire trucks was enclosed by a ring of about twenty ambulances. The ambulances were painted white, blue, yellow, or red, and were parked on a large patch of dry, barren earth that surrounded the crater. The ambulances were in turn ringed by perhaps thirty Los Angeles City Police Department and Los Angeles County Sheriff's black and white patrol cars. Mixed among the patrol cars were a few vehicles that looked like unmarked police cars.

Paramedics, forensic techs, and cops stood by the ambulances and police cars, apparently waiting for some signal calling them to action. Since the explosion had taken place almost two hours ago, I took the fact that the medical personnel and ambulances were *waiting* and *not doing* as a bad sign.

Outside the rings of fire trucks, ambulances, and police cars, was yet another ring. That ring was about two hundred yards from the center of the crater and was made up of hundreds of spectators and at least six news vans. The spectators and news vans' crews were held in check by yellow police tape and sheriff's deputies. The combination of spectators and news vans was eerily reminiscent of the scene I had encountered at the stoning site in the Mojave Desert not much more than twenty-four hours before.

A NASAD helicopter was parked between the rings of ambulances and police cars on a large section of barren dirt that looked like it had been cleared for a landing zone. Donnie set our chopper down next to the other helicopter and shut off the engines. Donnie and I removed our headsets and unfastened our seat harnesses.

"Do me a favor, please," I said. "After we get out of the chopper, I don't want you anywhere near it. Go and find someplace safe for yourself while I try to figure out what's going on here. I don't want to have to save your fat ass again if someone tries to blow up this bird too."

Donnie stood up, reached behind his seat, and pulled out a cooler.

"Mind if I have a few cold ones while I wait?" Donnie said.

"You trying to kill off any brain cells the concussion missed?" I said.

"Who says it missed any?" Donnie said.

"You're right, it probably didn't," I said. "But, be that as it may, I don't think you should be drinking considering you got a cargo hold full of civilians instead of some whacked out Rangers you're gonna have to ferry back home."

"I won't drink more than a few six-packs," Donnie said.

"Only a few, huh?" I said. "Does it bother you at all that your boss, Dr. Lennon, is one of those civilians?"

"Nope," Donnie said.

I had a hard time believing Donnie was serious about getting drunk, but I wasn't relishing a fight with him over the cooler. Donnie seemed to delight in watching my mind whir as I tried to decide what to do next. Without taking his eyes off me, Donnie opened the cooler. It was filled with ice, cans of Coca Cola, and nothing else.

"Okay, you got me," I said. "Very funny, asshole."

Donnie looked surprised.

"What?" Donnie said. "You didn't think I was talkin' about beer, did ya'?"

"You know I did," I said.

Donnie laughed.

"Real eyes realize real lies," Donnie said.

"What the hell does that mean?" I said.

"I got no idea," Donnie said. "Saw it on the wall of a latrine at a landing zone in Mosul."

We exited the chopper. Donnie and I slid open the passenger compartment door and helped everybody out. Ray Carpenter and his two men formed a protective shield around Kate. Donnie, his job done for the moment, ambled about thirty yards away from the chopper and sat down on a rock that was lying amidst some dead weeds. He opened his cooler, grabbed a Coke, tore the tab off the top of the can, and took a few pulls.

The rim of the smoldering crater was about a hundred yards away from us. Freddy, Carter Bowdoin, Bryce Wellington, and Special Agent Burnette were standing close to the rim. They were accompanied by an escort of a dozen heavily armed FBI agents. I didn't recognize any of the agents in the escort. It looked like Burnette had put together a completely different team than the ones he had at the NASAD drone submarine manufacturing site and the Coso Junction rest stop.

"Burnette looks well protected," I said to Carpenter. "But I'd take you and your two men over his twelve anytime."

"Thanks," Carpenter said.

Kate seemed a bit uncomfortable with how closely Ray Carpenter and his men were guarding her.

"I appreciate all the attention," Kate said. "But do we really need to do this?"

I said, "We do unless you want to go back home."

"It looks pretty quiet to me," Kate said.

"As I remember it, it looked pretty quiet at NASAD's drone sub manufacturing site this morning too," I said.

Kate said nothing.

"Has your brain come up yet with even the slightest inkling of what the facility here was used for?" I said.

"No," Kate said. "I've never even been informed of its existence before."

"I would have thought you knew where all of NASAD's major facilities were," I said.

"NASAD has some top secret sites whose locations are shielded even from the board," Kate said.

I got a sinking feeling in the pit of my stomach. An explosion, massive casualties, and a NASAD facility completely unknown to Kate? Given all that had gone on, wasn't it likely that NASAD's top secret dark programmers would be a target of the brutal enemy I was chasing? What if that smoking crater was whatever was left of the dark programmers' workplace, and indeed, the dark programmers themselves? What if Nemo had been inside when it was blown up?

Suddenly, I detected movement within the crater. Near the crater's center, three men in yellow hazmat suits were climbing out of what seemed to be a hole in the ground. The men's hazmat suits looked like spacesuits. The suits appeared to be made of heavy-duty polyethylene coated fabric and had helmets with clear plastic faceplates. The men also wore self-contained breathing apparatuses on their backs.

The immediate question I had, of course, was where did that hole lead to? I guessed there must have been a NASAD workplace underneath whatever above ground structure had once existed on the site. The above ground structure had been reduced to ash, shattered hunks of concrete, and molten metal, but what of the below ground workplace? Had it been some kind of bunker with blast tolerances that had allowed it to survive the explosion?

I wasn't able to ponder that question for long, however, because I soon noticed that there was something very wrong with the hazmat team. At least with one member of the team anyway. That one member was the last tech up the stairs and he didn't have his breathing hose connected from his breathing apparatus to his helmet.

CHAPTER 79

I was sure that if any of the assembled firemen, paramedics, or policemen had noticed the hazmat tech's disconnected hose they would have called the tech's attention to it. But none of them said anything about the hose, nor did any of them seem to have even seen it. I assumed this was due to the fact they were all too preoccupied with their own concerns.

The responsible thing to do would have been to warn the hazmat tech about the disconnected hose myself, but after watching what happened next, I decided such a warning was unnecessary. What happened next was that the three hazmat techs washed down each other's protective suits, peeled out of their own suits, and then turned off their breathing apparatuses. The tech with the disconnected hose, however, had stared directly at the hose when he had turned off his breathing apparatus and had shown absolutely no reaction.

Which meant that either the tech was a fool or something else was going on.

What could that something else be?

I came up with two possible explanations.

Either the underground NASAD bunker was truly all clear of any dangerous chemicals and gasses, or, the techs' investigation of the bunker had been an elaborate charade from start to finish.

At that moment I had no way to tell which explanation was more likely to be correct.

Two of the hazmat techs, one of whom was the tech whose breathing hose had been disconnected, went off and joined some paramedics who were sitting on the hood of one of the ambulances.

The third hazmat tech - who also happened to be the tech I had seen unstrap a small camera from his forehead just after he had removed his protective suit - joined Freddy, Carter Bowdoin, Bryce Wellington, and Burnette. The third tech handed the small camera to Burnette and appeared to begin briefing all four men on what his hazmat team had found in the bunker.

I wondered about the photos contained on the small camera. I assumed that the hazmat team, in addition to their duties in regard to analyzing the bunker for any continuing health threats to the living, had also taken pictures of the dead to help with the identification of the bodies. If the bodies belonged to the dark programmers, and perhaps even Dr. Nemo as well, that was a tragedy for all of them. If the bodies belonged to the dark programmers and Nemo, it was also a harsh blow to my mission as I wouldn't be able to talk to any of the dead about the insurmountable edge. But I had to put any feelings I had about those two issues aside. I needed to consider the potential implications of the existence of that small camera and the fact that the tech had passed it to Burnette.

One. If the dark programmers and Dr. Nemo truly lay dead beneath the crater, were Burnette, Bowdoin, Wellington, and Freddy behind their massacre?

Two. If the dark programmers were dead, then had our enemy - and it was possible Burnette, Bowdoin, Wellington, and Freddy were all in the enemy camp - killed the NASAD dark programmers to cover up the programmers' involvement with the insurmountable edge?

Three. If Burnette, Bowdoin, Wellington, and Freddy were behind the massacre, were they checking the photos not just to identify the bodies, but to see if they'd killed every dark programmer they intended to kill?

Four. If Dr. Nemo had been killed in that crater, had he been a specific target of the four men? Or had he simply been killed along with all the rest of the dark programmers? Or was it vice versa - Dr. Nemo had been the target, but the other dark programmers had been killed in an attempt to get Nemo?

Five. If Dr. Nemo had been the target, wouldn't that confirm my suspicions our enemy had been aware of Dr. Nemo's attempts to contact Kate and thus had been hunting him all along? If my suspicions were true, and by some chance Nemo had escaped the massacre, wouldn't our enemy continue to hunt him?

I thought the best way to begin answering all of those questions was to talk to the hazmat techs as soon as possible about what they had found in the bunker. With Burnette close by, I didn't think that would be easily accomplished, but it was still worth a try. I turned back to Adelaide, Jeff, Kate, Ray Carpenter, and Carpenter's two FBI SWAT agents. I was about to tell them about my desire to talk to the hazmat techs, when I noticed that Adelaide's shoulders were starting to take on a lobster shell hue.

"Did you put sunscreen on, Adelaide?" I said.

"I don't burn," Adelaide said.

"Jeff doesn't burn," I said. "You burn, and in fact, are burning."

Kate reached into her purse, took out a tube of sunscreen, and handed it to Adelaide. Adelaide put an infinitesimal amount on her face and shoulders.

I spoke to Jeff and Ray Carpenter.

"Either of you see what I saw?" I said.

Jeff said, "I assume you talking about the hazmat tech with that hose that ain't connected?"

Ray said, "I was wondering about that too. What do you think it means?"

"Not sure," I said. "Either they knew it was safe before they went down that hole, they determined it was safe while they were underground, or the tech is completely incompetent and is going to be our canary in the coal mine."

Adelaide, who had been listening to our conversation while applying the sunscreen, said, "Canary in the coal mine?"

Jeff said, "He be referring to miners. They used to bring canaries down to coal mines as an early warning system. Canaries more sensitive to poison gas so they die before a human does. Miner see a dead canary, it mean time to get out."

Adelaide looked questioningly at me, as if she wasn't sure if Jeff was pulling her leg or not.

"Couldn't have put it better myself," I said.

Carpenter said, "If they knew it was safe before they went down there, then all this might be just another show."

"That's what I was thinking," I said. "Burnette, Freddy, Carter, and Bryce look like they're getting briefed by the hazmat tech. How about we join them and try to figure out what's what?"

"Sounds like a plan to me," Carpenter said.

Jeff said, "Might also be nice to see what's on that camera that tech give to Burnette."

"You saw the tech hand it to him too, huh?" I said.

Jeff nodded.

"Short of killing Burnette," I said, "you have any idea how we can get the camera from him?"

"Nope," Jeff said. "I said it be nice to see what's on the camera, not that it's possible."

Carpenter and I headed off towards Burnette, Freddy, Carter, Bryce, and the third hazmat tech. But before we had taken more than a few steps, Freddy appeared to notice us. He immediately broke away from the other four men and started walking in our direction. Carpenter and I came to an abrupt stop. We watched as Freddy moved towards us with his head down, carefully picking his way among the smoldering bits of ash, rocks, and gopher holes on the surface of the barren dirt patch.

When Freddy arrived at our side, he was breathing heavily and his face was covered with a sheen of sweat. His suit, untucked shirt, and shoes were layered with dust.

"Things aren't good," Freddy said.

Kate said, "What does 'aren't good' mean, Freddy?"

"There are no survivors," Freddy said.

I said, "You're sure?"

"The hazmat team was in the bunker for over an hour," Freddy said. "Everyone's dead."

"So there's a bunker under the crater?" I said.

"Yes," Freddy said. "Where the crater is now used to be a three-story office building. The bunker was under the building."

"The bunker is still intact?" I said.

Freddy nodded.

"The dead," I said. "Were they NASAD employees?"

Freddy sighed, nodded again, then tipped his head forward and down, seemingly studying his shoes. We waited for Freddy to continue. He didn't. Jeff, Kate, Ray, and I exchanged glances, but none of us said anything.

I think we all sensed that questioning someone under as much emotional stress as Freddy seemed to be under might be counterproductive. It was probably better to give him some time to regain his composure. Hopefully Freddy would find the words to express himself. Adelaide, however, appeared to be having trouble with the waiting process and quickly took matters into her own hands.

"Come on, dude!" Adelaide said to Freddy. "Tell us who was in the goddamn bunker!"

Freddy looked up. He studied her, as if he was trying to place who she was.

"Who are you?" Freddy said.

I said, "Sorry, Freddy. I should have introduced Adelaide and Jeff. Adelaide is my ward, and General Jeff Bradshaw is my good friend and colleague."

"What are they doing here?" Freddy said. "And why isn't she wearing any clothes?"

Adelaide said, "Not that it's any of your business, but we were at the beach."

I said, "Adelaide and Jeff are here to help me protect Kate."

I had fully expected this information to cause Freddy to go into a tirade, but it did not. In fact, the opposite seemed to be occurring - Freddy appeared like he might be going into something approaching shock. Just as I was thinking that, Freddy stared right at me. I was surprised to see what I was pretty sure was pleading in his eyes. The pleading was so out of character for Freddy, that I began to feel a completely different sensation than I had ever felt in Freddy's presence. I was worried about him.

"You okay, Freddy?" I said.

"I've been better," Freddy said.

"Do you need to sit down?" I said.

"No," Freddy said.

Jeff, who had carried his bag of potato chips with him when he left the chopper, extended the bag towards Freddy.

"Want some chips, Freddy?" Jeff said.

"Thanks," Freddy said.

Freddy put his hand into the bag, took out a big fistful of chips, put one chip in his mouth, and chewed.

I said, "Freddy, you said there were no survivors, correct?"

Freddy nodded.

"Do you think you can tell us who worked in the bunker now?" I said.

"No one was supposed to know," Freddy said. "Not even I knew. Dad set it up that way."

"But you know now?" I said.

Freddy nodded.

"The dark programmers," Freddy said.

The sinking feeling I had in my stomach since we had landed at the crater sank a whole lot lower.

"You're absolutely sure about that?" I said.

Freddy nodded.

"Fifty-five of them, plus the vice president of dark programming," Freddy said. "They worked in the bunker. All dead now."

"My understanding was that everything about the dark programmers was top secret," I said.

"It was top secret," Freddy said. "My dad put a system in place over thirty years ago. He made it so the NASAD vice president of dark programming is supposed to break the secrecy protocols only in the event of certain occurrences."

"A mass attack on the programmers being one of those occurrences?" I said.

"Uh huh," Freddy said.

"So that's what the vice president did?" I said. "He broke the secrecy protocols after the attack?"

"Not exactly," Freddy said.

"What do you mean 'not exactly'?" I said.

"The vice president didn't consciously break the protocols," Freddy said. "He's dead at the bottom of the crater with everyone else. His name was Rick Benavidez. He was a decorated war veteran. The records say Daddy would have trusted him with his life."

"If Mr. Benavidez didn't consciously break the protocols, how were they broken?" I said.

"Daddy's system automatically unsealed the records when Mr. Benavidez died," Freddy said.

"That was another good idea your daddy had," I said. "Is it safe to assume that means Mr. Benavidez was the first and only vice president of dark programming NASAD has ever had?"

Freddy nodded.

"How did NASAD learn Mr. Benavidez was dead?" I said.

"He wore a GPS device that also monitored whether he was alive or not," Freddy said.

"His death caused the device to notify NASAD of both his death and his location?" I said.

Freddy nodded again.

"But the device never sent any signals to NASAD before today?" I said.

Freddy shook his head. He wiped his nose with his finger.

"Were the names of the dark programmers also automatically unsealed when Mr. Benavidez died?" I said.

"No," Freddy said. "Their names are still locked up in the system. I don't know why Daddy set up the secrecy protocols that way, but he did."

So, the NASAD vice president of dark programming was dead. Since he was the first and only vice president, it seemed he most likely wasn't one of the bad guys, and was someone I could have trusted. I supposed I could have tried harder to reach him, as we might have had a productive conversation once I shared my thoughts with him about the possible connection between the Chinese insurmountable edge and the dark programmers' war games software. Perhaps Mr. Benavidez and the dark programmers might also still be alive if I'd been able to contact him. But I didn't know what else I could have done to have effectuated that contact. It seemed to me that the systems Mr. Benavidez and Milt Feynman had established to keep the identity of Mr. Benavidez and the dark programmers a secret, as well as make it nearly impossible to communicate with Mr. Benavidez about anything other than the business items Benavidez himself had already cleared as being essential to the dark programmer division, were the systems that ultimately helped seal the programmers' and Benavidez's fates. I felt terrible about their deaths, but there was nothing to be gained at that moment by dwelling on them. I needed to move forward, and Freddy's mention of the GPS signaling of Benavidez's location had raised some questions in my mind.

"Freddy, I understand the GPS communicated Mr. Benavidez's location to NASAD upon Mr. Benavidez's death," I said. "But someone still had to know where the dark programmers were before the attack, otherwise the attack could never have occurred in the first place."

"Someone would, yes," Freddy said.

"Do you know who that someone was?" I said.

Freddy didn't say anything, but that pleading look reappeared in his eyes.

Kate, who had been closely watching Freddy, said, "Do you know something you're not telling us, Freddy?"

Freddy's pleading look was replaced with tears, and his breathing became very shallow and was accompanied by soft wheezes. He shook his head and looked down at his shoes again.

I said, "Freddy, I know this must be very hard on you. I bet you're thinking about how upset your dad would be right now if he was still alive, aren't you?"

Freddy nodded, but did not look up.

"Did you know your dad and I were very close?" I said. "I could never miss him as much as you do, but I miss him a lot."

Freddy looked up at Kate. The expression on his face seemed to be asking her if what I said was true.

Kate said, "It's true, Freddy. General Wilder and Daddy worked closely together on many projects at NASAD years ago."

I said, "You're among friends here, Freddy. If there's something on your mind, you can tell us."

Freddy looked at me, then at Adelaide, Jeff, Carpenter, Carpenter's two SWAT team members, and, finally, Kate. He began to sob uncontrollably. Freddy shuffled over to Kate and put his head on her shoulder and his arms around her chest.

Kate said, "Freddy, if you have any inkling who was behind this, you should tell us."

"I...I...can't," Freddy mumbled between sobs.

Kate looked at me and silently mouthed, "What should I do?"

I mouthed back, "Give me a minute."

It was pretty clear to me that Freddy was on the edge of a nervous breakdown. As much as I wanted to find out who he thought might have known the bunker below the smoking crater was once the home of NASAD's dark programmers, I felt if I pushed Freddy any further I could lose him altogether. I thought about what I had seen since we had arrived at the site, especially about the hazmat techs who had come out of the hole in the crater's center and the fact that one of those techs had a disconnected air hose. I decided my best course of action would be to at least find out whatever else Freddy might know about the techs and what might lie beneath that hole.

"Freddy, I understand there are some things you just can't talk about right now," I said. "But can I ask you some other questions?"

Freddy nodded.

"Did Agent Burnette say what he thought had happened here?" I said.

"Terrorists," Freddy said.

"Okay," I said. "You said there was a bunker. Can you get to it by going through the hole I saw the hazmat men come out of?"

Freddy nodded again.

"Were the dark programmers in the bunker at the time of the blast?" I said.

"Yes," Freddy said.

"Were they incinerated in the blast?" I said.

"No," Freddy said softly.

"So the dead programmers are still down there?" I said.

"Yes," Freddy said. "Daddy designed the bunker."

"It must have been a very good bunker then," I said.

"Uh huh," Freddy said. "The building above the bunker was just a decoy. The dark programmers used it to enter and exit the bunker, but all the offices in the building were always empty. The windows were opaque, so no one ever knew that though."

"How did you find out the building above the bunker was a decoy?" I said.

"Daddy had another system in place to keep the dark programmers safe," Freddy said.

"Do you know how the system worked?" I said.

"If the GPS and EKG device detects that the vice president is dead in the bunker, a camera and sensor system automatically activates and analyzes the health of all the programmers," Freddy said. "If the system determines there is something wrong with the dark programmers, the system transmits that data to the NASAD head of security so he can send emergency help."

"But if the bunker is top secret, how does the head of security know he has to tell the emergency personnel to look inside it?" I said.

"The building's and bunker's architectural plans are sent as part of the transmission," Freddy said. "The head of security is told to look in the bunker."

"So until now, everything about the bunker, even including its architectural plans, had remained top secret?" I said.

Freddy nodded.

"And everything you learned today about the building and bunker, you learned from the emergency transmission the automatic system sent to NASAD?" I said.

Freddy nodded again.

"I assume the head of NASAD security must have known it was possible he or she might one day get such a transmission?" I said.

"Yes," Freddy said. "I was told today that the security head only knew that he might receive a transmission at some point. Once he receives it, though, he has to follow protocols Daddy put in place."

"But, again, those protocols did not include revealing the identities of the dark programmers?" I said.

Freddy shook his head.

"For reasons we don't know?" I said.

"Uh huh," Freddy said.

I thought about that for a moment.

"I guess it could be some kind of fail-safe system your dad designed, as putting in a fail-safe is something Milt would definitely have done," I said. "He may have worried the sensors could make a mistake, and wanted to protect the identities of any dark programmers who were unharmed in a catastrophe so they could continue working in the dark programming division. Your dad also probably didn't want to reveal the identities of any injured programmers since he might have thought there was a chance they could get medical care without having to reveal they worked in the dark programming division. If they were able to do that, they could come back to work when they were healed. As for the dead, your dad probably figured they could be identified from their driver's licenses or other form of personal ID."

"Maybe," Freddy said. "But since they're all dead, what difference does it make?"

Freddy was right, of course. Whatever system Milt had put in place really didn't matter at that point. What did matter was whether or not I could obtain the names of the dark programmers. If I could do that, I might be able to determine if Dr. Nemo was among the dead. But I didn't say anything to Freddy about that. I did, however, wonder what Milt's plan had been for replacing the vice president of dark programming if a vice president died before they could replace themselves. Would the NASAD head of security, or the NASAD board, automatically get a message outlining the proper protocol once there had been such an occurrence? It was a challenging problem to be sure, but not one I could afford to think about at that moment. I needed to concentrate on what had happened to the dark programmers and what their deaths meant to my mission.

"Does anybody know how the programmers died?" I said.

Freddy mumbled something.

"What was that, Freddy?" I said.

"No," Freddy said. "The hazmat man said they look like they're sleeping."

He wiped his nose with his suit sleeve. His sobs were slowly changing to whimpers and he seemed to be regaining his composure. Freddy still clung tight to Kate, however.

"Sleeping?" I said.

"Peaceful," Freddy said. "They're very peaceful."

"So the bodies are intact?" I said. "The hazmat team didn't say anything about the concussive blast of the explosion or the heat of the fire afterwards damaging any of them?"

"No," Freddy said.

If Freddy was correct, and the blast or the fire afterwards didn't kill the dark programmers, what did? Poison? Suffocation? And if they were killed by poisoning or suffocation, why go through the trouble of blowing up the building?

I put those questions on hold, however, because I quickly realized something might still be salvaged from the horrendous tragedy that had just occurred in the bunker. If I could get into the bunker, I could identify the bodies using the ID's in wallets, purses, or pockets. The ones I couldn't identify that way could be identified by MOM's state of the art facial recognition software.

The odds were one of those bodies would be Dr. Nemo's, but even if it was, it did not mean all was lost. There was still a chance something Nemo might have left behind - be it on his body or near it, in his home or car, on his phone or computer - might help me crack his code.

"Is hazmat letting anyone into the bunker?" I said.

"They said the air was probably safe but they wanted to run some fans for a while just to be sure," Freddy said. "But even with the fans, no one's getting in."

I checked on our canary in the coal mine hazmat tech. He seemed alive and well.

"Why isn't anyone getting in?" I said.

Freddy turned his head on Kate's shoulder to face me.

"Bryce Wellington is worried about booby traps and secondary explosions," Freddy said.

"The FBI must have a team out here that could clear that," I said.

"Burnette said he has one," Freddy said.

"And?" I said.

"Carter said he only wanted the best," Freddy said.

"Who's the best?" I said.

"Carter said he knew about an elite team at Quantico," Freddy said. "Demanded they come out here."

"Did Burnette say he'd get them?" I said.

Freddy nodded.

Ray Carpenter, who had been listening intently to our conversation, rolled his eyes.

"When will they be here?" I said.

Freddy wiped his nose with his sleeve again. He wasn't crying anymore and seemed more focused.

"Burnette called Quantico and found out the team is on a training mission in Israel," Freddy said. "Soonest they can be here is three days."

Three days? The war with China was set to commence in ten days. With so little time left, I couldn't afford to lose any of it standing around waiting to learn what had happened in the bunker. There was also no reason in my estimation, other than Carter Bowdoin's interference, not to use the Los Angeles FBI team to clear the bunker.

Was this another strange coincidence involving Carter, or something more nefarious?

I voted for more nefarious.

More nefarious, mainly for three reasons. One, if there really was a concern about bombs and booby traps in the bunker, would the FBI have let the hazmat team down there? Two, if there really were bombs and booby traps in the bunker, wasn't it likely the hazmat team would have already set them off? And three, Carter's insistence on waiting for the Quantico team made no sense.

Bomb clearing teams or no bomb clearing teams, as long as my canary kept singing, I wasn't going to wait.

I had to get into the bunker.

A glimmer of a plan was already starting to form in my brain.

Freddy wiped his nose with his sleeve once more and stepped away from Kate.

"I better get back to Carter and Bryce," Freddy said.

"Freddy, I had the impression earlier that you might have a hunch about how the dark programmers' location was leaked," I said. "Sure you don't want to discuss it before you go?"

Freddy looked down at his shoes.

"It was a crazy idea," Freddy said. "Not worth discussing."

"I have a hard time believing that, Freddy," I said.

Freddy looked up at me, but didn't say anything.

"Well, whatever you do," I said, "don't take any action on your own."

Freddy raised his eyebrows, smiled a tight-lipped smile, and shrugged.

"I'm serious, Freddy," I said. "It could be very dangerous."

"I gotta go," Freddy said. "Sorry about crying on your shoulder, Kate."

Kate said, "Freddy, if you know who got the dark programmers killed you have to tell us."

"I don't know," Freddy said.

"I can tell you're lying," Kate said.

"Shows how little you know me, then," Freddy said.

Freddy slinked away.

"Freddy, come back here," Kate said.

Freddy gave a dismissive gesture with his hand and kept moving without turning around.

"Jack, you have to stop him," Kate said.

"And do what?" I said.

"Make him talk!" Kate said.

"Just hold on a second," I said.

I turned to watch Freddy as he waddled away.

Adelaide said, "Freddy's just a little fat boy. He wouldn't stand a chance against me. You want me to bring him back here?"

"Stay put, Adelaide," I said.

Kate said, "We really need to make Freddy tell us what he knows, Jack."

"Now may not be the right time," I said. "We need a minute to think this through."

I didn't believe there was any way we could get Freddy to talk at that moment, and I felt it best just to let him keep going. I also had another reason for letting him go, though. There were some things I had just decided I needed to tell Kate, and I wanted to be sure Freddy was out of earshot when I did. If Freddy overheard what I was going to tell Kate, I was afraid that Freddy - because of his newfound suspicions - would, despite my earlier warning to him about not trying to take matters into his own hands, do exactly that. And probably get himself killed in the process.

The first thing I wanted to tell Kate was that I was pretty sure the person Freddy suspected was his beloved Carter. The next thing I was going to tell her was that I suspected Carter Bowdoin as well. Then I was going to share with Kate everything I knew about Carter and his connection to the nightmare that had enveloped NASAD.

Normally I wouldn't have said anything to Kate about Carter Bowdoin. But the risk parameters in my 'need to know' equation had changed. The downside to Kate learning of Jeff's and my suspicions about Carter was that Kate might slip up and somehow let Carter know we were on to him. If she did, Carter and his accomplices might be driven underground where I could never reach them. Worse, such a slip up might put Kate's life in even more danger than it already was.

The upside to telling Kate far outweighed the downside, however. Kate knowing about Carter might save her life. Since I'd made my way to Southern California it had seemed that Carter was never very far away from any of us. Both Kate and Ray Carpenter needed to know just how dangerous Jeff and I believed Carter was.

When Freddy was finally far enough away from us so I was sure he wouldn't be able to hear what I had to say, I turned to Kate and said, "I'm fairly certain Freddy suspects Carter Bowdoin."

Kate appeared taken aback.

"Carter Bowdoin?" Kate said.

I nodded.

"But...I don't understand," Kate said. "Why?"

Jeff said, "Because we suspect Carter too. He behind everything."

Kate said, "Everything? What do you mean everything?"

I said, "I'll explain. But first you have to promise me you won't leak a word of what I tell you, and you also have to promise - just like I warned Freddy - that you won't even begin to think about taking any action on your own." I turned to Ray Carpenter and his two SWAT cohorts. "Anything we say here is mission critical. You gotta keep it buttoned up."

All three of them nodded.

Kate, whose face and neck had gotten very red, said, "I'm not promising anything. Because if everything really means *everything*..."

"It's still just suspicions, Kate," I said. "We have no direct proof."

"Suspicions, huh?" Kate said.

"Yes," I said.

"Suspicions that Carter Bowdoin killed my father and husband?" Kate said.

"Not with his own hands," I said. "But, yes."

"And Sam and Lizzy, and Sarah Lennon, and Paul's parents, and my employees, and all those FBI agents this morning, and everyone who's dead in that bunker?" Kate said.

"Yes," I said.

Kate stepped up close to Ray Carpenter and pointed at the MP5 submachine gun on his shoulder.

"Give me that thing," Kate said.

"I'm sorry, Dr. Lennon," Carpenter said. "I can't do that."

"I'll kill him with my bare hands then," Kate said. She spun on her heels and headed off in Carter's direction.

Adelaide whipped her combat knife out of its scabbard and said, "I'll help you."

I jumped in front of both of them.

"Settle down you two," I said.

They both glared at me.

"Don't look at me," I said. "Look at Carter instead. Tell me what you see."

Kate, fuming, said nothing.

Adelaide said, "Which one's Carter?"

Jeff said, "He the one with the Little Lord Fauntleroy 'do."

I said, "How'd you know that?"

"I already figured out fat pig-eyed guy in the porkpie hat with the gold Glock on his belly gotta be Burnette," Jeff said. "And I done know who Freddy and Bryce Wellington is. Fourth one be Carter. Process of elimination."

"Nice," I said. "Kate, you still haven't told me what you see."

Kate, still fuming, did not respond.

Adelaide said, "You aren't worried about those twelve clowns standing watch over there with the Heckler and Koch submachine guns are you?"

Adelaide was clearly referring to the team of FBI agents guarding Freddy, Bowdoin, Wellington, and Burnette.

"I am," I said.

"Pussy," Adelaide said.

Suddenly, the air was filled with the sound of screeching tires and the whine of a high revving engine. We all turned in the direction of the sound.

A Volkswagen bus was careening towards us down the city street that provided access to the NASAD facility. The bus, a classic vehicle favored by hippies in the 1960's and 70's, was covered on its roof and sides with astrological signs painted in fluorescent Day-Glo colors.

We watched as the Volkswagen made a sharp, nearly ninety degree turn, went up on two wheels, and crashed back down. It then smashed into the curb lining the city street, and, going up and over the curb, sped its way across the dirt NASAD lot toward the Maginot Line of police and sheriff patrol cars forming the outer circle of the vehicles surrounding the smoking crater. I thought the driver might try to drive the bus right through the law enforcement barricade, but the Volkswagen slid to a halt ten yards short of the cops and about thirty yards away from me.

CHAPTER 80

The bus's driver door opened. A man, who looked to be in his late twenties and about six feet tall and one hundred and eighty pounds, leapt out of the bus. The man had wavy brown hair down to his shoulders, a full brown beard hanging close to his chest, and was wearing a red and black flannel shirt, blue jeans, and Teva sandals. As soon as his feet touched the ground, the man, looking extremely agitated, began running at the wall of police cars. The cameras of all six news crews, along with the eyes of the hundreds of spectators, instantly began tracking the man's every move.

The L.A. cops had reacted immediately when the bus jumped the curb. The cops were crouched behind the open doors of their police cruisers and pointing their handguns at the bearded man. Twenty cops shouted at once, "FREEZE!"

The bearded man looked momentarily bewildered, almost as if he hadn't expected anyone to try to stop him. He seemed to come to his senses, however, and froze, putting his arms up. I noticed that he appeared not to be looking at the cops, but over their heads. I followed the direction of his gaze. I was fairly certain he was looking at Freddy, Bowdoin, Wellington, and Burnette.

"Carter, you son of a bitch!" the bearded man screamed. "What have you done?!"

Jeff said, "Ah. A kindred spirit."

I said, "I think I recognize that guy."

Kate said, "You do?"

"I'm pretty sure he's one of the defensive programmers I saw in the NASAD Cyber Defense Hall this morning," I said.

"Why don't I recognize him then?" Kate said.

"With all due respect," I said, "it's probably because it's my job to pay closer attention to those kinds of things than you do."

"Okay," Kate said. "I suppose that's possible."

"If we're lucky, he might be proof of my hypothesis," I said.

Jeff said, "What hypothesis that be?"

"That one of the NASAD dark programmer offensive team members switched over to the defense," I said. "From everything I've heard about the impregnable security system protecting the dark programmers, I thought the most likely hole would be the human element."

"Because humans weak and like to shoot their mouths off?" Jeff said.

"Correct," I said.

"You think bearded guy know this place because he used to work here?" Jeff said.

I looked over at Freddy, Bryce, Carter, and Burnette. The bearded man seemed to have captured the four men's full attention.

"The dark programmers' location was supposed to be top secret," I said. "Even Kate and Freddy didn't know where it was."

Kate said, "That's true."

Jeff said, "Hmm...Bowdoin know all the defensive dudes, since he be gambling with them. Maybe bearded guy, if he used to be a dark programmer, might have linked Bowdoin up with the offensive dudes too."

"That's part of the hypothesis," I said. "I was thinking, that since Carter is betting on the war games and he hates to lose, maybe he didn't want to rely on just the defensive programmers in the Cyber Defense Hall for his information. Maybe he wanted to supplement the defensive team's information with whatever the dark programmers' offensive team could tell him."

"Seem like something Carter be doing," Jeff said. "How come you didn't share your hypothesis earlier?"

"I didn't have anything close to resembling proof," I said. "I considered it more a hunch than a hypothesis."

"Until bearded guy show up," Jeff said.

"Until the bearded man showed up, yes," I said.

Jeff appeared to think about what I had said. He seemed bothered by something.

"I can see how you don't mention your idea if you calling it a hypothesis," Jeff said. "But you never shy about sharing your hunches before."

"It was such a weak hunch, it almost didn't qualify as a hunch," I said. "Full disclosure, however - I did tell Haley about my hunch and ask her to investigate it."

"You told Haley but not me?" Jeff said.

"Yes," I said. "Not sure why."

"I know why," Jeff said. "You're a coward. You're afraid your hunch so weak, I'd give you a hard time about it if you told me. Haley less likely try to make you explain yourself than me."

"That's probably it," I said.

Kate said, "If it's any consolation, Jeff, Jack didn't tell me his hunch either."

Jeff said, "I guess I can forgive him then." To me, he added, "Haley's investigation turn up anything yet?"

"No," I said.

"With bearded man here now, we probably won't need it to," Jeff said. "If we assume your hunch/hypothesis is true, it's likely bearded guy is mad because he thinks Bowdoin killed his buds."

"Good point," I said.

"It also possible bearded guy might not only know something about Bowdoin, but also about our 'in versus out' thinkin'," Jeff said.

"It'd certainly be worth asking him if we get the chance," I said.

Kate said, "'In versus out'?"

"It's complicated," I said. "I'll explain later."

Jeff said, "'Course, our other hypothesis also in play."

I said, "Which one?"

"That Nemo be a dark programmer," Jeff said. "He might be in that bunker."

"I've been hoping he isn't," I said

Kate said, "Jesus, he better not be."

CHAPTER 81

The bearded man remained standing in place, his hands still above his head. I didn't like the bearded man's situation - there were far too many guns pointed at him - and I knew that things could very quickly get a lot worse for him. Indeed, it was highly likely he only had a few more moments to live.

I was about to grab Ray Carpenter and tell him we needed to get to the bearded man as fast as possible. But suddenly, completely against my will, my body felt like it was stuck in molasses, and time began to slow down for me under the late afternoon sun. I was fairly certain what was happening to me was a combination of Jeff's pointing of the CheyTac M200 sniper rifle at me, my gun battles over the last two days, Burnette's drugging me, my fight with the biker drug dealers, the murders of Sam and Lizzy, my death earlier that morning, and my overall exhaustion, but that understanding did me little good. I remained stuck. Time slowed down further, and I became acutely aware of how completely calm the air was and that the only sound I could hear was the muted rustling of distant traffic.

My eyes rotated haltingly in their sockets and scanned across the faces of all those assembled on that parched piece of barren earth. Kate, Jeff, Adelaide, Ray Carpenter, and Carpenter's two FBI SWAT team members seemed like statues to me as they gazed at the bearded man. Freddy, Bowdoin, Wellington, and Burnette were still staring at the bearded man, and they, like everyone else, appeared frozen in position. Even Donnie Kurtinsinger had taken a break from his Coke downing, his eyes seemingly focused on the bearded man.

A gunshot rang out.

The shot reverberated in my ears in what felt like a chain of tidal waves thudding on my eardrums.

My eyes slowly scanned back to the bearded man.

The man looked incredulous, but had not fallen.

The bullet, apparently, had missed.

I forced my head to turn in the direction from which the gunshot's sound seemed to have come.

I saw a whiff of gun smoke drifting up from one of the L.A. cops' handguns.

The cop holding the gun looked mortified.

And then, for reasons I will never understand, I suddenly became unstuck.

Everyone and everything instantly sped up to what felt like triple time.

"Hold your fire!" screamed a male voice.

The voice belonged to an L.A. police captain crouching behind the open door of one of the police cruisers.

The bearded man said, "What the hell?!"

"Shut your mouth, asshole!" said the police captain. "And keep your hands up."

A heated discussion seemed to break out among Freddy, Carter, Bryce, and Burnette. Carter looked in the bearded man's direction, then at Burnette, then back at the bearded man, then back at Burnette. I couldn't swear to it, but something about the way Carter's gaze kept shifting back and forth led me to believe he might know the bearded man. Carter then looked at the bearded man once more, his eyes lingering on the man a lot longer than they had previously. When Carter finally turned back to Burnette, he started gesticulating wildly and simultaneously appeared to raise his voice.

I got the distinct impression that Carter was panicking and that he was trying to get Burnette to take some kind of action in regard to the bearded man. Freddy, who seemed to be paying close attention to the dialogue between Burnette and Carter, suddenly looked like he was yelling at both of them. Burnette wagged a threatening finger at Freddy and Freddy charged at Burnette. Bryce Wellington stepped between Burnette and Freddy and held Freddy back.

Burnette shook his head in apparent disgust, then waved at his close by contingent of a dozen FBI agents. Burnette seemed to bark orders at them, but I couldn't hear Burnette's exact words. The twelve agents, raising their MP5's from where they were slung on their shoulders, slowly and carefully fanned out. They cautiously made their way through the ring of fire trucks as they headed directly toward the bearded man. The twelve agents' deliberateness made me believe they were afraid of the bearded man. Burnette, meanwhile, stayed put.

I presumed that Burnette, probably at Carter's instigation, had motivated the twelve agents' actions by imparting some kind of idiocy to them. But what was that idiocy?

That the bearded man was a suicide bomber intent on blowing us all to smithereens?

Sadly, that seemed likely given Burnette's habit of blaming terrorists for all the evils that had been visited upon NASAD.

In any event, no matter how slowly the agents were moving, there was no question they wouldn't stop moving until they had traversed the hundred yards then separating them from the bearded man and come fully upon him.

"I don't like what I'm seeing," I said.

"Me either," Carpenter said.

Jeff said, "That makes three of us."

I said, "We need to talk to the guy with the beard, which means we need to get to him before Burnette's yahoos do. You got any kind of jurisdiction here, Ray?"

"I could try to manufacture something," Carpenter said. "Don't know how long it would last."

I turned to Kate.

"Kate, Donnie told me it was the NASAD transportation department that informed you a NASAD helicopter was taking Freddy, Bowdoin, Wellington, and Burnette to this site," I said. "Was Donnie right about that?"

"Yes," Kate said. "I asked the transportation department to keep tabs on Freddy and the other three for me."

"That was smart," I said.

"Thanks," Kate said.

"Do you think Freddy, or anyone in his group, knew the transportation department told you what they were doing?" I said.

"No," Kate said. "I trust my contact in the department."

"And you have no reason to suspect any of them - Freddy, Bowdoin, Wellington, or Burnette - would think you had any idea they were coming here?" I said.

"No, I don't," Kate said. "Why are you asking me all these questions?"

"I want to be sure you weren't lured here," I said.

"Like into a trap?" Kate said. "Like this morning?"

I checked on Burnette's agents. They had maintained their fanlike positioning and were slowly, but steadily, moving towards the bearded man.

"Correct," I said. "Jeff, I don't see anything that makes me think a sniper is going to jump out of the woodwork. You?"

"All clear, brother," Jeff said.

"Ray?" I said.

"Nothing that worries me," Carpenter said.

"What about you two?" I said to Ray's men.

They both shook their heads.

"Okay, here's the plan," I said. "Ray, you give your vest and helmet to Dr. Lennon. Jeff, Adelaide, and your men will stay here and protect Dr. Lennon while you and I go and arrest the bearded man."

Kate said, "Wait a second. I don't want anything to happen like what happened this morning. I'm not letting anyone be put in a position where someone might shoot at Ray's men to get at me."

"Sorry," I said. "But you don't get a vote."

"No," Kate said. "I do get a vote, and I'm not allowing this."

"Kate, you do understand that if we don't get to the bearded guy first, Burnette's guys will probably kill him?" I said.

"Kill him?" Kate said.

Jeff said, "Burnette's boys moving like that's their intention."

"But why?" Kate said.

"I can't say for sure, but it looks to me like Carter has something to do with it," I said. "Carter seemed to be in a panic over the bearded man. I bet he insisted Burnette take action. Knowing Burnette, he probably told his agents the guy's a terrorist, maybe even that he's wearing a suicide vest."

Jeff said, "Carter Bowdoin is an important man Agent Pigeyes is supposed to be protecting. No way Pigeyes gonna let a terrorist threaten Bowdoin and live to tell about it."

Burnette's team continued their slow approach toward the ring of ambulances. They had seventy-five yards to go to get to the bearded man. Kate looked from Burnette's team, to the bearded man, and back to Burnette's team again.

I said, "We gotta go now or it's going to be too late."

Kate appeared to agonize over what she should do.

"You pretty sure the bearded man is a NASAD employee?" Kate said.

"A Cyber Defense Hall programmer, yes," I said.

Kate continued to look like she was thinking hard. She took a deep breath in and let it out.

"Go, then," Kate said. "And don't let those assholes lay a finger on him."

Ray Carpenter quickly took off his vest and helmet and helped Kate put them on. Adelaide, Jeff, and Ray's two SWAT team cohorts formed a protective ring around Kate. Ray and I ran toward the bearded man.

The bearded man seemed to be focusing intently on Burnette's advancing team. Since Burnette's team was coming at the bearded man from his front, and Ray and I were approaching the man from behind, I didn't think the bearded man would notice us until we were already upon him. It looked like Ray and I had a good chance to get to the bearded man before Burnette's team did, as we had started out closer to him than they had. Our chances were also improved by the fact that Burnette's team had also slowed down once they had gotten past the ring of ambulances and was cautiously taking up positions behind the barricaded police cars.

The bearded man screamed, "You coward Bowdoin! Just like you to send a bunch of hired goons after me. Why don't you come over here and talk to me yourself?!"

Burnette yelled, "Those aren't goons, you jackass. They're a highly trained squad of elite FBI agents!"

The bearded man said, "Who the hell are you?!"

"I'm Special FBI Agent in Charge Burnette," Burnette said.

"What are you in charge of?!" the bearded man screamed. "Killing innocent people?!"

Burnette shouted something back, but that time I was distracted and didn't make out his words. I was distracted because I was grabbing the bearded man's shoulders from behind while Ray Carpenter yanked down both the man's arms and cuffed his wrists. I seized the chain linking the two handcuff rings and held the bearded man steady while Ray stepped in front of him and got between the bearded man and the dozens of cops and Burnette's FBI agents.

"What the hell you doing?!" the bearded man said.

I said, "Saving your life. And the best thing you can do right now is shut up."

"You can't do this," the bearded man said. "I haven't done anything wrong."

I pulled sharply down on the cuffs' chain.

"Ow!" the bearded man said.

"I told you to shut up," I said.

The bearded man seemed like he was about to say something else, so I pulled again and sharply twisted the chain as well.

"Okay, okay, okay," the bearded man said. "Chill, alright?"

Ray addressed the cops and agents.

"You can all stand down now," Carpenter said. "I'm FBI Special Agent in Charge Ray Carpenter and I have taken custody of this man."

The cops and FBI agents seemed unsure of what they should do.

"Stand down, I said!" Carpenter said.

One of Burnette's FBI agents yelled, "He's got a suicide vest on!"

Which was pretty much what I had expected one of Burnett's agents would say. Keeping one hand on the handcuffs' chain, I reached around to the front of the bearded man's body and ripped open his flannel shirt.

"Hey!" the bearded man said.

"For the last time, shut up," I said. Then to Burnette's agent who had spoken, I added, "Sorry, I'm confused, agent. Is that an *invisible* suicide vest we're talking about?"

The agent, glaring at me, said nothing.

Carpenter turned to the LAPD captain who had moments earlier barked orders at the bearded man.

"Captain, I need to borrow your car, please," Carpenter said.

The captain nodded and gestured for Carpenter and me to bring the bearded man over. When we got to the captain's police cruiser, I pushed the bearded man's head down and shoved him into the back seat. The cruiser had a steel cage separating the back seat from the front seat and the rear doors couldn't be unlocked from the inside. The rear door on the other side of the car from the bearded man was closed. The door I had just pushed the bearded man through was still open, but I blocked the opening with my body. As long as I didn't move, the bearded man would be protected from any gunfire and he also wouldn't be going anywhere. Carpenter took up a position next to me, standing alongside the driver's door.

The captain said to Carpenter, "What do you plan to do with him?"

"As I am sure you are aware by now, Captain," Ray said, "due to the fact the facility that was blown up was a top secret NASAD site, we're in the middle of a touchy situation that may involve national security issues. I'm going to put a call into the FBI director's office and let them make the decision."

"Good enough for me," the captain said.

I said, "Thank you, Captain. We're also going to have to ask the man some questions. If you hear anything of what we say, it's possible you will be dragged into an investigation you probably don't want any part of."

"Understood," the captain said. "I'll leave you men alone."

The captain went over to talk with some of his officers who were standing in a small group in front of the line of police cars. Burnette's twelve FBI agents, their MP5's at the ready but no longer pointed at us, maintained their positions behind the police car line. One of the agents signaled to Burnette with his palms up in the universal gesture meaning 'what should we do now?' Burnette, still about a hundred yards away from us, looked even more enraged than usual. He refused to acknowledge his agent and began walking as fast as he could toward us.

I said, "Ray, you're not really going to call the director, are you?"

"No, he'd probably just screw things up for us," Carpenter said. "But we do need to decide what to do with this guy as soon as possible."

"I've got an idea," I said.

I took out my cell phone, searched my contacts, and pushed 'send'.

"Who you calling?" Ray said.

"My new friend," I said. "U.S. Attorney Vandross."

Vandross answered on the first ring. I told him what Ray and I were up to. Vandross and I came up with a plan.

A moment later Carpenter and I watched as Burnette, who was still walking toward us, reached into his pocket, took out his cell phone, and looked down at it. Burnette grimaced, but answered the call, stopping in his tracks as he did so.

Carpenter said, "Vandross on the other end of Burnette's call?"

"Uh huh, I said. "Vandross is on his way here as well."

"Chopper?" Carpenter said.

"Yes," I said. "Vandross was at the DOJ's Los Angeles office. They just happened to have one of their choppers parked on the roof."

"Well, it better be a fast chopper," Carpenter said. "Burnette is the kind of guy who might conveniently lose a cell connection and do whatever the hell he wants."

"Like kill this kid, even though we've got him cuffed in the back of a police cruiser?" I said.

"Exactly," Carpenter said.

I got into the back seat of the cruiser and sat down next to the bearded man.

CHAPTER 82

Up close, the bearded man seemed like he might be a pleasant enough fellow under circumstances different from our current one. He had a handsome face under the beard, and there seemed to be a deep intelligence behind his dark brown eyes.

I extended my hand to the bearded man and said, "I'm Jack Wilder and that man out there is Ray Carpenter. I'm a general in the United States Army and Ray is an FBI agent. What's your name?"

The bearded man looked down at my hand.

"Really, dude?" the bearded man said.

"Sorry," I said. I leaned out the back door of the cruiser. "Ray, hand me the key to the cuffs, please."

Ray handed the key to me. I unlocked the cuffs. The bearded man tugged the front edges of his flannel shirt together - his torso had remained exposed since the moment I had ripped open his shirt to demonstrate to Burnette's team that he wasn't wearing a suicide vest - and buttoned the lone remaining button that had survived my demonstration. He then rubbed his wrists.

"Why should I talk to you, asshole?" the bearded man said.

"Maybe because I just saved your life," I said.

"Yeah, right," the bearded man snorted.

"Carter Bowdoin just had everyone who was in that bunker killed," I said. "You think he was going to let you live?"

The man stared at me. He looked like he was trying to read my mind.

"I don't expect you to trust me, not yet anyway," I said. "But take a moment to reflect."

"Reflect on what?" the bearded man said.

"On what just happened," I said.

The bearded man didn't say anything.

"I'll help you get started," I said. "Those twelve guys in the suits out there with the Heckler and Koch submachine guns take orders from the pig-eyed fat guy in the porkpie hat. Fat guy in turn takes his orders from Carter Bowdoin."

The bearded man seemed to consider this.

"How do I know you're not in with all of them?" the bearded man said. "Maybe you guys were putting on an act together. Making it look like my life was in danger so you could step in, save me, and win my trust."

"We'd have to have known you were coming to do that, wouldn't we?" I said.

"What do you mean by that?" the bearded man said.

"You think that stuff about the suicide vest was something me and the guys with the Heckler and Kochs could have made up together on the spur of the moment?" I said.

The bearded man did not reply.

"Well, I don't think we could have," I said. "I think we would have had to plan it well in advance. Which, again, means we would have to have known you were coming. How could we have known that? My hunch is even you didn't know you were coming until a very short time ago."

The bearded man appeared to ponder this.

"You think the enraged look on Pigeyes right now is an act?" I said.

The bearded man said nothing.

I took a moment to check on how Kate was doing. She was still surrounded by her guard of Adelaide, Jeff, and Ray's two men. Kate looked safe enough. She appeared to be looking at me and the bearded man. I was tempted to wave, but did not. Donnie Kurtsinger, still perched on his rock, had three Coke cans on the ground beside him, and was popping open another.

"I don't think Pigeyes is acting," I said. "I think he's truly enraged. Want to guess what's making Pigeyes so mad?"

Again nothing from the bearded man.

"I'll tell you, then," I said. "It's because he knows the only way he's going to get to you is over Agent Carpenter's and my dead bodies."

A moment passed, after which the bearded man said, "I saw you this morning in the Cyber Defense Hall."

"I saw you too," I said. "Did you see me get introduced to Carter Bowdoin?"

"Yeah," the bearded man said.

"Did I seem like I was pretending not to know Bowdoin?" I said.

"Not really," the bearded man said.

"So, if I just met Bowdoin this morning," I said, "what are the odds, I'm, as you put it, 'in with' him now?"

"Pretty low, I suppose," the bearded man said.

"They're lower than low," I said. "They're zero. So I'd like it if we can please start talking for real. I want to get Carter Bowdoin just as much as you do, and I need your help to do that."

The bearded man still seemed like he wasn't sure what to make of me. I checked on what Burnette was up to. He was yelling into his cell phone. There was a good chance Vandross would be able to keep him at bay, but as long as Vandross remained offsite, as opposed to being right up in Burnette's face, I thought there was an equally good chance Burnette would just tell Vandross to screw himself at any moment. Which meant my window of opportunity to talk with the bearded man might be closing. Or worse, the bearded man's life might be ending if Ray and I couldn't keep Burnette and his team away from him.

I decided to go for broke. I was going to tell the bearded man something that, under normal circumstances, I would never tell him. I felt by telling him, however, he might start to trust me. If he trusted me, he might begin to open up to me and tell me what he knew. And I was pretty sure he knew a lot. About Bowdoin, the dark programmers, and many of the strange and terrible things that had been going on at NASAD.

Telling the bearded man what I was about to tell him wasn't as big a risk as it might seem. I figured it was unlikely he would be able to reveal to anyone what I told him - at least not to anyone who could affect the outcome of my mission. The reason I thought that was I believed there were only two possible scenarios for what would happen next. One, the bearded man was going to be dead at the hands of Pigeyes and his crew, and dead men tell no tales. Or two - which was by far the most likely scenario, given that Ray and I were protecting him - the bearded man would be taken into in protective custody by Vandross, and Vandross would keep him from talking to anyone until my mission was complete.

"Listen," I said. "We're running out of time. I don't think I can hold Pigeyes off for much longer. I'm going to let you in on a secret, okay?"

"If you want," the bearded man said.

"I assume, given the nature of your job, you're already cleared for top secret matters?" I said.

"Yes," the bearded man said.

"Well, this is a bit above your clearance level," I said, "but the reason they sent a general to run wild around the streets of Southern California is to try to stop China from starting a war in the Middle East. I'm sure you've seen the news reports about the possibility of war?"

"I've seen them," the bearded man said.

"Good," I said. "The United States Central Command believes that China thinks it has an insurmountable military edge, or it wouldn't even consider going to war against us. I believe that insurmountable edge has something to do with what you work on at NASAD."

"You're kidding, right?" the bearded man said.

"I wish I was," I said. "U.S. Central Command also believes China will commence hostilities a week from this Friday, the same day the NASAD war games are scheduled to commence, or at least were scheduled to commence before the deaths of the dark programmers. That could be a coincidence, but I don't think it is."

The bearded man again said nothing. What I had said to him so far clearly wasn't working, at least not as fast as I needed it to work.

I decided to try a different tack.

"Did you know Milt Feynman?" I said.

"Yes," the bearded man said. "He was a great man. He hired me to work for NASAD when I was seventeen years old and had just completed my Ph.D. at MIT."

"A seventeen year old Ph.D.," I said. "That's cool."

The bearded man shrugged.

"I thought Milt Feynman was a great man too," I said. "I worked with him for a long time. He was like a father to me. Everyone believes Milt died in an accident, but they're wrong."

"What do you mean, 'they're wrong'?" the bearded man said.

I looked out through the front window of the cruiser at Burnette's twelve men. The men were maintaining their positions but seemed to be growing antsy. Their Heckler and Koch submachine guns were all still lowered, however. Outside the police cordon, food trucks were arriving to feed the ever-increasing hordes of spectators.

"Milt was murdered," I said. "Look at this."

I took out my iPhone and played the video of Milt's plane being blown out of the sky.

"Jesus goddamned Christ," the bearded man said. "I recognize that plane. I saw it on the news. It's the Otter seaplane Milt Feynman and Paul Lennon were in when it went down in Alaska."

"I believe Bowdoin was behind whoever blew up that plane," I said. "Just like I believe that Bowdoin has somehow highjacked the dark programmers' war game software for the benefit of China."

"Why would Bowdoin do that?" the bearded man said.

"Now you're the one who's kidding, right?" I said.

The bearded man seemed confused.

"Here's a hint," I said. "Why does Carter Bowdoin do anything?"

A light seemed to go off in the bearded man's head.

"Bowdoin's being paid?" the bearded man said.

"Billions," I said. "Maybe trillions."

"Trillions?" the bearded man said.

"Could easily be, yes," I said.

"That goddamn greedy bastard!" the bearded man said.

The bearded man looked me in the eye. It was a hard look that made me feel like he was trying to parse my soul. I didn't turn away from his look. After a long moment, the bearded man finally seemed to satisfy himself, and extended his hand to me.

"I'm George Boole," the bearded man said. "Sorry if I was rude earlier."

I took his hand and shook it.

"No problem, George," I said. "Nice to meet you, too."

"What do you need me to tell you?" George Boole said.

"I want to go over some ideas with you," I said. "Tell me if you think I'm on the right track."

"Okay," Boole said.

"First off," I said, "you used to be a dark programmer, correct?"

Boole's eyes went wide.

"How the hell did you know that?" Boole said.

"You, or someone like you, is a key component of my hypothesis," I said.

Just then, in a virtual replay of what I had witnessed the day before at the stoning site in the Mojave, one of the two-person news crews broke through the police line and made a beeline for the cruiser George Boole and I were sitting in. Boole and I watched as two sheriff's deputies appeared seemingly from out of nowhere and tackled the two news people to the ground.

"Those news people are batshit crazy," Boole said.

"You'll get no argument from me on that," I said.

Boole looked away from the news crews and back at me.

"So, what's the hypothesis I'm a key component of?" Boole said.

"That Bowdoin had gained access to one of the most hidden, closely guarded secrets in the U.S. defense industry," I said.

"You mean the location of the NASAD dark programmers, don't you?" Boole said.

I nodded.

Boole put his face in his hands and moaned softly.

"I screwed up, didn't I?" Boole said.

"Let's table that for the moment," I said.

Boole looked up at me.

"I'm in a lot of trouble aren't I?" Boole said.

"George, chill, okay?" I said. "We may not have much time before Pigeyes starts to freak out and there are a lot of things I need to know."

Boole didn't speak for a moment. He was looking at me but didn't seem to see me. It was as if he was running some kind of calculations in his head. Finally, he said, "If I help you, you'll help me right? That's the way these things usually go, isn't it?"

"It is," I said. "And I'll certainly do my best for you."

"Is your best usually good enough?" Boole said.

"I like to think so," I said. "Now, I assume Bowdoin got you to help him to initiate contact with the dark programmers by saying something like he was getting tired of always betting only on the defensive programmers in the NASAD Cyber Defense Hall, and thought it'd be fun to spice things up by also taking some action on the dark programmers?"

Boole's eyes widened again.

"What are you psychic, man?" Boole said.

"No," I said. "I've just been giving a lot of thought to what I would do if I were Carter Bowdoin."

"You must have a very evil mind," Boole said.

"Let's table that one for the moment, too," I said. "My hunch is Bowdoin probably said he would up the ante on the bet as well?"

"Goddamnit, who are you man!" Boole said.

"I'll take that as a yes?" I said.

Boole took in a deep breath and let it out.

"The defensive and offensive teams had been betting under ten thousand dollars per war game," Boole said. "Bowdoin said he had a way to increase the pool to ten million dollars."

"Ten million dollars?" I said.

"Uh huh," Boole said. "Bowdoin said he had a big gambler who would bet five million dollars on our defensive team in the Cyber Defense Hall as long as Bowdoin gave him two to one odds."

"So if Bowdoin bet on the dark programmers' offensive team and lost, he would lose ten million dollars to the gambler?" I said. "But if Bowdoin won, the gambler would pay Bowdoin five million?"

George Boole nodded.

"Bowdoin told the dark programmers that if he won he'd split his winnings with them," Boole said.

"Bowdoin was going to give two and a half million dollars to the dark programmers?" I said.

"Yes," Boole said.

I thought about that for a moment. As I did, one of Burnette's agents seemed to grow even more antsy. The agent raised his H&P and pointed it at our police cruiser. Carpenter instantly drew his Glock and aimed it at the offending agent's head.

"Don't be stupid, asshole," Carpenter yelled. "Lower your weapon."

The agent grimaced, but the H&P came down.

Boole looked frightened.

"Don't worry," I said. "My buddy Ray out there knows what he's doing."

"You sure about that?" Boole said.

"I'm sure," I said. "Now, I assume Bowdoin also told the defensive team in the NASAD Cyber Defense Hall that if they were victorious in the war games, they'd share in the ten million dollars won by the gambler he'd found to bet against his position on the dark programmers' offensive team?"

"Yes," Boole said. "Bowdoin said his gambler friend wanted all of us in the Cyber Defense Hall to be as highly motivated as the dark programmers."

"How much was the defensive team going to get of his friend's share?" I said.

"A quarter," Boole said.

"A quarter of ten million dollars is two and a half million dollars," I said. "Which would make it the same as what the dark programmers would have won."

"Yes," Boole said. "Bowdoin told everyone in the Cyber Defense Hall they would split two and a half million dollars."

"Which means you would have gotten a part of the defensive team's two and a half million as well?" I said.

Boole nodded again.

"All of this was kept secret from everyone else at NASAD, I presume?" I said.

"Yes," Boole said. "Can you imagine the shit-fit the board would throw if they heard about it?"

"I can," I said. "However I'm not sure I want to. I'm also having a hard time believing the NASAD vice president of dark programming condoned it."

"He didn't," Boole said. "He didn't know about it."

"But I thought the vice president was the one who helped coordinate the bets?" I said.

"The smaller bets, yes," Boole said. "But no one told the vice president about the ten million dollar bet. Everyone was sure the vice president would also throw a huge shit-fit if he found out what Bowdoin was up to, a shit-fit that was even bigger than the one the board would have thrown if they found out."

"You were actually able to keep the vice president from knowing about the bet?" I said.

"The dark programmers were," Boole said. "The vice president was a good man, but he was getting old. The dark programmers knew how to keep him out of the loop if it suited their purposes. They didn't do it very often, and they wouldn't have done it if they thought it was something bad - after all, the vice president was like a father to most of them - but they didn't consider Bowdoin's gamble anything evil. It was just something they knew the vice president would never allow."

"In retrospect it certainly looks like they should have told him," I said. "Maybe they'd still be alive."

"You're probably right about that," Boole said.

"When did Bowdoin first come up with the bet?" I said,

"We have the war games up to seven times a year," Boole said. "Bowdoin proposed the bet about nine months ago, right after the games in September of last year. We've had a few games since, but Bowdoin said he would give the dark programmers plenty of time to get ready for the games where the big bet would be in play. The dark programmers said they were ready about three months ago, but the bet wasn't scheduled to be put in play until the games that were scheduled to start a week from Friday."

I checked again on Burnette's agents. They were back to holding steady. I then checked on Burnette himself. Vandross appeared to have been doing a great job with Burnette, as Burnette, even though he was still yelling into his cell phone, was also still stalled about fifty yards away from Boole and me. The question was whether or not Vandross, whose helicopter's ETA was probably about ten minutes at that point, could continue to keep Burnette out of my hair until the chopper arrived. I figured the chances were at best still fifty-fifty.

I returned my attention to Boole.

"You put Bowdoin in touch with a dark programmer sometime after Bowdoin proposed the bet in December?" I said.

"Immediately after," Boole said.

"Who was it?" I said.

Boole hesitated.

"Everyone in the bunker is dead, George," I said.

"Yeah, I heard you say that the first time," Boole said. "You're sure about that?"

"There was a hazmat team in the bunker for over an hour," I said. "They didn't find any survivors."

George Boole put his face in his hands again and shook his head. Tears fell down his face.

"It's all my fault," Boole said.

"No, it's Carter Bowdoin's fault," I said.

Boole said nothing. I looked over at Kate again. She still seemed well protected and she was still looking my way.

"You have to be strong right now, George," I said, "or we're never going to get Bowdoin."

Boole looked up.

"Hugh MacColl," Boole said. "He was my best friend."

"Did your relationship with Hugh have something to do with you knowing there was a problem out here today?" I said.

Boole nodded.

"Hugh and I had a competition going," Boole said.

"What kind of competition?" I said.

"To see who could get the most heartbeats in a day," Boole said. "We have an app on our phones that can monitor each other's hearts."

The mention of heartbeats reminded me of the hazmat tech who had the disconnected air hose. I took a look over at the tech. He was still walking around, the canary still singing.

"You were monitoring Hugh's heart today?" I said.

"Until it stopped," Boole said.

"You actually saw Hugh's heart stop?" I said.

"The app shows a rhythm strip like an EKG," Boole said. "I didn't even know the app had it, but there's also some kind of alarm that goes off when the heart beats abnormally."

"And you heard the alarm go off?" I said.

"Yes," Boole said. "I watched as Hugh's heart slowed down and went into what the app said was ventricular fibrillation. Then his heart stopped altogether. I thought it might be some kind of trick so I called Hugh to tell him to cut it out. But he didn't answer and I got worried. So I called everyone else I knew at this site and none of them answered either."

"That's when you decided to come here?" I said.

"I wasn't sure what to do," Boole said. "Like you said, this site is top secret. It wasn't like there was anyone I could tell that I thought there might be a problem with the dark programmers. Almost immediately, however, a rumor started circulating in the Cyber Defense Hall that a NASAD facility in the east San Fernando Valley had blown up. And I knew."

"So you jumped in your VW bus?" I said.

Boole nodded.

"All the way over I kept thinking it had to be Carter Bowdoin who had gotten Hugh and maybe everybody else killed," Boole said. "NASAD has kept this site a secret for decades. I didn't think it was a coincidence that, as far as I knew, the only person who was aware of its existence, and shouldn't have been, was Bowdoin."

More Bowdoin coincidences, I thought to myself. When do coincidences make a certainty? That was more of a question for a philosopher than for me. In any event, at that moment, I was convinced more than ever that Carter Bowdoin was the prey I had to pursue.

I thought for a moment about having Ray Carpenter arrest Carter Bowdoin and Bryce Wellington, load them into Vandross's helicopter once it arrived, and then have Bowdoin and Wellington taken somewhere I could question them. I quickly decided against taking Bowdoin and Wellington into custody, however.

My reasoning for not taking Wellington in was simple. I felt it was unlikely Carter would have told Bryce anything of significance about the insurmountable edge. Carter, like everyone else who worked with Bryce, would have determined that Bryce could only be trusted to handle a few narrowly defined responsibilities. The insurmountable edge wouldn't have been one of those responsibilities.

I had three reasons for not arresting Bowdoin, however.

One, I didn't have any hard evidence to use against Bowdoin to get him to believe there could be anything to be gained by confessing to his involvement with the insurmountable edge. I didn't believe torturing Bowdoin would work, but even if I had believed it would, torturing the son of the former president of the United States was a dicey proposition at best.

Two, even if Carpenter and Vandross arrested Bowdoin, I thought it probably wouldn't have any effect on slowing down what appeared to be a rapid acceleration of Bowdoin's, Dragon Man's, and their team of mercenaries' mission of death and destruction. It had taken Bowdoin, Dragon Man, and whoever they employed three years to rack up their first fourteen deaths - those of Milton Feynman, Paul Lennon, and the twelve NASAD engineers - but the number of deaths had suddenly grown to scores more with the murders of Sam and Lizzy, Lennon's other family members, the dead FBI agents at the drone sub site, and the massive numbers of slain dark programmers lying beneath the smoking crater only a hundred yards away from me. Dragon Man and the mercenaries, even without Bowdoin, would most likely continue to be motivated by the ever shortening amount of time left before the war with China would start and an apparent need to do away with anyone and anything that might throw a wrench into Dragon Man's and Bowdoin's plans.

My third reason not to bring Bowdoin in was probably the most important reason of all, however.

I thought there was a chance Bowdoin could lead me to Dragon Man. If that happened, and I could get Bowdoin and Dragon Man into the same room, it might be a whole new ball game. Again, even though I thought Bowdoin, on his own and alone with me, probably wouldn't confess or tell me anything of value about the insurmountable edge, my experience with bad guys the world over was that if given a choice between a painful death and rolling over on their associates, rolling over won out nearly every time. I saw no reason why Bowdoin and Dragon Man would behave any differently than all those other bad guys.

I made a mental note to ask Haley to have MOM put Carter Bowdoin under surveillance. I also planned, no matter what happened with Bowdoin's surveillance, to continue to follow up on every lead I already had, or might discover, that could potentially help me catch Dragon Man. Just as I also planned, of course, on continuing my quest to find Dr. Nemo. Catching Dragon Man - and putting him and Carter Bowdoin in a room together - or finding Nemo, or cracking Nemo's code, still remained MOM's and my best hope for discovering what the Chinese insurmountable edge was.

"Did Hugh MacColl tell you what the dark programmers had come up with for the war games?" I said.

"No," Boole said. "If Hugh had told me what they'd done, we could have programmed against it and beat him. Hugh was quite adamant about one thing, though."

"What was that?" I said.

"He was confident they were going to blow us out of the water," Boole said.

"Do you think Hugh would have told Carter what the actual dark programmers' plan was?" I said.

"I don't know if Hugh told Carter exactly how the plan would work," Boole said. "But I do know Hugh convinced Carter that it would work, because Hugh said Carter wouldn't bet unless Carter was sure he had a clear advantage."

"And Carter did ultimately bet?" I said.

"Yes," Boole said.

"When did you get confirmation Carter had made the bet?" I said.

"About three months ago," Boole said.

The Chinese had been massing their troops on the Saudi Arabian border for about three months. Another Bowdoin coincidence or...?

My money was on the 'or'.

"Is there any chance that Hugh might have sent Carter the actual programmers' work to evaluate?" I said.

"You mean the software itself?" Boole said.

"Yeah," I said.

"Jeez, I don't know," Boole said. "That'd be a huge breach."

"But with two and a half million dollars at stake for the dark programmers...," I said.

"I guess it's possible then, isn't it?" Boole said.

The headache I'd experienced on the beach at Malibu suddenly came back with a vengeance. My skull throbbed so badly I couldn't stop myself from squeezing my eyes tightly shut to deal with the pain.

Boole apparently noticed.

"You okay?" Boole said.

I kept my eyes shut and took some deep breaths. The pain dissipated. I opened my eyes.

"Yeah, I'm fine," I said. "Sorry. I got a little banged up this morning out at the NASAD's drone sub manufacturing site."

"I heard there were some explosions at that site," Boole said.

"There were," I said. "I actually had the pleasure of hearing the biggest one up close and personal."

"Ouch," Boole said.

"Ouch, indeed," I said. "How often do NASAD software updates get distributed to the U.S. military computer systems?"

"I think it can be as much as once a month," Boole said. "That's our job at the Cyber Defense Hall, to keep upgrading and improving the functionality of those systems. Even in the downtime between war games, we keep trying to find and fix potential problems."

I looked over at Kate again. She was still safely surrounded by Adelaide, Jeff, and Carpenter's two agents. Kate, and all four of the others, also seemed to be keeping a close watch on Boole and me.

"So the Cyber Defense Hall team programs an improvement to NASAD's military software, and then that improvement is uploaded to update the live operational military systems?" I said.

"After it is fully debugged, yes," Boole said.

"The war games are part of the debugging process, correct?" I said.

"They are," Boole said.

"I also understand the dark programmers get to study a copy of the latest version of the military's software – the version that will be uploaded into the military's computers after the debugging is complete - so they can work out a plan of attack prior to the war games' commencement," I said.

"They do," Boole said.

"Have you ever faced a situation where the dark programmers altered the copy they had been given and substituted that altered copy for the version of the software you expected to be defending during the war games?" I said.

"I've never heard of that," Boole said. "I doubt it's ever been done before."

"Would it be against the war games rules for the dark programmers to replace the war games software with an altered copy?" I said.

"I'm not aware of any rule against that," Boole said. "The war games are pretty much a free-for-all. What's that saying? 'All's fair in love and war'? It's kinda like that."

"Understood," I said.

"You know, replacing the copy with an altered one is an interesting concept, though," Boole said.

"Interesting why?" I said.

"It would suggest the dark programmers designed an attack that would come from inside the software," Boole said. "The defensive team and I would have been preparing to defend against an external attack."

"Like the Nasty Pandas' hacking attack I saw up on the Jumbotron in the Defense Hall this morning?" I said.

"Exactly like that," Boole said. "Of course, the dark programmers would have to upload their altered copy into the system used for the war games at the last possible moment. Otherwise we might detect what they had done before the games started."

"Makes sense," I said. "Would an attack from inside the software be harder to deal with?"

"Much harder," Boole said.

"Why?" I said.

"There would be the element of surprise, of course," Boole said. "But an internal attack would be almost impossible to defend against."

My eye caught movement near the roadway bordering the crater site. Two more food trucks and another news van were pulling up outside the police cordon. At least a dozen spectators were already dashing for the food trucks.

"Explain, please," I said.

"The only way to stop such an attack would be to find the software code the dark programmers had altered and then cut it out," Boole said. "But there are millions of lines of code and just finding it could take months."

"The war games don't last months, do they?" I said.

"A few hours at most," Boole said. "If the dark programmers did what you said though, that iteration of the war games would be over in a matter of minutes. The dark programmers would win for sure." He paused. "I have to take back what I said before about it being an interesting concept. It's actually a genius concept."

"That's pretty high praise," I said. "Your analysis would also suggest that if Bowdoin was shown what the dark programmers planned to do, he would feel his bet was pretty secure."

"I have no doubt about that," Boole said.

"How often would the dark programmers' software be uploaded into the military's live computer systems?" I said.

"That would never happen," Boole said. "The dark programmers produce attack software against our own systems. It is used only for testing purposes."

I didn't say anything, just stared at Boole. After a moment, I slightly raised my eyebrows.

"Did you just raise your eyebrows at me?" Boole said.

"Yes," I said.

I raised my eyebrows again.

"Why are you doing...?" Boole said, then stopped dead in mid-sentence.

Boole's eyes went wide.

"Is it possible?" I said.

"Oh shit," Boole said. "Oh shit, oh shit, oh shit."

"I'll take that as a 'yes,'" I said.

"Is that what you think Bowdoin did?" Boole said. "Load the copy of the military's computer systems software that the dark programmers altered for the war games into the live systems?"

"I repeat," I said. "Is it possible?"

"From a technical viewpoint, it would be a very difficult feat," Boole said. "So Bowdoin couldn't do it himself. But if he had a copy of the dark programmers' software, he could probably find someone who could."

"How would that someone do it?" I said.

Boole seemed to give my question some thought.

"Well, obviously there are incredible safeguards that are built into the system to prevent that kind of thing...," Boole said.

"But no computer security system is completely infallible," I said.

"No, it's not," Boole said. "If I were going to do it myself, I would probably try to insert the dark programmers' attack software into the live system somewhere in transit - before it was deployed, as it went from NASAD to the military for installation."

"Do you think one of the dark programmers would help Bowdoin insert the attack software in that manner?" I said.

Boole seemed to give my question some thought.

"I don't think so," Boole said.

"Why?" I said.

"It's one thing to build the attack software as part of the war games," Boole said. "It's quite another to actually participate in a scheme that could bring real catastrophic damage to the United States."

I saw that Burnette's two agents on the opposite ends of the twelve agents' semicircle formation were spreading out away from the rest of their team. I assumed they were going to try to make a play at getting behind the cruiser and 'surprising' Boole and me.

I leaned my head out the door again.

"Ray, you see that?" I said.

"Under control, General," Carpenter said.

"Good," I said. I turned back to Boole. "So there would be no reason for the dark programmers to believe whatever they designed would ever actually go operational and be used against the United States, then?"

"Any of the dark programmers who took the time to think about it would know it was a theoretical possibility," Boole said. "But, again, they were always told there were all manner of safeguards against such an occurrence, and that as dark programmers our job was to be as vicious as possible, just like an enemy would be."

"If the attack software the dark programmers designed for the war games was in the live software currently being used by the military, could you find it?" I said.

"It'd be hard," Boole said. "Like I said before, there's millions upon millions of lines of code and the dark programmers would be really good at hiding where they put it."

"How long would it take to find the attack programming code if the entire defense team in the Cyber Defense Hall was looking for it?" I said.

"Again, it could take months," Boole said. "Unless..."

"Unless what?" I said.

"Unless we knew what subsystem the dark programmers had decided to attack," Boole said.

Another two-person news crew made a dash through the police cordon. They, like their predecessors before them, were quickly tackled to the ground by sheriff's deputies.

Boole, nodding his head at the news crews, said, "They don't give up, do they?"

"Apparently not," I said. "So, do you have a hunch what subsystem the dark programmers might have chosen?"

Boole shook his head.

"No clue," Boole said.

"How many subsystems are there?" I said.

"Hundreds," Boole said.

"Hundreds?" I said.

"Hundreds," Boole said. "One each for every component of military functionality."

"You mean like weapons control, GPS, communications, navigation, and power systems?" I said.

"Yes," Boole said. "And each of those broad areas have subsystems of their own."

"A disruption in the normal functioning of any of those subsystems could cause major problems throughout our entire Armed Forces," I said.

"Correct," Boole said.

"Well, that's not good," I said. "Not with war about to break out in less than ten days."

"It's not good at all," Boole said.

"Do you know when the last update to the the military's live operational software was?" I said.

"I don't," Boole said.

"Do you know the process by which the updates occur?" I said.

"I don't," Boole said. "I don't even know who you could talk to."

"That's okay," I said. "I can get help from other people on that."

The 'other people' I was thinking of was actually just one person - Kate. I made a mental note to ask her how the updating process worked and what employees might be involved with that process.

Just then I saw Burnette's lips move in what looked like a loud 'Go screw yourself', after which he violently stabbed at his cell phone with his index finger, shoved the phone in his pocket, and started marching toward us. I checked my watch. Vandross's helicopter was still at least two minutes away.

I leaned my head out the door again.

"Ray, Burnette is on the move," I said.

"Yeah, I saw that," Carpenter said. "I guess that changes my metric a little."

Carpenter turned toward the agent from Burnette's team who was trying to sneak up on us from our right flank.

"Hey asshole," Carpenter yelled. "Get back to whence you came."

The agent glowered at Carpenter.

Carpenter waved his Glock at the agent.

"Now!" Ray yelled. He then turned to Burnette's agent who was coming up our left flank. "You too, asshole!"

The second agent glowered at Carpenter as well.

"I'd hate to shoot a fellow agent," Carpenter said. "But I will if I have to."

Burnette's two agents seemed not to know what to make of that. Carpenter waved his gun at them again.

"Move!" Carpenter said.

The two agents glowered for a moment longer, then both of them seemed to have a change of heart at almost the same time. Keeping their eyes on Carpenter, they slowly backed up towards their ten compatriots who had maintained their positions along the semicircle formation.

"Nice," I said to Carpenter.

I checked on Kate, Adelaide, Jeff, and Carpenter's two agents. Kate was still surrounded by the other four, and all five of them seemed to have witnessed the confrontation between Ray Carpenter and Burnette's men. They all appeared to be impressed by what they had seen.

I turned back to Boole.

"Obviously everything we've been discussing about the dark programmers, their war games software weapon, and Bowdoin could be deemed wild speculation," I said. "But I have a very strong hunch it's going to turn out to be reality."

"I agree with you," Boole said. "And if the dark programmers' software is truly in the live systems, then the Chinese would absolutely have that insurmountable edge you mentioned earlier." He paused. "You're going to do something about it, right?"

"I am," I said. "Now George, you ever heard of a dark programmer named Dr. Nemo?"

"Like in 'Twenty Thousand Leagues Under the Sea'?" Boole said.

"Yes," I said.

"I thought that was Captain Nemo," Boole said.

"It was," I said. "But I'm looking for Dr. Nemo."

"Sorry," Boole said. "I've never heard of him. Who is he?"

"I think he's a dark programmer who tried to warn Dr. Lennon about what Carter Bowdoin was up to," I said. "Is there any dark programmer you can think of who would be more likely than anyone else to take that kind of action?"

Boole appeared to give my question some thought.

"No," Boole said. "I can't think of anyone."

"Any of the dark programmers that stood out as possibly more brilliant than his or her colleagues?" I said. "So brilliant they could have come up with a software program for the war games that would be unbeatable, or as close to unbeatable as possible?"

Boole shook his head.

"Everyone there is really smart," Boole said. "I can't think of anyone who would stand out." He paused. "I suppose someone could have come after my time though."

"After your time?" I said.

"I left the dark programmers three years ago," Boole said. "I've been with the defensive team in the Cyber Defense Hall ever since."

"Understood," I said. "If you don't mind me asking, why did you leave the dark programmers and join the defense team?"

"My girlfriend lives in Thousand Oaks," Boole said. "I wanted to be closer to her."

"Good reason," I said. "Now George, you do realize you kinda screwed yourself by making that dramatic entrance, don't you?"

"Yeah," Boole said. "I was so pissed off I wasn't thinking. They'll figure I had something to do with all my friends getting killed, won't they?"

"Most likely, yes," I said.

Boole didn't say anything.

"As far as I'm concerned," I said, "I think you made a stupid mistake, but I don't think you intended to get them killed."

"No, no, of course I didn't," Boole said.

"And you were led down the garden path by Carter Bowdoin, a NASAD board member, and ostensibly your boss," I said.

"Will that make a difference?" Boole said. "Is it something you can use to help me out, at least a little like you promised me?"

"I think so," I said. "It wasn't like anybody forced the dark programmers to participate in Bowdoin's high-stakes bet either. I hate to say it, but they were in a way complicit in their own deaths."

"Doesn't make it any easier for me to deal with," Boole said. "I'm guilty. I deserve to be punished."

"I'm not sure I'd agree with that," I said. "And along those lines, I'd like to offer you some advice."

"Be my guest," Boole said.

"Very soon a good man by the name of Vandross will be arriving here," I said. "He's a U.S. Attorney. I asked him to come for your own protection."

Boole gave a nod toward the onrushing Burnette.

"From Pigeyes?" Boole said.

"Yes," I said. "Pigeyes means you harm."

"Sure looks that way," Boole said.

"Luckily for you, however, Vandross outranks Burnette in the hierarchy of the U.S government," I said. "I'll fill Vandross in on everything you told me. Burnette will probably lobby for you to be put away for life, but I think Vandross should be able to find a way to pretty quickly let you go. Even if Vandross does find that way, though, I still want you to stay in his custody for a while."

"He's going to put me in jail?" Boole said.

"Protective custody," I said. "It's not jail."

"Because Bowdoin and Pigeyes will try to kill me?" Boole said.

"I don't think Pigeyes would go that far, especially now that everyone here has seen you're not a suicide vest wearing terrorist," I said. "But Bowdoin is a different matter. If I were Bowdoin, I'd do whatever I could to make you dead as fast as possible."

"The evil part of your mind telling you that?" Boole said.

"Who said it was just a part?" I said.

Boole laughed.

"How long do I need to stay in protective custody?" Boole said.

"Maybe for as much as the next ten days," I said. "The Chinese are supposed to start their war with us in ten days, so this is a very important time for Bowdoin. He's obviously highly focused right now on trying to eliminate any and all threats to his success."

"I think what happened to my dark programmer friends in the bunker pretty much proves that," Boole said.

I nodded.

"What about after ten days?" Boole said.

"I'm hopeful by then I'll have enough evidence to put Bowdoin away for good," I said. "Especially if I find Dr. Nemo."

"What if Dr. Nemo is dead in the bunker along with the rest of the dark programmers?" Boole said.

"I might still be able to bring Bowdoin down without him," I said.

"What if you can't?" Boole said.

"Then you might have to enter a witness protection program," I said.

"Witness protection?" Boole said. "That would be for the rest of my life, wouldn't it?"

"It would," I said.

"Shit," Boole said.

Boole, not unexpectedly, looked extremely upset at the prospect that his life might be so severely disrupted. I felt for him. I considered telling Boole he didn't really need to worry about Bowdoin bothering him, since as far as I was concerned Bowdoin was a dead man. In my world you don't kill all the people Bowdoin killed - Sam, Lizzy, Sarah, Milt Feynman, Paul Lennon, the NASAD engineers and dark programmers, and everyone else - and get away with it. I was letting Bowdoin live for now only because, again, I believed he might somehow lead me to the Chinese insurmountable edge. After I found the edge, I was going to kill Bowdoin regardless of whether or not I ever gathered enough evidence to convict him in a court of law. In the end, however, I told Boole nothing about my plans for Bowdoin. Those plans were 'need to know', and Boole wasn't qualified to hear them.

"You seem pretty tough to me, George," I said. "Whatever happens, I'm sure you'll be able to deal with it."

"I hope so," Boole said.

"I know so," I said. "Now, you can talk freely to Vandross about what we discussed, but no one else. If any of our conversation leaks to anyone outside the three of us, it will greatly reduce my chances of bringing Bowdoin to justice."

"Okay," Boole said.

"I'm going to get out of the car and close the door now," I said. "That way Pigeyes can't get to you."

"Thank you, General," Boole said.

"No," I said, "Thank you."

I got out of the car, shut the rear door, and opened the front door so Boole would have some air.

Burnette was nearly upon us.

Carpenter stepped between Burnette and me.

Burnette, his face bloated and burning red, his eyes looking as if they might be about to pop out of their sockets, and spittle dripping from the corners of his mouth, said, "How dare you interfere with my investigation, Wilder!"

"Interfere?" I said.

"Do you deny it was you who called Vandross?" Burnette said.

"I did it for your own good," I said.

"My own good?!" Burnette said.

"Your boys there were about to kill an innocent civilian," I said.

"An innocent civilian who happens to be a terrorist who is part of the sleeper cell that murdered all those people in the bunker," Burnette said.

"You sure figured that out pretty quick," I said.

"Are you a moron, Wilder?" Burnette said. "In case you haven't noticed, terrorists are behind every single goddamn thing we've been dealing with for the last few days. Besides, if the guy's not a terrorist, why else would he show up here?"

"Maybe Carter Bowdoin asked him to come," I said. "The kid was yelling Bowdoin's name as soon as he got out of the car."

"Bowdoin said he'd never seen him before in his life," Burnette said.

I scratched my head.

"Hmm," I said. "There's only one possible explanation then isn't there?"

"What's that, asshole?" Burnette said.

"Bowdoin and the kid are part of the same sleeper cell!" I said.

Burnette grabbed Carpenter's shoulders and tried to shove him aside.

"Get out of my way, Carpenter," Burnette said. "I'm taking custody of the prisoner."

Carpenter flicked Burnette backwards, almost knocking Burnette on his ass in the process. Which was pretty impressive, considering how porky Burnette was.

Carpenter said, "Are you out of your mind, Burnette? Don't touch me again."

"Fine," Burnette said. "Have it your way."

Burnette gestured to his twelve nearby agents.

"Men," Burnette said. "Get over here."

I said, "Burnette, didn't you notice the half dozen news vans over there? You want them filming a shootout between FBI agents?"

"Do I look like I give a good goddamn?" Burnette said.

"Alright, fine, settle down, will you?" I said. "We're fighting over some kid who really doesn't have much to offer. His name is George Boole, and he's just some hothead who had some friends in that bunker. He came here looking for someone to blame for what happened to them. Boole didn't even know Bowdoin was here until he got here."

Burnette eyed me suspiciously.

"He didn't?" Burnette said.

"Nah," I said. "Boole knows who Bowdoin is since Boole works in the NASAD Cyber Defense Hall and he's seen Bowdoin there many times. There's no reason to think that Bowdoin has any idea who Boole is though. I mean why would he? There must be hundreds of programmers in the Defense Hall. I was just yanking your chain, Burnette."

Burnette didn't seem to know what to make of what I'd said. I, of course, didn't care what he believed. I was just trying to buy some time. But there was some secondary benefit to what I had told Burnette as well. Bowdoin was surely smart enough to figure out that since Boole and I had spent so much time together in the cruiser, it was pretty likely that Boole had told me everything that Bowdoin had been up to with the dark programmers. However, if Burnette told Bowdoin what I had just relayed to him about Boole denying he had any real, significant relationship with Bowdoin, there was a chance it might at least sow some doubts in Bowdoin's mind about what I knew. And as far as I was concerned, doubt in an enemy's mind was never a bad thing.

Burnette seemed to come to a decision.

"That's an interesting story, Wilder," Burnette said. "But until I decide otherwise, this Boole is still a terrorist. I'm taking him in." Burnette turned to his approaching agents. "What the hell's taking you jackasses so long? Get over here!"

Behind me, I heard the roar of a helicopter. Burnette and I turned to look. The Department of Justice chopper was fast approaching us. I estimated it would be at the site in at most fifteen seconds.

"I'm pretty sure Vandross can already see us from the chopper," I said. "Are you willing to gamble he'll approve of you messing with his prisoner?"

"Shit," Burnette said. "I didn't think Vandross would get here so fast."

"Just another of the so, so, many things you've been wrong about, Burnette," I said.

Burnette lunged at me. Carpenter flicked him away again.

Burnette's twelve agent escort finally arrived at their commandant's side.

"Sir?" one of the agents said.

Burnette ignored him. Instead, he watched as the helicopter - emblazoned on its side with the Department of Justice logo - set down next to the two NASAD choppers.

"Screw this," Burnette said, and turning to his agents, added, "Let's get out of here."

Burnette led them away. The DOJ helicopter's door opened, a ladder was let down, and Vandross climbed out.

I turned to Carpenter.

"As soon as Vandross gets Mr. Boole out of here, I'm going to need you to help me with a plan," I said.

"What kind of plan?" Carpenter said.

"A plan to get inside the bunker under that crater," I said.

CHAPTER 83

Vandross, after exiting the Department of Justice helicopter, immediately headed toward me. He looked as dapper and handsome as when I had seen him the day before in the Lancaster jail. His eyes were also just as sharp and clear, his black skull just as glistening. He wore a perfectly cut dark blue designer suit, a blue and white striped dress shirt, and a brilliant crimson tie.

Vandross, being no fool, had also brought a half dozen U.S. Marshals on the helicopter with him. I spoke with Vandross while the marshals, along with Ray Carpenter, loaded George Boole into the helicopter. Burnette and his team of agents joined Freddy, Carter Bowdoin, and Bryce Wellington back at the crater.

"Didn't expect to see you again so soon," Vandross said.

"What can I say?" I said. "I missed you."

Vandross smiled.

"So you want me to hold this Boole kid for ten days?" Vandross said.

"I think that's the safest thing for him," I said.

"Will do then," Vandross said. "Boole know something about the drone subs?"

"Drone subs?" I said.

"Isn't that what you're working on?" Vandross said. "Drone subs and the Chinese insurmountable edge are all Hart was talking with us about yesterday."

Damn. I'd been so focused on what I thought was the real insurmountable edge - the dark programmers' war game programming - that I'd completely forgotten that Vandross had been with me in Lancaster when Hart had been going on and on about the drone subs. Slipping up like that in front of Vandross, especially when I wasn't sure how close he was to Hart, was clearly a sign my brain had gone to mush.

"Right, the drone subs," I said. "The drone subs are..."

"The insurmountable edge lies elsewhere, huh?" Vandross interrupted.

"Well...," I said.

"Look, you don't want to tell me, it's okay," Vandross said. "I know how Hart likes to micromanage. I always keep him on a need to know basis so he'll stay out of my hair." Vandross paused for a moment, then added, "Actually, even if you're considering telling me, don't."

"Don't?" I said.

"Hart can read me like a book," Vandross said. "Hart will figure out I'm hiding something from him and then he'll mercilessly pound on me until I tell him everything I know."

"Since you put it that way," I said, "I guess I better not tell you then."

"Were you going to?" Vandross said.

"Fifty-fifty," I said. "I'm a 'need to know' guy too."

Vandross laughed.

Ray Carpenter, having finished loading Boole into the DOJ helicopter, joined us. He slapped Vandross on the back.

"Good to see you, Vandy," Carpenter said.

"You too, Carpman," Vandross said

Vandross and Carpenter bumped chests.

"Carpman? Vandy?" I said. "I think I'm missing something."

Carpenter said, "That suit U.S. Attorney Vandross is wearing is very misleading. Inside that finely tailored cloth beats the heart of a stone-cold killer. We saw combat together in the Korengal Valley."

Vandross said, "Carpman got a Silver Star."

"So did you," Carpenter said.

"That's right, I did, didn't I?" Vandross said.

I said, "General Hart clearly chose his team for MOM well."

Vandross said, "The general chose best when he chose you and General Bradshaw."

"That's the beauty of America, isn't it, Vandross?" I said.

"Sir?" Vandross said.

"Everyone is entitled to their opinions no matter how ass-brained those opinions might be," I said.

Vandross and Carpenter laughed.

I looked over at Kate, Jeff, Adelaide, and Carpenter's two agents. Kate gave me a look that seemed to say 'What's going on?'

I mouthed, "Be with you in a minute."

Kate appeared to have understood me.

Vandross said, "I guess I probably should be getting out of here before Special Agent Burnette changes his mind and decides to start shooting at us. Is Boole ready to go, Ray?"

"He is," Carpenter said.

"Gentlemen, until we meet again," Vandross said.

Vandross saluted us, started to walked away, then stopped.

"General, I forgot to ask," Vandross said. "Did you recover well enough from that elephant tranquilizer Burnette gave you yesterday?"

"I'd forgotten all about that," I said. "I'm fine now though. Thanks."

Carpenter said, "The elephant tranquilizer pales in comparison to what happened this morning."

I said, "Come on, Carpenter."

Vandross said, "What happened this morning?"

"General got blown up," Carpenter said. "Dead seven minutes."

Vandross looked at me.

"Seven minutes?" Vandross said.

"How would I know?" I said. "I was dead."

Carpenter said, "It was definitely seven. Dr. Lennon was there and the number came from her."

Vandross said, "Impressive. Must be some kind of record. Not that it's the kind of record I'd want to own..."

"Goodbye, Vandross," I said.

Vandross smiled and continued on his way to the helicopter. As I watched him walk, I felt like I'd forgotten to ask him something important, but couldn't remember what it was. I kept trying to come up with whatever it was, but I gave up a minute later when the DOJ helicopter's doors closed with Vandross inside and the chopper quickly became airborne and headed for parts unknown.

Ray Carpenter and I made our way towards Adelaide, Jeff, Kate, and Carpenter's two FBI SWAT team cohorts. Most of the nearby fire trucks and ambulances were slowly pulling away, presumably heading back to their home bases.

"How hard is it going to be for Burnette to explain to Carter Bowdoin that losing Boole wasn't really his fault?" I said.

"Real hard," Carpenter said. "I could see Burnette spending the rest of the afternoon out here trying to do that. You might have to wait awhile until you can get inside that bunker."

"I was going to wait until dark, anyway," I said.

"Dark is always good," Carpenter said. "Nightfall won't be for about three hours though. What are you going to do in the meantime?"

"You pretty antsy to get Dr. Lennon back to her estate?" I said.

"I am," Carpenter said. "She'll be much safer there."

"Maybe I'll go with you to Malibu and come back later," I said. "Do you have a vehicle at Kate's estate that I can borrow?"

"I do," Carpenter said.

As we continued to approach Kate and the others, I told Ray about the key points of my conversation with George Boole of which he was not already aware. Across the field the news crews were packing up and preparing to depart. The crowd of spectators was thinning out as well, but the food trucks were still doing a brisk business. Donnie Kurtsinger was on his seventh Coke.

We joined Kate and the others.

Kate said, "What's the Department of Justice going to do with that poor kid?"

"Keep him alive," I said.

"It looked like they were arresting him," Kate said.

"All for show," I said.

My phone rang. It was a FaceTime call from Haley.

"Sorry," I said to Kate. "I have to take this." To Ray, I added, "Ray, will you please bring everyone up to speed on our new friend George Boole?"

"Happy to," Carpenter said.

I stepped away from the group and answered Haley's call.

Haley was resplendent, her brown locks falling in a big curl across her shoulders, her big brown eyes laughing, and her fine white teeth sparkling between her beautiful lips. The lights of the NORAD computer banks still twinkled behind her.

"Still stuck at NORAD, huh darlin'?" I said.

"I can go back home anytime I want, sweetheart," Haley said. "But if I went back home that would mean I'd have to waste valuable time traveling, time that could be better spent working for you."

"That's very kind of you," I said.

"Thank you," Haley said.

"Normally right now is when I'd ask you what you have for me, but

I'm not sure I want to know," I said.

"Damn," Haley said. "My smiley face didn't work, huh?"

"Nope," I said.

"What gave it away?" Haley said.

"If I told you," I said, "you'd try to hide it from me the next time."

"I would indeed," Haley said. "Anyway, it's bad."

"How bad?" I said.

"Before I answer that, why don't you tell me how bad things are where you are?" Haley said. "Your phone's GPS says you're at the NASAD site that just blew up."

"This is supposed to be an ultra top secret site," I said. "How do you know about it already?"

"Oh, I don't know, maybe it's because we're monitoring all NASAD communications, and two NASAD helicopters just happen to be parked on the ground right next to you?" Haley said.

"When you put it that way, I guess there's not any 'maybe' about it," I said.

"You're right," Haley said. "There's not."

"Good," I said. "I love being right. As to how things are here, they're bad. Real bad." I pointed my iPhone camera at the crater. "All the NASAD dark programmers might be dead inside a bunker at the bottom of that crater. The vice president of dark programming too. His name was Rick Benavidez. He was highly trusted by Milt Feynman and he had been the only vice president of dark programming the dark programming division had ever had."

"That's awful," Haley said.

"It is," I said.

"It's bad for us too," Haley said. "It probably would have been incredibly valuable to communicate with Benavidez or one of the dark programmers. It's too bad their security protocols were so tight we couldn't reach Benavidez. Maybe he and the programmers would be alive if we had."

"I had those same thoughts," I said.

"You think our man Dr. Nemo might be in the bunker with all the others?" Haley said.

I turned the camera back around to focus on me.

"There's always a chance he isn't," I said. "But the odds say he is. I'm going in there after dark to look around."

"May God bless those programmers' souls," Haley said. "But it'll certainly help my Dr. Nemo hunt if you can get me some ID's and pictures of their faces."

"That was the plan," I said. "It will be best if you can work quickly after I give you the pictures. Burnette was handed a camera by the hazmat guys who were down in the bunker, which means Burnette probably already has his own pictures of the dead. We need to beat Burnette to the punch if he's also looking for Nemo."

"When have I ever not worked quickly?" Haley said, giving me a bit of a nasty look.

"Sorry," I said. "I should know better than to say something like that."

"You should," Haley said. "By the way, I already know what your next request is going to be, so you don't have to make it."

"You do?" I said.

"Weren't you just about to ask me to look for footage from any security cameras that might have been recording outside the bunker to see if we can identify who the assholes were that blew up the site?" Haley said.

"I was actually," I said.

"Good," Haley said. "I'm already on it."

"Thank you," I said. "Next subject then. I'm thinking that even if Nemo is dead, I might still be able to find something in the bunker that will help us break his code."

"That would be great," Haley said. "But my gut says that's going to be too much to hope for."

"It's worth a shot anyway," I said. "I should also tell you, that if something produced by NASAD is the source of the Chinese insurmountable edge - and so far everything we've seen, from Dr. Nemo's warning, to all of Hart's China intel, points to NASAD being the source - then I'm sure that Carter Bowdoin and his associates are the ones who gave the Chinese the insurmountable edge."

"'Sure' is pretty strong language coming from you," Haley said. "Why are you sure?"

"I just spent the last many minutes interrogating a former NASAD dark programmer," I said. "His name is George Boole and he is currently a programmer in the NASAD Cyber Defense Hall. Boole is the missing link we've been looking for, the person who provided Carter Bowdoin the ability to interact with the dark programmers. My discussion with Boole provided me with plenty of details to support a theory of how and why the insurmountable edge was created. That discussion also makes me believe the edge has already been inserted into the military's live computer software systems."

"It's *in* the military systems, not an attack *on* the systems?" Haley said.

"Correct," I said.

"That could be very bad for us," Haley said.

"Very, very bad," I said.

"Did Boole tell you how the insurmountable edge works?" Haley said.

I checked in on Kate. She seemed to be closely focusing on what Carpenter was telling her.

"Unfortunately, he doesn't know," I said. "Which is why we still need to focus on finding Nemo or cracking his code. I assume there's still no evidence that anything even remotely resembling an insurmountable edge is already at work against us? All U.S. military systems still working normally?"

"All U.S. military systems are working normally, including all computer systems," Haley said.

"Good," I said. "Now what's the latest on your end?"

"Another Doctors of Mercy plane landed in the U.S.," Haley said.

"When?" I said.

"About four hours ago," Haley said.

"Where?" I said.

"Oklahoma City," Haley said. "But there's a problem."

"What is it?" I said.

"The plane is no longer in Oklahoma City and I don't know where it went," Haley said. "I screwed up."

"Major Marian Haley never screws up," I said.

"This time I did," Haley said.

"I'll be the judge of that," I said. "What happened?"

"Well, after I told you that we'd figured out that the first Doctors of Mercy flight had dumped all those mercenaries off in Pixley," Haley said, "and that whoever dropped them off had succeeded in hiding what they were up to by most likely using the same radar eluding and location falsifying technology that was used to make Feynman and Lennon's plane crash look like an accident, I kept looking for any other flights that might have landed in the U.S."

I took a quick glance across the field. The hazmat team, which had been relaxing near the crater, was picking up their gear from where they'd left it piled on the ground. I assumed they were planning on leaving soon. The canary still looked fine.

"I remember we both thought that was a good idea," I said.

"It was," Haley said. "The only problem is I only looked for planes that had already landed and never even stopped to think about any additional ones that might be on their way."

"But you did think about any additional ones that might be on their way at some point?" I said.

"Yes," Haley said. "But by the time I thought about them, it was way too late. The second Doctors of Mercy flight took off from Herat nineteen hours ago. Like the first flight, it stopped at Almaty International and refueled in Hong Kong. Unlike the first flight, however, it landed in Oklahoma City, not Dallas. It cleared customs about three hours ago, only I didn't start looking for it until about two and a half hours ago. By then it had taken off and headed for San Francisco."

"The same place the first Doctors of Mercy flight ultimately landed," I said.

"Correct, after the first plane's detour through Pixley," Haley said. "I've scrambled some F-16's out of Hill Air Force Base in Ogden, Utah. They're following the second flight's radar trace."

"Let me guess," I said. "The plane is not on the trace?"

"No, it's not," Haley said.

"Which means they must have turned on the location falsifying system the moment they left Oklahoma City," I said.

"That's what I think," Haley said. "If I'd been more on the ball, I would have been anticipated there might be a second flight and kept eyes on Herat. Then I would have scrambled something out of Bagram, then Kadena and Honolulu, and had a visual from start to finish."

"And taken them into custody after they landed in Oklahoma City," I said.

"Would have been nice," Haley said.

Behind me I heard more car engines starting up. I turned to look. About half of the police cruisers were slowly pulling off the lot onto the bordering street and heading away.

"Who was on board the second flight?" I said.

"Thirty orthopedic surgeons according to their documents," Haley said, "but if you look at their customs' photos from Oklahoma City..."

Haley flashed pictures of the men who had gotten off the plane in Oklahoma City onto my iPhone screen.

"Afghans and Kazakhs," I said. "The Kazakhs look just like the Kazakhs who've been shooting at me, except they're wearing suits and ties, and the Afghans fit the descriptions Bobby and Timmy gave me."

"Those two little boys did a pretty good job for us, didn't they?" Haley said.

"They did," I said.

"Jack, I know you figured that since you killed seven of the twenty-nine from the first flight, that you only had twenty-two hostiles left," Haley said. "But now you've got fifty-two."

"Is that what twenty-two and thirty add up to?" I said.

Haley rolled her eyes.

I checked on Carter Bowdoin, Bryce Wellington, Freddy, Burnette, and Burnette's twelve man squad. They were still standing next to the crater. Bryce and Carter were both yelling at Burnette. Carter was also repeatedly jabbing his finger towards the sky, the path of his jabs in line with the direction Vandross's DOJ helicopter had taken when it flew away. I felt it safe to assume that Carter and Bryce weren't too happy that Boole had escaped their clutches.

"At least my odds have improved now that Jeff and Adelaide are here," I said. "Fifty-two to three is better than twenty-two to one."

"You sure Jeff is an asset?" Haley said.

"Jeff is always an asset," I said.

"God, I hope so," Haley said. "Nothing I would like more than for General Jeffrey Bradshaw to be on the mend."

"Agreed," I said.

At that point, I wanted to know more about the Doctors of Mercy plane, but I could tell Haley was still beating herself up about her mistake.

Haley could beat herself up worse than just about anybody I knew. That didn't mean she deserved to suffer as much as she seemed to be suffering. Cheering her up was a long shot, but it was worth a try.

"And Haley...," I said.

"Yes, Jack?" Haley said.

"Please don't keep blaming yourself for the second plane," I said. "I never considered there might be another one and I doubt anyone else would have either. The fact you not only considered it - even if you were a little late - but also found out where it landed and who was on it, puts you light years ahead of mere mortals."

"That sounds like you're trying to cheer me up," Haley said.

"It might," I said. "But that doesn't mean what I said isn't true."

"Hmmph," Haley said.

"Don't 'hmmph' me," I said. "There's no reason for you to be so god-damned hard on yourself."

Haley took in a deep breath and let it out.

"Okay," Haley said. "I feel better. Sort of."

"Good," I said. "I don't want us to give up on trying to figure out where that plane is now, however. I assume you're tasking the satellites to look for it?"

"I've done that," Haley said. "But we've got nothing yet. There's a huge thunderstorm over the entire Midwest that extends to most of eastern California and I'm sure they're flying the plane under the clouds to avoid detection."

I checked again on Burnette, Bowdoin, and Wellington. Things seemed to have continued to heat up between the three of them. Freddy appeared to be trying to make peace, but with no success I could discern.

"You said their flight plan says they're headed for San Francisco, right?" I said.

"Yes," Haley said.

"When are they due?" I said.

"They were due ten minutes ago," Haley said.

"Damn," I said. "That means they've probably already dropped off the mercenaries, I mean doctors, by now."

"But we don't have a clue where," Haley said.

"Seek and ye shall find," I said.

"Knock, and it shall be opened to you," Haley said.

"Is that really the next line?" I said.

"Yes," Haley said.

"I didn't know that," I said.

"Now you do," Haley said. "We're obviously going to keep looking for that plane. If we find it, we'll get Vandross to take the crew into custody for interrogation after it lands. You have to promise me you'll keep something in mind from now on, though."

"What?" I said.

"We both know that the mercenaries have already targeted you," Haley said. "But I think it's moved beyond just lying in wait like they did at the NASAD drone sub manufacturing site. There's a high probability they're actively searching for you now. So be watching your own ass and not just Dr. Lennon's."

"O, beware, my lord, of jealousy," I said. "It is the green-eyed monster which doth mock the meat it feeds on."

"Maybe I am a bit jealous," Haley said. "But you still better be careful."

"I will," I said. "What else you got for me?"

"This," Haley said. "It's from one of the security cameras at the Beverly Wilshire Hotel in Beverly Hills, California."

A photograph came up on my iPhone screen. It showed a very long line of people - perhaps more than a hundred - waiting to be checked in at what appeared to be a charity event at the hotel. I recognized twelve of the people in line. They were the twelve dead NASAD drone sub engineers. I also recognized the man who was standing off to one side of the line and seemed to be taking a cell phone picture of the twelve dead NASAD engineers. The man was Carter Bowdoin.

Carter Bowdoin wasn't alone in the photograph, however. He was standing next to a shorter man. The shorter man had his back turned to the hotel security camera that had taken the photograph Haley was showing me. The shorter man wore his short, straight black hair in what looked to be a very expensive cut, and his blue suit and dark alligator shoes also looked extremely expensive. His entire style was very 'GQ' except for one thing. The short man was wearing yellow socks.

Yellow socks?

"That's a charity event, isn't it?" I said.

"For 'Save the Whales," Haley said. "NASAD has heavily supported it ever since Greenpeace accused them - falsely accused them, I might add - of harming whales with their sonar devices. NASAD buys tickets for all their top managers who want to attend."

"Where did you get the photo?" I said.

"We fished around everywhere we thought we might find photos of the twelve dead NASAD engineers," Haley said. "We hacked into the private computers of all their friends and relatives, scanned online photo albums of every NASAD employee, and looked for any camera that might have recorded a NASAD event. We processed what we found with facial recognition software."

I quickly checked on Kate. Carpenter was still talking to Kate, Adelaide, Jeff, and his agents. Kate seemed to have her doubts about something. She appeared to ask Carpenter a question. I couldn't hear what she said. Donnie Kurtsinger, still sitting on his rock, was chugging on another Coke.

"I never thought to look outside the NASAD archives for a photo like this, but you did," I said. "Good work."

"Thank you," Haley said.

"Dr. Lennon showed me pictures of all the dead NASAD drone sub engineers yesterday morning," I said. "That's them lined up one after the other in the sixth through seventeenth positions from the front of the line, isn't it?"

"Bingo," Haley said.

"I also know the guy standing off to the side and taking pictures of the engineers with his cell phone is Carter Bowdoin," I said. "Did you figure out who the short guy standing next to Bowdoin is?"

"No clue," Haley said. "We were able to identify everyone on the guest list that night except him."

"Bowdoin's friend wasn't on the guest list?" I said.

"No, he wasn't," Haley said. "His shoes turned out to be of interest, however."

"They look like nice shoes," I said.

"They're five thousand dollar Ferragamos," Haley said. "That model is only made for the Ferragamo stores in Beijing and only sold in those stores."

"How many people go all the way to China just to buy shoes?" I said.

"Not many," Haley said. "The suit, by the way, is also sold only in Beijing. It costs ten thousand dollars."

Over by the crater, the argument going on between Bowdoin and Burnette seemed to be escalating. Freddy got between the two men and Bowdoin immediately shoved Freddy aside. Across the field from Bowdoin's group most of the police cars had left and the hazmat team was loading up their van.

"Based on what you just told me, I don't think we'd be going out on a limb if we assume Bowdoin's friend is Chinese," I said. "You think Bowdoin's friend could be our elusive Asian connection?"

"Best candidate so far," Haley said. "We did a biometric analysis of the man himself - Bowdoin's friend, as you call him - for size and weight. We also estimated his age from skin wrinkling. In this case we used the skin exposed above his collar."

"And...?" I said.

"Five foot eight, one hundred and forty pounds, and thirty-six years old," Haley said. "Which would make him the same age as Bowdoin."

I again studied the picture of the activity outside the 'Save the Whales' event.

"Pretty amazing, isn't it?" I said.

"What?" Haley said.

"We've been looking for some special connection among the dead engineers," I said. "Something to explain why they, among all the NASAD drone sub engineering project managers, were murdered and the other project managers weren't. But it looks like it all came down to chance."

"Chance, yes," Haley said. "They just happened to be the drone sub engineering project managers who were standing in line together when Carter Bowdoin and his Chinese buddy took a picture of them. They were in the wrong place at the wrong time."

I sighed.

"Carter and his pal probably thought it was a devilishly funny idea too," I said. "Must've got a sicko kick out of it, knowing what fate was in store for them."

"No doubt," Haley said. "It sure makes your guess that the drone subs are really just a diversion look better and better."

My eye caught some movement over to my right. On the other side of the police cordon, the food trucks were being packed up and readied for departure. The crowd of spectators had diminished to less than a quarter of what it had been, and I assumed the food trucks' owners had decided it was time to look for greener pastures.

"I suppose it does, doesn't it?" I said. "You'll remember to keep that under your hat, right? Not a word to Hart about that or about my theory that the insurmountable edge relates to the possible insertion of the dark programmers' war games software into the live military computer systems."

"Puhleeeeease," Haley said. "Who do you think you're talking to?"

"Sorry," I said. "I don't even know why I mentioned it. What else you got for me?"

Haley removed the photo of the charity event from the screen and reappeared in all her glory.

"We've scoured Paul Lennon's personal, business, and military life," Haley said. "The idea being to find someone who would hate him so much that they'd want to kill him and his whole family. We've found nothing so far. We're at a complete dead end."

"Paul's only relatives left alive are his sister, Dr. Lennon, and Dr. Lennon's two children, right?" I said.

"Correct," Haley said. "FBI has the sister under guard at her home in Claremont."

"Even though you can't find the person doing all of the hating, hate has to remain part of the equation," I said. "I can't think of anything else that would explain Dragon Man's murders of Sam and Lizzy, their mother Sarah, and Paul's parents."

"I agree," Haley said. "I said we were at a dead end, not that we've stopped searching."

"Good," I said. "Because I think it's very likely that when we find the identity of the person who holds a deadly grudge against Captain Lennon, we'll also have found Dragon Man."

"We've already found Dragon Man, though, haven't we?" Haley said. "We can't identify him by name, but we know who he is."

"You're referring to Carter's friend in the photo at the charity event who we decided was Chinese?" I said.

"You know I am," Haley said.

"Hmm," I said. "So you're saying that just because Bobby and Timmy said Dragon Man was wearing a Chinese Dragon mask and spoke English with a Chinese accent, that Dragon Man, just like Bowdoin's friend at the charity event, is Chinese?"

"Stop it," Haley said.

"Of course," I said, "we also know that Dragon Man - again wearing a Chinese dragon mask - was watching the attempted assassination of Kate at the NASAD drone sub site using an app that connected him to the cell phone of one of the Kazakh snipers, and that Bowdoin seemed to know about the assassination attempt in advance. So, I suppose there's a good chance Bowdoin and Dragon Man know each other."

"Didn't I just tell you to stop?" Haley said.

"Fine, I'll stop," I said. "May I assume you are also in agreement with me that Carter's charity event friend is not only Dragon Man but is also probably Carter's partner in the insurmountable edge? And that we can proceed under those assumptions unless facts come to light that dictate otherwise?"

"You may," Haley said.

"Very good," I said. I paused. Something had just occurred to me. "Damn. I can't believe I didn't think of this before."

"What?" Haley said.

"I'll bet Carter's Chinese friend is also a princeling or some such shit," I said. "I mean, after all, don't all those sons and daughters and grandchildren and great-grandchildren and who knows what of Mao's underlings own every goddamn thing of value in China now?"

"They do," Haley said. "The Chinese company that Carter would be partnering with would probably be at least as big as Pennsylvania Avenue Partners, otherwise how could they pull off the deal we think Carter and his Chinese friend must have made? And big means valuable. So it would be right up a princeling's alley."

"Or a 'princessling's'," I said.

"Is that a word?" Haley said.

"If it isn't, it should be," I said.

"So now I'm looking for someone in the family tree of a princeling or princessling who hates Paul Lennon?" Haley said.

"I don't think you really have to limit it to that, but at least it gives you more places to look," I said.

"Okay," Haley said. "My job then is to find someone who hates Paul Lennon, is associated with both Carter Bowdoin and a big Chinese defense or engineering company, and is descended from a relative who was a member of Mao's quasi-royal court. If I do that, there's a good chance we'll have found Dragon Man's true identity. Once we know Dragon Man's true identity, we'll try to track him down here in the United States. If we succeed in tracking Dragon Man down, we might be able to force him to tell us what the insurmountable edge is. And if we do that, maybe we can stop a war."

"I couldn't have said it better myself," I said.

"Of course there's always the chance I could figure out who Dragon Man is some other way," Haley said.

Across the field from me, the three techs who made up the hazmat team were continuing to load their van. The tech whose hose had been disconnected was still alive and well.

"If anyone can, you can," I said. "Which brings me back to what I was going to originally ask you to do."

"Which is?" I said.

"Put Carter Bowdoin under surveillance," I said.

"In the hope he leads us to Dragon Man?" Haley said.

"Yes," I said. "Right now he's standing about a hundred yards away from me, so it should be easy for you to start your tracking."

"Consider it done," Haley said.

An idea began to form in the back of my mind in regard to something I could do to supplement Haley's investigation into who might hate Paul Lennon enough to murder his entire family. The idea was a long shot, but time was running short and it was one of the few shots I had left.

"You going to tell me what you're thinking?" Haley said.

"How did you know I was thinking something?" I said.

"Gimme a break," Haley said. "Same way you knew I had bad news."

"Good point," I said. "There are some things I have to check out."

"What is it you have check out?" Haley said.

"The house where Sam, Lizzy, and Sarah Lennon used to live," I said. "And Paul Lennon's parents' house too."

"The murder sites?" Haley said.

I nodded.

"I know the address of Sarah's house in Claremont," I said. "Claremont is close by, right?"

"Yes," Haley said. "Parents' house is also close by. They lived in Montclair, which is right next to Claremont. You think you might find something in the houses that will give you an idea of the source of Dragon Man's grudge against Paul Lennon?"

"There's a chance," I said. "A small one, but a chance. Paul Lennon's sister is a professor at Pomona College and she lives in Claremont too. I should probably pay a visit to her as well."

"The theory being, we've got so little to go on, we have to follow up on any lead?" Haley said. "Even the ones you're manufacturing out of thin air."

"Haley giveth and she taketh away?" I said.

"No, really, it's a good idea," Haley said. "When you going to do this?"

"Now," I said. "Unless you have something better for me to do between now and when I get inside that bunker."

"I don't," Haley said. "Do you have the addresses of the professor's and Lennon's parents' homes?"

"No," I said.

"I'll text you the addresses as soon as we hang up," Haley said.

I took another look at Freddy, Bowdoin, Burnette, and Wellington. Their argument seemed to have further intensified. Burnette's twelve FBI agents remained gathered around the four men.

"Thanks," I said. "Getting back to George Boole - the former NASAD dark programmer and current NASAD Cyber Defense Hall programmer - and my conversation with him regarding the insurmountable edge. If the Chinese are truly relying on the NASAD war games doomsday software as their insurmountable edge, then, as you and I discussed, the software must have somehow found its way into the currently operational military computer systems. Which means that on top of looking for Nemo and trying to crack his code, I'd like you to stop searching for any weaknesses such as backdoors that could be exploited by an external attack on the military's systems and instead start looking within those systems for any software code that could function as a doomsday weapon/insurmountable edge. I'd also like you to try to find out how the military's live systems get updated."

"We'll get on it immediately," Haley said.

"Thanks," I said. "I apologize, but now I've got a stupid question for you."

"What is it?" Haley said.

"If we decide it's likely that the military's current systems have been updated with the software that contains the insurmountable edge," I said, "could we potentially replace the current live operating software with an older, previously installed version?"

"That's not a stupid question," Haley said.

"Phew!" I said,

"Ever since you told me about the NASAD dark programmers and Dr. Nemo and asked me to start looking into potential weaknesses in the military's computer systems, we've been trying to come up with ways to shore up any such weaknesses we might find," Haley said. "We've already explored replacing the software as a potential solution."

"And?" I said.

"For highly technical reasons," Haley said, "the two most important of which are the fact that there have been hardware updates that won't work with the old software, and the high likelihood almost all data would need to be recovered from backups, reinstalling previously used system software is a very messy task that would take weeks to accomplish. It therefore won't work in our present circumstances."

"Oh well," I said.

"Oh well is right," Haley said. "Now, back to your request that we try to find out how the military's live systems get updated with the latest software version. We could do it, but I suggest it would be faster for you to just ask your girlfriend, Dr. Lennon. It should be pretty easy for her to find someone at NASAD who can tell her how it's done."

"How'd I go from staring at Dr. Lennon's ass to her being my girl-friend?" I said.

"Because everyone says she is," Haley said.

"Everyone in the whole world?" I said.

"Everyone in the whole galaxy," Haley said.

"That many, huh?" I said. "I guess for their sakes I better ask Dr. Lennon then."

"For their sakes, yes," Haley said. "What part of the military's software should I start looking for the edge in?"

My eye was drawn again to movement on my right side. The last of the food trucks was pulling away. A few straggler spectators appeared to be staring in the direction of the crater, perhaps waiting for the last of the smoking patches of burned out grass to die out. Three sheriff's deputies were manning posts along the yellow crime scene tape surrounding the crater. They appeared to be a more than adequate force to control the remaining onlookers. I refocused my attention on Haley.

"Don't know," I said. "Could be anywhere."

"Anywhere?" Haley said. "That's millions of lines of code."

"That's the best I can tell you right now," I said. "However, I'll bet if you decrypt Dr. Nemo's message the answer will be right in front of you."

"Nemo's code is as unbreakable as they come," Haley said. "We still haven't even made a dent."

"Two impossible tasks then," I said. "Right up your alley."

Haley smiled.

"What alley would that be?" Haley said.

"Not the alley you're thinking of," I said.

Haley smiled again.

"Jeez, Major, your mind is truly in the gutter," I said.

"Yeah, well I've been up for forty-eight hours," Haley said. "What's your excuse?"

"I wish I had one," I said.

"Call me after you've checked out the houses of Lennon's relatives," Haley said. "Bye."

"Bye," I said.

"Damn, hold on," Haley said. "I forgot to tell you something."

"Yes?" I said.

"We've been looking at the cracked cell phone you sent us from the NASAD site with Dragon Man's picture on it," Haley said. "The cell phone's signal was routed via hundreds of fake IP addresses. We aren't going to be able to determine where Dragon Man was when he made the call."

"Understood," I said.

"Bye for real this time," Haley said.

"Bye," I said.

Haley clicked off.

I rejoined Kate, Adelaide, Jeff, Ray Carpenter, and Ray's two men. Kate was still wearing Carpenter's helmet and bulletproof vest.

I said, "Am I interrupting anything?"

Carpenter said, "I was just finishing up the George Boole story as I know it."

"Good," I said. Then pointing at the SWAT helmet atop Kate's head, I added, "That's a nice look for you."

"Shoot," Kate said. "I forgot I still had this stuff on."

Kate took off the helmet, wiggled out of the vest, and handed both to Carpenter.

"Ray, that vehicle I asked you about earlier?" I said.

"Yes?" Carpenter said.

"I need it now, please," I said.

"'Now', now?" Carpenter said.

"Yes," I said.

Ray looked over at the policemen gathered around the few cruisers and unmarked cars remaining on the lot.

"I know one of those plainclothes detectives," Carpenter said. "Erwin Bleckley. He used to be a Seal. Maybe Bleckley will lend us his car and he can get a ride home with a buddy."

"Or maybe Donnie Kurtsinger can take Bleckley home in the NASAD chopper," I said.

"Bleckley will lend us his car for sure then," Carpenter said. "Especially if we let him rappel down from the chopper into his backyard."

Adelaide said, "Rappelling? That's a great idea. I'll bet I can get into that old guy's backyard before he's halfway down the rope."

"Bleckley's only thirty-five," Carpenter said.

"Like I said," Adelaide said. "Old."

Jeff said, "Adelaide, don't you know by now that children should be seen and not heard?"

"I'm sorry, Jeff," Adelaide said. "I didn't realize I was interrupting some vital discussion regarding national security."

"You would if you be paying closer attention," Jeff said.

"You do understand that no matter how close attention I pay, I still won't be able to hear the voices in your head," Adelaide said.

I said, "Okay, I think that's enough of that. You're both staying with me, so the rappel or not to rappel discussion is moot." To Kate, I added, "That okay with you? Not the rappelling part, but the ride for Bleckley part?"

"As long as we have enough fuel," Kate said.

Carpenter said, "Bleckley lives in Simi Valley."

"Right on the way," Kate said. "Perfect."

"I'll go ask him," Carpenter said.

Carpenter left.

I noticed that the hazmat techs had almost completed the loading of their van.

Kate said to me, "What do you need a car for?"

"I probably shouldn't say, since I'm afraid it might conjure up some unpleasant images for you," I said, "but I think I better take a look at the homes of Sarah Lennon and Paul Lennon's parents."

Kate grimaced.

"Why do you have to go there?" Kate said.

"I'm still convinced the killings are personal," I said. "I'm hoping I'll find something the FBI or police missed that might give me a clue who the killer is. I'm going to try to pay Professor Margaret Lennon a visit too."

"Maybe I should go with you then," Kate said. "I've been to everyone's homes. I know Margaret well. There might be something I can help you with."

"Too dangerous," I said. "I want you back at the estate please."

"After what I've been through in the last two days, I'm pretty sure I can handle a visit to Sarah's and Paul's parents' houses," Kate said. "I'm not afraid."

"I believe you," I said. "But I've actually got a more important job for you to do."

Kate raised her eyebrows.

"You remember what we said about the dark programmers' war game software and how Carter Bowdoin was gambling on its success in the upcoming NASAD war games?" I said.

"Of course I remember," Kate said. "I just talked about it with Ray. I can't believe the bet between the dark programmers and the Cyber Defense Hall programmers got upped to ten million dollars." Kate paused. "Damnit, you do realize, don't you, that the dark programmers might still be alive if they hadn't kept the vice president of dark programming out of the loop?"

"I think that's probably true," I said. "They also might be alive if Mary Beth had been able to get Mr. Benavidez to contact us."

"It makes me wish my dad and Mr. Benavidez hadn't done such a good job when they designed the secrecy protocols for the dark programming division," Kate said.

"Your dad and Benavidez did do a great job," I said. "They were right to think the dark programmers might be subject to attack, and their system would have worked fine if the dark programmers had stuck to protocol. But there's no use crying over spilt milk. Right now, we need to stay focused on our mission."

"I understand," Kate said. "What's the job you need me to do?"

"It relates to the dark programmers' software," I said. "What I need you to do is find out how NASAD normally updates its software into the military's live systems. It's important."

"You're not just saying that so I'll go back home, are you?" Kate said.

"No," I said. "I really need to know."

"Why?" Kate said.

"I think the dark programmers' war game software might have been inserted into the military's currently operational systems," I said.

Jeff, cutting in before Kate could respond, said, "That Boole kid confirm Nemo and the dark programmers' war games software worked like we thought it might? That it's an attack coming from within the military's systems, not an attack coming from outside the systems?"

"Boole has never seen the dark programmers' software, so he couldn't actually confirm that's how it works," I said. "But my discussion with Boole leads me to believe you and I have definitely been on the right track."

Kate said, "Hold on a second. Are you really saying that Dr. Nemo and the dark programmers figured out a way to get their war games software into the live military computer systems?"

"I'm pretty certain Nemo and the dark programmers didn't intend for it to get it into the live systems," I said. "But I do think that's what happened."

"Could the fact their software got into the live systems be the grave threat Nemo warned of?" Kate said. "The insurmountable edge that CENTCOM is so worried about?"

"I'm afraid so," I said.

"Are you serious?" Kate said.

"I'm so serious I can only joke about it," I said.

"What?" Kate said.

Jeff said, "He just mangled something Werner Heisenberg said."

"Oh," Kate said.

"Still mean he serious though," Jeff said.

"If the software is in the live systems we're probably looking at a disaster, right?" Kate said.

I said, "Disaster would be putting it mildly."

"I guess I don't have a choice then," Kate said. "I suppose it shouldn't be too hard for me to track down someone at NASAD who can tell me how it's done."

"Good," I said.

"Something's been on my mind I have to ask you about, though," Kate said.

"What is it?" I said.

"If Carter Bowdoin had all the dark programmers killed," Kate said, "why didn't he have George Boole killed too?"

"I think Carter will have Boole killed if he can figure out a way to do it," I said.

"I meant before today," Kate said.

I considered what Kate had said for a moment.

"That's a good question," I said. "Leaving Boole alive does seem like a mistake on Carter's part, doesn't it?"

"It does," Kate said.

"However, if I had to guess what was going through Carter's mind, I'd say he probably planned on killing Boole later and never thought Boole would show up here," I said. "If Carter had Boole killed before he had the dark programmers in the bunker killed, Carter might have thought he'd run the risk of tipping off the dark programmers that they could be next."

Kate seemed to think this over.

"That would make sense," Kate said. "There's no way we'll ever know for sure though, is there?"

"I don't see how we could," I said.

Kate looked over at the crater.

"Bryce Wellington's story about there being booby traps in the bunker is probably bullshit, isn't it?" Kate said.

"Yes," I said. "It's probably just an excuse to keep people out of the bunker. There's no reason to wait for a Quantico bomb squad when the Los Angeles team could do just as well. Also, I hate to say this, but if there were any booby traps in the bunker, the hazmat team would have set them off."

"Those 'people' they're trying to keep out are probably us, right?" Kate said. "They don't want us to see what happened down there?"

"That's probably the case, yes," I said.

"So when are you going into the bunker? Kate said.

"What makes you think I'm going to do that?" I said.

"Jack," Kate said, "we both know Nemo might be dead in there. You have to look. Don't tell me you didn't already think of that."

"I did," I said.

"So when then?" Kate said.

I turned to Adelaide.

"How is our canary doing?" I said.

"He looks fine to me," Adelaide said.

I looked back at Kate.

"Tonight," I said to her. "After dark."

Adelaide said, "Me too?"

"Yes," I said. "You too."

"Cool," Adelaide said. "What are we going to do with Jeff though?"

"Jeff is also coming," I said.

"Damn," Adelaide said.

CHAPTER 84

Ray Carpenter convinced former Seal and current LAPD detective Erwin Bleckley to give us his car. Ten minutes later Bleckley was flying away in the NASAD helicopter and Adelaide, Jeff, and I were in Bleckley's Crown Victoria heading south on the 5 Freeway towards Pomona. Before we left the NASAD site, Carpenter had also made some calls that would smooth the way if we ran into any law enforcement authorities during our visits to Paul Lennon's relatives' homes.

The Crown Victoria was a specially modified undercover unit - it had been souped up under the hood and had a heavy-duty suspension. The sound of the engine's hum filled the passenger cabin, while at the same time the engine's vibrations passed up through my seat and rattled and warmed my body. Gas fumes from the freeway traffic seeped into the cabin through gaps in the window seals. We had put the car's moveable red police light on top of the roof. The light was flashing and spinning inside its clear plastic case. The two yellow lights on the shelf above the car's back seat also flashed on and off.

Adelaide was driving, mainly because she had insisted on doing so and Jeff and I hadn't had the energy to argue with her. With the rush hour traffic at a near standstill, Adelaide zipped along the freeway's right shoulder at ninety miles an hour, occasionally using the unmarked police car's siren to scare away any poor soul who had wandered into her path. I wondered if any of those souls had tried to divine what kind of case required a detective to go undercover as a nearly naked teenage girl.

Jeff and I were both firmly buckled up. Jeff was in the back with his head out the window enjoying the wind on his face. I was in the front next to Adelaide and digging my fingers into my seat.

It was standard practice among us that the driver had choice of music. Adelaide was listening to Metallica's 'Creeping Death' which I found appropriate for the situation.

Respecting Haley's fear that the mercenaries might be actively searching for the three of us, both Jeff and I were keeping a look out for tails. Neither of us had seen anything suspicious.

Adelaide said, "Do you think the hazmat team knew before they went into the bunker that it was safe?"

"You mean because of the disconnected hose?" I said.

Adelaide nodded.

"Not sure," I said. "If they knew or didn't know, the fact it was disconnected still has to be an oversight. If the hazmat team was a bluff to make us think the bunker was dangerous in order to scare us away from going inside, they certainly wouldn't want us to see the disconnected hose. And if they didn't know if the bunker was safe, then the hose being disconnected could still have been unintentional - dangerously unintentional, but unintentional nonetheless."

"But either way you think it's safe to go down since the canary was still singing?" Adelaide said.

"Yes," I said.

"And that the booby traps already would have gone off?" Adelaide said.

"Yes," I said. "And the fact the whole booby trap idea came from Bryce Wellington, who probably just said it so that he, Bowdoin, and Burnette could justify stalling anyone else's entry into the bunker while they waited for the Quantico team."

"So we won't die when we go into the bunker?" Adelaide said.

"Highly unlikely," I said.

"Is highly unlikely worth the risk?" Adelaide said.

Jeff said, "A 'highly unlikely' from General Jack Wilder gonna be as good as it ever gets. No guarantees in our line of work."

"Okay," Adelaide said. "I'm in."

A silver Prius drifted out of the freeway's right lane and onto the shoulder. Adelaide blasted the siren. The Prius didn't move. Adelaide didn't slow down, just squeezed between the Prius and the edge of the freeway. I dug my fingers harder into my seat.

A few moments later, after my fingers had uncramped, I took out my iPhone. I pulled up the picture of Carter's Chinese friend in his ten thousand dollar suit, five thousand dollar shoes, and yellow socks and handed the phone to Jeff.

"Haley sent this to me," I said. "He's our best candidate for Dragon Man."

Jeff studied the photo.

"Yellow socks," Jeff said. "Interesting."

"That 'interesting' sounds like you think it's more than just a fashion statement?" I said.

"Yellow is the official royal color of the Chinese emperor," Jeff said.

"Aha," I said. "I didn't know that."

"Lots of things you don't know," Jeff said. "When we gonna talk to your two witnesses already?"

"Bobby and Timmy?" I said.

"Um-hmm," Jeff said.

"Hand me the phone," I said.

"You forgot to text Vandross again didn't you?" Jeff said. "I told you not to delete that text when we was on the beach."

The bad news was that Jeff was right. I had forgotten. The good news was that at least I'd figured out what it was I was trying to remember to ask Vandross as he was leaving the NASAD site earlier. I certainly wasn't going to share either news with Jeff, however.

"Just hand me the phone," I said.

"Guess I can forgive you since you were dead this morning," Jeff said. "Seven minutes a long time, even for you."

Jeff handed me the phone. I texted Vandross asking him to set up a call with Bobby and Timmy and put the phone back in my pocket.

A stalled car suddenly appeared on the shoulder about fifty yards in front of us. Adelaide quickly slowed down, turned on the siren, and laid on the horn. Miraculously the cars to the left and ahead of us in the freeway's right lane moved onto the shoulder. Adelaide slipped into the narrow space in the right lane created by the cars' moving, rapidly accelerated around those cars and the stalled car, then swerved at high speed back onto the shoulder. I had dug my fingers so hard into my seat I thought I had snapped a few tendons.

Jeff said, "I been thinking about why Dragon Man wanna kill Paul Lennon's family."

"What'd you come up with?" I said.

"I say I be thinking about it," Jeff said. "I didn't say I come up with anything."

"Sorry," I said. "I just naturally assumed that since you brought it up, you had something constructive to relate."

"I didn't say I didn't come up with nothing neither," Jeff said.

"So which is it?" I said.

"I done come up with something," Jeff said.

"You done come up with something?" I said.

"You making fun of the way I speak?" Jeff said.

"Absolutely," I said. "Yes. Without a doubt."

"Glad you man enough to admit it," Jeff said.

"Thank you," I said. "I repeat, what'd you come up with?"

"I think it's personal," Jeff said.

"As I remember it, we already discussed that issue and we were both in agreement," I said. "It's definitely personal."

"I mean real personal," Jeff said. "Like real, real, real personal."

"What does real, real, real personal mean?" I said.

"Like maybe since Dragon Man be killing Paul Lennon's family, maybe Lennon killed one of Dragon Man's own clan," Jeff said.

"Hmm," I said. "I kinda like that. Except the most likely place Lennon would have killed someone was on a mission. Haley already looked into that and couldn't find anything."

"Maybe Haley is missing something," Jeff said.

"Unlikely, but not impossible," I said. "What do you want to do?"

"Might be good if we start from scratch," Jeff said.

Another stalled car appeared in front of us on the shoulder. The car's driver was fixing a flat tire. Adelaide slowed nearly to a stop, and laid into the horn and siren again. The cars to our left miraculously pulled onto the shoulder once more. Adelaide slammed the pedal to the floor, shot into the empty space in the right lane created by the cars' moving, and back onto the shoulder unscathed. That time I was sure I'd snapped some tendons.

"Okay, let's do that," I said. "How about we start by assuming Dragon Man really is Chinese?"

"Yeah," Jeff said. "Let's be assuming that."

"If Lennon killed someone in Dragon Man's family, probably means Lennon killed a Chinese person," I said.

"Some folks may claim we're being prejudicial in deducing that, but I'm okay with it," Jeff said.

"You ever heard of any missions special ops ran that involved a fire-fight with Chinese military personnel?" I said.

"Meiyou," Jeff said.

"That 'no' in Chinese?" I said.

"Shi," Jeff said.

"That 'yes' in Chinese?" I said.

"Shi," Jeff said.

"Can we switch back to English now?" I said.

"Shi," Jeff said.

"That doesn't mean one didn't occur though," I said.

"Oui," Jeff said.

I rolled my eyes.

"I suppose there could even have been an off-books mission," I said.

"Hai," Jeff said. "That's what I was thinking."

"If you were thinking that all along why didn't you just say that from the start?" I said.

"Wanted to see if you got there without me intruding on your thought processes," Jeff said.

"Fair enough," I said. "Off-books means Lennon would have had a code name. Even with a code name, Haley should have found it though."

"Unless code name got screwed up," Jeff said.

Adelaide hadn't appeared to be paying much attention to us, but at the mention of a code name, her ears seemed to perk up.

"Wouldn't have been the first time that happened," I said.

"Nope," Jeff said.

"If Haley looked at all of Lennon's missions and his code name got screwed up," I said, "then she wouldn't find the mission."

"Even if she find a mission could have involved Chinese military and Lennon was on it, she wouldn't have known it since it be the wrong code name," Jeff said.

Adelaide looked over at me and said, "I hate to admit it, but you two idiots might actually be making some sense right now."

"Thanks, Adelaide," I said. "But keep your eyes on the road, please."

Jeff said, "What'd I say about children being seen and not heard, Adelaide?"

Adelaide whipped her head to face forward again and said "Screw you, Jeff," then floored the gas pedal. The Crown Victoria quickly went from ninety to one hundred and ten miles an hour. A green overhead freeway sign said our exit for the 134 East was coming up in one mile.

I said, "Uh, Adelaide?"

"What do you want asshole?" Adelaide said.

"We need to take the 134 to get to Claremont," I said. "Exit is coming up."

"I see it," Adelaide said.

"The curve for the turnoff looks a little sharp," I said. "Perhaps you might be going just a teensy-weensy bit too fast?"

"It's under control," Adelaide said.

Adelaide kept the pedal to the metal and by the time we hit the exit ramp we were going one hundred and twenty. Adelaide jerked the steering wheel to the left and the Crown Vic went up on two wheels, sliding along the ramp at a forty-five degree angle to the ground. Directly in our path were a dozen or so yellow water-filled safety barrels that were guarding the sharp corner at the end of the ramp's side rails. I braced myself, sure we were going to hit the barrels. I figured we wouldn't die, but it wasn't going to be pleasant either. But then, just before impact, Adelaide feathered the steering wheel and the car fell back on all four tires. We missed the barrels by the barest of inches, exited the ramp, and, somehow, having lost none of our speed, joined the 134 Freeway heading east.

"Adelaide," I said. "A hundred and twenty is a little too fast for my taste. Bring it back under a hundred please or I'll take over."

"I don't understand why you're the boss of everything," Adelaide said.

Jeff said, "He's older and bigger than you."

"That's the way the world works, huh?" Adelaide said.

I said, "Pretty much. Now, slow down."

Adelaide slowed down.

"Well, it won't work that way when I'm in charge," Adelaide said.

"How will it work when you're in charge?" I said.

"I haven't decided yet," Adelaide said. "But when I do, you'll be the last to know. Speaking of which, why are you so high and mighty you think you're going to find something in Claremont the FBI and cops didn't find?"

"I might not," I said. "But I think it's worth a try."

Jeff said, "He's leaving no stone unturned. It's a key rule in the book known as 'The Philosophy of General Jack Wilder.'"

Adelaide said, "Uncle Jack never wrote a philosophy book."

"Be a book in his head," Jeff said. "I read it because I can read his mind."

"I bet there must be a lot of other dumb sayings in that stupid book," Adelaide said.

I said, "Thank you Adelaide." I turned to face Jeff. "We were on to something earlier before we got interrupted, weren't we?"

"I think next thing we was going to do was decide to ask Major Marion Haley to be looking for any special ops teams that got in an off-record shooting match with Chinese troops," Jeff said.

"And if she finds one, then see if there might be a code name that got screwed up," I said.

"And then see if that screwed up code name might be Paul Lennon's," Jeff said.

"I think I'll do that right now," I said.

"I believe you should," Jeff said.

I took out my iPhone and texted Haley asking her to please do some research along the lines of Jeff's and my latest thinking. Knowing how sensitive Haley could be to any notion that she might have made a mistake, I made it clear we believed it would have been next to impossible for her first searches to have found a connection between Dragon Man and Lennon of the kind Jeff and I thought might exist, as there were just too many unknown variables. The odds were good Haley would still beat herself up if she found such a connection, but at least I felt comfortable I had given it my best shot at keeping her from doing so. I also texted Kate asking her if she had ever heard of any mission that might have brought Paul in contact with Chinese military personnel.

The traffic traveling east up the hill on the 134 out of Glendale remained congested, so Adelaide continued along the shoulder. To our left, the foothills rose steeply to meet a soft blue sky that was speckled with small wisps of white cloud. To our right, the grade dropped off sharply into a canyon that seemed to fall all the way to downtown Los Angeles. Homes like little boxes dotted the canyon and sat among thick greenery of short, leafy trees and shrubs. The downtown high-rises glittered gold, red, and orange in sunlight that fought its way through the late afternoon haze. The 134 became the 210 and we sped past the towns that lay at the base of the mountains that held the Angeles National Forest - Pasadena, Arcadia, Azusa, and Glendora - and turned off the freeway at Towne Avenue in Claremont.

We took Towne to Foothill Boulevard, turned left, then right on Indian Hill. We came to the little village of Claremont where candy and ice cream shops, pizza and Japanese restaurants, and record and gift stores catered to the college students who attended the local colleges. Sam, Lizzy, and Sarah Lennon had lived on Spring Street which was just off the main drag. We quickly found their house, pulled up in front of it, and parked.

CHAPTER 85

I stared at Sam, Lizzy, and Sarah's house. I didn't really have any idea what I expected a search of the house might reveal that could be of value in my hunt for Dragon Man. I only knew that I needed to conduct such a search in order to satisfy myself that, as Jeff had said, we had left no stone unturned.

The house was two stories high. It had been constructed of wood beams and slats in the craftsman style that had been popular over fifty years ago. The beams were painted yellow, the slats blue. The house had a sharply sloping roof. A covered veranda lay along the front of the house and also along both sides of the house halfway to the backyard. The veranda's roof threw most of the first floor's exterior into shadow. The front door was dark maple with a large window cut into its center.

A front yard sloped gently upwards to the veranda. The yard was covered by a vibrant green lawn. A concrete walkway traversed the lawn from the sidewalk to the veranda. The walkway was intermittently broken up by sets of two or three brick stairs. Pink, red, and yellow flowers bloomed in flowerbeds that lined the walkway. Tall elm and redwood trees were scattered about the yard.

If it weren't for the yellow crime scene tape strung in big haphazard 'x's across the veranda, Sam, Lizzy, and Sarah Lennon's house would have looked like any other well kept, small town home.

Adelaide, Jeff, and I got out of the car. We were instantly struck by a hot, dry heat. It was at least ten degrees hotter than the San Fernando Valley had been and the light was much brighter too - so bright it was hard to see for a moment. The heat evaporated all the moisture from our eyes and seared the inside of our noses even as the flowers' fragrance wafted up to us. A few birds that had taken refuge in the shade of the upper branches of the front yard's trees chirped out a warning song to us.

Adelaide seemed to be studying the crime scene tape.

"I don't think going in there will turn out to be what I'd call fun," Adelaide said.

"Why not?" I said.

"It looks spooky," Adelaide said.

Jeff said, "Sounds like you a scaredy-cat to me."

"Call it what you want, asshole," Adelaide said.

I said, "Adelaide, you're welcome to stay out here."

Jeff said, "Yeah. If you too chicken, be best you do that."

Adelaide said nothing.

I said to Jeff, "Should we make a big spectacle of ourselves and bust through the crime scene tape and break down the front door, or see what the backyard has to offer?"

"That a question?" Jeff said.

"No," I said.

The house's backyard had a lush, well-manicured lawn surrounded by a six foot tall pine plank fence. A child's swing set, two children's bicycles, and an above ground portable blue plastic pool were on the lawn. One of the bikes was green, medium in size, and had fat white-walled tires. Multicolored streamers trailed from the ribbed blue grips on the bike's handlebars. The second bike was nearly identical to the first one except it was pink, and smaller in size. The bikes had clearly been Sam's and Lizzy's. I thought about the fact that Sam and Lizzy would never ride the bikes again, swing on the swing set, or swim in the pool. I was sad and angry at the same time.

I took a closer look at the pool. The pool's waterline had fallen half-way down from the pool's top edge. A small rubber raft, missing a bit of its air, gently rocked on the water, stirred by a mild breeze. Leaves littered the water's surface and also lay in clumps at the bottom of the pool. Death had been recent, but nature was already taking its inexorable course.

Adelaide, Jeff, and I stood in the backyard and looked up at the rear of the house. The roof atop the second floor had two sloping sides that formed the letter 'A'. There were three windows on the second floor and one large picture window on the bottom floor.

Ten wooden steps led up to a ten foot by ten foot rear porch. The porch was about nine feet off the ground, made of two-by-fours, and bordered by a wooden rail. The back door, which opened onto the porch, was made of pine that had been painted white. The door also had a brass doorknob and a window cut into its top half. The window was covered by a blue and white checkered curtain.

We climbed the steps, the wood sagging and groaning beneath our feet. Jeff tried the brass doorknob. It was locked.

"We gonna kick it in?" Adelaide said.

The large bottom floor picture window was to our left, three feet beyond the porch rail and level with it. It too was covered with a blue and white checkered curtain. The curtain fluttered slightly as the breeze crept in through a tiny gap between the bottom of the window frame and the sill.

I said, "Might be an easier way."

I leaned over the porch rail and put my left palm on the window. I jiggered it back and forth. The window was stuck in its rails, but I didn't think it could be locked and still have the gap I observed. I jiggered the window some more, then pressed hard, and slid it open until the gap was about two feet wide.

"Adelaide, do you think you can get yourself in the window?" I said.

"I'm not going in alone," Adelaide said.

Jeff said, "Still chicken, huh? That don't portend well for your future as a cold-blooded warrior, girl."

"I am a cold-blooded warrior," Adelaide said. "Just not when it comes to haunted houses."

"Who says it's haunted?" Jeff said.

"Who says it's not?" Adelaide said.

Realizing Adelaide and Jeff could continue to argue on their current topic of contention well into the foreseeable future, and that such argument would surely lead nowhere, I decided it best to take matters into my own hands. I climbed over the rail, stood on the landing on the other side of the rail, leaned sideways out into space, and grabbed the bottom of the windowsill with both hands.

My next maneuver was going to be to leave the landing and swing out below the sill.

I knew it could hurt, so when I did it, I did it as gently as possible.

Gently didn't help, however.

After the swinging part was complete, I was left hanging below the sill and supporting the full of my weight with just the tips of my fingers.

Both my shoulders felt like they were ripping out of their sockets, and I was sure my fingers were about to break all at once.

Jeff said, "Oooh, that look like it be painful. Don't think I ever seen a general do that before."

"Yeah, well when the troops are spoiled rotten, sometimes you just gotta do things yourself," I said.

Adelaide said, "You better not mean me."

Jeff said, "Who else here a troop?"

I ignored them. I hung on the sill for a few moments taking some deep breaths and hoping the pain would subside a little before I put myself through my next stupid move. Then, grunting, I pulled myself up, hooked a leg over the sill, and rolled into the house. I found myself in the kitchen, lying on a ceramic-tiled counter next to the sink.

I let myself down off the counter and onto the kitchen floor. The kitchen table was bare and its chairs were all neatly in place around it. The cabinets and drawers were all closed. The refrigerator door was also closed and the refrigerator was humming. There wasn't a single dish, clean or dirty, in the sink. In short, the kitchen was immaculate and everything was where it belonged. Which made sense to me if the mercenaries had invaded the house sometime in the middle of the night long after dinner had been eaten, and well before breakfast would be prepared.

I took a few steps toward the center of the house and stood in the kitchen's interior doorway. The doorway opened onto the living room. The living room was in complete disarray. Lamps and tables had been up-ended and lay on the floor. A couch was slit open and on its side. A heavy woolen throw rug that had most likely covered the center of the walnut living room floor appeared to have been flung against the wall. A few oil paintings depicting harbor scenes and forest landscapes lay in a corner of the room, the paintings' canvases torn and their frames smashed.

I didn't know what to make of the living room's condition. Had someone been looking for something and become enraged when they didn't find it? If they had been looking in the living room for something, was it something they did not expect to find in the kitchen? Or had they found what they were looking for and simply left the kitchen alone?

The fact that someone might have been looking for something at all, however, made me feel like the decision to come to the house had been a good one. If we could find out what that something was, there was a reasonable chance it might turn out to be a clue that would lead us closer to Dragon Man.

Jeff's and Adelaide's voices floated in from outside.

"You okay in there?" Jeff said. "Adelaide's worried about you. She thinks a demon got you."

"He's lying," Adelaide said. "I never said anything about a demon."

"Ghost, demon, ain't no difference," Jeff said.

I walked back to the kitchen door, unlocked the dead bolt, and opened the door. Jeff came in, followed by Adelaide.

"Don't let the kitchen's immaculate condition fool you," I said. "There's a mess in the living room. A big mess."

I led Jeff and Adelaide from the kitchen into the living room. We surveyed its contents.

"Look like someone be looking for somethin'," Jeff said. "Maybe they're mad when they don't find it, or they're mad when they does, but either way they're mad."

"I agree," I said. "Let's see if we can figure out what they were looking for."

We spent the next few minutes examining the ruined couch, lamps, paintings, and tables. We found nothing that we believed could help us discern what Sarah Lennon's murderers were looking for. We moved out of the living room and into the house's front entry lobby.

The front door was at one end of the entry lobby and at the other end was a staircase that led to the second floor. The entry lobby had the same walnut floor as the living room. A mirror lay in shards under a narrow table that stood against one of the lobby's walls.

Adelaide said, "What could they possibly think could be hidden in a mirror?"

"I believe that mirror goes more towards what Jeff said about them being mad since they hadn't found what they were looking for," I said.

"Not yet, anyway," Jeff said.

On the side of the lobby opposite the entrance to the living room was a sitting room. The sitting room had a wide arched entrance and a large picture window that looked onto the street. A beige muslin floor-to-ceiling curtain covered the window. Vases, picture frames, tables, and chairs lay smashed on the floor. A green felt couch and a brown Naugahyde chair had had their upholstery slashed to ribbons and their interior stuffing was strewn about. It looked as if someone had driven a threshing machine right through both pieces of furniture.

All in all, the sitting room looked pretty much the same as the living room. There was one important difference, however. The difference was a chalk outline of a body that had been drawn just below the picture window's curtains. A maroon-tinged pool of coagulated blood stained the floor inside and outside the chalk boundaries.

Since I hadn't heard of anyone else being murdered in the house other than Sarah Lennon, I assumed the body represented by the chalk outline was hers. The chalk outline depicted a body that was different than most bodies one might find at an average crime scene, however. The body had no head, only a line across the top of the shoulders.

Adelaide walked into the sitting room. Her flimsy sandals made her close to barefoot, and she appeared to be trying to protect the exposed tops of her feet by making sure only the bottoms of her sandals came into contact with anything on the floor. She crouched next to the chalk outline.

"This body doesn't have a head," Adelaide said.

Jeff said, "Mighty powerful observational skills you got there. Aren't you being a tad bit hasty though?"

Adelaide looked at him in a manner that was at once both annoyed and questioning. It was a look I believed she had perfected at birth, and of which I had seen her make abundant use.

I said, "I think what Jeff means is you might want to consider broadening your horizons."

"Really?" Adelaide said. "That's what Jeff means? Well, perhaps you'll understand what I mean when I say you can both go screw yourselves if you can't speak plain English."

Jeff and I looked at each other and shrugged. We both gingerly raised our right hands and pointed with our index fingers at a spot about ten feet to her left, close to the front corner of the room. Adelaide turned her head and followed our indicated line. Her eyes opened in horror.

"Oh my God!" Adelaide said.

What she was looking at was a chalk circle the size of a honeydew melon. The circle was filled nearly entirely with coagulated blood. The blood spilled out over the chalk circle just as it had with the chalk line marking Sarah's body.

"That's where the head was, isn't it?" Adelaide said.

Jeff said, "Give the girl credit. She recovers quickly."

I said, "Remarkable pick up."

Adelaide said, "You guys are assholes."

We all surveyed the room for another moment.

"I don't see anything here that clues me in to what the killers were searching for," I said. "Either of you got any ideas?"

Adelaide said, "No."

Jeff said, "Not about what they're searching for. But I do have something heavy on my mind."

I said, "What is it?"

"I'm having a hard time dealing with the notion those two kids, Sam and Lizzy, seen their momma get her head cut off," Jeff said.

Adelaide said, "What's wrong with you Jeff? Did you really have to bring that up?"

"That thought never occur to you?" Jeff said.

"No," Adelaide said. "It's too awful to even consider."

I said, "I considered it. But what the killers did to Sam and Lizzy already has me mad enough. I didn't want to dwell on the idea the killers made them watch what they did to their mother and make myself even madder."

"That's probably not a bad idea," Jeff said.

A thought crossed my mind.

"Actually, I think it's unlikely Sam and Lizzy were forced to watch the decapitation," I said.

"Why do you say that?" Jeff said.

"The killers knew what they were going to do to Sam and Lizzy in the desert," I said. "I think they wanted the kids fresh and lively for the festivities they had planned…"

"That pitching contest?" Jeff said.

I nodded.

"The pitching contest," I said. "If those kids watched their mom being killed I think they would have gone into shock. Fresh and lively goes out the window. I also think that when Sam was out there in the desert, he wasn't sure what the killers were going to do to him. If he was sure - and seeing his mother killed would have made him sure - then Sam never would have dug his own grave. Sam was a brave kid. I think he would have fought to the death well before that grave was finished."

Adelaide said, "That's a pretty awful idea too."

"It is what it is," I said. "But the truth is we'll probably never know what actually happened. Let's go check out the second floor."

We walked up the staircase at the end of the entry. The stairs creaked beneath our feet. There was a landing at the top of the staircase encased by thin wood posts. The posts had been painted white and were topped by a pine rail that had been stained a mahogany hue.

Three doors to three bedrooms bordered the right side of the landing. All three doors were open. A sudden unexpected loud clang emanated from the doorway of the bedroom closest to us. All three of us, young and old, experienced and inexperienced, shuddered involuntarily.

Jeff said, "That be just a wind chime, right?"

I said, "I think so."

Jeff's and my shudders apparently did not escape Adelaide's notice.

"Cold-blooded warriors my ass," Adelaide said.

Jeff said, "Even cold-blooded warriors get the heebie-jeebies."

"Heebie-jeebies?" Adelaide said.

I said, "Swahili for screaming meemies."

Jeff said, "You speak Swahili, bro?"

Adelaide said, "God, am I sorry I asked."

We stepped into the bedroom where the sound had come from. It was clearly Sarah Lennon's room. Sheer white curtains fluttered in a window that was on the wall opposite from where we stood. The wind chime that had frightened us was hanging just outside the window's frame. The chime had a little buddha sitting in a bronze temple guarded by dragons. Tubular bronze bells and red cords dangled beneath the bronze temple.

The wind once again hit the chime's bells. The sound the chime made was peaceful and meditative. The condition of Sarah's room stood in sharp contrast to the chime's sound, however.

A king-size bed that was beneath the curtained window had had its mattress sliced and shredded just like the chair and the couch in the sitting room. The drawers of the room's dresser had all been opened, and their contents of socks, underwear, bras, scarves, and sweaters had been strewn on the floor. The doors of the room's closet had been ripped from their rails, and the closet's contents of dresses, jeans, coats, sneakers, boots, and high heel shoes lay in scattered piles.

Sarah Lennon's bathroom was in the same shape as the bedroom. The mirrored door of the medicine cabinet above the sink looked like someone had taken their fist to it - cracks in the shape of a spider web spread out from the mirror's center. Pill bottles had been opened and dozens of pills littered the pink tile bathroom floor. Cosmetic jars had been emptied, their powders staining the white porcelain sink.

We searched both Sarah's bedroom and the bathroom but found nothing that would help us determine what the killers were looking for. We left Sarah's room and entered the center room of the three bedrooms on the second floor.

The center room had obviously been little Lizzy's room. Her room was also a mess. A small wooden dressing table and mirror had been hacked to bits. The mattress of Lizzy's bed looked like it had been ripped off its frame and hurled across the room. Childlike watercolors and crayon drawings appeared to have been torn from the walls, stepped on, and kicked aside.

Jeff said, "I still can't tell yet what they looking for. But I'm pretty sure about something."

"Yes?" I said.

"If it was in this house, they found it," Jeff said.

We searched Lizzy's room but could still find no clue what the killers were looking for.

We moved to the third room off the landing. There was no question it was Sam's bedroom.

Sam's room looked like it had been pulverized. The floor was strewn with ripped up posters of Los Angeles Lakers and Dodgers players, a few small, shattered trophies for participating in football and basketball summer camps, a PlayStation - to which someone appeared to have taken a hammer - and a little wooden picture frame.

I moved through the rubble to the picture frame. The frame's glass was broken and behind it was a photograph of Sam and his father Paul Lennon. Paul had his arm around Sam and Sam was wearing the red and white of a St. Louis Cardinals Little League uniform. Sam also had a bat slung over his shoulder. Sam and Paul were smiling broadly. I imagined I could see pride in Paul's features, and Sam's face seemed to be full of love for his dad. I was wiping a tear from my eye, when I heard Jeff's voice come from somewhere behind me.

"You best take a look at this," Jeff said.

I turned to see Jeff studying a photograph that was in a frame hanging crookedly on the wall next to one of the room's windows. I walked over to Jeff's side. The glass in the frame had been smashed just like the frame on the floor, but I could nonetheless identify the two people in the photograph. The people were Jeff and me, and we were standing close together, our inner arms around each others' shoulders and our outer arms holding aloft our M16's. We were both smiling, our faces swathed in camouflage paint, and our bodies dressed in dust-covered, full combat regalia. I recognized the battlefield on which we stood as being in Iraq. The smoking ruins of Fallujah were in the distance behind us.

Jeff said, "We took out 200 hostiles that day. Didn't lose any of our own. How'd Lennon get that picture?"

"Don't know," I said.

I can't explain why, but as soon as I had answered Jeff, the vision I had had yesterday out at the stoning site in the Mojave Desert was once again filling my mind. I saw Sam trying to be strong, trying to protect his little sister Lizzy as the stones were flying. I saw him comforting her, telling Lizzy things would be alright.

Then, suddenly my vision of Sam and Lizzy disappeared, and I heard a little boy's voice in my mind. The boy's voice said, "Help me, General Wilder. Help me, General Bradshaw. Please come. I need your help."

The boy's voice echoed in my mind. Each succeeding echo grew softer and softer until the sound of the boy's voice dwindled into a forlorn, infinite silence.

The silence was interrupted by a new voice floating up to me. I recognized the voice as Jeff's.

"You okay?" Jeff said. "You look like you're going out on me."

"It won't stand," I said softly.

"What'd you say?" Jeff said.

"It won't stand," I said.

"What won't stand?" Jeff said. "What you talking about?"

I realized I must have fallen into a trance. I shook myself out of it and turned my face towards Jeff.

"They killed those little kids, Jeff," I said.

"Sam and Lizzy?" Jeff said.

"Yeah," I said.

"Don't worry, bro," Jeff said. "You're right. No way that gonna stand. We're gonna get them."

Adelaide called from behind us, "Hey, don't you two have medals like these back home?"

Jeff and I both looked at Adelaide. She was kneeling beside an over-turned desk. In her hands was a wooden box she appeared to have taken off the floor. Jeff and I walked over to her.

Adelaide held the box up to me and pointed at one of the box's medals.

"This is a Bronze Star isn't it?" Adelaide said. "You both have some of these, don't you?"

Jeff and I nodded.

"Do you mind if I take a closer look at the box?" I said.

Adelaide handed the box to me. It had had a glass cover of which only a few shards remained. Inside the box were three medals lying on a padded red cloth backing. The medals were a Bronze Star, a Distinguished Service Medal, and a Purple Heart.

The wooden box, however, had clearly once held a fourth medal that was no longer there. The fourth medal had been between the Bronze Star and Purple Heart. I could tell the missing medal had been there, because the outline of the medal's shape showed clearly on the cloth, the interior of the outline being a deeper hue of red than the faded cloth that surrounded it.

"There was another medal in the box that's not here now," I said. "You didn't take it out did you, Adelaide?"

"What?" Adelaide said. "You think I'm a thief?"

"No, I don't think you're a thief," I said.

"It's obvious there's a missing medal," Adelaide said. "You think I'd be so stupid as to show you the box if I took it?"

"No, I just wanted to make sure you didn't take the medal out to look at it," I said.

"I didn't take it out," Adelaide said.

"You didn't happen to see the medal anywhere around here on the floor, did you?" I said.

"Wouldn't I have told you if I did?" Adelaide said.

"Yes, you would have," I said. "Sorry I asked."

I looked at Jeff.

"You thinking what I'm thinking?" I said.

"I believes so," Jeff said.

"We better not jump to any conclusions before we make a thorough search," I said. "Adelaide please help us look for the medal."

The three of us spent the next fifteen minutes scouring the room from top to bottom.

We didn't find the missing fourth medal.

"Well, it doesn't seem like the medal is here," I said. "But at least we've probably discovered what it is that the killers were looking for."

Jeff said, "It does appear that way."

Adelaide said, "You two think the killers tore apart most of this house looking for the missing medal?"

I said, "Yes. As we all discussed in the car, Jeff and I believe that Paul Lennon may have participated in a special ops mission that involved him in a firefight with troops from China's People's Liberation Army. We have no record of the mission yet, but it's possible the missing medal may have been awarded to Paul for his performance during the mission."

"I heard part of what you two were saying in the car about Lennon's code name, but I didn't hear anything about why the mission is so important," Adelaide said.

Jeff said, "We think Paul Lennon killed one of the Chinese troops."

"So what?" Adelaide said. "That's what special forces captains do. They kill enemy troops."

"Yeah," Jeff said. "But it's not every day they kill a troop that be near and dear to Dragon Man."

CHAPTER 86

I took a picture of the three medals that were still in the box and sent them to Haley. I hoped that if Haley could somehow identify the missing medal from the group, she might be able to find a record of the off-books special forces mission on which we believed Paul Lennon had killed one of Dragon Man's relatives.

Having sent the photo to Haley, there was nothing more for Adelaide, Jeff, and me to do at Sarah's house. We exited the rear kitchen door and made our way to the front yard. It had gotten hotter, the birds were more subdued in their chirping, and the scent from the flowers was more intense.

"So Adelaide," I said, "if Dragon Man knew Paul Lennon had been awarded a medal for killing one of his relatives, do you think he might be mad enough to go through all that time and expense to rip up Sarah's house to find it and destroy any last trace of the medal?"

"I don't like it when you ask me questions you already know the answer to," Adelaide said.

Jeff said, "You do admit we're pretty smart to figure out what's going on with Dragon Man though."

"I might think you're smart if you actually catch him before we go to war with China," Adelaide said. "But given what I know of the two of you, I'd say that's never going to happen."

"You be wrong about that," Jeff said. "And when you see that you are, I suspect you gonna cry like a little baby."

"The day I cry is the day I die," Adelaide said. "What you got, ten days left?"

I said, "Adelaide, you do realize you're only insulting yourself, don't you?"

"If you only knew how stupid you sound," Adelaide said.

"I brought you down here to help me get this job done," I said. "So what you're saying is your presence is meaningless and that despite whatever contributions you might add to our team, we're still doomed to failure."

Adelaide studied my face for a moment.

"Say that again," Adelaide said.

"You're an integral part of this team," I said. "I'm expecting you to make up for any deficiencies that Jeff and I might possess."

Adelaide studied me once more, then spit on the ground.

"You're just blowing smoke up my ass," Adelaide said.

"No, I'm not," I said.

"I'm not buying it," Adelaide said. "However, I probably will wind up saving both your butts. Not that either of you deserve it."

We made our way back to the front lawn of Sarah's house. As we crossed the lawn and approached the Crown Vic, three preteen boys on bicycles came rolling down the sidewalk in front of us. They took one look at Adelaide in her bikini, screeched to a halt, and stared at her with their eyes wide open.

Adelaide said, "What you clowns looking at?"

The one in the middle, a carrot topped, freckle-faced kid with arms and legs so long he looked like a starving stork, said something that made the others laugh.

Adelaide gave them a hard look.

"You think something's funny, do you?" Adelaide said.

Carrot Top said, "Yeah. Your ass."

All three boys giggled.

"How 'bout I kick your ass," Adelaide said, "then me and my FBI buddies toss you in the squad car and take you downtown for making inappropriate comments to a minor."

Jeff whispered to Adelaide, "Downtown?"

"Shut the hell up, Jeff," Adelaide said.

The boys looked at the Crown Vic, then at Jeff and me, doubt growing on their faces.

Carrot Top said, "We didn't mean anything by it."

"Next time, think before you speak," Adelaide said. "Now get out of here. Go back home to your mommies before you really piss me off."

The boys spun around on their back tires and high-tailed it away from us.

Jeff said, "Wow. You showed them. They must be at least eight years old."

"I didn't like how they were looking at me," Adelaide said.

I said, "I could be completely wrong about this, but it might have something to do with your outfit."

"I'm sorry," Adelaide said. "Did you hear me ask for your opinion?"

Adelaide strode off the lawn and onto the steaming asphalt of the street. She marched around the back of the Crown Vic, opened the driver's door, slipped herself into the seat, and slammed the door.

"Women," Jeff said.

I said, "Does a seventeen year girl old meet the definition of a woman?"

"If it's female," Jeff said, "a seventeen month old meet the definition."

"Hmm," I said. "There might actually be some truth in that."

The Crown Vic's engine cranked to life. Adelaide gunned it a few times. She set the red roof light whirring and the back seat shelf yellow lights flashing.

"She be communicating to us?" Jeff said.

"Seems so," I said.

"Probably ain't a good idea to ignore her," Jeff said.

"Unless we want to walk home," I said.

We dashed to the car. I got in the front passenger seat and Jeff got in the back. Adelaide shifted into drive and floored the accelerator. The car's tires screeched as we sped away from the curb. Adelaide blew the first stop sign we came to and kept right on going. I prayed no one pulled out of a driveway. An old man wearing a windbreaker and Pomona College cap was walking a poodle on the sidewalk. The man stared at us as we went by.

"Don't you want to know where we're going next?" I said.

"Not particularly," Adelaide said.

"Okay," I said. "But if you do change your mind, it's the other way."

Adelaide didn't say anything, just whipped the steering wheel hard left. The Vic's rear end fishtailed around as I held on for dear life. After the car completed its full 180 degree turn, Adelaide floored the gas pedal and took off in the opposite direction. We passed the old man and the poodle again. I waved to them.

Adelaide continued to speed through Claremont's residential streets and I shouted directions at her. After five more blown stop signs, three up on two wheel fishtailing turns, and four blasts from the Vic's siren, we arrived outside a one-story, two bedroom stucco house in Montclair, a small town that bordered Claremont.

The one-story house had been the home of Paul Lennon's parents. The front lawn was bright green fescue and well-manicured. A palm tree grew on its right edge. A faded red brick walkway led up to the house's front porch, which, like Sarah's home, had yellow crime scene tape strung across it. Jeff and I opened our doors and got out. Adelaide kept the engine running and made no move to exit.

"You coming?" I said.

"What's the point?" Adelaide said.

"Suit yourself," I said.

Jeff and I walked across the lawn towards a six foot high wooden fence protecting the side yard. Some birds were in a small pine tree with browning needles on the other side of the wooden fence. The birds weren't visible, but they were singing the same subdued song as the birds had been singing at Sarah's house. Jeff and I had gotten about halfway to the fence when we heard the Vic's engine cut out. The car's door opened and slammed shut.

Jeff said, "What's she doing?"

"There isn't enough money in the world to get me to turn around and find out," I said.

We arrived at the fence and saw that it had a three foot wide gate. I tried the gate's handle. It was locked. I reached over the top of the gate, felt around, found a string, and pulled it. The gate unlocked. I opened it. Adelaide glided wordlessly by me and into the backyard.

Jeff said, "Don't let us hold you up."

"Shut up," Adelaide said.

We let ourselves in through an unlatched window at the back of the house and searched the house from room to room. Each room was completely trashed and, all in all, what we found differed in only three ways from Sarah's house.

One, there were four chalk circles instead of two - two bodies and two heads.

Two, the photographs in the smashed and shattered picture frames had different people in them. The photograph that struck me the most was almost a duplicate of what I had seen in Sarah's house, only this photo had Paul Lennon's father with his arm around a very young Paul in a Minnesota Twins Little League uniform. Paul must have been nearly the same age as Sam had been in Sam's own Little League photo with Paul.

Three, we found absolutely nothing to suggest the killers had discovered anything during their search of Lennon's parents' home that might have had the equivalent meaning to Dragon Man as the missing medal that was taken from Sarah's house.

Jeff said, "Don't look like the killers find anything worth taking, but I'm wondering if maybe they came here first, before they go to Sarah's?"

"Why do you say that?" I said.

"If they came here second, they'd already have the medal," Jeff said. "They kill Paul Lennon's parents, but don't need to waste all that time trashing the place."

"I can see that," I said. "Hard to believe the killers were searching for anything other than the medal they took from Sarah Lennon's home."

We left the house and piled back into the Crown Vic. Adelaide rolled down her window and started to put the domed red light on the roof. I reached over and stopped her.

"Let's take it a little easier," I said. "We don't have far to go. Lennon's sister's house is very close."

Adelaide frowned and reluctantly put the light back in the car. I gave her directions to Paul Lennon's sister's house. She pulled away from the curb and we were off.

Adelaide said, "Thanks so much for making me feel like a ghoul for the last hour. I really enjoyed it."

Jeff said, "That because you don't understand."

"Don't and don't want to," Adelaide said.

"The science of leaving no stone unturned is a precious science," Jeff said.

"I didn't see any stones in there," Adelaide said. "And I didn't see any in the first house either."

"Taking a metaphor literally is a sign of schizophrenia," Jeff said. "Learned that in Walter Reed."

"So you're calling me a schizophrenic?" Adelaide said.

"Just saying," Jeff said.

"What does that make you 'Mr. Running Through The House Half Naked At Midnight' shouting while he looks for IED's under the furniture?" Adelaide said.

I said, "Cut it out, Adelaide."

Jeff said, "Ain't schizophrenia. Be Post-Traumatic Stress Disorder."

"Though the wonderful, caring doctors at Walter Reed seem to easily confuse the two," I said.

"Which is why you my doctor," Jeff said.

"And a damn good one, I might add," I said.

"Amen to that," Jeff said.

Adelaide said, "Whatever."

We made it back to the center of Claremont Village again. Streams of college kids were walking on the sidewalks to and from the Claremont colleges. We came to a red light at the intersection of Bonita and Indian Hill. Adelaide repeatedly gunned the engine as we waited.

"Is that really necessary?" I said.

"Yes," Adelaide said.

The light changed to green. Adelaide floored the accelerator and the tires screeched on the asphalt, the rubber burning as I was thrown back in my seat. It wasn't quite as bad as riding in Donnie Kurtsinger's chopper, but it was close. I reached over, turned off the ignition, removed the key, and held it in my fist.

Adelaide struggled to control the car without power to the steering and brakes. She was finally able to get the car against the curb in a red zone. That was fine with me. I figured even though we weren't cops, we had a cop car, and cops always parked their cars in red zones.

Adelaide fumed. Jeff and I sat quietly. I let a minute go by, then spoke.

"Adelaide, I said we weren't in a hurry," I said.

Adelaide ignored me.

"I've told you this before, but it seems like it's time to say it again," I said. "Being a success in your chosen profession is not just about who can shoot the straightest, fight the hardest, run the longest, or jump out of airplanes with perfect technique. You need to be able to use your mind."

"How did you and Jeff make it then?" Adelaide said.

"Very funny," I said.

We sat silently for another moment.

"Alright, what's your point?" Adelaide said.

"It's one thing to be going hell-bent for leather...," I said.

"Hell-bent for leather?" Adelaide interrupted.

Jeff said, "Don't you watch no westerns, girl?"

"Westerns?" Adelaide said.

"You never seen 'High Noon'?" Jeff said.

"I don't watch cartoons, Jeff," Adelaide said.

"Ain't no cartoon," Jeff said. "'High Noon' about honor."

I said, "I think we're getting off subject here, Jeff. And I'm not sure anyone was going hell-bent for leather in 'High Noon.'"

"Adelaide still need to learn about honor," Jeff said.

Adelaide said, "I don't need to watch a cartoon to learn about honor."

"I told you it ain't no cartoon," Jeff said. "It's a movie starring Gary Cooper."

"Is Gary Cooper one of those dead movie stars you're so fond of?" Adelaide said.

"Gary Cooper immortal," Jeff said.

"So he *is* dead," Adelaide said. "I told you a hundred times I don't care about your goddamned dead movie stars."

"Go on home to your kids, Herb," Jeff said.

"What?!" Adelaide said.

I said, "It doesn't make any sense unless you watch the movie. Now listen, 'hell-bent for leather' means you're moving so fast it's reckless. It's one thing to be racing on a freeway or on empty residential streets, but if you kill someone in the middle of this crowded village, it's going to hurt our mission."

Jeff said, "Mission always come first."

Adelaide looked at both of us.

"Wow," Adelaide said. "What a great lesson. I can't thank the two of you enough. Can I have my keys back please?"

I said, "You're going to slow down?"

"Do I look like someone who wants to kill someone and ruin your precious mission?" Adelaide said.

I turned to Jeff.

"I don't think she's being sincere," I said.

Jeff said, "I suppose my best attribute, if you want to call it that, is sincerity. I can sell sincerity since that's the way I am."

"John Wayne?" I said.

Jeff nodded.

Adelaide said, "That's another dead movie star, isn't it?"

Jeff and I said nothing.

"Give me the goddamn key," Adelaide said.

I handed her the key.

Adelaide put the key in the ignition, turned it, placed the red light back on the roof, flicked on the yellow rear window light flashers, and repeatedly gunned the engine.

I said, "Goddamnit, Adelaide!"

Laughing, Adelaide put the car in gear, looked both ways, and slowly pulled away from the curb and into traffic. She made a full stop at the next stop sign on Bonita Avenue.

"You have to have a little faith in people," Adelaide said.

Jeff said, "That Tracy in 'Manhattan'?"

"Yep," Adelaide said. "Mariel Hemingway ain't dead."

A group of college students walked through the crosswalk in front of us. A pimply faced, gangly boy with short hair and a backpack stopped and stared at Adelaide. Probably just another person wondering about teenage girl cops in bikinis. Or maybe he just liked the bikini. Adelaide smiled at him then gave him the finger.

I said, "You're going to give the cops around here a bad name."

"Good," Adelaide said.

When the crosswalk cleared, Adelaide gradually accelerated and we continued at a slow pace through Claremont Village. We were going so slow cars were stacking up behind us. No one dared honk or otherwise complain.

CHAPTER 87

Professor Margaret Lennon's house was on Olive Street. It was a one-story Spanish colonial with a sloped red-tile roof, small arched windows, and a flagstone walkway leading to the front door. Three huge pine trees on the front lawn cast so much shade that the lawn and house were thrown into darkness. Pine needles littered the lawn and gave it an unkempt appearance. A blue jay, the crest on its head rising to a sharp peak, its body plumed in blue, white, and black, sat atop one of the pines, alternating its whistles with occasional hawklike cries. An oscillating sprinkler attached to a hose sprayed water from an aluminum tube that moved back and forth, the water hissing in the heat as it fell in droplets on the grass and flagstones. Magenta rhododendrons, orange poppies, and red fuchsias bloomed in a flower bed that lay at the base of the front wall of the house. Overhead the sun remained bright in a grey-blue sky, the air silent and still.

An FBI sniper was on the roof next to the stucco chimney, and an unmarked FBI car, a Crown Vic nearly identical to ours, was parked on the street under the shade of one of the pines. Two FBI agents sat in the Vic's front seat. All four of the Vic's windows were rolled down, I assumed to soften the heat. The agents watched us as we exited our car. They both appeared to check out Jeff's beach attire, but seemed to pay extra special attention to Adelaide - undoubtedly to assure themselves she wasn't carrying any concealed weapons inside her bikini.

We walked over to the FBI agents' Vic. Both agents had Heckler and Koch MP5 submachine guns across their laps. Cardboard trays with empty sandwich wrappers and coffee cups were on the Vic's front dash. There was the distinct smell of hamburgers and fries.

"That's a mighty spiffy combat unit you have there, Generals," the FBI agent in the passenger seat said.

"Don't let the clothes fool you," I said. "Ray Carpenter told you we were coming?"

The agent nodded.

"Will Professor Lennon see us?" I said.

He nodded again.

"Thanks," I said.

We turned to go.

"Hold on," the agent said. "Don't want you getting shot."

The agent picked up a walkie talkie and mumbled something into it. I saw the FBI sniper on the roof say something into the microphone mounted on his shoulder.

"Okay, you're clear," the agent in the car said.

We continued our way up the flagstone walkway, waited a couple of seconds for the sprinkler spray to oscillate away from our path, and climbed the few steps to the red brick landing which led to the front door. The door was oak with a small window. The window had a black cast iron grille and interior flap. A cast iron door knocker that matched the grille was beneath the window. I lifted the knocker and rapped it against its plate.

For a moment there was nothing but silence. Then we heard a soft squeaking noise followed by even softer footsteps. The window flap opened and two eyes peered out. The flap closed again and I could hear a dead bolt sliding out of its strike box followed by a heavy, old door-knob being turned. The door opened and Paul Lennon's sister, Margaret Lennon, stood before us.

We had been told Margaret Lennon was a poetry professor at Pomona College. There was nothing in the way she looked that made us doubt that. She was tall and pretty with finely sculpted cheekbones. Margaret appeared to be in her mid-forties, which meant if Paul was still alive she would then have been at least ten years older than him. She wore no makeup or jewelry, and her long brown hair was braided and fell down her back. She was dressed in a black knit ankle length dress that fully covered her arms. Open leather sandals were on her feet and a green-eyed grey cat with black tiger stripes was in her arms. Margaret's blue eyes were red rimmed, as befitted a woman who had lost her parents, a niece, a nephew, and a former sister-in-law within the last forty-eight hours. I introduced Jeff, Adelaide, and myself to her.

"Nice to meet all of you," Margaret said. "Please come in."

The front door opened directly into a living room. The room was dark with only a few shafts of sunlight escaping through heavy, drawn wood blinds. A hallway went off to what appeared to be three bedrooms on the left and there was a door directly in front of us that opened into a kitchen. The living room floor was solid oak stained a deep brown with a hemp throw rug in its middle. The walls were lined with bookshelves holding mainly the work of poets. I made out Shelley, Browning, Spenser, and Milton.

A grand piano was in a corner closest to the window, its lid and lyre shiny with black lacquer. On the lid sat gold and silver framed photos. I recognized Paul Lennon, Sarah Lennon, Sam, Lizzy, Paul and Margaret's parents, and also Kate and her kids, Carolyn and Dylan, in the photos.

Margaret, stroking the cat, led us to a couch of crushed maroon velvet that backed up against the front window. We sat down. In front of the couch was an antique cedar coffee table. Atop the coffee table was a silver tea kettle in a silver stand and next to the kettle was a china teacup in a matching china saucer. A linen doily was beneath the saucer. On the other side of the coffee table was a rocking chair. Margaret started to sit down in the rocking chair but stopped herself.

"Can I get you anything?" Margaret said.

"No, thank you," I said. "We would like to express our sincere condolences on your loss."

"Thank you," Margaret said.

Margaret sat down in the rocking chair, lifted the teacup to her lips, took a sip, and put the cup back down on the saucer. She stroked the cat, which purred softly in return. Margaret didn't say anything, just looked at us through her soft eyes. Her gaze lingered a bit on Adelaide's ankle monitoring bracelet, but there was nothing in her expression that revealed any thoughts the bracelet might have engendered. She seemed completely unfazed by the African American surfer in her midst. Outside, the sprinkler continued to hiss and the blue jay to whistle and jeer.

Margaret said, "As I understand it, you gentlemen are generals providing security to my sister-in-law, Kate."

"You are correct, ma'am," I said. "We are also helping Kate investigate the trouble at NASAD."

"I don't much like that company," Margaret said. She faced Adelaide. "Where do you fit in, young lady, if I may ask? It seems like dangerous work."

Adelaide looked questioningly at me. I said nothing. I was curious to see how Adelaide would answer on her own.

"I'm their trainee, ma'am," Adelaide said.

"What are they training you to be?" Margaret said.

"An Army Ranger," Adelaide said.

Margaret didn't say anything, only trembled slightly. Her grief-stricken face seemed to become even sadder. Adelaide appeared not to have picked up on the change in Margaret's features, because she simply forged ahead with her own question. It was a question I wouldn't have asked because it was a question I would have thought would have only poured salt into Margaret's fresh wounds.

"If you don't mind my asking, ma'am, why don't you like NASAD?" Adelaide said.

"I am opposed to war in all its forms," Margaret said.

"Don't you think it's naive to believe that there aren't people out there who will do anything to achieve their goals, including slaughtering the weak and the innocent?" Adelaide said.

I said, "Adelaide, please."

Margaret said, "It's fine General. I'd like to hear what Adelaide has to say." To Adelaide, she continued, "There are certainly people like that."

"You don't think they should be stopped?" Adelaide said.

"Not if the price is one's own soul," Margaret said.

"Well," Adelaide said, "that's easy for you to say. You're a poetry teacher. You live in a fantasy world of others' making."

I said, "Adelaide!"

Margaret said, "I am not offended, General."

Margaret took in a deep breath through her mouth and let it out, then gently stroked the cat.

"I have recently had a great loss," Margaret said. "My father and mother, my niece and nephew, and my former sister-in-law were all murdered. But it has not shaken my faith."

And her brother, Paul, too I thought. But that was not the time to tell her that Paul's death was also no accident.

"Their murderers should go free?" Adelaide said.

"Their murderers are not free," Margaret said. "They are trapped by their own karma. Perhaps one day they will break free of the cycle they are in."

"And in the meantime it's okay if they kill more people?" Adelaide said.

I was tempted to try to quiet Adelaide again, but I held my tongue.

Margaret leaned forward over the cat in her lap and picked up the teacup. She took a long sip and put the cup back on its saucer.

"Perhaps I can explain it better if I describe to you what I believe is the path for mankind that will bring us out of this endless cycle of war and killing," Margaret said.

"I'm listening," Adelaide said.

"General Bradshaw, do you mind if I use you as an example?" Margaret said to Jeff.

"Please do whatever you like, ma'am," Jeff said.

"Here is a strong, intelligent man," Margaret said. "And by the way he moves, I sense he is an athlete, perhaps even a great athlete. And yet this man has been cut down in the prime of life." She paused. "You suffer from post-traumatic stress disorder do you not, General?"

"It's that obvious, huh?" Jeff said.

"I volunteer in the mental health department at the Loma Linda VA hospital," Margaret said. "I have worked with hundreds of men suffering with the same issues. You all share a certain look in your eyes."

"I'm getting better," Jeff said.

"With all due respect, that is doubtful," Margaret said. "The disease has a poor prognosis. Do you know what the suicide rate is in the U.S. military?"

"Be about the same as combat casualties, ma'am," Jeff said.

"That is correct," Margaret said. "So for every soldier we lose in combat, we lose another at his or her own hand. The death rate for our wars is double what it appears to be."

"I believe you're right, ma'am," Jeff said.

"When we factor in all the lost lives such as your own, not to mention all the soldiers who will never be the same due to their physical injuries," Margaret said, "clearly it is a system that cannot work."

Neither Adelaide, nor Jeff, nor I, said anything. Margaret took another sip of her tea.

"I assume you were in Walter Reed Army Hospital, General

Bradshaw?" Margaret said.

Jeff nodded.

"How did you escape the system?" Margaret said. "I would have expected the Army to give someone of your status continued care, or at least what they call care, until they had deemed you cured."

Jeff tilted his head in my direction.

"My friend here come and get me," Jeff said.

"They let General Wilder take you out of Walter Reed?" Margaret said.

"No letting's about it, ma'am," Jeff said.

"He broke you out?" Margaret said.

Jeff nodded. Margaret appeared to think about that for a moment.

"Actually, I believe I heard that story," Margaret said. "I thought it was apocryphal. It is quite commendable, General Wilder."

I said, "Thank you, Professor Lennon."

Adelaide seemed annoyed with the turn the conversation had taken.

"If you don't mind, ma'am," Adelaide said, "can we get back to that alternate path for mankind you spoke of?"

"Sorry dear," Margaret said. "Of course we can. All human life is equally valuable. Our so-called enemies in war suffer the same, and most times, worse casualties than we do. It is a great and unnecessary waste. I believe salvation comes in understanding the ways of the Jains."

"I don't see you wearing a mask over your face," Adelaide said.

"I see you know the Jains," Margaret said. "I admit I cannot go as far as the Jains do, though I wish I could be just as committed. It is wonderful to me that they believe so deeply in nonviolence that they wear the masks to be sure they do not even accidentally kill an insect that might fly into their mouths. Just imagine if everyone on earth was like that. There would be no war. The Jains' purity of thought is the only way to reverse the natural predatory state of homo sapiens."

Outside, the blue jay made its hawklike cry.

"About how many Jains are there?" Adelaide said.

"I believe there are six million," Margaret said.

"Maybe the Jains only exist because people like us protect them," Adelaide said. "Maybe without us, the human predators roaming the earth who consider its seven billion homo sapiens mere prey would be shooting the Jains like fish in a barrel. And maybe the ones they didn't kill, they'd just enslave. With all due respect Professor Lennon, maybe you should put aside those poetry books for a while and read a little history."

"I understand your point," Margaret said. "You sound like my brother. He would have made similar arguments. But if we do not at least try another way, what future do we have?"

I interrupted before Adelaide could continue her argument with the professor. There was, after all, a purpose behind our visit, and it was time to get to that purpose.

"Thank you, Professor," I said. "We don't often hear words like yours in our world. There is a specific reason for our visit, however, and I would please like to get to it."

Margaret stroked the cat's back and gave a few rubs to its ears.

"And what is that reason, General?" Margaret said.

"Actually, before I get to the reason," I said, "I need to clear something else up first. That is, if you don't mind?"

"Okay," Margaret said.

"The killings of your parents, Sarah, Sam, and Lizzy all occurred yesterday morning," I said. "The FBI told me that when they found you, you said you had been out all day. Would you normally have been home in the morning?"

"Normally, yes," Margaret said. "I don't teach my classes at Pomona until the afternoon."

"Why weren't you home yesterday morning?" I said.

"An elderly neighbor friend of mine who lives down the street was not feeling well," Margaret said. "She asked me to drive her to the doctor."

"What time did you get back home?" I said.

"Not until late this morning," Margaret said. "The doctor decided my friend needed to go to the hospital, so I drove her there and waited until she was admitted. Then, once she was in her room, she said she was scared and asked if I would stay with her through the night. I called the college and told them to cancel my classes. I stayed with my friend, only leaving the hospital for an hour or so to get dinner."

Jeff said, "Lucky."

"I wouldn't call her lucky," Margaret said. "I am sure she could have found someone else if I wasn't available."

Adelaide said, "He doesn't mean the neighbor."

Margaret looked puzzled. I wasn't surprised she hadn't immediately recognized the obvious, that her trip to the hospital had saved her life. I have seen people with much bigger blind spots when it came to their own mortality. Margaret's failure to recognize the obvious didn't appear to last long however, as, a moment later, her face drained of color and she brought her right hand up to her neck, cradling the cat with her left. The professor also looked like something might have caught in her throat, that she might be having trouble breathing. She swallowed a few times, moved her head from side to side, and seemed to clear whatever it was that was bothering her.

Still looking pale, Margaret said. "You're saying it was me who was lucky? I would be dead if I had been home?"

I said, "I'm sorry, but yes, we do believe that."

"I don't know why I didn't think of that before," Margaret said.

Margaret leaned forward and picked up the teacup. She took a sip, and then held the cup in both hands, slowly lowering her arms until they rested on her lap so that the cat lay between the 'v' of her arms and the cup. She seemed to think things over.

"No one has yet discussed with me why my family was killed," Margaret said. "I would like to know what you think, General."

I hesitated for a moment. We had just forced Professor Lennon to confront the possibility of her own murder and I wasn't sure how direct I should be in regard to the murders of her loved ones. I decided she was strong enough to handle whatever I told her.

"We believe it was revenge," I said. "We think someone has waited a long time to take vengeance upon your brother Paul."

"Do you know who?" Margaret said.

Jeff said, "Man who wear a dragon mask. He wants to be emperor of Saudi Arabia."

Margaret looked at Jeff as if he were a very odd duck, but then seemed to catch herself, as if she remembered his difficult history. I also looked at Jeff, the expression on my face clearly saying, 'Please shut up'. Jeff shrugged.

I said, "Professor Lennon, what General Bradshaw said is correct, even though it might sound a bit confusing to someone such as yourself who is not as close to the situation as we are. We believe the person behind the killing of your relatives is most likely a Chinese man who had a member of his family killed in combat by Paul, or by someone in a squad that Paul was leading. Did Paul ever talk to you about any missions he was on in which he might have engaged the Chinese military?"

"My brother knew I had no interest in such matters and we never discussed them," Margaret said.

"I assume then he never gave you a gift of any of his military memorabilia?" I said. "Medals, combat photos, diaries?"

"Heavens no," Margaret said. She seemed to consider something for a moment. "The news has recently been full of stories of an impending war with China and also attacks on NASAD. Do you think there is any connection between those events and the murder of my family?"

Jeff said, "Uh huh. They be killing two birds with one stone."

I gave Jeff a harsh look. He gave me another shrug in return.

Margaret turned to Adelaide and said, "You see my dear don't you? The general has made my point for me. Endless cycles of violence and retribution. War will never stop unless we make it stop."

Adelaide said nothing.

I said, "Thank you, Professor Lennon. You've answered all my questions and I think we've taken up enough of your time. I'm going to give you my cell number and I would appreciate you giving me a call if you think of anything else you believe could be of value to us."

I was about to tell Margaret my cell number when outside, the blue jay, which had up until then only been making whistles and jeers, suddenly started rapping its beak into the pine tree, making a loud knocking sound.

Jeff and I looked at each other.

We both knew that jays don't knock like that unless they are annoyed, unless something has invaded their territory.

I quickly turned from Margaret, got up off the couch, and went to the front window.

"Is something wrong?" Margaret said.

I didn't answer. As I parted the window's blinds, there was a loud thump on the roof above me. The thump was followed by the sound of something large and heavy sliding along the roof's tiles. A moment later, I watched the heavy thing that had been sliding along the roof fall through the air and smack into the flower bed with a deep, dull thud. The thing was the body of the FBI sniper that had been on the roof. A red stain formed in a puddle between the flower stems on the ground surrounding the sniper's head.

I looked out at the two FBI agents sitting in the Crown Vic that was still parked on the street in front of Professor Lennon's house. They must have heard the sound of the sniper's body hitting the ground, as their heads were turning toward me. Those turns were never completed. The agents' heads disintegrated in nearly simultaneous clouds of pink spray. There had been no sound of gunshots. The rounds had come from silenced weapons.

I turned back to face Margaret.

"Do you have a basement?" I said.

"Why, what's wrong?" Margaret said.

"I'm sorry," I said. "No time for discussion. Do you have a basement?"

Margaret pointed at one of the doors off the hallway that led away from the kitchen.

"Adelaide," I said. "Take the professor into the basement. Find something to barricade the door and don't open it under any circumstances unless I tell you to."

"I'm not going anywhere unless you tell me what is going on," Margaret said.

"The three FBI agents that were guarding you were just killed," I said. "Unless you get in the basement, you'll be next."

Adelaide moved around the table, put her arms around Margaret, and moved her out of her chair. Adelaide then hustled Margaret, who was still cradling her cat, towards the basement door.

"I won't countenance any killing in my name," Margaret said, looking back over her shoulder as her body was ushered forward by Adelaide.

I didn't respond. Adelaide opened the basement door with one hand, pulled Margaret and her cat in through the door with the other, then kicked the door closed.

I looked back out the window, being careful to stay to the side of the window's frame, using the frame and surrounding wall as a shield. There was no movement on the street or in the yard.

Jeff said, "Hitters staying invisible?"

I nodded my head.

"They're waiting to show themselves until they're sure sniper ain't got no life in him," Jeff said.

"Agreed," I said. "My gut says three guys. When they come, it will be two through the front and one through the back."

"Three guys sound good," Jeff said. "How we gonna do this?"

"Don't relish the idea of doing it barehanded," I said.

"Always the kitchen," Jeff said.

"You think Margaret has automatic weapons in the kitchen?" I said.

"I would think that is highly unlikely," Jeff said. "However, I believe there is a very good probability we will come across some knives in the food preparation area."

"How come your grammar suddenly got so good?" I said.

"Just felt like teasing you," Jeff said. "Making sure you stays loose."

We ran into the kitchen. The sink was bordered on both sides by a black and white tiled countertop. Beneath the countertop were wood cabinets that had been painted white. Jeff and I each took a cabinet, opening doors and pulling out drawers. The third drawer I opened had a set of steak knives in it. I grabbed a knife for myself and tossed another one to Jeff. Jeff caught the knife, then pulled out a meat cleaver from one of the drawers he had opened. He held the knife and the cleaver out in front of him, weighing the relative merits of each one.

"Which you like better?" Jeff said.

"Why not both?" I said.

"Both it be," Jeff said.

"Might I suggest a plan?" I said.

"It a good one?" Jeff said.

"Don't know," I said.

"Least you honest," Jeff said.

"I stay here, jump the guy who comes in through the kitchen door from the backyard," I said. "You go down the hallway to the bedroom, turn on the shower."

"I already took a shower today," Jeff said.

"Doesn't smell like it," I said. "After you turn on the shower you get yourself someplace safe. Hopefully the two guys coming in the front door think the professor's in the shower. I'll use kitchen back door guy's gun to take out the front door guys from behind as they walk down the hallway to the shower."

"That the whole plan?" Jeff said.

"You don't like it?" I said.

"I didn't hear no contingency portion," Jeff said.

"I don't have one yet," I said. "But you'll be the first to know if one comes to mind."

"Hmm," Jeff said. "I suppose that seems fair, especially given the celerity with which the present situation done come upon us."

"Is celerity a word?" I said.

"Wouldn't be using it if it ain't," Jeff said.

"Of course you wouldn't," I said.

Jeff turned to dash off.

"Hold on," I said.

"Yes?" Jeff said.

"You gonna be okay?" I said.

"I told you I'm getting better," Jeff said. "Too bad you didn't let me bring a gun down here with me though. It be nice if we had one."

"Yes, it would be nice," I said. "Shall we begin?"

"We shall," Jeff said.

He took off.

The kitchen door that led to the backyard had two windows on either side of it. The upper half of the door itself had small glass panes framed by crosshatched wood bars. The door and kitchen windows were covered with red and white gingham curtains. I moved aside the window curtains covering the window to the right of the door and surveyed the backyard. No one there. Yet.

I turned around, looked for a place to hide. Opening the refrigerator door and crouching behind it was a possibility, but I figured that no matter how stupid the guy was who came in from the backyard, he would still think it strange the refrigerator door was open and that someone's feet were poking out below the door's bottom edge. I thought about standing on one of the counters on either side of the kitchen door and leaping on the killer when he entered, but the killer would probably see me when he opened the door and it would not be a hard thing to just sweep his gun toward me and fire off a burst into my chest. I also considered climbing atop the Tiffany lamp of red, green, and purple glass that hung from a brass chain of large linked rings above a small, pine, farmhouse-style kitchen table that was surrounded by four matching wooden chairs, but nixed that as well. Even if the chain held, which was doubtful, I didn't want my last thoughts to be wondering how bad it would hurt when I hit the floor as I fell from my badly chosen perch - though I would probably be dead before I hit the ground anyway.

I decided my best choice was to crawl under the kitchen table. I thought the killer wouldn't immediately look under the table as there was no reason for him to suspect that a poetry professor spending a nice quiet evening at home would do so under her kitchen table. Hiding under the table would also place me in a spot that would give me clear sight lines to the front and kitchen doors.

Having decided where to hide, I then looked for an object I could use to distract the killer's attention from my location. Drawing on my extensive training and experience in diversionary tactics, I decided one of the aluminum pots in the sink would do just fine. I grabbed the pot, and holding it in my left hand and the steak knife in my right, I got under the table. I drew the table's chairs around me, made myself as small as possible, and waited.

I didn't wait long.

The sound of shattering wood came from the direction of the front door. I turned and saw that the front door lock had been blown out and that the door was slowly opening. Two men dressed in white pants, white t-shirts, and white Sherwin-Williams caps came into the house. As they moved closer to me I noticed that their pants, shirts, and caps were spattered with multicolored paint - perhaps they believed the paint splatters were some kind of clever suburban camouflage. Due to their method of entry, I had already pretty much assumed the men weren't there to paint the house, but if I had had any doubts about that assumption - I didn't, but if I did - those doubts would have been quickly dispelled by the fact the men were not carrying any brushes, rollers, or masking tape, but rather Russian AK-12's with high-tech optical scopes and silencers. The men's boots, which had no paint on them, looked exactly like the boots on the Kazakh mercenaries who had attacked us at the rest stop in the desert. Both men also had short brown hair and their haircuts were identical to the haircuts worn by the Kazakhs.

The first man through the door swept the room with his weapon, then signaled to his partner using his hands and arms. The signals - fore and index fingers pointing to his eyes, followed by pointing in the distance, and then some kind of fast circling motion with his forearm - looked remarkably similar to the signals used by actors playing SWAT team members in American television shows. Undoubtedly they had American television shows on local Kazakhstan television stations - or maybe it was just the internet? - but either way, I didn't know what the signals meant and I didn't care. It should be noted, however, that the assassin painter giving the signals looked just as silly as the TV actors did when they used them.

The men ran by the kitchen towards the sound of the water spraying from the bedroom shower.

Right on cue, I heard glass breaking in one of the panes of the rear kitchen door. Shards from the door pane fell on the kitchen tile and splintered into a hundred little glass pebbles. A hand reached in through the empty pane, grabbed the doorknob, and twisted it. The door opened and the predicted third killer, another painter who was not a painter, entered, AK-12 first. The killer had the same boots, haircut, and paint-spattered clothes as his compatriots. He stepped carefully and slowly, sweeping the kitchen with the gun's barrel. I had hoped he would give some hand signals, but, alas, he did not.

It was time to put my plan in motion.

I watched the mercenary sweep the barrel of his AK in an arc over my head and across the kitchen. When the barrel was pointing at a spot that was left of both the killer and my location, I threw the aluminum pot as hard as I could against the kitchen wall that was just to the right of the killer and outside his vision. The crash of the pot hitting the wall made the killer turn to the source of the sound. The killer's turn was my cue. I sprang from my hiding place under the table, my knife poised in my right hand, and before the Kazakh had even realized I was there in the room with him, I was able to cover the space between us. I clamped my left hand over his mouth so that no sound could escape from his lips and turned his head sharply to the left.

I quickly drew the blade of my knife across his neck, feeling his neck tendons, veins, and arteries give way.

A fountain of the mercenary's arterial blood shot upward, some of it splattering the ceiling, while the rest fell down like rain onto the kitchen floor.

The man died in the next instant.

I let his corpse down slowly and it settled in a heap on the floor. I reached for his gun, but as I did so, I heard a very unsettling sound.

I looked up.

Jeff's and my prediction had been wrong.

I ascribed my slip up to being out of practice - just as I had similarly ascribed my earlier slip ups - but no excuse was going to do me much good just then.

A fourth gunman, same haircut, shoes, and paint stippled clothes as the others, was entering the front door, his AK-12 turning towards me. I didn't have enough time to get the dead Kazakh's gun off the floor and aim it at the new gunman, so I began to coil my legs as a prelude to diving behind the wall that was next to the doorway between the kitchen and the living room. I knew it was nearly impossible I would make it to cover before the soldier fired a fatal burst at me and I remember thinking this was not going to be a good way to die but it was how it was going to happen.

Everything from that point on seemed to move in slow motion. I watched the assassin's eyes focusing on me and then moved my own gaze down to his trigger finger. The finger appeared to me as if it had been magnified a hundred times, and as the barrel of the AK-12 swung to face me, I watched the finger slowly contract around the trigger.

The finger had perhaps a millimeter to go when I saw, out of the corner of my eye, something bright and silver whooshing through the air.

Had a bird flown into the house?

The soldier didn't see the bright and silver thing as he only had eyes for me.

The bird kept flying, flapping its silver wings, moving like an airborne metallic torpedo, and the killer's AK kept sweeping, my eyes locked on it, even as my body launched, and moved sideways across the doorway.

Just before the AK was aimed directly at my chest - and while most of my body was still framed in the doorway, a big easy target if there ever was one - the bird flew directly into the killer's Adam's apple, hitting the killer's neck with such force the killer's head snapped back and then flew clean off his shoulders. The last thing I saw before I cleared the doorway was another bright red arterial fountain, this one shooting up at the living room ceiling.

Time sped up to normal as I hit the kitchen tiles shoulder first, the impact sending a wave of pain into my shoulder and neck. I rolled as I hit, came to my feet, and, propelled solely by instinct, covered the few steps back to the AK-12 that lay next to the body of the commando I had killed in the kitchen. I snatched up the gun and carefully peered around the door frame.

Everything I had just seen in the living room suddenly made sense.

Lying on the living room floor and cradling the body and severed head of the killer who had come in the front door, was Jeff. On the couch next to Jeff was the bird. The bird was as lifeless as the assassin, only it wasn't a bird, but the meat cleaver, silver and laced in blood. Jeff must have thrown the cleaver, then made it across the room fast enough to catch the head and body before they could hit the floor and make any sound. Jeff had thrown the cleaver in a way only he could, combining its angle of attack with just the right amount of rotational speed and force so that the cleaver had done its job and then fallen soundlessly to the couch.

My body became weak as I was overcome by emotion, first at the fact my friend had saved me for the umpteenth time, but then almost immediately followed by fear for Jeff and what his actions might do to his fragile mental state.

Jeff saw me standing in the doorway and smiled. He slowly wriggled out from under the body, grabbed the dead painter assassin's AK-12, got to his feet, and hoisted the gun to his side.

Breathing slow and deep, I attempted to gain control of the feelings coursing through my body. Holding my newly acquired AK, I moved across the living room floor as silently as I could and came to Jeff's side.

"Thought I told you to hide somewhere safe," I said in a hoarse whisper.

"What made you think I was gonna listen to you?" Jeff whispered back.

"Good point," I said.

"Besides, your contingency plan be crap," Jeff said.

"I didn't have a contingency plan," I said.

"Exactly," Jeff said.

"Well, I'm glad you had one," I said.

"We both glad," Jeff said.

"What was it you wound up doing?" I said.

"I turned on the shower," Jeff said. "Then I come back in the living room and hid under the coffee table so I could see the front door."

"Not exactly safe, but definitely smart," I said.

"Thank you," Jeff said.

I paused for a moment, didn't say anything, just looked into Jeff's eyes, studying them. As I did so, my deep breathing finally began to have the desired effect. I started to feel like I was in control of my body once again.

"You okay?" I said.

"Can't say for sure," Jeff said.

"You look okay to me," I said.

"We'll see," Jeff said.

A sound came from the end of the hallway. I raised my right hand, pointed my index and forefingers at my eyes, then flicked my wrist and gestured down the hallway like I had seen the painter assassins do.

Jeff said, "What the hell does that mean?"

"Don't know," I said. "The two in the bedroom did it when they came into the house."

I circled my forearm in the air.

"Same thing?" Jeff said.

"Same thing," I said.

"Got any more?" Jeff said.

"No," I said.

"Good," Jeff said.

"Think they figured out nobody's in the shower by now?" I said.

"If they haven't already, it be soon," Jeff said.

"And when they do, I would expect they'll most likely come sauntering out the bedroom door into the hallway," I said.

"Sauntering?" Jeff said.

"Don't like it?" I said.

"Word good," Jeff said. "But it's a little advanced for you."

"I can accept that," I said.

"Wanna try to take them alive?" Jeff said.

"Nice idea," I said. "But..."

"Most likely that ain't gonna happen," Jeff said.

"Probably not," I said.

"Give them a chance though," Jeff said.

"Always," I said.

We raised our newly acquired AK-12's and stepped closer to the front wall of the living room. From there we would be out of the hallway's sight lines and thus not immediately visible to the other two killers when they exited the bedroom.

"Need to ask you a favor," I said.

"Shoot," Jeff said.

"Now?" I said. "Because honestly I was going to wait until I saw the whites of their eyes."

Jeff shook his head.

"Oh man, that's bad," Jeff said. "That's really bad."

"Sorry," I said. "Anyway, the favor is this. Toying with a meat cleaver is one thing..."

"But a fully loaded, silenced automatic Russian AK-12 assault rifle be another?" Jeff said.

I nodded.

"How about you let me handle this?" I said.

"You saying there's no reason to push it?" Jeff said.

"That's what I'm saying," I said.

Jeff seemed to think for a moment.

"Guess that probably a good idea," Jeff said.

Jeff put the AK-12 he had lifted from the headless commando back on the floor where he found it.

"Want to take a seat on the couch?" I said.

"Couch is good," Jeff said.

"Professor's rocking chair be fine too," I said.

"I like the couch," Jeff said. "Fabric got a nice pattern."

"Loved it the minute I saw it," I said. "Watch out for the cleaver."

Jeff walked to the couch, sat down, crossed his legs, leaned back, put his hands behind his head, his elbows akimbo, and closed his eyes.

"Nighty night," I said. "Sleep tight."

My gun was silenced after all.

Outside the blue jay resumed its whistling and hawklike cries. As far as the jay was concerned all was well again.

I checked the safety of the AK-12. It was off. I checked the fire position. It was on full auto. Three shot burst would be nice, and perhaps more professional, but no reason to take chances. I left it where it was. I tightened down the silencer with a twist of my wrist. I raised the rifle's butt end to my cheek and sighted it to my left at the entrance to the hallway that led to the bedroom. I waited.

A moment later I heard two sets of footsteps.

I assumed from the sound of the steps that both of the Kazakh killers had exited the bedroom and were moving down the hall towards me.

I wondered if they were giving hand signals.

If I had to bet, I would have said yes.

I sighted the AK-12's scope at the center of the hallway at what I predicted would be about chest height for the approaching painter assassins when they first became visible to me. I stepped to my right directly in line with the hallway and both men came into view. The first man was slightly in front of and to the side of the second man. The muzzles of both men's guns were pointing down. My assumption that the painter assassins would be relaxed since they believed they had already cleared the living room and hallway appeared to have been correct. I lowered the AK so the scope was exactly on the first man's center mass right where his heart would be behind his sternum, but I didn't have to lower it much - my first chest height approximation being only a half inch off from his actual center mass.

"Freeze!" I yelled.

My voice was as commanding and loud and violent as I could make it. It was the way I had been trained to handle that type of situation and it was the way I always did it. Get their attention. Shock them. Jeff sometimes added 'please' but that wasn't my style. I had never tested my voice against a grizzly, but I was pretty sure it would have stopped him in his tracks. At least for a few seconds before he charged and tore me to pieces.

If a man was going to stop at all, then my voice and the sight of a rifle muzzle aimed directly at him should have done the trick.

This guy didn't stop.

He started to raise his AK-12.

I fired a silenced burst. The first man went down in a heap. His comrade behind him got his own AK a little higher than his friend had - though not by much - before my second burst blew him back and down.

"Take it they unwisely decided to shoot it out," Jeff said, his eyes still closed.

"Unwisely," I said.

"Gave them a chance," Jeff said.

"I did," I said.

"Was a mighty good freeze," Jeff said.

"Coming from you I take that as a great compliment," I said.

"Think about adding 'please'?" Jeff said.

"Wouldn't wanna jock your style," I said.

"Respectful," Jeff said.

I walked across the living room and, keeping my AK trained on the first Kazakh's body, moved into the hallway until I stood over him. I kicked his rifle away, bent down, and felt for a carotid pulse. There wasn't one. I pulled back his ear. A cobra and crucifix insignia was tattooed on the skin there. I repeated the same procedures with the second soldier. Same result.

"Let's see how the ladies are doing," I called to Jeff.

Jeff didn't answer. I slung the AK-12 over my shoulder and walked back to the living room. Jeff was where I had left him, sitting on the couch, leaning back against the cushions. His eyes were still closed, but his breathing was slow and irregular and his body was gently shivering. I had seen him like that too many times before. I knew he was trying to shut down visions of terrible things, trying to quiet demons that chased him down the hallucinatory halls of a nightmare world.

I also knew it was best to leave him alone.

I returned to the hallway, rapped on the door to the basement.

"It's safe," I said into the door. "Please open up."

I heard shuffling on the floor below, then footsteps climbing the stairs. The footsteps were followed by the scuff of wood on metal which

I thought was probably the sound of Adelaide removing whatever she had wedged against the door to keep it closed. The doorknob rattled a little and the door opened inwards. Adelaide stood in front of me holding aloft a thick, ancient, ironwood walking cane that was topped by a brass elephant handle. The cane looked like it had been made in India. Maybe Margaret was a traveler.

"The professor is not happy," Adelaide said softly.

"Not much I can do about that," I said.

Adelaide turned and led me down the oak plank stairs towards the basement's floor. I noted an indentation in the drywall a few feet away from the door and level with the door's knob where Adelaide had probably braced the cane's head. It looked like it would have held well against the weight of a man trying to force open the door. A burst of automatic weapon fire would have been an entirely different story.

The basement was very clean. The cool, still air smelled of chlorine bleach. The lighting came from a single yellowed overhead bulb operated by a pull chain. There was a white porcelain utility sink mounted on the far wall. The sink had a stainless steel faucet. Boxes of canned cat food and paper towels were stacked against the wall to my left.

Margaret, her face pinched with displeasure, stood on the cement floor at the base of the stairs looking up at me. She held the cat in her arms, stroking it. I reached the bottom of the stairs. Margaret gestured to the AK-12 on my shoulder.

"Please don't bring that down here," Margaret said.

"Sorry," I said.

I climbed back up the stairs, left the gun propped up against the hallway wall, and walked back down.

"What happened up there?" Margaret said.

"We're okay now," I said.

"That's not an answer to my question," Margaret said.

I took a long breath in and let it slowly out.

"You're right," I said. "Four Kazakh special forces soldiers, most likely in this country illegally and acting as hired mercenaries, are dead upstairs. I believe they are, if not the same ones that killed Sarah and your mother and father, at least from the same team. I believe other Kazakh members of that team also attempted to kidnap Kate, and that their Afghan cohorts killed your nephew Sam and your niece Lizzy. The dead soldiers upstairs were heavily armed and came here to kill you. They would have done so if we did not stop them."

"You don't know that," Margaret said.

I could see Adelaide trying to hold her tongue. I knew that would never work.

I said, "No I don't, ma'am. I thought it highly likely though and that it was best not to take that chance."

"I told you I would not countenance killing in my name," Margaret said.

"Yes, you did," I said.

Adelaide could hold back no longer.

"Professor, we'd be dead if Jeff and Jack didn't stop them," Adelaide said.

"Please do not interrupt, Adelaide," Margaret said. "Perhaps the men only wanted to talk to me."

"You're right," Adelaide said. "We should have just asked them in for tea."

"Adelaide, please," I said.

Margaret looked harshly at Adelaide but did not say anything. She seemed to be thinking things over. Her features softened a bit.

"The FBI agents that were guarding me are definitely dead?" Margaret said.

"I'm sorry Professor Lennon, but yes, all three are dead," I said.

Margaret bowed her head and trembled.

"Seven dead men," Margaret said. "For what?"

I didn't say anything.

In the distance I could hear approaching sirens. I assumed it was the local police. Perhaps a neighbor had seen the dead FBI agents and called it in.

Margaret said, "Is Jeff okay?"

"I believe he will be," I said.

"Is he hurt?" Margaret said.

"No," I said. "He's resting."

"This can't be good for someone in his condition," Margaret said.

"Maybe, maybe not," I said.

Margaret looked at me questioningly.

"Jeff did an amazing thing today," I said. "He was his old self for a little while for the first time in years. He saved my life. He probably saved all of our lives."

Margaret nodded, then seemed to think about something for a moment.

"I can't say I approve of such a thing, but I've heard people are experimenting with immersion therapy for PTSD," Margaret said. "You think it's possible the experience might help Jeff recover?"

"I don't know," I said. "Immersion therapy is actually something Jeff has been thinking about lately. Be that as it may, I wrestled with whether or not it was a good idea to bring Jeff into this mission. Now that I have brought him in, I still don't know if it was a good idea. I'm pretty sure, however, he couldn't keep going the way he was. Jeff is active, but in comparison to his former life, his current life is more like that of an invalid. If Jeff makes it through this okay, I'm hoping he'll come out stronger."

"And if he doesn't make it out okay?" Margaret said.

"He'll be in very bad shape," I said.

"Let's hope he makes it then," Margaret said.

The approaching sirens were becoming louder.

"Things are going to get very crazy around here in a minute," I said.

"Yes, I believe they will," Margaret said, then paused. "Actually, I just remembered something you probably should know."

"What is it?" I said.

"A man from NASAD called me and said they were doing a tribute to my brother and that I was invited," Margaret said.

"When was this?" I said.

"Three days ago," Margaret said.

"Did he say when the tribute would be?" I said.

"No," Margaret said. "He said I would get an invitation in the mail and he needed to know my address and how to title it."

"Title it?" I said.

"He wanted to know if I went by Margaret or some nickname like Marge or Margie," Margaret said. "I told him I prefer Margaret."

"Did he give you his name?" I said.

"Yes," Margaret said. "I remembered it since I thought for a moment he might be kidding. He said his name was Dr. Nemo."

CHAPTER 88

Adelaide, Jeff, Margaret, and I regrouped in the living room. I was strongly encouraging Margaret to go to a safe house - and she was steadfastly refusing to even consider the idea, saying that she wasn't going to let anyone intimidate her, and that she needed to stay at home to teach her classes at the college and in case her friend in the hospital needed any further assistance - when four squad cars from the local Claremont Police screeched to a halt outside Margaret's home.

I quickly called Ray Carpenter and told him about our fight with the Kazakhs and that I was trying to get Margaret to go to a safe house. Ray told me he would begin the arrangements for a safe house in case I was successful in convincing her she needed to be in one. He then hung up and called the Claremont police commander and explained our situation to him. The commander, being an ex-special forces lieutenant, was only too happy to send us on our way without delay.

Before we left, however, Professor Margaret had insisted on finding something for Adelaide to wear. Margaret was of the opinion that Adelaide's off-beach exposing of her bikini-clad, nearly naked body was lacking in modesty. Adelaide and the professor disappeared for a few minutes. While they were gone I checked the two dead mercenaries that were in the kitchen and next to the front door and confirmed they both had crucifix and cobra tattoos behind their ears. When Adelaide and Margaret returned, Adelaide was wearing a tie-dyed, pink and purple cotton hippie dress. The dress came down to Adelaide's ankles.

I made another attempt to get Margaret to go to a safe house, and she made another refusal. I thought Margaret was probably as mentally tough as she seemed to be, and that she truly believed her reasons for staying at home were sound. But I also thought there was a good chance her mental faculties had been overwhelmed both by what we had just experienced with the mercenary attacks, and her grief over the deaths of Sam, Lizzy, Sarah, and her parents. In any event, I knew that I wasn't going to make any progress in getting her to a safe house at that moment. I gave Margaret my cell phone number and asked her to please call me if she remembered anything that could be of use to me on my mission. I then texted Ray Carpenter to update him on Margaret's continued refusal in regard to the safe house, and to ask him to arrange for security for Margaret in her home instead. I felt Margaret would be properly protected until Ray did that, given the fact the Claremont cops had just arrived. After giving our confiscated AK-12's to the cops, Adelaide, Jeff, and I said our goodbyes and left Margaret's house in Bleckley's Crown Vic.

With Adelaide driving, me sitting next to her in the front seat, and Jeff reclining in the back, we quickly retraced our steps through the Claremont streets. It was around 8:00 p.m. by the time we made the turn from Towne Avenue onto the westbound 210 Freeway and headed back towards the site in Sylmar where the NASAD dark programmers had been massacred. Still respecting Haley's fears, Jeff and I continued to keep a lookout for tails. As of yet, we had seen nothing that made us concerned.

Even though the hour was late, the sky above the foothills to the north was just beginning to turn from blue to orange. The heat had not yet subsided and the smell of ozone rose from the cars heading east on the other side of the freeway, cars that were barely moving and were packed like sardines in the never-ending Los Angeles after work rush hour. A river of white light shone in our faces from the cars' headlamps.

The Crown Vic's red rooftop light was whirling and the yellow rear deck lights were flashing. Adelaide was again using the freeway shoulder as her own private roadway. As instructed, she was keeping the car at under a hundred miles per hour. Adelaide appeared, however, to be having a hard time fighting off the urge for more speed.

"When we get to the NASAD site the plan will be to get in and out as quickly as we can," I said. "First we'll take photos of the dark programmers' faces and their ID's to send to Haley. After we do that we'll give a quick look around and, if we're lucky, maybe we'll find a clue that will allow us to unlock Nemo's code. But that's it. We don't linger."

"I'm hoping Nemo ain't dead," Jeff said.

"Me too," I said. "But it might take some time for Haley to figure out whether Nemo is alive or not, even after we get her the ID's and photos."

Adelaide said, "Because we don't know what Nemo looks like?"

"Correct," I said.

"If we don't know what he looks like then how can Haley figure it out at all?" Adelaide said.

Jeff said, "Haley gonna match up what we give her with her Nemo psychological profile."

"Haley's already got a profile for Nemo?" Adelaide said.

I said, "Young, male, mathematical genius."

Jeff said, "Of course that probably fit every dead man in the bunker."

Adelaide said, "How is she going to know if any of them are Nemo then?"

"Haley profile actually much more complicated than we been implying," Jeff said. "I bet she got her algorithm so fine-tuned that there's a good chance she gonna able to tell us if Nemo is dead in that crater or still out among the living."

I said, "If anyone can, Haley can."

Adelaide said, "We have ten days, right? Haley will be able to figure it out in that amount of time?"

"One would think so," I said.

"Well, as much as I like math, I still hate that we have to rely on some goddamn algorithm," Adelaide said.

Jeff and I exchanged a look.

"You like more direct action I take it?" I said.

"Damn right," Adelaide said.

Jeff said, "I like the way you think girl. We might make you a soldier yet."

"I already am a better soldier than either of you will ever be," Adelaide said.

The last thing I wanted was to be trapped in the car with the two of them going at it again. I gestured to Jeff with a finger to my lips. Jeff rolled his eyes, then nodded.

"Anyway," Jeff said, appearing to take a deep breath, "that algorithm don't work, we always got option number two."

I said, "Option number two?"

"You," Jeff said.

"Me?" I said.

"I'm thinking maybe you get one of your hunches once we in that bunker," Jeff said.

"Since when have you been a fan of my hunches?" I said.

"Whenever all we got is hope," Jeff said.

"You think it's already come to that?" I said.

"When it come to this Nemo dude, I'm starting to think that most likely be the case," Jeff said.

Adelaide said, "We should just give up right now then. 'Cause Jack's hunches ain't worth shit."

I said, "Thank you, Adelaide, for the compliment. I hope you realize, however, that we never give up."

Jeff said, "Give up ain't even in our vocabulary."

Adelaide said, "Good for you. Sounds to me, however, like the sooner we check out that NASAD bunker, the sooner we'll know what's going on with Dr. Nemo. I consider it my duty to inform you that we'll get there a lot faster if you let me open this puppy up."

I said, "One hundred is plenty fast, Adelaide."

"Maybe for a couple of old fogies like you and Jeff," Adelaide said.

"We got to be old fogies because we don't like taking unnecessary risks," I said.

"Unnecessary risk, huh?" Adelaide said. "Sure seems like an unnecessary risk to me that we're traveling around unarmed."

Jeff said, "That because you don't understand the law."

"What law?" Adelaide said.

"It illegal for U.S. Army personnel be conducting missions on American soil," Jeff said.

"That's a stupid law," Adelaide said. "No wonder you know about it."

I said, "It's also against the law in California for anyone to carry a weapon in public without a permit."

"What if the next time we're attacked Jeff can't find a meat cleaver?" Adelaide said.

Jeff said, "We all going to die."

I said, "That's the spirit."

Adelaide said, "What the hell is wrong with you two?"

Jeff said, "Actually, more I think about it, probably woulda been smarter if we took those Kazakhs' AK's."

I said, "You're probably right."

Adelaide said, "Jesus goddamn Christ."

"We just being honest, girl," Jeff said.

Adelaide slammed on the brakes. Jeff and I were thrown violently against our seat belts. The car shimmied and swayed, its tires screeching against the shoulder's asphalt, until we finally came to a stop after traveling at least four hundred feet. Adelaide twisted around in her seat to face both Jeff and me.

"Didn't you idiots ever stop to consider those assholes at the house might have been coming for us and not the professor?" Adelaide said. "And that they might be on our tail right now?"

"Good question," I said, then turned to Jeff and added, "Did we consider that?"

"Hmm," Jeff said. "I'm trying to remember. If we didn't consider it we probably should have though."

Adelaide shifted the car into reverse, floored the gas, and whipped the steering wheel around so that the car did a full 180 degree turn. She then started speeding along the shoulder against traffic, going the opposite way we had been heading.

I said, "Whoa, whoa, whoa. Where do you think you're going?"

"Back to the professor's house so I can get myself an AK," Adelaide said.

"Stop the car, okay?" I said. "I'm sorry. We were kidding."

Adelaide didn't slow down.

"What do you mean you were kidding?" Adelaide said.

Jeff said, "We just testing you."

"Testing me about what?" Adelaide said.

"See if you be worrying about the important things," Jeff said.

Adelaide kept the gas pedal floored.

"Really?" Adelaide said. "How am I doing?"

I said, "You're doing great, okay? Now stop the car."

Adelaide slammed on the brakes. Jeff and I were once again thrown against our seat belts. The car came to a stop along the shoulder.

"What are the important things?" Adelaide said. She put the gearshift into neutral and gunned the engine. "And this better be good."

"You're right to worry whether we were also targets of the attack at Professor Lennon's house," I said.

"Jeff said 'things,'" Adelaide said. "With an 's.'"

"An 's', yes," I said. "You're also right to be worried about whether or not we're being followed."

"Damn right I am," Adelaide said.

"And about the fact that we're unarmed," I said.

Jeff said, "Other than what we be finding in someone's kitchen."

We were still parked with the Crown Vic pointed the wrong way on the shoulder. Cars whizzed by going in the opposite direction from us. It seemed to me many of the cars' drivers gave us curious glances, but their faces came and went so quickly I couldn't be absolutely sure about that observation.

Adelaide said, "Why aren't we doing anything?"

"About what?" I said.

"About being followed!" Adelaide said.

Jeff said, "Who said we ain't doing anything?"

I said, "What Jeff means to say is that ever since we left the NASAD site where the dark programmers were killed we have been very careful to make sure we're not being followed."

Adelaide said, "You were checking to make sure we weren't followed, huh? How come I never saw you doing that?"

Jeff said, "Because we professionals."

Adelaide appeared to study both our faces.

"So we're not being followed then?" Adelaide said.

I said, "We're not. And since very few people knew we were going to Professor Lennon's house..."

Jeff said, "Three of who be dead."

Adelaide said, "Dead? What are you talking about?"

I said, "He's referring to the FBI agents in the car outside the house and the sniper on the roof."

"Oh, right," Adelaide said.

"And given the fact the only other people besides the dead FBI agents who knew we were planning on visiting Margaret were Ray Carpenter, his two men at the NASAD site, Haley, and Kate, I find it highly doubtful the Kazakhs would have known we would be there," I said.

Adelaide seemed to think this over. A car shot by us with a little kid in the back seat. The kid stuck his tongue out at us.

"I'll buy it," Adelaide said. After a pause, she added, "Am I supposed to bring up the fact Dr. Nemo might be a bad guy?"

"A bad guy?" I said.

"Neither of you has said a word about it," Adelaide said. "I would have thought you'd at least think about it after what the professor said about Nemo calling her. Isn't he a potential threat?"

"Actually, we're not worried about that either," I said.

"Why not?" Adelaide said. "What if he called to make sure Professor Lennon was home so he could set up her killing?"

"Nothing of what we know about Nemo so far would lead us to believe he would do such a thing," I said.

Jeff said, "Plus we got an alternate theory."

Adelaide said, "You do?"

Jeff was about to speak, but I interrupted him.

"Adelaide, I think it might be a good idea if you make a stab at trying to figure out what our theory is," I said.

"You want me to figure out your theory?" Adelaide said.

Jeff said, "Yeah. Since this be about your education and all."

Adelaide snorted.

"Well, since it's probably a completely idiotic theory, that shouldn't be so hard," Adelaide said.

A highway patrol car sped by. The patrolman seemed to be looking at us and was frowning. Maybe he was trying to figure out how it could be possible that there were three undercover cops stupid enough to wind up going the wrong way on the freeway.

I said, "Why don't you give us one that's not idiotic?"

Adelaide rolled her eyes.

"Fine," Adelaide said. "I'll give you my own version, not yours."

Adelaide's eyes narrowed. She seemed to be concentrating.

"Okay, I got it," Adelaide said.

"Go ahead," I said.

"No one, other than you and Jeff, would be so stupid as to ask such a dumb question as 'do you have a nickname?' and then leave their own name," Adelaide said.

"Why?" I said.

"Because all it would do is draw attention to you," Adelaide said.

"Then when the person who you called was killed you would be the prime suspect."

"That's a good start," I said. "What else?"

"Since it's very unlikely it was Dr. Nemo who called, it means someone was trying to frame Nemo for Professor Margaret's murder," Adelaide said.

"Who would that be?" I said.

"Probably the person who sent the Kazakhs to kill Margaret," Adelaide said.

Jeff said, "Carter Bowdoin and Dragon Man."

"You buttheads know a lot more about the details than I do," Adelaide said, "So fine, I'll go with that. Carter Bowdoin and Dragon Man. They're the ones that left Nemo's name with Professor Lennon."

I said, "There's one more important thing that maybe is not so obvious."

"Maybe not to you," Adelaide said.

"You sound pretty confident you know what that thing is," I said.

"Carter Bowdoin and Dragon Man must know who Dr. Nemo is, or at least that he exists, otherwise they wouldn't leave his name," Adelaide said. "Since you guys have told me all about Nemo and how important he is to our mission, that probably means Nemo's life is in danger."

Jeff said, "I'm impressed. Need to give you a gold star, girl."

I said, "I'm impressed too."

Adelaide beamed. She put the Crown Vic in gear, made a three point turn, pointed the car back west towards the NASAD site, and quickly accelerated to one hundred miles per hour.

"There's one problem, however," Adelaide said.

"What's that?" I said.

"What if it's a double reverse?" Adelaide said.

"You mean Nemo actually made the call, but he did it so we would go through all that analysis and convince ourselves it couldn't have been him, and thus miss the fact he really is a bad guy after all?" I said.

"Yeah," Adelaide said. "Nemo could be completely misleading us. We spend all this time tracking him down and miss what the bad guys are really up to."

"As in, he's just another diversion?" I said.

Adelaide nodded.

"Jeff and I have considered that too," I said.

Jeff said, "We have."

"But we've convinced ourselves there's something that mitigates against that," I said.

Adelaide said, "Mitigates?"

Jeff said, "Mean it be unlikely."

"Okay," Adelaide said.

I said, "And I would think you, Adelaide, of all people, would pretty easily see what that something is if you really take a close look at Nemo and what he's done."

Adelaide narrowed her eyes again. She also screwed up her upper lip. She seemed to think long and hard.

"I think I know," Adelaide said a moment later.

"Tell us then," I said.

"It's the way Nemo encrypted the file he sent Kate," Adelaide said.

"Elaborate," I said.

"The encryption is uncrackable," Adelaide said. "If Nemo was a diversion, the encryption would be hard to crack, but not impossible to crack. That way, when we cracked it, we would follow whatever false information the file contained and be even more misled. But since we can't crack it, we can't be following any false paths. Ergo, Nemo is not a bad guy."

Jeff said, "How you know 'Ergo'?"

"Cogito ergo sum," Adelaide said. "I think, therefore I am."

"You reading Descartes?" Jeff said.

"What's wrong with that?" Adelaide said.

"It's good," Jeff said. "I was gonna give you another gold star for figuring out why the way Nemo encrypted that file was the clue to his good intentions, but now I gotta give you one more for Descartes. Make three in one day."

Adelaide twisted around in her seat. Since we were going a hundred miles an hour, that did not seem like a great idea to me. I put my hand on the steering wheel, at the ready if a course adjustment became necessary.

Adelaide, speaking to Jeff, said, "Is something wrong with you?"

"Why you say that?" Jeff said.

"You're being so nice," Adelaide said.

Jeff cackled.

"Won't last," Jeff said. "Enjoy it while you can."

Adelaide shook her head, turned back to face forward, and knocked my hand off the wheel.

We reached the bottom of the pass that ran through the hills just before Glendale. The reds and yellows of the setting sun over the Pacific Ocean still glowed in the distance and the lights were coming on in the windows of the downtown Los Angeles skyscrapers.

"We need to take the exit for the 5 Freeway heading north," I said. "It's coming up soon."

Adelaide nodded. She slowed the Vic and seemed to cautiously search for the ramp we needed to take. Was this cautious driving the birth of a new Adelaide? I doubted it. I figured her behavior was more along the lines of what Jeff had just said - I should enjoy it while I can, it won't last.

Adelaide said, "Something else is bothering me."

"What?" I said.

"All of us were together when Professor Lennon told us what Nemo had said on the phone," Adelaide said, "So how come you and Jeff know all about this so-called 'alternate' theory and I didn't hear anything about it?"

Jeff said, "I told you. I can read his mind."

I said, "Jeff and I talked about it while we were waiting for you and Margaret to find that dress you're wearing."

"Why you telling her our secrets?" Jeff said.

We came to the intersection of the 5 and the 210. Adelaide steered the Vic to head north on the 5. A few minutes later we took the Roxford Street exit, then traveled a few blocks on the Sylmar surface streets.

"Turn off the headlights and the flasher, then turn right and keep moving as slow as you can," I said. "The goal is to not draw any attention to ourselves."

Adelaide's expression seemed to say 'well this might get interesting', and she did as I asked without complaint. We continued a short distance and arrived at our destination.

"Stop the car and cut the engine," I said.

She did.

The spot we then found ourselves upon was atop a hill about two hundred yards away from the site of the crater formed by the NASAD explosion we had visited earlier in the day. It was pitch black except where the soft green rays of an occasional streetlamp glowed and illuminated conical sections of the earth near the lamps. Smoke arose in scant streams from small, isolated patches of still smoldering brush, the streams swirling in the gentle night breeze. The crater was as we left it - surrounded by yellow crime scene tape mounted on stakes. Circular tubes that were the height of small children, and that looked like giant cloth covered Slinkys, were connected on their front ends to the open door of the underground bunker and on their back ends to huge fans. The fans were sucking massive volumes of air out of the underground bunker. The low-pitched hum of electric generators at work was barely discernable.

An LAPD police cruiser and a blue forensic crime scene van parked on the site were the only vehicles visible. Two police officers leaning against the side of the cruiser and two forensic techs working near the van were the only people on the site.

The forensic techs appeared to be finishing up. They loaded some equipment chests into the back of the van, slammed shut the double doors, said something to the officers, then each opened a front door, one right, one left, and climbed into the van. The van's engine started, its lights came on, and it rolled across the parched dirt of the site, over a curb onto the street, and drove off. The two cops chatted for a while and got back into the cruiser. The cruiser's nose faced the street.

Adelaide said, "We've been counting on the fact the canary was fine to make us comfortable with the idea that the air is okay to breathe in the bunker, but those fans make it even more unlikely we'll have any trouble, correct?"

"Yes," I said. "And if someone was really worried about booby traps then they never would have let anyone take the risk of installing the fans."

"So our odds of having a problem are even better than 'highly unlikely'?" Adelaide said.

"Correct," I said.

"Great," Adelaide said. "When we going in?"

"After you tell me what's wrong with the scene," I said.

"This still part of my test?" Adelaide said.

Jeff said, "Test never ending unless you die."

"Got it," Adelaide said.

Adelaide stared out at the crater. She furrowed her brow and puckered her lips. I assumed she was thinking.

"Only two cops to secure the whole area?" Adelaide said.

"Two cops is enough," I said.

"I don't like the lighting," Adelaide said. "They need more light."

"You're getting colder," I said.

Adelaide scrunched up her face in displeasure. Jeff, who had slumped back into his seat, came forward again and leaned his elbows on the top of the seat between Adelaide and me.

Jeff said, "Where the cops be looking?"

"At the street," Adelaide said.

"What they guarding?" Jeff said.

Adelaide furrowed her brow and puckered her lips again. More thinking. A light seemed to go off in her head.

"They're guarding the entrance to the underground bunker," Adelaide said. "Only they're not looking at it. They're looking at the street where they think someone might come from and that's not how we're going to do it."

I said, "Bravo."

Jeff said, "Molto bene."

"Molto bene?" I said. "That seems a little tame for you."

"Was gonna say bahuta acha," Jeff said.

"What's that?" I said.

"Punjabi for molto bene," Jeff said.

"Punjabi, huh?" I said. "Actually, I think I knew that."

"Why you asking me then?" Jeff said.

"I mean, I knew it in English," I said. "Didn't make the Italian connection."

"You usually pretty good with translating," Jeff said. "Maybe you missed it because you died this morning."

"That must be it," I said.

I turned to Adelaide. She appeared to be beaming with pride despite Jeff's and my linguistic digression.

"What do you think, Adelaide?" I said. "Can we get by the cops?"

Adelaide was about to answer, then stopped herself. She was learning. She thought it over.

"That's a trick question," Adelaide said finally.

I didn't say anything. Jeff was mum.

"Too risky," Adelaide said. "You guys are big on diversions..."

"As well we should be," I said.

"So I vote for a diversion," Adelaide said.

Jeff said, "All you gonna do is vote?"

"I did all the driving," Adelaide said. "I gotta do all the thinking too?"

"You be on your own one day," Jeff said. "What if we be indisposed when you call for advice?"

"You plan on being indisposed?" Adelaide said.

"Might be eating," Jeff said. "Or sleeping."

I said, "Odds are he done be doin' one or the other."

Jeff gave me a look.

"What?" I said. "You the only one can talk like that?"

"I talk like that since that's who I is," Jeff said. "Besides you only allowed to make fun of my dialecting once a day. You already use up your once."

"Sorry," I said. "What do you suggest, Adelaide?"

"I know what we're not doing," Adelaide said. "I'm not taking off this hippie dress and running past the cops in my bikini no matter how entertaining, effective, or humiliating you two think that might be."

"Are you admitting running around this afternoon in just a thong and flip flops might not have been the wisest of choices?" I said.

"No, that is not what I said," Adelaide said.

"We weren't going to suggest you take off the dress," I said.

Jeff said, "Never be crossing our minds."

"Uh huh," Adelaide said. "I have a better idea anyway."

"It involve me taking my clothes off?" Jeff said.

"Yuck," Adelaide said.

I said, "Double yuck."

"Coffee," Adelaide said. "And doughnuts."

CHAPTER 89

"Question is," Jeff said, "who gonna do the delivery?"

"Don't look at me," Adelaide said.

"Be your idea," Jeff said.

"True," Adelaide said. "But I can't be two places at once and I'm going to be down inside the bunker."

"Sure you can handle that?" Jeff said. "Lotta dead people in there."

"I can handle it," Adelaide said.

Jeff looked at me.

"What you got to say about that?" Jeff said.

I didn't say anything.

"Cat got your tongue?" Jeff said.

Actually the cat did have my tongue and had tied it into a neat little knot. Because I didn't want to tell Jeff what I was thinking. Because what I was thinking was, while it might be rough on Adelaide to go down into the NASAD bunker, it would probably be a lot rougher on Jeff. The last time Jeff had been around that many dead people at once was the last time he had seen combat. Which was also the day before he had entered the U.S. Army hospital system, a system he was in for six months before I finally took him out of it. I was worried about what might happen to him when he got down into the bunker. I was also pretty sure what had happened at Professor Lennon's house was probably stress enough for one day.

"You a coward," Jeff said.

"I am?" I said.

"You are," Jeff said. "Because you're too afraid to tell me what's on your mind."

I said nothing.

"You really gonna make me say it for you?" Jeff said.

"No," I said.

"Say it then," Jeff said.

"Maybe you shouldn't go down into the bunker," I said. "Maybe Adelaide should go with me instead."

"I agree," Jeff said.

I studied his face. He looked sincere.

"You do?" I said.

"Professor's house no walk in the park," Jeff said. "But this be the gates of hell."

"Gates of hell," I said. "Yes."

"Just like we said when we were in Professor Margaret's house," Jeff said. "No reason to push it."

"So you really don't want to go down there?" I said.

"Nope," Jeff said.

"That was easier than I expected," I said.

"Yeah, well that be your last get out of jail free card," Jeff said. "Next time maybe it won't be that way."

"Understood," I said.

"Now you two get the hell outta my car," Jeff said. "I got to do some shopping."

Adelaide and I exited the Crown Vic. Jeff started up the engine. He kept the lights off as he slowly drove off. I watched the Vic until it disappeared from view. As soon as it had, I began to have a problem.

Because I couldn't breathe.

And my heart was racing.

And my chest was constricting.

Adelaide said, "Come on. Not you too."

I turned to face her. It was so dark it was hard to see her. But the darkness alone could not explain what happened next. Adelaide seemed to be vanishing.

"Not me too what?" I said, doing my best to appear as if nothing was wrong, even as Adelaide continued to dematerialize.

"You look like Jeff when he's having one of his spells," Adelaide said.

"Hardly," I said.

"Hardly?" Adelaide said. "I can hear you breathing like a hundred times a minute."

She took out her cell phone and briefly flashed my face with the faint light of its screen.

"Don't do that," I said. "The cops will see us."

"I can see your pulse in your carotids," Adelaide said. "It's going twice as fast as your breathing. And your eyes look like one of those goddamn Asian squirrels."

"A tarsier?" I said.

"Yeah," Adelaide said.

"Must have been something I ate," I said.

Something I ate? Hadn't I used the same excuse with Kate a little over twenty-four hours ago? I was going to have to find a better excuse or stop having these spells as Adelaide had so kindly put it. Finding a better excuse was probably the way to go, since the spells...well, they seemed to have a life of their own, didn't they?

"You better pull yourself together," Adelaide said. "I'm not going into the bunker alone."

Adelaide's voice had been loud and clear, but she had become completely invisible to me.

"I'll be fine," I somehow managed to say. "Let's just sit down until Jeff gets back."

"Whatever," Adelaide said.

We sat down on the hilltop where we could see both the crater and the cops. It was still warm. The lights from the valley's tens of thousands of homes obscured the sky and no stars were visible. The only sound was the distant hum of traffic and soft rush of the breeze. The lingering smoke overwhelmed any other smells there might have been. I tried to slow both my breathing and my heart rate but nothing worked. In fact things only seemed to get worse. My chest constricted even more, filling with pain as it did so, and my head throbbed. The only positive thing was that, for reasons completely unknown to me, Adelaide's visage stopped its vanishing act and slowly stabilized back into its normal tellurian substantiality.

I thought back to the moment when all the symptoms started. I realized I had been thinking about what I might find in the bunker. The dead. The dead shouldn't have bothered me. My job was to deal with the dead. But 'shouldn't' wasn't an operative word for me anymore. Something had gone haywire inside of me. Maybe I was getting as bad as Jeff. Would it all get worse down in the bunker? If it did, could I handle it?

I suddenly heard the high-pitched sound of an approaching siren. I assumed it had to be Jeff, but I hadn't expected him back so soon. I looked down at my watch. Twenty minutes had gone by since he left. It had felt like seconds. Had I passed out and not realized it? I looked over at Adelaide. She was still staring down at the cops. If I had passed out, wouldn't she have said something? Throbbing head, racing pulse, chest pain, rapid breathing, and now time distortion too? I'd heard LSD could do that but I'd never taken LSD. I knew PTSD could also do it. But Hart and Vandross had said I had a stress reaction, not PTSD. Could a stress reaction do all that too?

I put those thoughts aside and instead tried to follow the siren's shrill peal back to its source. It took me a moment, but I finally saw a rapidly approaching flashing red light trailed by less distinct flashing yellow shafts. The sound of the siren was then quickly joined by the whine of a redlining engine and the screech of sharply turning tires. The Crown Vic passed beneath us a minute later.

The light of one of the streetlamps illumined the Vic's cabin for a fraction of a second. I could see Jeff in the cabin, his eyes wide and staring straight ahead. His right hand was on the wheel, and left hand and arm were casually draped on the sill of the open driver's window. The Vic's siren quickly dropped in pitch, the rotating silver fin of the red roof light became visible, and the flashing yellow rear lights shot sharp beacons into the night.

Jeff rocketed the car over the curb bordering the NASAD lot and raced across the empty lot towards the squad car. The Vic's lights lit up the interior of the squad car and the cops' faces looked more curious than annoyed or frightened. I assumed they must have believed the approaching Crown Vic, with its blaring siren and flashing lights, was one of their own. Jeff executed a high-speed 180 and came to a suspension rocking, brake squealing halt that left the Vic three feet away from the squad car. The 180 also left the Vic parallel to the squad car and the Vic's nose facing the squad car's tail. Jeff's window was thus directly in line with the window of the cop in the squad car's driver's seat.

"Pretty slick," I said to Adelaide.

"180 is kinda lame," Adelaide said.

"Lame?" I said.

"Geezer move," Adelaide said.

"What's worse?" I said. "Geezer or old fogey?"

"No difference," Adelaide said. "I'd kill myself if I was either one."

"Is that what Jeff and I should do?" I said. "Kill ourselves?"

"If the shoe fits," Adelaide said.

Jeff, coffee and doughnuts in one hand, and flashing his Army ID in the other, exited the Crown Vic. The cops seemed happy to see him. Actually they were probably happy to see the doughnuts. The cop in the driver seat twisted around, opened the back passenger door, and gestured for Jeff to take a seat. Jeff climbed in and passed around the provisions.

"Time to go," I said to Adelaide.

Adelaide and I stayed low to the ground, half slipping, half stepping down the loose earth below our hillside perch, setting off small landslides of dirt and gravel as we went. We reached the street, and, moving in the shadowed darkness between the lights from the streetlamps, made our way to the rear of the crater.

We stopped when we reached the crime scene tape and checked on Jeff and the cops in the police cruiser. The cops looked like they were on their second doughnuts, or maybe even their third. Adelaide and I ducked under the tape, and still staying low, circled around the rim of the crater. When we got to the rim's front edge, we left the rim and headed down into the crater and towards the stairs that led to NASAD's underground bunker.

The hum of electric generators and the whir of the giant fans pulling the air out of the NASAD underground bunker grew louder the closer we moved to the stairs. Adelaide and I reached the top of the stairs and began climbing down the bunker's long, steep staircase. We had to avoid the generator cables and also squeeze between the small space that existed between the walls of the staircase and the large Slinky-like portable air ducts through which the air was flowing out of the bunker.

Adelaide and I finally reached the bunker's door when we were about fifty feet below the base of the crater. The door was open to let the cables and air ducts inside the bunker. The door was made of two foot thick hardened steel hung on powerful hinges and was surrounded on its top, bottom, and both sides by three foot thick blast proof concrete. We stepped over the generator cables, slipped in through the space between the air ducts and the bunker's doorway, and found ourselves standing on a landing just inside the doorway.

The landing was raised fifteen feet above the floor of a massive room that was more like a warehouse. The room was at least one hundred feet long, one hundred feet wide, and thirty feet high. Because the generators were bringing power to the room, the room's lights were on. In some ways I wished those lights had not been on, because I found myself having a hard time dealing with what they illumined.

CHAPTER 90

I had seen mass graves in Serbia where skeletal bones poked through dead, rotting flesh that had once been animated and alive. I had seen death camps in Somalia where flies were feasting on the tiny corpses of babies locked in the final embrace of their slaughtered mothers' rigor stiffened arms. I had seen the bodies of entire families - grandparents, parents, uncles, aunts, and children - hung on meathooks swaying in the dry heat of the Syrian desert. I had seen countless other dead in countless other places, but for me, perhaps selfishly, what I saw in that NASAD bunker, was worse.

Worse because I felt indebted to the dead young people in that room. They had been among America's best and brightest - brilliant men and women of all races and creeds who had come to the bunker from the finest schools in the land. They had come to the bunker in order to help keep the U.S. military's technology the best of any fighting force in the world. That technology had in turn helped keep our soldiers alive on any killing field in any war-torn country on the face of the earth.

It made me sick to think those young men and women had been murdered. Murdered just like their NASAD cohorts - Milt Feynman, Paul Lennon, and the drone sub engineers - had been murdered over the last few years. Murdered just like Sam, Lizzy, their mother Sarah, Paul Lennon's parents, and a slew of FBI agents had been murdered over the last two days.

And then I remembered something that transformed the sick feeling I was having into a dread bordering on panic.

My body began to wobble.

I feared I might pass out once again.

What I remembered was what Mary Beth had said.

Some of the dark programmers had started to work at NASAD when they were only thirteen or fourteen years old.

None of the faces I had seen so far looked anywhere near that age. I wasn't sure I'd be able to handle it if any of the victims in the bunker turned out to be children so young. I prayed there wouldn't be any. I took a few deep breaths and slowly regained control of my emotions.

I looked over at Adelaide. She seemed deflated, as if all her usual vibrant, over-the-top energy had vanished into thin air.

"You okay?" I said to her.

Adelaide didn't respond, just slowly swiveled her head to face me. She looked as if she didn't see me.

"This is a tough scene," I said. "Maybe one of the toughest I've ever come across."

Adelaide still said nothing.

"You want to go back up top?" I said. "There's no shame in it if you do. I'll find a way to handle this by myself."

There was an almost imperceptible shake of Adelaide's head.

"No," Adelaide said in a near whisper.

"Okay," I said. "We need to get started now, though. We don't have much time."

Adelaide gave a very small nod.

"Take this," I said to Adelaide.

I handed her my cell phone.

"What should I do with it?" Adelaide said softly.

"Pictures," I said. "All of them."

"I can use my own phone," Adelaide said, still softly.

"No," I said. "We have to use mine. Everything has to be sent secured. Follow me."

We walked down the stairs to the floor of the bunker. The bunker was neither corporate nor military in design. It was a playroom for young adults. There were no cubicles, just desks and chairs in haphazard groupings. The chairs ranged from standard issue office chairs to lounge chairs, butterfly chairs, and easy chairs. The desks ranged from the common single person gunmetal grey variety to wooden antique partner desks, along with desks that seem to have been lifted from schoolrooms. There were even a few roll tops.

Every desk appeared to have both a desktop computer and laptop computer. Some of the desktop computers had three or even four screens attached to them. The screens were all lit up and populated by screen savers, the savers running the gamut from simple word phrases, to photographs, to colorful, undulating designs.

The dead were scattered about the room. Some bodies were seated in chairs at the desks, the bodies' heads and shoulders resting on the desktops. Other bodies lay in the aisles between the desks. Still others were on the floor in front of a table where a coffee bar had been set up. Those bodies were surrounded by shattered coffee cups and dried puddles of coffee.

The bodies were all casually dressed. Many of the women were in shorts and halter tops, and many of the men were in jeans and t-shirts. Some of the t-shirts were emblazoned with pop music bands, ancient and current, obscure and known. The dead programmers had mostly worn open-toed sandals, running shoes, or hiking boots, though some were barefoot. Coffee stained the pants, shirts, and shoes of the bodies near the coffee bar.

The men's hair for the most part was longish. There were many beards, kempt and unkempt. The women had mainly worn their hair long and simply cut, often in ponytails, though there were some who had dyed their hair bright and unnatural colors. There were eyeglasses of all shapes and sizes, framed and frameless.

In one corner of the warehouse-like room, far from the work desks, was an area set up as an arcade. The men and women in the arcade had apparently spent the last moments of their lives playing ping pong, shooting pool, rolling balls up the inclined lane of a Skee-Ball, or controlling the flippers of pinball machines. The pinball machines' upright screens still flashed red, green, yellow, and purple. The machines' dead players lay crumpled beside their chosen games.

On the edges of the arcade, bodies of dead programmers reclined lifelessly in beanbag chairs. The beanbag chairs seemed to have been placed to facilitate intimate conversations, conversations whose participants were silenced by death, and whose words had been lost forever.

None of the dead had yet appeared to be under the age of eighteen. I found some solace in that, though admittedly, not very much.

Adelaide and I walked over to the body that was closest to us. It was that of a young Latino woman who looked to be in her early twenties. Her cheeks were red and rosy and she had two earrings in each ear. There were beaded bracelets on both her wrists, flip flops on her feet, and she was clothed in a red pin-tucked crepe dress with white doves printed on it.

Adelaide's energy appeared to have returned, at least for the most part, and she seemed to study the young woman's body.

"She's young," Adelaide said.

"Not much older than you," I said.

Adelaide gestured to the other bodies in the room.

"All these people were dark programmers?" Adelaide said.

"Yes," I said.

"And their job was to look for any weaknesses in the design of NASAD's military products and systems?" Adelaide said. "And then see if they could exploit those weaknesses?"

"Yes," I said, "The goal being that NASAD would fix those products and systems before they became operational."

"But now you think it's possible the dark programmers actually created a weakness that's become operational in the military's systems?" Adelaide said.

"Correct," I said. "My fear is that weakness might actually be able to take down the entire U.S. military. We're working to make sure that doesn't happen."

"How could the dark programmers have let it become operational?" Adelaide said.

"I think they unwittingly let it happen," I said. "I don't believe it was truly their fault."

"You think it's Carter Bowdoin's fault, right?" Adelaide said.

"Yes," I said. Then it was my turn to gesture to the dead. "As far as I'm concerned, all these people are heroes. Their work helped make missiles fly on course, jets stay in the air, and warships navigate the seas. Their efforts also helped guide rescue missions to the wounded and ensure communications couldn't be intercepted. The dark programmers were the best of the best."

"I wish they weren't dead," Adelaide said. "Sounds like they were just the kind of people we need working with us."

"Yes," I said.

"That why they built this place the way they did?" Adelaide said. "Because they were the best of the best?"

"Not sure what you're talking about," I said. "You mean the game-like atmosphere?"

"No," Adelaide said. "I mean the walls. Somebody wanted these people alive. It looks like they could withstand a nuclear bomb."

"Not a direct hit, but...," I said.

"I didn't mean a direct hit," Adelaide said.

I was about to respond to her, but I was suddenly unable to speak. My eyes lost focus and I felt woozy.

Adelaide noticed my condition.

"Hey!" Adelaide said. "You're doing it again! Not down here asshole. I'm spooked as it is."

I said nothing.

"Shit," Adelaide said, then gave me a sharp slap across my cheek. The pain snapped me out of whatever spell had taken over me.

"Thanks," I said.

"You gotta stop that crap," Adelaide said.

"I'm fine," I said. "Where were we?"

"You were giving me a hard time about saying this place could withstand a direct nuclear hit," Adelaide said. "But that's not what I said."

"Of course you didn't," I said.

"Are you screwing with me?" Adelaide said.

"I know you're too smart to think anything like that," I said.

"You better," Adelaide said.

"Anyway, it's my job to give you a hard time," I said.

"Well, you're really good at it," Adelaide said.

"Thank you," I said.

"It wasn't a compliment," Adelaide said.

"I'm sure it wasn't," I said. "Let's get back to work."

I bent down over the young Latino woman, then gently lifted and turned her head so that she was directly facing us. I carefully opened her eyes so that we could see their color. They were a deep brown, but flat and lifeless, the pupils dilated.

"We only need one picture per person as long as you make it clear and sharp," I said.

Adelaide took the picture with my iPhone. I closed the woman's eyes and laid her head back down on the desk. Adelaide studied the image on the phone's screen.

"She looks like she's still alive," Adelaide said. "Her skin looks healthier than a lot of people I know."

"What do you make of that?" I said.

Adelaide didn't answer right away. She seemed to be thinking about my question. She looked out at the other bodies that were nearby.

"They all look the same," Adelaide said. "Their cheeks are red, like they just came back from a run. How can that be? They're all dead."

"What else do you see?" I said.

"What else do I see?" Adelaide said.

"Yes, what else do you see?" I said.

Adelaide slowly scanned the entire room. She appeared to be looking for something that might help her figure out an answer to my question. Nothing seemed to come to her. She looked frustrated.

"Can I give you a hint?" I said.

"No," Adelaide said.

I raised my eyebrows.

"Alright, fine," Adelaide said. "If it will make you feel better."

"When we were here this afternoon, they told us something happened," I said. "Do you remember what it was?"

"They said there was an explosion followed by a fire," Adelaide said. "But it doesn't look like either of those killed them."

"Why do you say that?" I said.

"If the explosion killed them it would have been due to the concussive forces the explosion produced," Adelaide said. "But if there was a concussive force strong enough to kill them, that force would have shattered other things in the room as well. The glass on the pinball machines, the cups on the coffee table. But the only shattered cups I see are the ones that hit the floor."

"Very good," I said. "What about a fire?"

"Fire wouldn't explain things either," Adelaide said. "None of the bodies have any blisters, charring, or anything else to suggest high heat. Also, the heat or smoke from the fire probably wouldn't have killed them instantaneously. You would think they would have made a run for the exits, but everyone seems to have gone down at their posts. There are no bodies piled up at the door. There are not even any bodies heading in the general direction of the door. These people look like they dropped where they were."

"Also very good," I said.

"The question is then," Adelaide said, "what gives dead people rosy cheeks and kills them in their tracks."

I didn't say anything.

"Well, what is it?" Adelaide said.

"Hell if I know," I said.

"You do know," Adelaide said.

"Well at the risk of sounding smug and condescending...," I said.

"Why should this day be any different than any other day?" Adelaide said.

"Carbon monoxide," I said. "At very high concentrations - much higher than can be achieved by sitting in your car in a closed garage or running a hose from your tailpipe into the passenger compartment - carbon monoxide will cause unconsciousness and death in a person in a matter of seconds. It is colorless, odorless, and tasteless so the victim will not have even the faintest clue something is wrong before they pass out and die. Maybe a few of the programmers lasted a second or two longer than the others and saw what was happening to their comrades, but that wouldn't have been enough time for them to do anything about it."

"Does the carbon monoxide also make their skin red?" Adelaide said.

"Yes," I said. "The carbon monoxide combines with the hemoglobin in a person's blood to make a chemical called carboxyhemoglobin. Carboxyhemoglobin in human tissues is seen as bright red."

"You ever use it?" Adelaide said.

"Carbon monoxide?" I said.

Adelaide nodded.

"Once or twice," I said.

"How about the truth?" Adelaide said.

"Four or five times?" I said.

"The truth I said," Adelaide said.

"It works," I said. "Let's leave it at that."

"How'd whoever did this get the carbon monoxide in here?" Adelaide said.

"Most likely pumped it into the air vents," I said. "Before we leave, we'll see if we can find whatever is left of the vents down here in the bunker and estimate where the vents exited the building."

"You mean the building that was above us, but is no longer here?" Adelaide said.

"Correct," I said.

"How will that help?" Adelaide said.

"We might find a hose or tire track where it shouldn't be," I said.

"Or we might not," Adelaide said.

"There's that," I said.

Adelaide appeared to be thinking something over.

"Why didn't they just blow it up?" Adelaide said.

"Come again?" I said.

"Why go through all the trouble of pumping carbon monoxide in here and also blowing up the building that used to be just above us?" Adelaide said. "Why not just blow up the bunker as well?"

"Depends what you think their motive was," I said.

"It wasn't to kill the dark programmers?" Adelaide said.

"It probably was," I said. "But I'm pretty sure they were especially worried about one specific one."

"Dr. Nemo?" Adelaide said.

"That's my guess," I said.

"So, if they blew everything up they risked not being able to identify the bodies?" Adelaide said.

"Uh huh," I said.

"And if they couldn't identify them, then they couldn't be sure they killed Nemo?" Adelaide said.

"Exactly," I said.

Adelaide appeared to consider this.

"That brings up the opposite question then," Adelaide said. "Why not just pump in the carbon monoxide? Why blow up the building too?"

"No telling what's inside the mind of a terrorist," I said.

"Terrorist?" Adelaide said. "But I thought you said only that idiot Burnette thinks terrorists are behind everything that's going on? You said that the bad guys are trying to make it look like terrorists did everything as a cover for their own actions."

"I did say that," I said. "I still believe it too. So that being said, the bad guys have to keep the terrorist cover going, don't they?"

Adelaide seemed to think about this as well.

"I get it," Adelaide said. "Nothing's changed then? Whoever did this are the same people who are killing everyone else and they just blew up the bunker with a bomb to make it look like terrorists did it?"

"Yes," I said.

"Carter Bowdoin and Dragon Man?" Adelaide said.

"Better be," I said.

"Better be?" Adelaide said.

"If it's not Carter and Dragon man, then my theory about the Chinese insurmountable edge being the dark programmers' war games software is wrong," I said. "If my theory is wrong, then the edge is something else entirely, and I don't see how we're going to be able to figure out what that something else is, let alone neutralize it, in less than ten days."

Adelaide looked back out over the dead bodies strewn across the room.

"Hope Dr. Nemo isn't in here," Adelaide said.

"I hope so too," I said. "But even if Nemo is in here, there's still a chance he left us a clue we can use. Now, please start getting us a picture of everyone's face and of their ID's as well. While you do that, I'm going to take a closer look around."

"Do I have to open their eyes every time I take a picture?" Adelaide said.

"Yes," I said. "I realize it's not the most pleasant of tasks, but I'm sure you can handle it."

I left Adelaide to her work, then moved among the dead. Every one of them that I came across looked the same - young, rosy cheeked, appearing almost like they were asleep. I scanned each of the dark programmers' desks, looking for anything that might stand out, anything that might speak to me of Dr. Nemo, his code, or the software changes I thought might be the basis for the Chinese's belief they possessed an insurmountable military edge.

The first dozen or so desks held no interest for me. But then I came to a desk that was shoved up against a wall. The desk was about halfway across the room from the doorway that Adelaide and I had used to enter the bunker.

The desk was the type of desk one might have found in a high school in midwestern America during the early half of the twentieth century. It was made of yellowed wood that was faded and scratched. The desk also had large drawers in both of its side pedestals.

No one was sitting at the desk. There was, however, a tall, well-padded, black leather office chair on casters shoved in close against the desktop between the two pedestals.

The body of a young man lay on the floor near the desk. The man had long blond hair, an earring in one ear, and had been wearing a loose cotton shirt with a green and blue checked pattern, Levi's, and hiking boots. His eyes were open in death and they were blue. I couldn't tell if the desk belonged to the man or if he had simply been passing by it when he died.

What had drawn me to the desk was not the man, however, but the movie posters mounted on the wall above it. The movies were 'The Conversation', 'Babel', 'Blow Up', 'Inception', 'Kill Bill', and 'The Matrix'. I sensed there was something about the posters - or perhaps just one of them? - that was trying to tell me something, even though I had no idea at the time what that something was. There wasn't a poster for 'Twenty Thousand Leagues Under the Sea', but I suppose that would have made things too easy wouldn't it have?

The posters had drawn me to the desk, but the object I found on top of the desk intrigued me even more. It was an object with which I was well acquainted as I had learned about it in one of my courses at West Point.

I pulled out the desk chair and sat down so I could more closely study the object. The object was sitting next to a computer that had four large monitors attached to it. The monitors were running screen savers showing clips from video games like 'Call of Duty', 'Grand Theft Auto', and 'Halo'. The video games were what I would have expected a dark programmer to amuse him or herself with during work breaks, but the object was wholly from another era. The 1920's to be exact.

The object was in a black steel case, had what looked like typewriter keys atop its upper surface, and could easily be mistaken for a hundred year old typewriter. The machine was definitely not a typewriter, however. The things that looked like keys were actually circular buttons mounted on levers. There were three rows of buttons and each button had a letter on it. Other than for the 'L', 'P', 'Y', and 'Z' buttons, the buttons were positioned where they would be expected to be found on a typewriter. There were no buttons with numbers or punctuation, however.

Above the three rows of buttons were three rows of letters that could light up when the machine was in use. These letters were the twins of the letters in the three button rows and were in the exact same position in their rows as their button twins were in their own rows. The letters that could light up were used as signals only, and, unlike the buttons, were not meant to be pushed.

Above the rows of letters that could light up were three dials that looked like the dials on a bicycle combination lock. The three dials did not have numbers like bicycle locks have, however, but instead were imprinted with all the letters of the alphabet.

On the front face of the machine was another set of three rows of the letters in the alphabet. Those letters were also in the same positions in their rows as their twin lights and buttons were in their own rows. Each of the letters on the front of the machine had a hole beneath it that was in fact an electrical connector into which one end of a patch cord could be inserted.

There were at that time six patch cords in use, and each patch cord was connecting a pair of letters together. For example, 'A' was connected to 'D' and 'G' was connected to 'T'. The patch cords were not permanently fixed in those positions, however. The machine's operator could, if he or she so desired, move the patch cords to connect different pairs of letters together.

The machine's power cord had been pulled out of the electrical outlet. I was about to plug it back in when I heard a strange sound coming from behind me. I turned around to look and found the coyote I had first encountered in the desert standing atop a desk a few feet away from me. He was accompanied by Foster Mom's dalmatian and the two of them sang the same 'Rainbow' song they had been singing the last time I had seen them -

At the end of a dream

If you know where I mean

When the mist just starts to clear

In a similar way

At the end of today

I could feel the sound of writing on the wall

It cries for you

It's the least that you can do.

The coyote smiled at me, and just like that, he and Foster Mom's dalmatian disappeared. I felt a soft touch on my shoulder and warm breath upon my ear. I turned my head.

Grace was standing there.

"Grace?" I said.

"Yes, my love," Grace said.

"I'm glad you're here," I said.

"Thank you, my love," Grace said. "I'm glad I'm here too."

"I love you, Grace," I said.

"I love you too, Jack," Grace said.

"Did you hear the coyote and the dalmatian singing?" I said.

"Yes," Grace said. "You need to pay close attention to them."

"I did," I said. "I don't know what their singing means though."

"I know you'll figure it out sweetheart," Grace said. "But Jack..."

"Yes?" I said.

"Your life is in grave danger, my darling," Grace said. "You need to be very careful."

"It is?" I said. "I mean, yes...I'll be careful."

"Good," Grace said, and kissed me on the lips.

Grace suddenly disappeared. I reached for where she had been, but my arms found only empty air. Tears began welling in my eyes and then instantly became a torrent. I felt my body becoming soaked in the tears. I began to shake violently. It was as if some monstrous giant had grabbed my shoulders and was tossing me to and fro.

A voice said, "You promised me you wouldn't do this."

I turned to the sound of the voice, but the tears were obscuring my vision and I saw nothing. I struggled to gain control of my arms despite the uncontrollable shaking of my shoulders. I was able to get one arm up to my eyes and use my sleeve to wipe away the tears. I saw Adelaide standing over me, her hands on my shoulders. I realized my head and the front of my chest were resting on the desk in the same position they would be in if I'd fallen asleep in the desk chair.

Adelaide said, "What the hell is it with you?"

"I was taking a nap," I said.

"I thought you were a goddamned general in the U.S. Army," Adelaide said.

"Generals take naps," I said.

"That was no nap," Adelaide said. "You were passed out."

"Hardly," I said.

"Oh yeah?" Adelaide said, and pointed at an empty plastic bottle of water on the desk. "I poured this whole bottle on your head and you didn't even flinch. I thought you were dead."

"Clearly I'm not dead," I said. "Why don't you get back to work? I've got some things to check out on this desk."

"I'm already done," Adelaide said.

"You already got a photo of everyone's faces and ID's," I said.

"Yes," Adelaide said.

"You checked the restrooms too?" I said.

"Yes," Adelaide said. "Two dead in the men's room and one in the women's room."

"Good, you were very thorough," I said. "I guess that must have been some nap I took."

"Quit with the nap story okay?" Adelaide said. "'Cause you're so full of shit I can see it behind your eyeballs. And by the way, I *was* very thorough. I found an old dead guy behind that door over there."

Adelaide gestured with her thumb to a door in a wall that was all the way across the room from where we were. I hadn't noticed the door before, as that area of the room was darker than the rest of the bunker and the door was hidden in the shadows of some file cabinets that were flanking it.

"An old guy, huh?" I said. "How old?"

"Maybe sixty," Adelaide said.

Hearing the man's age reminded me anew that NASAD had hired some of the dark programmers when they were only thirteen or fourteen years old. The dread I had felt at the thought that children so young might be among the bunker's dead returned once again. I asked Adelaide a question I truly did not want to ask.

"Sixty?" I said. "That is old. You didn't happen to come across anyone really young, did you? Say thirteen or fourteen?"

Adelaide looked at me like she thought I was out of my mind.

"What are you talking about?" Adelaide said.

"NASAD scoured the country for geniuses they could employ in the dark programmer division," I said. "Some of them were only thirteen or fourteen when they started working."

"You're kidding right?" Adelaide said.

"No," I said. "Paul Lennon, Kate's deceased husband, used to help mentor them when they would first come on board."

Adelaide shook her head.

"I didn't see anyone who looked close to being that young," Adelaide said. "Everyone appeared to be at least eighteen. And I'm glad that was the case. I'm not sure I could have handled it if it wasn't."

"I understand," I said. "I'm also glad that was the case. I *know* I couldn't have handled it."

Adelaide seemed to think for a moment.

"Since we didn't find anyone that young, do you think maybe the youngest dark programmers are working somewhere else? Adelaide said.

"I doubt it," I said. "From everything I know about the dark programmers, it seems very likely all of them worked in this bunker. As to why there isn't anyone that young down here, my best bet is the program either slowed down during the last few years or NASAD didn't find anyone that age they felt they could hire during that time."

"Makes sense to me," Adelaide said.

"How about we go take a look at the old guy now?" I said.

"First tell me what this thing is," Adelaide said pointing at the machine on the desk with all the buttons, dials, and levers.

"Let's go see the old man first, then I'll explain," I said.

"Is it a typewriter?" Adelaide said.

"How do you know about typewriters?" I said.

"I saw a picture of one in a book," Adelaide said.

"It's not a typewriter," I said. "Typewriters don't have all these dials and lights and wires."

"If it's not a typewriter, what is it then?" Adelaide said.

"Old man, then the machine," I said. "Come on."

CHAPTER 91

Adelaide and I entered the room at the far side of the bunker that she had pointed out to me. Adelaide had been right about the dead man in the room. He appeared to be about sixty years old. The dead man was slumped over his desk and the exposed skin of his hands and face was the same crimson color as the skin of the dead NASAD dark programmers in the main room of the bunker. The man's right hand clutched a red plastic telephone handset. The handset was still in its cradle, so either the man had placed it there after making a call, or he had never made one at all. As the carbon monoxide had wreaked its deadly havoc on the dark programmers in what appeared to be a nearly instantaneous fashion, I saw no reason to believe the man's fate had been meted out any differently. I thus went with the latter option - the call had never been made. The phone, connected by a cord to an outlet in the wall next to the desk, had no keypad and so couldn't be dialed. Because of the phone's red color and the fact it couldn't be dialed, I assumed the phone was some kind of hotline, and that the call, if it had been completed, would have gone directly to NASAD.

Of course, as soon as Adelaide had said there was a dead older man in the room, I had instantly thought 'NASAD vice president of dark programming'. At sixty years old or thereabouts, not only was the dead man unlikely to have been doing the same work as the young genius hotshot programmers, but he also would be close to the same age as Milt Feynman would have been if Milt was still alive. Freddy had confirmed what I'd been thinking ever since Mary Beth had told me about the duties of the vice president of dark programming - that the vice president was a contemporary of Milt's, someone Milt had known and trusted for a very long time. The man slumped over the desk in front of me clearly fit the bill age-wise, and, if there had ever been any doubt in my mind that the man truly was Vice President of Dark Programming Rick Benavidez - I actually never had any such doubt, but *if* I had - then three of the items in the room would have made such doubt impossible.

The first item was a framed photograph of the dead man with Milt

Feynman in which the dead man was wearing a black baseball cap upon whose crown was emblazoned 'NASAD Vice President of Dark Programming' in gold letters. Milt and the man both appeared to be in their thirties when the photograph was taken, which meant the photograph could be nearly thirty years old.

The second item was what appeared to be the hat itself resting on a hook on the wall behind the man's head.

The third item was the device the dead man was wearing on his wrist. The device was in the shape of a watch, but it wasn't a watch. It was a combined GPS and electrocardiograph. The device was clearly the device that the vice president of dark programming wore to alert NASAD in the event of his death - the same device Freddy had told me about earlier that day.

There was a screen on the device that was divided into two smaller screens. One screen showed GPS coordinates in blinking green numbers. The other screen was labeled 'EKG' for electrocardiograph. The EKG screen was flashing a solitary flat red line.

Adelaide said, "You think this man was Rick Benavidez, the NASAD vice president of dark programming that Freddy was talking about?"

"It certainly looks that way," I said. "You didn't find any identification on him?"

"I didn't," Adelaide said. "He's the only person down here that doesn't have any."

"I'm not surprised," I said. "Dark programmers must have come and gone, but this man was on this job for over thirty years. Due to the need for secrecy in order to protect both him and the dark programmers, I doubt the programmers even knew his real name."

"What did he actually do?" Adelaide said.

"As the vice president of dark programming, Mr. Benavidez was the dark programmers' boss," I said. "Since this was a top secret facility, he was also the programmers' only liaison, as least as far as their professional responsibilities were concerned, with the outside world."

"He was a pretty important guy then?" Adelaide said.

"Yes," I said. "He was fiercely loyal to both Milt Feynman, who founded NASAD, and to NASAD as well. His job also had profound effects on our country's ability to defend itself."

Adelaide appeared to think this over.

"Freddy said he was a highly decorated soldier," Adelaide said. "Sounds like a true patriot to me. But now he's dead. We're not going to let that stand, are we?"

"No," I said. "We're not."

"Good," Adelaide said.

"You took a picture of him?" I said.

Adelaide nodded.

"We'll send it off to Major Haley along with the other pictures you took of the dark programmers' faces and ID's," I said. "I don't see any way this man isn't Benavidez but it can't hurt to have Haley confirm it." I looked around the room. "I can't think of anything else we can do for him now. Let's go back into the main bunker and I'll explain to you what that machine is."

Adelaide and I left Vice President of Dark Programming Rick Benavidez where he lay and made our way back to the desk with the strange machine full of buttons, dials, levers, and lights.

CHAPTER 92

"What is it?" Adelaide said.

"It's a machine the Nazis used to send coded messages in World War II," I said. "By changing the dials and the patch cords, the Nazis could create ten quadrillion different combinations. Each combination would code a message differently."

"An Enigma machine, huh?" Adelaide said.

"How did you know that?" I said.

"I read about it in a book," Adelaide said. "Do you know how it works?"

"Yes," I said.

"Are you going to tell me?" Adelaide said.

"Yes," I said. "But please pay close attention because it's kind of complicated and I don't want to have to repeat myself."

"I'm all ears," Adelaide said.

"Okay," I said. "First you set the machine to scramble your message by adjusting those dials that look like bicycle combination locks and using the patch cords to connect a few pairs of letters. Then you type in your message using the buttons with the letters on them. Those rows of lighted letters above the buttons will light up depending on what button you hit. The whole secret behind the machine's ability to code, however, is that because the dials and patch cords scramble the letters, the lighted letters will not light up with the same letter as the letter on the button you hit, but will instead light up a new, different letter. Essentially you are creating a code letter to represent the letter on the button. You write down the letters that lit up as you typed your message, then send those letters to whomever you want to decode your message. The person you send the letters to must also have an Enigma machine just like this one. As long as that person sets the dials and patch cords to exactly match the settings on your machine, when they type in the letters in your coded message the original letters you typed in will light up. They then copy down those letters and read your message."

"Cool," Adelaide said. "Let's try it."

I plugged the machine in, turned it on, then put my fingers over the buttons.

"Tell me what to type," I said.

"No bozo, I don't want to code a message, I want to decode one," Adelaide said.

"I just told you it doesn't work unless you have a message from another machine," I said.

"I understood that," Adelaide said. "What makes you think we don't have one?"

"A message or another machine?" I said.

"I know you died this morning, and you just passed out, and God knows whatever else you've been through in the last two days," Adelaide said, "but have you really forgotten you've been carrying around a message in your pocket ever since you left the ranch? Take it out."

"Message?" I said. "What message?"

"Dr. Nemo's message!" Adelaide said. "The one on your phone in the file that Kate transferred to you!"

I don't think I had ever felt so stupid in my life. My only excuse was the one to which Adelaide had alluded - stress. I'd been under a lot of stress ever since Jeff pointed the rifle at me. The Taser, the elephant tranquilizer, running around at the morgue and the stoning site in Lancaster, being blown up and dying, all the gunfights, and now being confronted by the dead programmers in the bunker, had probably only made the stress worse. Still, all I could think about was that I should have done better.

"You must think I'm a moron," I said.

"What else is new?" Adelaide said.

I reached into my front pants pocket to get my phone. But my phone wasn't there. I checked my other pockets, but the phone wasn't in them either. I started to get anxious. Where could my phone possibly have gone?

"Looking for this?" Adelaide said, laughing and extending me my phone. "Remember? You wanted only secure photos."

"Right, thanks," I said.

I opened Nemo's file.

"Grab a pen and paper," I said. "I'll type in the letters in the cipher-text and you write down the letters that light up."

Adelaide found a pen and sheet of paper in one of the desk drawers. I began to type. With each button I hit, a letter lit up on one of the rows on top of the Enigma machine. Adelaide copied the letters down as the lights came on. I typed in twelve letters, figuring that was enough to get some idea of where we stood.

"Please read me what we have so far," I said.

"Letter by letter?" Adelaide said.

"There aren't any recognizable words?" I said

"Is 'grxypltzmwqn' a word?" Adelaide said.

"Let me see that please," I said.

Adelaide handed me the sheet of paper. I studied the string of letters. I read them forwards and backwards. I held them upside down. I did a few quick reconfigurations, trying to find a word, any word. I couldn't find any English words, at least any I knew.

But I didn't want to give up.

I raced through all the other earthly languages I could conjure. None turned the meaningless, unpronounceable gibberish into any kind of intelligible communication.

"You speak Martian?" I said.

"You think it's that bad, huh?" Adelaide said.

"Couldn't be worse," I said.

"Maybe the dials were moved," Adelaide said. "Or the patch cords in front. Should we try some different combinations?"

"That would be a good idea," I said. "Except..."

"Except what," Adelaide said.

"I wasn't kidding when I said there were ten quadrillion possible combinations," I said. "Would take billions of years."

"A journey of a thousand miles begins with a single step," Adelaide said.

"I thought you were reading Descartes?" I said.

"You have a problem with Lao Tzu?" Adelaide said.

"I just didn't realize you were reading both," I said.

"I'm reading a lot more than just them," Adelaide said.

"I'm impressed," I said.

"Thank you," Adelaide said. "So what should we do?"

"About what?" I said.

"About Dr. Nemo's code," Adelaide said.

"I think we should take the Enigma machine with us when we go," I said.

"You think Nemo may have coded his message on it after all?" Adelaide said.

"Yes," I said. "Especially since I just remembered something Nemo said in his voicemail to Kate."

"What did he say?" Adelaide said.

"Nemo was talking about being worried about going to prison for breaching security protocols," I said. "But he prefaced what he had to say with 'I apologize for the enigmatic way in which I have contacted you'..."

"Enigmatic as in 'enigma'?" Adelaide said.

"It's a shot," I said. "We can get the machine to Haley and maybe she can figure out a way to shortcut the ten quadrillion possible combinations."

"I guess that means this is probably Nemo's desk then too," Adelaide said.

"Probably," I said.

Adelaide gestured to the posters on the wall.

"Good taste in movies," Adelaide said.

I didn't share my hunch with Adelaide that one or more of the posters might hold some meaning for us in regard to our search for Nemo and what he was up to. I didn't share it mainly because the hunch was so amorphous I wasn't sure how to explain it.

Just then my iPhone played the tone it makes when I have an incoming message. I looked down at the phone's screen.

"It's a text from Jeff," I said. "He's almost out of doughnuts. We better take a quick look for the air vents and go. We've been down here too long as it is."

I picked up the Enigma machine. The body of the blond man on the floor was blocking our path to the bunker's exit. Adelaide was about to step over the body, then stopped.

"You don't think this is Dr. Nemo do you?" Adelaide said.

"The desk chair was pushed all the way in when I got here, so I don't think he was sitting at the desk when the carbon monoxide was pumped in," I said.

"So this guy might not be Nemo, but some other guy who was just walking by right before he died?" Adelaide said.

"God bless his soul, yes," I said. "Of course, he could be Nemo, and he might have been leaving on a break or coming back from one when he died."

"I guess there's no way to tell?" Adelaide said.

"No," I said.

"But we at least have a fighting chance Dr. Nemo is still alive though?" Adelaide said.

"It's a small one," I said. "But yes, I think so."

Continued in Book Three of *THE INSURMOUNTABLE EDGE...*

Made in United States
North Haven, CT
03 December 2022

27761321R00264